MURDER AND THE MASQUERADE

MURDER AND THE MASQUERADE

BOOK 1 OF THE DOROTHY PHAIRE ROMANTIC MYSTERY SERIES

Dorothy Phaire

Author of *Almost Out of Love*

iUniverse, Inc.

New York Lincoln Shanghai

MURDER AND THE MASQUERADE
BOOK 1 OF THE DOROTHY PHAIRE ROMANTIC MYSTERY SERIES

iUniverse books may be ordered through booksellers or by contacting:

iUniverse
2021 Pine Lake Road, Suite 100
Lincoln, NE 68512
www.iuniverse.com
1-800-Authors (1-800-288-4677)

Because of the dynamic nature of the Internet, any Web addresses or links contained in this book may have changed since publication and may no longer be valid.

This is a work of fiction. All of the characters, names, incidents, organizations, and dialogue in this novel are either the products of the author's imagination or are used fictitiously.

ISBN: 978-0-595-44787-9 (pbk)
ISBN: 978-0-595-89105-4 (ebk)

Printed in the United States of America

Masqueraders

My grief will still allow me to complain,
But you who chant the Pollyanna strain,
Or whistle shrill glad lyrics in the dark,
Why did they force you to the wall? What stark
Lean precipice do you peer down of nights ...
What is this ragged edge your scared soul flaunts
For courage, that you wing your head in face of pain?
                    —Margaret E. Haughawout (1929)

This book is dedicated to a woman that I most admire for her charm, grace, beauty and generous nature—my mother, Sylvia Mosby Herring. She has always encouraged me to not give up and to live my dream as a writer. I remember one day when I became so frustrated by all the non-writing obligations tugging at me that day and one particular cruel rejection letter. I was near tears while talking to her on the telephone when she told me that it didn't matter what others thought about how good or bad your work is, but more importantly—you must keep striving and not give up.

Author's Note

In 2001, I completed my first novel, **Almost Out of Love** while working full-time and maintaining a busy household schedule. That writing project resulted in 4 draft versions stretched across 8 years to arrive at a publishable product. It also took attending writing seminars and workshops, networking with other aspiring writers, reading works I admired, and sitting down to a disciplined writing schedule of between 1½ to 2 hours a day. In those early draft phases of my first novel it was difficult to allow my own voice to come through, but I kept hearing a recurring message in my mind to write what you know; give of yourself; reveal yourself. I began to take risks and finally developed the courage to reveal my character's truth. However, the release of my first book did not even begin to tap the full potential for distribution due to time demands, other commitments, and lack of funds to invest in touring to reach new readers. After only a year on the market, I made the difficult decision to remove my first book from print, and I then started an extensive rewrite. While early readers enjoyed **Almost Out of Love** when it was first published, I knew I could make this story even better as I continued to learn and hone my craft for several years. To read some of the early praise for **Almost Out of Love**, see readers' comments from 2001 that can be found after the acknowledgment page.

As a writer I feel that I have a responsibility to my readers to write the best story I can write. Today, I continue to find new ways to see and improve my writing. After undergoing professional editing and another revision, I believe this new version entitled **Murder and the Masquerade**, approaches the high standards I have set for myself. Readers, who enjoyed **Almost Out of Love** in 2001, will find new scenes, deleted and modified text, without losing the characterization and plot development that they previously found entertaining. Readers who missed

Almost Out of Love since it was removed from print early, can meet these characters for the first time in its rewrite, **Murder and the Masquerade**. This book reflects my determination to have the courage to write boldly and not be paralyzed by a fear of rejection. I believe it reflects my growth as a writer. I am on a writer's journey that has nothing to do with getting a book deal from a major publisher or getting on best seller lists. On this writer's journey I will live the life I have chosen for myself, not a life someone else or circumstances have chosen for me. An elder once told me, "If you don't know what you want, somebody else will!" Through my setbacks, retries, and successes I do know what I want. I will sit in my small, cluttered office at the top of the stairs, where the sofa print does not match and the shelves come from IKEA and simply have the courage to write every day. I hope you will enjoy reading my new work. To give you a preview of more to come, visit my website at www.dorothyphaire.com for updates about the sequel that I expect to be released next year, 2008. There is also a list of Discussion Questions for Reading Groups or Book Club meetings at the end of this book. Thank You for entering my world!

Acknowledgements

There is an old Nigerian proverb that says, "One tree cannot make a forest." I owe many people thanks for their encouragement and expertise without whom I could not have gotten this far. I am grateful to my editor, Valerie Jean for helping me to see the novel in a new light and for her willingness to be honest in her professional critique and editing work. I want to thank Charlene Ridley, an early reader during the lengthy revision phase, who anxiously waited to receive each revised chapter and continually offered her encouragement along the way. My publicist, Denise Laing, a talented writer in her own right, helped me conceive a working title and offered literary advice; I am grateful for her creative energy and positive spirit. During my research phase many people generously shared their time and answered my questions on a number of topics. I would like to personally thank Charles Dean, Lori Herring, Angela Khan Thomas, Pamela Mosby, and LeeAnn Robinson for their insight and knowledge. I would like to thank Cedric Herring for sharing his thoughts from a teenage male's perspective that helped me develop one of the young characters in the book. While too many to name here, I'd like to thank the dozen or so avid reader friends whose opinions I sought. I feel blessed and thankful for my parents for being such wonderful role models and for their giving spirits. Of course, making a commitment to a disciplined writing schedule requires people close to you in your life who are willing to make a sacrifice and understand your need to create without being unnecessarily demanding. So finally, I would like to thank my husband, Austin and daughters, Danielle, Amber, and Mia for allowing me space to live in my writing world during my creative periods.

Praise from Readers for the 2001 release of ALMOST OUT OF LOVE
Source: Amazon.com's Reader Reviews, 2001

FANTASTIC!
Inspiring and heartwarming. The author took it to another level by adding the mystery to the romance. The ending was so good. It didn't have the typical ending that romance novels have.
A Reader from Washington, D. C.

I enjoyed every moment I spent reading this novel. I finished it last night and I'm more eager to have my friends read it SOON so that we can get together and discuss. Also, the murderer was not who I expected! Great job!!!
A Reader from Silver Spring, Maryland.

I like how the writer threw in facts about the D.C. area. The characters also seem to know police language and psychology (good research!). From what I've been reading in trade magazines, the black romance lines are being flooded, but the mystery, horror, and a few other genres are still wide open (good move with Almost Out of Love!)
A Reader from Maryland.

The characters are in my mind when I let my mind relax from my technical/medical thoughts. The author has a colorful manner to her writing and I'm enjoying the use of pop culture throughout the writing.
A Reader from Maryland.

The book was wonderful. It held my attention the entire time. I would arrive early to work and would sit in my car in the parking lot and read. I didn't want to stop reading to go into work. I had a hard time putting it down. Whenever I had spare time I was reading it. I can't wait for the next one to come out!
A Reader from Maryland.

I liked Renee, admired her courage. She wasn't happy and floundered a bit as we all do in her search for meaning and hence purpose in her life. She was willing to explore the idea of becoming an adoptive mom at 44, leave a marriage if need be

and have an affair with a man several years her junior. She was my favorite char-acter.
A Reader from Washington, D. C.

I thought Veda's issues were definitely real … having to hit rock bottom to see that LaMarr was not worth the time of day. I also liked the fact that she had a true sister/friend who had her back and vice versa. I enjoyed reading this book. Waiting for the next one.
A Reader from Washington, D. C.

Vivid, detailed character development. Contemporary themes (romance, profes-sional growth, employer racism, social issues); Suspenseful; Plot develops at a progressive pace. It's hard to put the book down.
A Reader from Maryland.

I just finished reading ALMOST OUT OF LOVE. I know me, if it had not kept my interest I would have not finished it. Well, I couldn't put the book down. I was there!!!!! I put myself on the set. Only a good book can do this to me. I'm looking forward to the next book from this author and will share "ALMOST OUT OF LOVE" with my friends!"
A Reader from Maryland.

I like the way it weaves the mystery and romance into the story! I'm so happy someone is writing my kind of book. It's more than a mystery, romance—it's also a thought-provoking book about so many areas of life. I am an avid reader—probably read 3-4 or more books a month, mostly mystery, romance, suspense, and intrigue. Can't wait for the next book!
A Reader from Maryland.

PROLOGUE

---▼---

Bill heard the front door slam shut, the garage door open, and his wife's car speeding off. Renee was gone before he could get up the nerve to ask who had paged her and where was she going. How the hell could he reason with a woman who would leave her home in the middle of the night to meet her lover whenever he called?

Thinking about the sound of panic in Veda's voice, Renee thought ahead of her treatment options if she was faced with the worst case scenario—signs of suicidal tendencies. In that situation, Renee knew she would have to recommend that her patient be committed to Washington Hospital Center for observation. This was the only way to ensure that she was in a safe environment. Renee hoped it didn't have to come to that, but if so she was prepared to follow through. She wouldn't take even the slightest chance of losing a patient. Renee started to notice some of the landmarks that Veda had told her to look for and felt relieved. About ten minutes later, she drove through the parking lot of Madison Towers, a luxury, high-rise, condominium complex. Even in the dark, the condominium complex appeared to be elegant and the grounds looked massive and well kept. After finding a place to park, she hurried out of the car and stood in front of the building's entrance. She peered through the thick glass palladian windows of the lobby because the building required a security pass card to open the door and Veda was no where in sight to let her in. She dialed Veda's cell phone number, but there was no answer. Renee felt foolish and started to turn around and leave. Suddenly a well-dressed man with a brief case walked up behind her.

"Locked out, huh?" he asked. Renee nodded and smiled.

"Happens to me too sometimes," he said and used his pass card to unlock the door.

He held the door open for her to walk through then disappeared to his own apartment on the first floor. Renee scanned the lobby. It was completely deserted, except for a security guard, who was dozing in a chair with his feet propped up. The guard snored heavily into the open textbook resting on his chest.

Renee pulled out the piece of paper with the address that Veda had given her. Apartment number 620 it said. Renee passed the sleeping guard and considered waking him so that he could come up to 620 with her, but she quickly decided against it. Better to check it out for herself first. She located the elevator and headed up to the apartment.

She knocked gently on the door of apartment 620 without getting any answer. She tried the doorknob and was surprised to find the door unlocked. As soon as she stepped inside the foyer, a strange combination of odors hit her in the face. One scent smelled like freshly smoked pipe tobacco. She couldn't discern the rest. Renee called out several times and inquired if anyone was home. No response. She ventured forward slowly. The apartment's entire color-scheme was black and white contemporary. A state-of-the-art sound system, big-screen flat panel television, and other expensive gadgets filled the room. Renee noticed a white dress shirt and silk tie thrown across a chair. Gold-threaded monograms adorned each cuff. A bench press with weights and a stationary bicycle leaned against one wall. She sniffed and took in the pungent smell of something resembling a combination of alcohol and cooked-meat. Not the appetizing aroma of filet mignon—one of her favorite meals at Fat Jack's on M Street—it smelled more like the fetid stench of rotten meat. Suddenly, Renee felt dizzy and nauseous from the odor. She leaned against the back of a white leather recliner to steady herself.

If Veda had been there she was gone now and no one else was home. Renee turned around to leave the apartment, anxious to get outside and breathe some fresh air. As she turned, she happened to glance down. That's when she saw the spattering of red stains on the white, plush carpet. She bent down to check the stain. At first she thought it was paint because the color was a vibrant red, but as she inhaled the odor, she realized it smelled more like fresh blood.

Renee stood up and looked around her. She saw that the door, to what must be the master bedroom, was slightly ajar. She went over and pushed the door open. The room was dark. Cautiously, she stepped through the doorway. She felt for the light switch on the wall and flicked it on. Renee gasped in horror and covered her mouth to suppress the screams.

What she saw was a young, black man sprawled on a king-sized bed. One of his arms dangled off the side of the bed, and the other lay across his chest. Long muscular legs jutted and spread out on the bed. Dark, lifeless eyes bulged out of their sockets and stared out at Renee with a permanently molded look of surprise. He was nude, except for a hand towel soaked with blood that covered his penis. Renee's shocked gaze traced a puddle of blood that settled on the black silk sheets and trailed down the sides of the bed onto the white carpet. A huge, gaping wound exposed the insides of his abdomen and a faint scent of stomach acid. Renee covered her mouth and swallowed down her own vomit rather than throw-up.

She knew she had to check him even though he already appeared to be dead. Trained as an emergency room nurse, her medical instincts kept her calm. She leaned over and placed two fingers at his throat. No sign of a pulse. She laid her ear to his chest. No sound or sensation of a heartbeat. She held his wrist. Again, nothing. His hand flopped down on the bed with a thud when she let it go. He didn't feel cold yet so she surmised that rigor mortis had not set in. He couldn't have been dead too long.

The sickening smell became unbearable. Still, she couldn't figure out what it was. Renee backed up to leave the room and nearly tripped over an empty bottle of Cutex nail polish remover that had been lying on the floor. She picked it up. The top was off and the strong scent of alcohol penetrated her nostrils. The open bottle of Cutex explained the alcohol smell. But she still couldn't figure out where that foul odor was coming from. The victim couldn't have been dead long enough for his body to start decaying because he still felt warm. The odor had to be coming from something else. She took a deep breath and willed herself to move closer. There was dead silence in the room, except for the sound of her rapid breathing and the sensation of her heart pounding. Slowly, she approached the victim and lifted the edge of the towel. That's when the source of the smell exploded in her face. Renee drew back in horror. His genitals swam in a pool of blood. His penis looked like it had been completely burnt off. That's when she screamed.

CHAPTER 1

▼

Midnight covered the sky in a thick, smoky blanket. Flickering bulbs in the lampposts lit up the winding lanes of Northwest Washington's Foxhall Crescent Estates. Bill Hayes drove through his sleeping neighborhood of sprawling French Colonials, pillared Georgians, and Tudor-style homes. The purplish trees he passed faded into murky shadows and the wind was like the fast, erratic breathing of an intruder lurking behind a door ready to strike.

Bill pulled into his driveway and sat in his Range Rover, which was often his refuge from home. The stately brick French Colonial house he lived in, the custom-fitted, designer suits he wore, and the yacht club Rolex on his wrist, were all symbols of his wife's success and constant reminders of his failures.

It was late and Bill wondered if Renee would still be up. What the hell. He'd wake her if he had to. He couldn't even remember the last time they had made love. They'd both been too busy, too tired, too absorbed in other things. Sometimes an entire day passed without them even speaking to each other or crossing paths. Tonight he needed the release of sex, but he wasn't going to cheat on his wife—though he had opportunities. Sitting in the car, with the music turned down low, he remembered the blonde from TechVenture, where he'd worked eight years ago. Daphne was her name. He had just been promoted to project manager and had been working through lunch at his desk when she walked in without even knocking. All Bill knew about her was what he overheard around the office in idle chitchat. He never paid much attention. Supposedly, she was married to a wealthy Atlanta businessman and didn't have to work, but she preferred not to sit home or spend her time with other wealthy socialites. Every now and then she accepted a temp agency arrangement; off and on she showed up around the office. He had heard that she worked just to pass the time because her husband was out of town a lot.

Before he could look up from his paperwork, she was in his face. Daphne sat on his desk and leaned her body towards him. Bill slid his swivel chair back away from her. That's when she swung around behind his desk and stood in front of him with both hands on her hips. Bill stared up at her. The blond raised her skirt slowly. Bill's gaze followed her hand upwards. She stopped and held her skirt just up to her waist. Bill saw she wasn't wearing any underwear or pantyhose under her skirt.

"I wanted you to see what you could be getting tonight," she whispered.

Bill was speechless and paralyzed in his chair. The hair between her legs was the same glistening yellow as the hair on her head. This was no bottled blond. Daphne was pure natural. He wanted to say something like 'What the hell are you doing,' but he couldn't get any words out. She let her skirt drop, reached into her side pocket and pulled out a piece of paper. She stuffed a note with her number and address on it into his hand and headed for the door.

"Think about it," was all she said as she left.

Bill thought about it and nothing else all that entire day. He decided he'd be a damn fool to mess with that white woman and risk his career and his marriage to Renee. He didn't call her and avoided any contact with her from then on. That was eight years ago. Nothing like that had ever happened to him again. It was just as well. An obsessed white woman in the workplace could spell trouble for a black man trying to move up in his career. There were already enough obstacles standing in the way. No need to add another burden.

Tonight he wanted to be with his wife. All he needed was someone to come home to who cared about how he felt and was interested in what he had to say. Often Renee acted like she didn't give a damn anymore. She complained about him spending too much time on his own business. According to her, eight hours at EduTech, the computer training center where he taught, was enough for one day. True, they didn't need the money. She was right about that, but she was dead wrong about this being a waste of time. Renee said he lacked the organization skills and aggressiveness that it took to start a business and keep it going. What she could not understand was that he needed to accomplish this goal for himself, not just to make more money. He needed to recoup the thirty thousand dollars he lost three years ago. This time he'd make it work and he'd do it without any help from her.

Bill didn't know what Renee wanted from him anymore and he gave up trying to find out. She complained he never talked to her, stayed isolated and too absorbed in his PC. Talk about what for christsakes? After maybe two or three benign words, she'd hit him with the subtle hints of what he could try, should be doing, or how someone else did it better. And then there were her eyes. Bill couldn't bear to look at them anymore for more than a few seconds. Her pain and disappointment reflected too clearly in them. He felt like Renee didn't even want him to touch her. What the hell was he supposed to do? Well, he wouldn't need her participation to enjoy himself tonight. He just needed to release stored up energy and tension. Thinking about screwing motivated him to lift his tired body out of the Range Rover. Who was he kidding? Bill knew he loved Renee so much it hurt. But he didn't want to think about love now. And forget about conversation. There'd be none of that tonight. Talking sometimes just made him feel worse.

Renee heard the sound of the automatic garage door opening. She curled under the covers and lay motionless, pretending to be asleep. She had no idea what time it was, but it didn't matter. Renee knew exactly what Bill's habits were and what he'd be doing to waste more time downstairs before coming to bed. He might grab the stack of envelopes off the table, fix himself a drink to unwind, and go hideaway in his office to sort through his mail. After that, he'd flip on his laptop computer to check for e-mail messages. If she didn't know better, she'd suspect him of engaging in one of those ridiculous Internet romances. But Renee didn't think Bill would fall for that kind of crap. The real truth was that he simply had no interest in sustaining any kind of meaningful relationship with her.

Renee heard her husband creep up the stairs to their darken bedroom. She recognized the familiar clanking of his keys as they hit the dresser. She listened as he pulled out his change and dropped them, unbuttoned and ripped off his shirt and trousers. After he took a quick shower, he crept over to the bed, and Renee felt the left side of the bed sink from his weight as he slipped under the sheets next to her. She smelled the mixture of Hennesey and the stale Lagerfeld cologne. No amount of soap or toothpaste could wash those familiar scents away.

Renee felt Bill's hand grip the inside of her thigh. Without so much as a *hello* or *how was your day*, he turned her over to face him and climbed on top of her. He rubbed his pelvis hard across hers in a circular motion in an attempt to get her excited and locked both her hands into his. Renee felt the weight of his body and tried to lift her head from the pillow as he covered her face with quick, hard kisses. Is this what he thought she wanted? Or, like the Hennesey, was she too just another convenient habit? A warm body? Only convenient for sex to help *him* unwind? It was obvious to her that Bill had no idea what an intimate relationship between a man and a woman was all about. She had grown weary through the years trying to teach him. She felt so alone and resentful. Others had found their soul mate, why couldn't she? She wanted a man that was crazy in love with her and she in turn with him. Her parents had felt that way about each other up until her mother's death, so she knew what it looked like and knew she didn't have it. She didn't think Bill had ever truly loved and cherished her the way her father had loved her mother, though in the beginning she convinced herself that she was in love with Bill. She always felt like she had passed an examination and met all his basic qualifications of a refined wife who would enhance his climb to career status and power.

She managed to turn her face to the opposite side to avoid his lips, but not ready to give up, Bill freed one of his hands and began tugging fiercely at the elastic band of her silk pajama bottoms attempting to remove them. Renee quickly slid her body from under him, but as soon as she managed to slip free, he moved on top of her again. She shoved him back and held her hand up against his chest to try to prevent him from moving towards her again. But she couldn't stop his tugging and groping. At fifty-one, Bill was still physically fit. He managed to retain his upper body strength and strong leg muscles from weekly workouts on the tennis court. Renee's fingers dug into the bulging muscles in his arms, but there was no holding him back. She felt like he was unleashing all his stored up anger and frustration on her. There was nothing she could do to stop him.

She punched her fist into his chest and screamed, "You bastard. Get the hell off of me!"

Bill ignored her words. Renee felt a sudden thrust of pain as he pushed and entered the dry, swollen walls of her vagina. Her body did not yield to him but he kept up a pounding pace nonetheless. Trying to suppress the pain, Renee counted silently to herself in rhythm to his rapid movements. She knew it would be over soon. It never lasted too long after extended intervals between their lovemaking when it was consensual. It had been months since she had felt the urge to have sex with him. After reaching the number ten, Renee felt a warm, thick liquid settle in and ooze down her thighs. Bill continued to ram his penis inside her but now she barely felt him because he was losing his erection. He appeared to be getting tired. Renee pushed hard against his chest and this time he willingly collapsed on his back away from her.

Free of Bill's weight, Renee sat up and turned on the lamp. She felt used and couldn't believe what he had done. She glanced at the clock and saw that it was almost 1 AM. Renee didn't bother to inquire about where he'd been because she already had a good idea that he'd gone to that makeshift warehouse that he called his new business and was there long after he should have been home. Instead of coming home at a decent hour and spending quality time with her in a loving way, he strolled in whenever he damn well pleased and forced himself on her like some wild beast. He rolled over, turning his back to her and pulled the sheet over his shoulders.

Renee punched him in the arm. "What the hell do I look like to you?"

He lifted his head and turned slightly, giving her an angry look. "You're my wife. The last time I checked a wife has duties, which you haven't been performing." He pummeled his pillow and sunk his head back down into it, then turned on his side away from her.

Her voice still clipped in anger, "My body doesn't belong to you to use at will. I'm not your possession. Maybe you need the law to remind you of that fact. I should go straight to emergency right now so they can collect a semen sample as evidence and then I'll bet they send your black ass straight to jail."

He shrugged his shoulders and yawned. "Do what you gotta do. I'm going to sleep."

Renee turned off the light, and sunk back down on the bed, but threw aside the covers. She felt her muscles tighten. She tried to focus on the rotations of the ceiling fan to relax but it was no use. She was hurt and angered by Bill's callousness and complete lack of sensitivity. It was getting more difficult for her to fake any kind of desire for him. Most of the time she would just lie there under him and count the seconds until it was all over just like she did tonight. Renee knew she had no interest in making love to Bill ever again, especially after what had just happened. She thought of leaving him, often. Even at forty-four years old, why was she willing to settle for an unfeeling android like Bill? Was it fear of loneliness? Insecurity? When she knew the answer to that question maybe she'd have the strength to change her life.

Renee glanced past Bill and frowned at her surroundings. She felt suffocated by the magenta, olive green, and gold canopy that hung from the brass rods above their bed posts. The walls were covered with a contrasting magenta and green patterned fabric. With so much ornate yardage of fabric and elegant formality around her, Renee suddenly felt trapped.

They first moved into this house eight years ago after her psychology practice took off and the royalties from her self-help books on relationships began to pay off. Renee had lacked the confidence to reflect her own tastes into their home and instead hired an interior decorator. Bill had never liked the results. He said it was too ostentatious—that there was nothing about their place that felt like it belonged to him. For once, she had to agree with him. Over the years Renee had grown to hate it as well. Given enough time and money, she knew she could fix the decor of the house. Her plan was to throw everything out and start over and make it their own. But she had come to realize that she could never start over from scratch with Bill.

There was no way she would be able to sleep through the sound of Bill's snoring, especially considering that her anger remained unabated. As the minutes passed, she remained wide awake and grew more and more annoyed. She kicked her husband in his side a few times but it didn't help ease her anger and frustration or his snoring. She shifted her body back and forth to get comfortable enough to fall asleep but couldn't stop the intrusion of her introspection and self-analysis. Why couldn't he figure out that all she wanted was to be important in just one person's life. For once, she just wanted to experience what it would feel like to be someone's priority, not their property or a mere afterthought. She decided Bill needed to be taught a lesson. She leaned over, clicked on the lamp and picked up the phone on her nightstand. She punched in the numbers 911 and waited for the operator to come on.

"Hello 911. What's your emergency?" asked the female voice on the other end.

Renee glanced over at Bill and then whispered into the receiver, "My name is Dr. Renee Hayes. I live at 127 Foxhall Road in the Foxhall Crescent subdivision. Can you send an officer out here right away so I can file a police report?"

"What's the problem ma'am?"

Renee hesitated, trying to find the right words to explain.

"Ma'am?" said the operator in a concerned voice.

"Well … it's … I've been raped." Renee blurted out the word and couldn't believe she had uttered it. The consequences briefly flashed before her mind, but it was too late to take it back. She had said it.

"Would you like me to send out an ambulance to take you to emergency?" offered the operator.

"No. No. I don't want to disturb the neighborhood. I just want an officer to come out. Please. I'm not …" Renee's voice broke; she was on the urge of tears.

The 911 operator reassured her that she would call it in and an officer would be there shortly to find out what she wanted to do. Renee hung up the phone and collapsed back down on the bed. She was torn between wanting Bill to pay for what he'd done and making it all go away by pretending that it never happened. Time passed, but while Bill slept, Renee remained wide awake. Her thoughts raced ahead in full, vivid animation. She laid still and listened above his snores to the sounds a house makes in the middle of the night. Twenty-five minutes later, the phone rang. Bill remained in his deep, satisfying sleep, so she knew the phone wouldn't wake him. Renee picked up on the second ring.

"Officer Stevens here. What's your emergency ma'am? You placed a call into the police," said the officer in a curt tone that Renee took as accusatory.

Renee cleared her throat before speaking. "Yes I called you. I'm Dr. Renee Hayes. I thought someone would be here by now. I've been waiting for 30 minutes. I want to file a complaint."

"What's the problem?"

"I've been … violated."

"Can you describe the perpetrator? How tall is he? What was he wearing? Is he Caucasian? African-American? Hispanic?"

"Well you see. He's my husband."

"Huh? Look lady, this is a busy night."

Renee's voice cracked as she spoke. "He forced himself on me. It was not … consensual."

"Where's your husband now?" the officer asked.

"Asleep. The phone didn't wake him."

Renee heard the officer's indifference from the monotone pitch of his voice. "Listen, Mrs … Dr.… Ma'am. We've got a burglary at 7-11 to respond to right now, but we'll be there in about 45 minutes."

"If that's all …" Renee heard the phone click before finishing her sentence or asking if they could send someone else. She put down the receiver. She got out of bed and clicked on the bathroom light. She was just about to run a tub of warm bath water when she thought she heard a strange noise coming from downstairs. It sounded like something had been knocked over. Renee turned off the light and pressed her cheek against the bedroom door to listen more closely. She imagined she heard footsteps downstairs and feared an intruder had broken in. The thumping of her heart quicken its pace. Her breathing came and went in brief, rapid spurts. Renee prayed this was only a dream. She'd had the same dream before but didn't know why it kept reoccurring. *Lying alone in bed, in the middle of the night, a prowler dressed in all black breaks in. Next, he's inside her bedroom, standing over her, close enough to smell his breath. He touches her with a black leather gloved hand. She reaches for the telephone on her night stand to dial 911 but the intruder grabs her wrist and snatches the phone from the wall outlet.* Renee always awakens at that moment, in a sweaty panic. She heard the noise downstairs again. She couldn't be dreaming. Not this time.

Renee tiptoed over to the bed and shook Bill's shoulders. "Bill? Bill? Wake-up. I think I hear something." She didn't want to make any loud noises to alert the possible intruder, but whispering Bill's name repeatedly and shaking him wasn't working. He wouldn't budge. It was useless trying to wake him. Renee knew nothing short of an earthquake would wake him up.

She reached for the telephone to dial 911, but stopped. They probably wouldn't believe her if she called again. If the cops showed up and found no signs of a break-in, they'd really think she was a nut job or even worse charge her for making false complaints. Since she couldn't wake up Bill, she'd go check it out herself. It was probably nothing more than an overturned plant or a book that had fallen off the shelf.

Renee retrieved a flashlight from the bottom of the closet. They kept no weapons in the house. She hated guns and insisted that Bill not keep any even though he had wanted to for protection. She prayed it was only her imagination and she'd find everything peaceful and safe downstairs. She didn't think ahead of what she'd do if actually faced with a dangerous intruder.

She crept out of the bedroom in her bare feet and descended the spiraling staircase. The beam from the flashlight guided her path. She passed by the entrance of the foyer where two French baroque busts sat on top of marble pedestals. A shiny, black Steinway baby grand sat in the corner of the living room. The piano was another vital accent piece that the decorator had insisted they purchase although neither she nor Bill played. All appeared still and quiet. After she had checked nearly every room, Renee began to feel relieved.

Their home had the look and feel of historic Europe imprinted throughout almost every room. Valuable paintings, mahogany antique reproductions, fine furnishings, and silken-threaded rugs covered all the hardwood floors. The house reflected nothing of their African-American heritage and the humble beginnings they both came from. For a potential burglar, it was a gold mine, full of expensive trappings.

Renee finished checking every room on the main floor and started down the stairs leading to her basement office. She found nothing amiss until she reached the door to her office. Flashes of light appeared under the doorway. Perhaps she had forgotten to turn off the lamp. Suddenly, the light disappeared. Her heart pounded against her chest as she unlocked the door. She slowly pushed the door open and stood still in front of her darkened office.

She waved the flashlight across the room slowly. She saw piles of patient folders and notes scattered all across the floor.

Slowly, a figure emerged from the shadows. Renee dropped the flashlight. She tried to scream but no sound came out. The intruder approached. She was frozen; feet cemented to the floor. Her palms began to sweat. The moonlight from the window cast a beam of light across his face. Renee clutched her pajama top together. She had on nothing but her silk top and panties and felt completely exposed. She hugged herself and shivered. Not from her near nakedness or the drafty night air, but from a paralyzing fear of being murdered. The only thing that might save her was that she couldn't make out his face. The man wore a coffee-bean colored stocking over his face, which made his features appear distorted. He breathed slowly through the thin, netted holes of the stocking. He appeared to be a thin man of average height, dressed in dark-colored blue jeans, a black shirt and black gloves. A gold medal hung from his neck. In his hand he brandished a gun.

Renee expected to die at any moment as the seconds elapsed. But instead of killing or raping her, he stared at her. Wisps of long, blond hair peaked out from the back of his neck. She dared not take her eyes away from him because at that moment she believed he would shoot her. In a weak, shaken voice she finally managed to speak.

"What … what do you want?" As she asked this question, the idea shot into her head that perhaps Bill had hired a hit man to break in and kill her and make it look like a burglary. He'd get everything she had worked hard for and be rid of her at the same time. That would explain why he hadn't bothered to get a home security system installed, even after she mentioned it to him a number of times. The security system was just one of many requests that he ignored because he hadn't remembered or was too busy. The hired hit man theory would also explain why she couldn't wake him to come downstairs and investigate the noise. It all made sense to her now. The bastard planned to sleep right through her murder then innocently inherit all her money.

The man still did not speak. He squinted at her through the stocking mask. She could tell he was a young man, probably in his late twenties.

He pointed the gun close to her throat. She didn't move a muscle or utter a sound. She knew she was soon going to die.

Suddenly, he pushed away her hands and ripped open her top, exposing her large breasts. He guided the gun slowly downwards from her throat and held it against the underside of her left breast.

Finally, he spoke. "Forget about callin' the cops 'cause I'll come back here. Ya hear me, darlin'?" He had a slight Midwestern accent, "To kill ya next time." The man turned around and picked up a stack of patient records from off the floor and gave her a final warning. "Already done killed me a couple a lil' girls in Nam. Liked it too."

Renee held her breath as he disappeared suddenly out the back door. She felt as though she had been standing before him, naked in the cool night air for hours. But it couldn't have been more than a few seconds. She pictured his masked distorted face and a cold chill ran through her. She believed the part he said about having already killed before and liking it. Renee ran upstairs, screaming for Bill to come quick.

CHAPTER 2

▼

Renee woke up restless in one of the spare bedrooms reserved for guests. She stretched her arms behind her head and tried to massage her stiff neck and shoulders. Despite the goose down pillows lining the brass headboard and the lush Pierre Cardin sheets, she hadn't slept for more than thirty minutes at a time. The dark figure from her nightmares had finally become a reality. She recalled what had happened last night, first her husband's assault that he viewed as lovemaking and then the break-in. The police showed up nearly two hours after her second 911 call to report the Breaking and Entering. She could only assume that they regarded the call as non-urgent since the perpetrator had already left. Or more likely they assumed she was some type of delusional lunatic. Two emergencies in the span of an hour—one an alleged spousal rape and the other a burglary with no valuables taken in a home full of rare art and expensive objects? She could hear them snickering now ... yeah right lady. No wonder the police probably didn't take her seriously.

When an officer finally did arrive last night, Bill stood in the foyer next to her and drew her close. The officer halted just inside the doorway and carried a notepad. He noticed the way Bill held onto his wife, rubbing her shoulder for comfort. Renee glanced up at Bill, surprised at his show of protectiveness towards her. His medium-brown complexion was carved with lines from years of too much sun. He still had most of his dark brown hair, but now it was sprinkled with gray at the temples. She still found him attractive after all these years.

The officer looked cynically at Renee before he spoke, "We received two emergency calls from this number this evening. Would you like to tell me the problem, ma'am?"

Renee told the officer everything she could recall about the break-in—about how she was not able to wake her husband when she heard a noise downstairs, and that she decided to investigate it for herself, thinking that something had simply fallen from the bookshelf in her office. She did not mention what had happened with Bill earlier that night. She never intended to press charges against him; she only wanted to teach him a lesson. She kept her gaze fixed on the officer's hand as he scribbled down everything she said on his notepad—how the young man looked, what he had on, his distinct cowboy accent. Thoughts of Bill wrestling on top of her and not being able to push him off flashed through her mind at the same time she was describing finding her patients' confidential records scattered across the floor. Then, instead of playing back the memory of the intruder's face, she saw her husband's droopy, blood-shot eyes. Whenever he'd worked too many long hours, they looked like the eyes of a sad St. Bernard dog. But at other times when determined to get what he wanted, he'd display the determined look of a pit bull. Renee told herself that what happened with Bill wasn't as traumatic as having a stranger break into her home. Her husband had never done anything like that before. She told herself it would never happen again.

The officer looked up from his pad. "Is that all this guy took? No cash, no jewelry? No other valuables, just some files?"

Renee stiffened. "Officer Stevens, did you say? I'm a clinical psychologist. Those stolen files contain confidential information about my patients. So indeed they are valuable to me and to my patients' privacy. This is a grave concern. I need this matter investigated and given the utmost priority."

Bill chimed in, "My wife is right. We wanna see some immediate follow through. This is damn serious."

Renee didn't want to think about the threat of a potential civil liberties case if a patient decided to take action against her for negligence. She could find herself facing a malpractice suit.

The officer nodded at Bill and turned back to Renee, "Do you happen to know whose file got stolen, ma'am?"

"No, not yet. I'll have to compare each file one by one against my recorded tapes from the sessions. There's no easy way to find out the patient's identity."

Renee assured herself that she had done the right thing by reporting the thief, but she was in no hurry to tell her patients what happened. She decided it would be better to wait until she knew for certain whose records had been stolen. No need in worrying everyone unnecessarily, especially with all the identity theft going on these days.

"One more question, Dr. Hayes. Did the intruder say anything important that you can recall before he left?"

Renee picked at the chipped clear polish from her nail and frowned as she pondered the question. There was one thing that she found particularly troubling. The officer's question brought back something strange that the burglar had said last night. She remembered the intruder's boasts of killing young girls when he was in Viet Nam and enjoying it. He threatened to come back and do the same to her if she called the cops. The strange thing was he only looked to be about 25 or 29 at the most. When he first said it, the inconsistency didn't register because she was too busy worrying about whether she was going to live or die. And until that moment she had not remembered anything he said. But now that she could give it more thought, there was no way this man could have served in the Viet Nam War. He would have been too young. Renee figured at most he would have been somewhere between five and ten years old in 1973, about the time that war ended. She told the police officer that the burglar must have been either high on drugs or out of his mind. She really wouldn't place any credence to what he said about being in Viet Nam.

After the officer left Bill assured her that he would call ADT Security systems and have them install the works. He'd been dragging his feet because they lived in a gated community, so he didn't see the urgency in getting home security. But now that there had been some recent complaints about the automatic gate taking much longer to close, he realized he needed to get this done right away. People who didn't belong there were now managing to slip through the gates before they closed. Bill insisted that Renee come back to bed with him, but she had refused and headed straight for the guest room. After the officer left she no longer had to pretend that everything was fine between them. She didn't want to wake up lying next to him; her hurt and humiliation from his actions last night still festered.

Renee sat up in bed and tried to make sense of everything that had happened last night. Who was that young man and why would he want to steal her patient files? Whose file had he stolen? From her window she caught a glimpse of the morning sun—a neon red sphere, announcing the arrival of dawn. She watched as it ascended upward into a hazy blue, cloudless sky. The flame-colored ball of fire slowly lifted itself, then sat suspended in a gray fog. Renee witnessed a new day come alive and felt mesmerized by it.

Here was proof there must be a God somewhere although she believed God had long since abandoned her. Or more likely, she had abandoned him. It didn't really matter to Renee who had given up first. Her soul felt just as dead inside.

She longed for a resurgence of spirit like this pre-dawn erupting forth with new hope.

Renee didn't even know where to begin to search for joy and peace in her life. She had grown accustomed to her hectic daily routine and meaningless rituals. She didn't know anymore how to give her husband what he needed or if she even cared to try.

At her last gynecological exam last year, she had confided to her physician that she'd lost interest in sex and wanted to know if this was normal for a woman her age. She had hoped the problem was something physical that could easily be fixed with a prescription, and not something mental, requiring she and Bill to go through counseling. She knew Bill would never agree to that. Renee longed to feel the intense passion she had experienced in the early years of their marriage. The fact that they barely spoke two words to each other in the course of any given day had to be a contributing factor. But she didn't tell her physician about the lack of caring and intimacy in her marriage. And God knows she would never want to reveal that he had forced himself on her. Some things do need to be left behind closed doors. Besides he would never do anything like that again; she just knew he wouldn't. Renee was not surprised when her doctor advised her to seek professional counseling. She felt embarrassed revealing these problems to her doctor; after all, *she* was a trained clinical psychologist herself and should be able to fix these things.

Fourteen years ago when she and Bill were first married, she was in her early thirties and still felt young and attractive. The seven-year difference between their ages didn't matter. Now at forty-four, she saw her body gradually aging, from the fifteen extra pounds and the flecks of visible gray in her sable brown hair to the signs of sadness around her once vibrant dark eyes. Time was running out. Renee had not been able to conceive children during her marriage to Bill. She believed this cast a distance between them. Now they behaved more like roommates than husband and wife. Renee was amazed that she'd been able to resist taking an overdose of pills herself. Sometimes, she felt she had just as much reason to gulp down a handful of barbiturates as any one of her suicidal patients. She struggled against acknowledging any similarities between her life and the pitiful lives of the patients that came to see her. She had always been able to block out these feelings before and accept things the way they were. She refused to succumb to the same emotional turmoil that her aunt suffered through all her miserable life. But lately she found it more and more difficult to accept living a lie and pretending that everything was okay. Happiness, peace and fulfillment were too important to do without forever. If she couldn't get what she needed from Bill, perhaps adoption would satisfy her inner need to be a central part of someone's life and to feel loved. She decided she was ready to do almost anything to satisfy the hunger for love and add meaning to her life.

Renee watched the sun metamorphosize from a mass of rutilant flames into a mellowed-out goldenrod of warm light. Like the sun announcing the beginning of another day, Renee Janette Hayes vowed to emerge anew. She would not accept a tranquilized body, void of spirit and passion—a lifeless shell. There would be no more feigning happiness and no more loneliness. She felt a renewed determination to go after what she believed would bring joy and meaning to her life—an adopted child to love and care for. For that reason, if for none other, she'd have to hold her marriage together. She didn't know if it was fear of being faced with death that brought this on, but whatever had caused her to feel this way she welcomed it. From the clock on the nightstand Renee saw it was almost 7:30 AM. She leaped from the bed, and rushed to her own bedroom to try to catch Bill before he left for work. She hadn't told him yet about their two o'clock interview that afternoon with a social worker from D. C. Public Health and Human Services to qualify them for adopting a baby. Bill still wasn't too keen on the idea of adoption so she hadn't given him any advance notice and extra time to think about it.

When Renee entered the bedroom she saw that he was already gone. He had left a note on her side of the bed. It was brief. "Had an early meeting. Didn't want to wake you. Will call later, Bill." She balled up the note and threw it in the wastebasket. Why hadn't he stopped in the guest room to check on her? She probably wasn't asleep anyway and would have appreciated a kiss good-bye. She could have been murdered last night by that intruder and lying in a pool of warm blood. She knew she had been lucky that all the intruder wanted was her patient's records. But how could she expect someone as thoughtless and preoccupied with his work as Bill was to see that she needed him right now? He probably wouldn't even have missed her until her body started rotting away downstairs in her office.

Renee called Bill at EduTech Computer Training Center and was told by the secretary that he was teaching a class. The secretary switched her to Bill's voice mailbox. She left a message, hoping he would return the call in time to come home for their two o'clock appointment that afternoon. Last month, Renee had filed an application to re-open her request for adoption and had scheduled an interview with Health & Human Services without Bill's knowledge.

She hoped she wasn't deluding herself about being able to one day offer a safe, loving, and stable two parent-environment—the kind of upbringing neither she nor Bill had known growing up. One of the main reasons Bill had always been against the idea of having children or, of even adopting when they found out Renee couldn't conceive, was because of his own neglected and dysfunctional childhood. He said that there were too many scars left over to risk inflicting the bitterness he felt onto a child. At her insistence, he kept telling her that he would think about it but his thinking had already carried them into fourteen years of a childless marriage.

Renee feared there would be many other things standing in the way of this adoption besides Bill's flat out refusal to even discuss it with her anymore. She realized her chances were slim but it didn't stop her from hoping. That's why she had to keep her marriage intact no matter how unfulfilled she felt being married to Bill. If they were ever approved for adoption, she had to be ready to offer a child what she had missed.

She believed Bill couldn't deny her this one chance to be a mother after all the years of unhappiness she put up with in their marriage. He would have to go along with it, if HHS actually presented them with a beautiful, healthy baby, wouldn't he? She had put up with Bill's moods, his isolation, and total lack of interest in anything she cared about for much too long. Now it was her turn to take charge of her life and go after what she wanted, no matter what Bill said.

Several years ago, she had tried pursuing adoption through a private agency. Bill balked at the $10,000 cost. The money was his convenient excuse for turning her down. Renee had to admit, she really didn't see any notable difference in services between the private agencies and Health & Human Services agencies to warrant a $10,000 fee, but nothing would stop her from seeing the entire process through this time. She was already forty-four years old and not getting any younger.

Seated at her vanity table Renee flipped open her appointment book and called patients who had scheduled counseling sessions for that day. She didn't feel up to focusing on other people's problems after last night. She managed to reschedule them all except for two of her newer patients. One was a shy young man named Kenneth Blackwell who could not be reached and had provided no way for her to leave a message. The other was a patient named Veda Simms whom she had only seen a few times and didn't want to cancel with her so early in her treatment. Veda was a 38 year old, divorced, African-American female suffering from depression and suicidal tendencies. Fortunately, the first session with Veda wasn't until four o'clock later that afternoon, so she'd have time to get herself together and meet with the social worker.

Since her calendar remained open all morning, she'd have plenty of time to prepare for the social worker's visit. She took a quick shower and dressed in a casual but elegant white double-breasted pantsuit. She applied her trademark shade of ripened burgundy lipstick which complimented her tender brown complexion. She emphasized her eyes with forest green eyeliner pencil. Afterwards, she made a quick run to the florist, picked up several bouquets of fresh flowers, and arranged them strategically throughout the foyer and living room. She prepared a light refreshment in case the social worker hadn't eaten lunch.

Several hours later, she was downstairs in her office, matching files against their taped recordings and waiting for the social worker to arrive. To her dismay, Bill had still not called and it was getting late. Piles of patient records and tapes were stacked high on the floor where she had begun to organize them. When the doorbell rang, Renee stepped over the files and rushed upstairs to answer it.

Mrs. Matilda Addison, the social worker was an ample woman in her early sixties with a friendly smile, hazel eyes, and a neatly pinned chignon in the back of her hair. The scent of Lavender soap sifted through Renee's nostrils as she led Mrs. Addison to a chair in the living room. Renee immediately felt comfortable with her. She brought out the refreshments and poured her a cup of herbal tea. She did not mind the personal nature of the social worker's questions. She told Mrs. Addison that she suspected it had been difficult for her to get pregnant because she waited until her thirties to get married. What she didn't reveal to the social worker was that her husband had been far from thrilled at the news of her last pregnancy five years ago. As it turned out it was an ectopic pregnancy that had to be aborted. The doctors told Renee that after having already gone through several unsuccessful attempts, her chances of bearing a child were slim. Her only hope of becoming a mother now was to adopt.

Renee skirted around Mrs. Addison's question about where Bill was. She told the social worker that her husband was tied up in a meeting at work but would be happy to speak to her at another time. She answered the social worker's barrage of questions, giving details about her education and background. She told Mrs. Addison that she had worked in the evenings and weekends as an Emergency room nurse for three years while attending Georgetown University during the day to pursue an MA degree in clinical psychology. She had seen enough people die on the table her first year in the Emergency room to know that she didn't want to practice nursing. Two years after completing her Masters in clinical psychology, she continued her studies at Georgetown University and received a doctorate in psychology. Then after answering all her questions, Renee asked Mrs. Addison the one most important to her.

"How long will I have to wait for a healthy African-American baby, Mrs. Addison?"

Renee knew Bill wouldn't even consider a boarder baby or one that was not perfectly normal and healthy in every way. For the past two years Renee had volunteered in the Court Appointed Special Advocate or CASA program where she worked with many abused, neglected or HIV-positive children. Recently, she had grown attached to an eighteen-month-old AIDS-infected baby girl, residing in the home of her foster mother. As a volunteer, Renee had been the baby's court-appointed special advocate since December and visited her every Saturday. In just a few days, she would have to face little Susanna's dark, listless eyes again but now Renee only wanted to focus on the image of a healthy child. Bill had always been adamantly opposed to her bringing Susanna or any of her past CASA children home for even a short visit. She knew Bill would never agree to adopt anything other than a healthy child. Mrs. Addison looked up at Renee from her notepad and pushed her glasses back from off the tip of her nose.

"Well, Dr. Hayes, to be perfectly honest with you," she said, "a healthy African-American infant could take as long as two years."

"Two years? I can't wait that long." Renee felt slapped. Her upbeat mood sank.

"Unfortunately, Dr. Hayes, as you must already know from your volunteer work with CASA, many of the children needing homes have been exposed to drugs, HIV, or alcohol or all of these complications. And another thing, the majority of these children are older, anywhere from two to sixteen."

Renee fought back tears as she felt her dream of becoming a mother slipping away.

"But, I would suggest that you not indicate healthy on your application," said Mrs. Addison, "because a low birth weight baby or one with a pre-existing condition, such as asthma or allergies could be presented to you in as little as six to eight months."

"Really? That soon?" said Renee.

Mrs. Addison nodded as she spoke, "These children are not necessarily unhealthy although HHS labels them unhealthy due to their allergies and whatnot."

Renee agreed to remove the healthy stipulation and savored Mrs. Addison's promise of six to eight months. She trusted Mrs. Addison to present them with a baby diagnosed with nothing more than a few minor health problems. She knew this was her only chance of getting Bill to agree to take on the responsibly of fatherhood at his age.

"A few years ago after becoming a child advocate with CASA, I started looking into adoption," said Renee, "I read somewhere that giving up a healthy infant for adoption appears to be mainly a white, middle-class occurrence. Do you think this is still the case today, Mrs. Addison?"

"I really couldn't say for sure, Dr. Hayes. But I do know that the number of special needs children far outweigh the healthy ones. One positive trend is that African-American couples who can provide good homes, such as you and your husband, are considering adoption more," said Mrs. Addison, "and of course we're very pleased about that because there are so many children who need love and a stable home." She paused, shifting her papers.

"But there's still a lot more steps involved before you and your husband qualify and get approved," said the social worker, "I'd like to ask you some additional questions, if I may."

"Yes, of course."

"First, tell me about your upbringing Dr. Hayes—about your parents."

Renee had been doing great until that point. It was easy to ask the social worker questions and to talk about her academic or professional accomplishments and her volunteer work but recalling childhood memories was another matter. Even in her patients' counseling sessions, Renee minimized the use of the typical Freudian, 'What happened in your childhood?' approach to psychotherapy as much as possible. Unless a patient had severe emotional problems stemming from childhood, she focused on what was going on in the patient's life right then and there. She gave them techniques for dealing with their day-to-day anxieties and ways to cope. Now the social worker wanted to open up old wounds from her past.

"Would you say you had a happy childhood, Dr. Hayes?"

Renee told Mrs. Addison that her mother had been a showgirl and her father a jazz musician when she was growing up. Her parents maintained an average of thirty-five to forty weeks a year on the road touring throughout the U.S. and Europe and making public appearances. Once they had even performed onstage with Lena Horne. Neither her father nor mother wanted to sacrifice his or her dream for Renee. So she ended up being raised by Aunt Clara, her mother's older, unmarried sister and seeing very little of her parents. Renee never really understood her parent's strong desire to be entertainers.

Aunt Clara had taken care of Renee from the time she was just a baby while her younger sister pursued a career in show business. Aunt Clara was a strict disciplinarian who had never been married and had no children of her own. The only time Renee dared get out of hand was on those rare occasions when her mother showed up because Renee knew her Aunt Clara *did not play.*

Mrs. Addison got up and removed an antique-framed picture from the piano ledge. She sat back down next to Renee and held the photo out to her. "Your parents, I presume?"

Renee nodded and stared at the photo for a moment. It was a black and white picture taken in 1962, the year they first met and fell in love. The two stood arm in arm under a canopy of autumn leaves. Renee's father, LeRoy Curtis, at twenty-one years old, wore a pencil-thin Clark Gable mustache, hair parted on one side and slicked down. LeRoy Curtis stood as tall as his slender 5'9" body would allow—with both legs spread slightly apart and one hand clasped around his beloved saxophone and the other arm around his sweetheart. Renee recalled how he would often raise one of his arched eyebrows when curious or crease them both together in a frown if pretending to be angry or hurt. She couldn't help laughing at his funny faces when she was a little girl. In the picture, his head tilted mischievously to one side and he wore the same boyish smile that her mother fell in love with. Next to him in the picture, stood Renee's mother, Bettina, a petite caramel-colored, eighteen-year old beauty whose sunlit face smiled back at Renee. She had on a long, floral dress that billowed around her legs from the fall breeze, exposing a well-shaped thigh. Bettina's thick, dark hair blew freely from her face. Renee stared lovingly at the picture and agreed with her Aunt Clara's constant insults, the child had inherited none of her mother's remarkable beauty. Nor did Renee possess her mother's chameleon ability to transform herself into virtually any man's desire and fantasy.

Renee's father, LeRoy, was the only one in the family who sympathized with Bettina's drive to sing and dance in show business. It was LeRoy who advised her to change her name from Bettina Johnson to a more befitting stage name of Tina Joye.

Thinking about her parents reminded her of just how lonely she'd been all these years despite being married to Bill and why she felt she needed a child to make her life worthwhile. Bill was far from being obsessed with her the way her father had been for her mother.

"Your mother, Dr. Hayes," asked Mrs. Addison as she positioned her pen on the questionnaire form, "still living or deceased?"

"Deceased."

"Oh, I'm so sorry," said Mrs. Addison and adjusted her eyeglasses to continue, "illness or accident?"

"She was killed in a bus accident on March 5th, 1970 while traveling with her tour group. I was only seven at the time."

"That must have been terrible for you," said Mrs. Addison, shaking her head slowly.

Renee nodded and poured more tea for herself and her guest, "Yes, it was."

"And when is your date of birth, Dr. Hayes?"

Renee told her, welcoming the change of subject. "Actually, that was just nine months after this picture of my parents was taken. It was love at first sight for them. But they never bothered to get married though. My mother was a true free spirit."

Renee thought about the love her parents shared for one another and realized she'd probably never experience that kind of intensity with Bill.

"What can you tell me about your father?"

Renee glanced back down at the photo sitting on the coffee table.

The handsome, young man in the picture would be almost 66 years old now. Renee recalled the last time she saw her father. It was over two years ago when LeRoy Curtis showed up unexpectedly one Christmas, loaded with gifts for his daughter and one ugly tie for Bill. Two years ago, LeRoy's complexion still looked youthful even at the age of sixty-four. His polished dark brown skin bore only a few wrinkles, but the hair on his head was practically gone. All that remained from a full head of once dark, shiny hair was speckled, gray fuzz. His eyes still sparkled, and he hadn't lost the up-turned brow or the crooked half smile of a young boy who looked like his hand had been caught in a cookie jar.

Renee's father had always disliked Bill. She never wanted to tell him anything negative about her husband because she knew he mistrusted his son-in-law and found him too cold and aloof. Whenever he visited them, Renee tried to pretend that her marriage was good and that she was happy. But her father saw through this facade. LeRoy believed Bill married his daughter for all the wrong reasons. He told Renee that after loving her mother, he could recognize when a man truly loved a woman. He insisted that Bill Hayes did not display those signs towards her. Renee realized her father meant well but his words stung deep.

Now, nearly two and a half years later, she worried everyday about where her father was and if he was getting along okay. She prayed that he'd call or write again. But just as it had been throughout her childhood, LeRoy Curtis's first dedication was always to his music. He had loved only three things in his entire life; his music, Bettina, and his only daughter, Renee.

When Renee was little, she and Aunt Clara could count on LeRoy to send money home whenever he played a steady gig. But as a child Renee never knew when to expect her father to call or actually show up. Not much had changed over the years.

She used to get a phone call or a card at Christmas from different places and occasionally a request to wire him some money. But this past Christmas Renee didn't hear from her father at all and that worried her.

"I haven't heard from him in over 18 months," said Renee, "I believe he's missing."

Mrs. Addison looked up, "Missing?"

"I've filed a missing persons report but the police say nothing has turned up yet. They warned me not to get my hopes up because it's difficult with transients who travel around a lot. For the last twenty years, my father's never been in Washington D. C. for more than six months at a time."

"Have you tried a private investigator?" asked Mrs. Addison.

"Yes, but he hasn't been able to find out much. The last letter I received from my father was postmarked somewhere in Germany. Unfortunately, the PI's tracking experience doesn't extend that far."

"I do wish you luck in locating your father, Dr. Hayes," said Mrs. Addison.

"Thank you," said Renee, "But I'm afraid at this point I've just about given up hope."

"You must never give up hope," said Mrs. Addison and patted Renee's hand as she stood up to leave, "You're in my prayers, my dear. You and your father. Now, I really must be going. I've got several more appointments this afternoon."

"Thank you," said Renee politely and escorted Mrs. Addison to the door.

A lot of good prayers will do me thought Renee feeling hopeless behind a bright smile.

"What's our next step, Mrs. Addison?"

"Well, the next important step, Dr. Hayes, is to speak to your husband. I really can't finalize the paperwork until I meet with him. Then we can proceed from there."

"But can't you do anything else in the meantime?" Renee pleaded.

"Not much. I forgot to mention, you'll both need to get finger printed and background checked."

"Yes, of course," nodded Renee.

"One more thing, while your application is being considered, HHS now requires prospective parents to attend a ten week class on parenting skills. It starts at 6:30 in the evening, once a week for three hours," said Mrs. Addison, "Please contact me when your husband is available for an interview, Dr. Hayes. I prefer to go over all those details with both of you at the same time."

Renee felt this sudden jerk back to reality like a smack of lightening. How would she ever convince Bill to go through with all these qualification requirements for something he's not even interested in doing in the first place?

CHAPTER 3

▼

After Mrs. Addison left, Renee placed the picture of her parents back on the piano ledge and gently stroked the edge of the frame. She thought about how nice it would be to have her father in her life. She missed his sense of humor and his easy way of dealing with disappointments. LeRoy Curtis always had a joke handy and a few words of wisdom to pass out. If only she knew how to get in touch with him; with any luck, she might be able to convince him to stay in the area for awhile. The last letter Renee mailed to her father had been forwarded back to her and stamped "returned to sender." He was no longer at that address and Renee had no idea where he was now.

Leroy never understood the importance of a closeknit family. His own *bourgeoisie* as he called it, middle-class upbringing had been too reserved. His parents disowned him after he dropped out of Howard University to become a bum according to his father. Renee believed her father's sacrifice to music was too great.

He never fulfilled his dream of reaching national and worldwide attention, but that didn't stop him from trying. He lived by the same advice he gave his daughter. Renee recalled what he had written years ago in one of his more serious letters, "*Daughter, you must never give up. A timid effort accomplishes nothing, so keep at it. The long and steady pull of the mule is what does the trick.*" His advice on perseverance carried her through undergraduate and graduate school. Over the years, his words had helped her deal with many disappointments, fatigue, and attacks of self-doubt. But the impact of his words had lost its meaning when it came to dealing with her marriage. Giving up on happiness had seemed easier than fighting for it.

Mrs. Addison's questions forced her to think about growing up in Aunt Clara's house. Aunt Clara passed away soon after Renee graduated from college. Usually, Renee tried not to think about her or what it was like growing up in the Twentieth Street duplex in North East Washington, D. C. Dredging up her past brought out old scars from tucked away childhood memories.

Renee retrieved a photo album that had belonged to Aunt Clara from the back of her bedroom closet. She blew the dust away and flipped it open. She stared at the faded pictures glued beneath their plastic coverings. One of the photos showed a picture of her when she was about 5 or 6. A pair of thick, shoulder-length pigtails and neatly pressed bangs outlined her chubby face.

Next to that picture was a rare photo of Aunt Clara, actually smiling. The matronly looking woman's brown complexion accented her shiny black hair. Aunt Clara had always worn her hair one way, parted down the middle and pulled back in a neat bun. Like her hairstyle and clothing, Aunt Clara's life and her household were always neat and orderly. That is, until Renee's mother, Bettina, dropped in every blue moon and ruined her older sister's strict routine.

Years later, after becoming a psychologist, Renee realized that her spinster aunt resented being placed in the position of having to raise her sister's child. She always seemed full of pent-up anger and out-right meanness. Renee always felt like everything her aunt did for her was an extreme sacrifice, from taking her to purchase new school shoes, washing and braiding her hair, to scheduling routine dental and doctor appointments.

Life with Aunt Clara was an endless recycling of the same tasks week after week. It was unheard of for them to do something spontaneous or just for fun. Aunt Clara wrote lists of chores for herself and Renee. She wouldn't stop moving until everything on her list was checked off. Even if it took all day, Renee couldn't play nor do anything else until everything on the list was done.

Saturday was their serious cleaning day. Everything had to be scrubbed until it glowed. Even the garbage cans had to be wiped down inside and out. A strictly enforced rule was to put everything away in its proper place when not in use. Sundays were reserved for sunrise service at St. Augustine's, followed by an hour of catechism class, as well as, devotion and prayers throughout the day. During the week, Aunt Clara taught seventh grade at Bethune Junior High School. In the evenings, she stayed closed up in her bedroom, grading school papers and preparing for her class the next day.

Renee remembered thinking as a young girl how she would someday get married, have a house full of children, and never feel lonely and unwanted again. But despite marriage, a thriving career, and a beautiful home, things were not much different now than they were during her childhood in Aunt Clara's house. Loneliness still held its grip on her.

She passed by the antique mirror that had belonged to her aunt, and caught sight of her own image. She stopped to gently finger-comb her soft, thick hair. The mirror was in desperate need of re-silvering. Tiny specks dotted its glass. Even through cloudy, translucent film, signs of gradual aging and depression stared back at her.

It was clear she needed a change—needed to do something for herself. Perhaps a little color to rinse out the few stubborn strands of gray, she thought. Renee remembered she already had an appointment at the hairdresser's that evening. Her beautician recommended a shorter cut, insisting that it would take years off her face. But Renee refused to listen. Now that her hair had finally grown to her shoulders, she wasn't about to cut it off no matter what Cha-Cha recommended. The full, layered style she wore often gave her hair a carefree, windblown look. Although it didn't quite match the mature wisdom of her face, Renee held onto her shoulder-length hair like an old dog with a chewed up bone. Was it because Bill had once said he liked her hair long? Or because Renee's mother, a natural beauty, had always worn hers long?

According to Aunt Clara, Bettina had good hair, unlike Renee. Aunt Clara had reminded Renee every chance she could that she was nothing at all like her beautiful, talented mother. Bettina's hair was the kind that needed only a slight touching up with the straightening comb, a teaspoon full of My Knight hair pro-made and a few bends with the marcelle curlers. When Renee was growing up, her aunt would complain every Saturday night when it was time to wash and press her short, thick hair for church the next day. What was it she always said? *'Lord have mercy, child. Not enough hair in this kitchen to work with ...'.*

The doorbell ringing interrupted Renee's thoughts. She approached her bedroom window, squinted through a ray of sunlight reflecting off the glass and looked down below. An unfamiliar car sat parked in her driveway. She glanced at her watch and saw that it was nearly 3:30. The first patient scheduled that day wasn't due until 4 o'clock. She wondered who it could be at the door. Probably someone trying to sell something she didn't want like a miraculous new cleaning product or even worse, the salvation of her soul. Renee headed towards the foyer and fixed her mouth to tell whoever it was she was on her way out. She jerked open the front door. Instead of speaking, she stood there transfixed and gaped at the handsome, young man standing on her front steps. At that moment, something stirred in her that she believed had long since died.

"Dr. Renee Hayes?" he said and removed his sunglasses, "I'm Detective Sergeant Degas Hamilton, homicide."

The detective showed his badge as he spoke, "I'm investigating the deaths of three victims in this vicinity. Do you mind if I ask you a few questions about the break-in you reported last night?" He returned the badge to his suit jacket.

Renee didn't hear a word he said after hello and his name. She gazed into his eyes that were as black and fluid as an ocean at midnight.

"Ma'am?" he repeated. "May I come in? I'd like to ask you some questions just in case the burglar you encountered last night has the same M.O. as the perp I'm after?"

Did he say *Degas* like the French artist thought Renee? Even his name sounded exotic. He couldn't have been much older than thirty, if that. Detective Degas Hamilton must have skipped his morning shave because a new growth of facial hair framed his chin and jawline. The tiny stubs of hair only enhanced his sex appeal and masculinity to Renee. She found this raw, untamed look exciting.

He had well-formed, almost perfect, features. His complexion displayed the smooth, even toned brown of a paper lunch bag. Like his eyes, his hair was jet black and cropped close so that small, soft ripples covered his scalp. The hair at the nape of his neck had grown a bit too long for her taste, but he sported a well-trimmed mustache. Renee noticed a great deal in the span of a few mesmerizing seconds. She heard him calling her name again and snapped out of her trance.

"I'm sorry Detective. Did … did you just say a homicide?"

"Yes, I'm investigating a murder and looking for similarities with the case you reported. It also started with a break-in. May I come in just the same, Dr. Hayes? I'll see to it that another investigator follows up on your B&E report."

"Of course. Please do come in," said Renee, a bit too eagerly, "I apologize for my rudeness."

She held the door open wide, and he stepped inside. Detective Hamilton retrieved a hand-held Personal Data Assistant from the breast pocket of his beige linen suit. She noticed the revolver tucked inside a shoulder holster under his jacket.

He glanced down at his notes. "I read the report, but why don't you tell me again what happened," he said, yawning wearily. "Sorry Doc, guess I'm a little beat."

He explained. "It was my squad's turn to pull the midnight shift this week. They've already got four principal detectives working on this murder case and a dozen other people involved, including me. And to top that, I had to testify at a grand jury this morning. Fun day, huh?"

When he smiled down at her, Renee noticed the dimples piercing each cheek.

"That's quite all right, Detective. I've had a long night too," she said, "Why don't you come in and sit down."

He followed her through the foyer into a large, step-down living room. He gave his surroundings an admiring glance and whistled softy. "Not too shabby, Doc."

Renee stole periodic glances at him when she thought he wasn't looking. He was quite tall compared to her 5 feet 4. Renee guessed he had to be about 6'2". He was trim and muscular, but not bulging like those weight lifters she had seen on television sports shows. Despite his drop-dead good looks, Detective Hamilton did not appear to be the least bit conceited or arrogant. His tie was loosened casually at the neck. Instead of a cop, he looked more like a GQ cover model or a daytime TV character on 'The Bold and the Beautiful.'

"Sorry to bother you with all this again Doc, but like I said, there's nothing solid to go on with any witnesses in my case, so I guess I'm grasping at straws here."

"I understand," said Renee, "but I don't know what else I can tell you, Detective."

"Let me get this straight, you said the only thing stolen was some patient records from your office?"

"That's correct."

He nodded and made a notation on his electronic notepad. She leaned forward pretending to get a better look at what he punched onto the tiny data screen. She found herself stalling in order to prolong his inquiry. When it appeared Detective Hamilton had no more questions to ask and she thought he was preparing to leave, Renee began asking him questions to detain him. From her prodding he explained that he had been temporarily assigned to the three high-profile homicide cases until the FBI would get involved sometime within the next few days. He said the chief also intended to beef up the manpower in many exclusive neighborhoods reporting a rash of break-ins. He'd be back to his regular homicide squad on Monday, working on his own active cases. Renee detected a sign of relief from the young detective. But for her own part she felt disappointed that she probably wouldn't see him again. Someone else from B&E would be following up with her after today.

Renee didn't understand her interest in the physical details of a complete stranger and a homicide detective at that. She suspected Detective Hamilton was displaying his best public servant behavior and could actually be quite crude in his own, natural habitat of serious police work. After all, he was really a homicide detective. For some reason, that excited her even more.

It took less than fifteen minutes for Detective Hamilton to take down her information about what happened last night. Renee didn't have much information to tell, but didn't mind repeating her story for him. She couldn't describe the burglar because he had worn a stocking over his face. She estimated his height, weight, and approximate age as best she could. She said the intruder had threatened her at gunpoint but couldn't identify the type of gun. Renee still hadn't finished the inventory of her patient data so she didn't even know whose records had been stolen.

"Do you mind if I take a look at your office before I go so I can check for forced entry?" he said.

Renee nodded and gladly led him downstairs to her office.

"What A Difference A Day Makes … twenty-four little hours …" The words from a late 50's Dinah Washington melody crooned out of the recessed speakers from the ceiling in Renee's office. While Detective Hamilton checked the windows and rear door leading to the back of the house, Renee stood close by and watched him. Dinah Washington's silky voice floated over them and Renee agreed with the words in the song, "What a difference a day makes."

"It didn't take much effort to break in here," said Detective Hamilton, looking at the window and pointing to where the point of entry must have been.

"My husband's planning to get a security system installed next week," she said.

"Good Idea. You say you don't know which files were stolen?"

"I'm afraid not, Detective. First, I need to inventory all my patients' files and match them against their corresponding taped sessions to see whose files are missing. That's probably going to take quite awhile. I still have to keep my regular appointments, you know."

Detective Hamilton glanced down at the piles of patient files stacked on the floor and shook his head.

"You know Doc, you could use some type of document management system and scan in all these files. It'd be a hell of a lot easier to find whatever you're looking for with a search engine," said the Detective as he glanced around the office, "but I see you don't even have a computer."

"I do, but my husband hasn't had time to set it up for me yet," she explained, pointing to two large boxes in the corner.

"Bill teaches programming at a computer training center in Arlington, Virginia and works late most nights on his own computer business" said Renee, "Do you know something about computers?"

"Yeah. Something. I used to be an IBM techie in a past life," Detective Hamilton walked over to the boxes and pointed, "How old is this PC?"

"I think I bought it about six months ago. Bill tried to talk me into getting a laptop, but I certainly have no intention of carrying an office around with me. And forget about email," she said waving her hand away, "What a time-waster. Besides, I prefer personal interactions." She looked at him with what she called a seductive 'come hither' glance, but obviously she was out of practice because he simply looked at her strangely, completely missing the signal.

With her approval, he bent down and ripped open one of the boxes.

"I hope you didn't pay much," he said, "You've only got a low end model here."

"I don't know anything about computers, Detective," she said, "I thought the color would match the peach tone in my office."

"Hum, I see," he nodded, "Well, just in case at some point you want to purchase a better PC, you could make this one a client. That might not be such a waste. But in the meantime, I can set this one up and connect your printer for you in about ten minutes if you like."

"Yes, of course, that would be nice. Thank you, Detective Hamilton," said Renee, happy to extend his visit even for ten more minutes.

Detective Hamilton took out his cell telephone and laid it down. He removed his jacket and rolled up his shirtsleeves. She noticed his arms were covered in short, fine hairs laying diagonally across his arms in neat rows. Renee fought against the impulse to touch his arm and stroke it, as she would rub the soft fur on a kitten's back. Instead of brief glances, Renee caught herself staring at his bronze-tinted arms, slightly glazed from droplets of perspiration. She felt guilty but couldn't take her eyes away from him.

He lifted all the computer equipment from the boxes, connected all the cables and tested the printer. It took less than ten minutes to set everything up just as he said it would. Renee tried not to think about how little effort Bill had put into meeting her request. When he finished with the installation, he went over a few basic operating instructions with her. He recommended that she go through the built-in tutorials for the operating system and its word processor program. He reached into his pocket and pulled out a card with three different numbers and his e-mail address written on it. One number was for the police precinct, another was a home number, and the third was to his cell telephone. The detective gave his card to Renee.

"Guess I'll be heading on home now, Dr. Hayes," he said, "It's been a long day for me. Time to take off the shackles. I'm due for a little R & R."

"Thank you so much, Detective," she said, "It was thoughtful of you to go out of you way."

"No problem. Call me if you think of anything else before Monday," he said and grabbed his cell phone from her desk, "and good luck with your PC."

A little Rest and Relaxation thought Renee. Who would he be enjoying that R and R with she thought? No doubt with some beautiful twenty-something year old—one with soft skin, a curvy figure, and hair flowing down her back. Probably not unlike one of those video dancers on T. V. that grind and shake to the latest hip-hop and rap music. Yes, that was probably his type—not a dried up, bookworm on the brink of middle age like her. She pictured him at home in ecstasy having hot, fluid sex with the video dancer. Renee felt long overdue for a little R and R herself, but had no clue how to get it, other than through her own imagination and daydreams.

"Well, thanks for answering my questions, Dr. Hayes" he said, "I'm sorry I took up so much time."

"No. Thank you, Detective," she said and wished she could think of something meaningful to say to keep him there longer, "I'm sorry … but what did you say happens after Monday?"

"Another detective from B&E will be in touch with you. I can't say exactly when or who it'll be," he explained between yawns, "Like I said, I only get interested when there's a dead body involved."

Renee reluctantly followed him to the back door of her office. She felt an uncontrollable tinge of desire for this man and didn't know why.

"Would you mind telling me your first name again, Detective."

"Degas. Blame my grandmother for that one," he smiled, "She was from Martinique. But people who know me pretty well call me Deek. Not much improvement, huh?"

"I like it," she said and offered her hand as a farewell gesture, "I like it a lot."

Detective Hamilton grasped her hand firmly in his and she saw he wasn't wearing a wedding ring. He hesitated as if he wanted to say something else but decided against it. Renee locked her eyes into his and he returned her gaze for a brief moment.

He stood so close, the scent from his cologne made her dizzy. It had a subtle, earthy, masculine smell, not at all flowery or too heavy. The natural spices of the fragrance mixed with his own sweat enhanced its sensual affect on her. She struggled to keep her composure and not let her imagination run wild, but she could not resist her fantasies.

Instead of letting go, she pictured herself guiding his hand to her lips and placing a lingering kiss on each of his fingers. Her feelings of guilt were strong. Aunt Clara had instilled enough guilt through the years. But it was not strong enough to stop her from fantasizing about this man who was much younger than she was.

Renee wanted to blame Bill for her pathetically unfulfilled state, but she knew her problem reached far back in time long before Bill. It began years ago with all the '*Thou shalt nots*' from Aunt Clara that echoed in her mind daily for years and years. Aunt Clara had warned her to fight against sexual passion as fiercely as she would battle with the devil. *Get thee behind me Satan* was one of her favorite expressions. Passion only made a woman need a man too much. And then he'd end up hurting her. Aunt Clara said Renee had only to look at her own mama to see proof of that. She felt like saying to hell with her and doing what she damn well pleased. Just see what the ghost of Aunt Clara would have to say if she invited this total stranger to her bed.

When Detective Degas "Deek" Hamilton stepped outside the door and put on his sunglasses, reality sunk in. The handsome young Detective was only there to do his job and hopefully had no idea of her desire for him. Long after he left, Renee recalled the deep tone of his voice and the smell of his cologne. She completely forgot about the Breaking & Entering, Mrs Addison and the adoption.

CHAPTER 4

▼

Deek turned off his digital phone to make sure those idiots at the precinct wouldn't bother him. The phone would store all his incoming calls for up to 72 hours so he could retrieve his messages later. He ran a quick mental inventory to check what games were on tonight but couldn't recall anything worth getting excited about, so he decided to stop off at Blockbusters and rent the latest action movie before heading home to his modest rowhouse near 23rd and Alabama Avenue. With the pizza parlor being conveniently right next door, his weekend was set. Tonight, he and Tyrone would zone out for the rest of the evening and watch movies. Tomorrow morning, they'd go get a haircut and later kill some time on the court in a little one-on-one basketball. Sixteen-year old Tyrone had become too much for the boy's mother to handle alone, so when Deek offered to spend more time with him whenever he had some time off, the single Mom jumped at the opportunity to provide her son with a positive male role model. For his part, Deek enjoyed the responsibility of being a mentor.

Deek cruised through traffic in his black, two-seater vintage Mercedes convertible while a relaxing jazz tune accompanied his thoughts. No matter how hard Deek tried he couldn't stop thinking about the doctor. If the department had her as its shrink, he wouldn't mind turning in his weapon and getting evaluated with one of those stupid psychological tests after popping a cap in some perp's ass. With Dr. Hayes as the department's shrink, at least those sessions wo   complete waste of his time.

          w the black lace bra had peeked out from under her silk
          ntrasted well with her honey brown complexion. He had
          gly across the curved mounds of her breasts when she

bent down to watch him connect the PC monitor and printer to the system unit. When she caught his eyes focusing too long on her ample cleavage, her fingers fumbled with the top button to fasten it. To his enjoyment, it had taken her awhile to locate the tiny buttonhole on her blouse. Deek wanted to believe this was all on purpose and that she had meant for him to see her breasts. But he dismissed his suspicions; Dr. Hayes was a lady and too modest to have deliberately revealed her breasts.

As Deek pulled up in front of his house, he heard a loud, redundant beat coming from inside. He climbed the steep, gray concrete steps while balancing two large pizzas and a movie under his arm. With each step closer, the pounding rhythm from a synthesized bass grew louder. The angry voice of some rap artist in the background chanted the word "ENRAGED" repeatedly. Deek felt the thump, thump, thump of the bass in sync with the throbbing of his head. *Now, I feel old*, thought Deek as he sensed the makings of a headache in progress.

Tyrone sat close to a teenage girl on the couch and didn't notice Deek come in. Deek watched as their heads bobbed up and down, feet tapped, and shoulders swayed from side to side in harmony with the rap music. Deek had told Tyrone more than once not to have friends over when he wasn't home. He cleared his throat to get Tyrone's attention since he didn't want to embarrass the boy in front of his company. He'd definitely talk to him about it later. Tyrone turned around and saw Deek standing in the hallway. He immediately jumped up and turned down the CD player.

"Hey, Deek. Me and Desiree was just sittin' here breezin' and checkin' out this new CD," explained Tyrone quickly.

"Did you have to blast it all over the neighborhood?"

"Sorry, man. Hey what you got?" Tyrone snatched the movie out of Deek's hand and checked out the title cover.

"Damn, I seen this one already." He turned up his nose and threw the movie on the counter.

"Watch your mouth Tyrone. You know Sondra wouldn't tolerate that kind of talk out of you if she were here."

"Yeah, but she ain't. And when she was, it was sure okay for her to use it."

Tyrone went back and sat down next to Desiree, a tall, slender girl with a rosy, healthy glow who appeared to be about Tyrone's age. Probably no more than fifteen. Where was this child's Mama and did she have any idea where her daughter was? They almost looked like brother and sister to Deek. Both teens had the same golden-brown skintone and the same intense, dark eyes. But when they looked at each other, it was clear they weren't brother and sister.

Her outfit showed off her youthful figure … jean shorts with a wrap-around skirt flap over the front and a form fitting T-shirt with a pink heart in the middle. Her hair was pulled back revealing a pretty, child-like face. A ponytail of dark, spiraled curls touched her shoulders. Her full lips, painted in raisin-tined lipstick, formed a sweet smile. Deek knew his plans with Tyrone were shot for the rest of the day. Damn. This kid was getting more play than he was. He put several slices of pizza on a paper plate and grabbed a beer from the refrigerator. Just as well. Looked like it was going to be just him, the movie and a cold pizza.

Deek called out to the kids from the kitchen, "I brought pizza. You guys want some?"

"Yeah, that's cool," Tyrone hollered back, "Pan crust, with extra cheese, right? By the way, Sondra called."

"Damn," said Deek to himself.

He juggled his plate of pizza, the cold beer, and the movie between his arm and headed upstairs to his bedroom. "The pizza's on the kitchen counter. Help yourself. But you might have to nuke it a little first."

Deek turned on the DVD player and sank into a soft leather chair. He positioned his laptop on the edge of the bed and powered up the PC to check e-mail while the movie credits rolled by. Waiting for the movie to start, he fixed his eyes on the tiny laptop monitor and gulped down his beer between huge bites of pizza. Deek accessed the Internet's on-line directory at four11.com to see if Dr. Renee Hayes was listed. He already had her phone number and address but just wanted to see her name show up on screen. In a few seconds her name appeared, right next to her husband's, William P. Hayes. He was immediately jealous of this William P. Hayes and he didn't even know the man.

Deek clicked off the laptop and settled in to watch the movie. He was glad he decided to take off for a few days. It wasn't just the long nights and grueling demands of his job as a homicide detective that was getting to him. He never complained about hard work or a challenge. It was the senseless violence springing up everywhere that he couldn't take anymore. And the perpetrators on the streets were getting younger and younger. Nothing but young thugs trying to earn a reputation. Deek felt helpless to do anything about it. The summer months were particularly bad. These young people needed a job, recreation centers in their communities, and ways to keep them in school. They got their training in crime early by imitating their older siblings, and by watching their childhood friends become gang members; these became their role models. Deek knew that simply locking them up didn't work either, because when they got out they were worse. The judges that saw these kids in juvenile court said they needed to learn how to deal with their frustrations and anger and to communicate with others in nonviolent ways. Deek agreed, but just as important as anger management, he understood that a young person needed to have hope and dreams in life. A young person without dreams or hope was a dangerous combination. So he decided that since Tyrone's own father was no longer around, if he could help in some small way by guiding Tyrone through the minefields of his youth then at least he had done something meaningful with his time. Deek gradually took on the self-appointed role of father-figure to Tyrone.

As far as he could tell Tyrone and Desiree looked like they were having innocent fun. Deek decided not to be too hard on the boy. It certainly could have been much worse than walking in and finding them blasting the music on the CD player.

It was just last year that Deek had to convince Tyrone to stop hanging out with those hoodlum buddies of his and go back to school. Deek knew that Tyrone Wallace was not like the typical sixteen-year old boy from his Southeast neighborhood. Most of the kids Tyrone's age and many a lot younger belonged to crews. There was a lot of pressure to join even when you didn't want to. Deek could tell that Tyrone's heart wasn't into gang wars and drug running. He felt that there was a chance to turn this kid around.

Tyrone's Mom struggled to keep a steady job and raise four children alone. Most employers were not that forgiving when it came to missing work because of a sick child, no babysitter, or doctor appointments. Tyrone said he knew his mother loved them but it still wasn't enough. He always felt inferior and unworthy of anyone's love because of his father's desertion when he was seven years old. He was thirteen years old when he stopped hoping and praying for his Dad to come back home. That's when he first began to get into trouble and started hanging with the wrong crowd.

But this time last summer Tyrone had listened to Deek and returned to school. Deek's argument hit close to home after one of Tyrone's boys named Junior was killed by his own crew. Deek and his senior partner investigated the murder scene where Junior was slain last summer. The evidence made it easy to draw a clear picture of what happened. Junior, crouched down with his hands tied behind his back, knew the split second when his young life would be snuffed out. All because former crew members wanted to teach him a lesson for trying to leave the fold. As Junior knelt on the ground crying and pleading for his life, one of the flunkies calmly stuck a pistol to his head and pulled the trigger.

Tyrone saw just how far those punks would go to control its members. But the idle summer months had worried Deek. Although, Tyrone was being raised in a loving household with a religious foundation, the temptations he faced in the streets were great. On top of that, he lived with his three half sisters, ages five, six, and eight, a diabetic grandmother and a mother who worked two jobs. There would be little, if any, supervision at home during the summer months.

They first met last year when Deek visited Tyrone's high school for career day. Tyrone seemed to hang on Deek's every word during the presentation. Deek told the students about the police cadet program whereby 11th grade students can apply and if selected they go through a training program administered by an instructor from the department. After the presentation, Tyrone sought out Deek as he was leaving the school to ask him more questions. Deek gave the kid his home number and address. Since then the two were inseparable.

Earlier that year, Deek thought that letting Tyrone stay with him and Sondra on weekends during the summer would be a good cooling off period for Tyrone from temptation he faced everyday in the streets. Time enough for him to get his life back on track. Sure Sondra was pissed when he brought Tyrone home that first weekend right after school let out in June. Sondra accused Deek of running a homeless shelter for juvenile delinquents. But he felt strongly that a young person's future was more important than Sondra's pissed-off attitude, which she always had anyway.

At twenty-eight, Deek had never been married, didn't have kids, and as of a few weeks ago, no longer had a girlfriend. His longtime relationship with Sondra ended bitterly when she moved out of his house. He knew it was a combination of things, but bringing Tyrone home was probably the last straw.

He had gotten in late from the station one night and went through the typical routine of reading his e-mail, sending out responses, and checking out the game scores that he'd missed. He found Sondra's note on the middle of the dining room table just as he headed upstairs to bed. It was short and to the point.

"Deek, I'm tired of waiting for your sorry black ass to commit to something other than your damn job, your PC, and time on the court. We've been together for four years now and I warned you many times this would happen. Four years is long enough to wait for any fool to make up his damn mind. Goodbye, Sondra."

It was just like Sondra to leave such a note. That woman was so uncompromising. Every other sentence coming out of her mouth had to be peppered with some type of profanity or criticism. She didn't see the contradiction when she admonished Tyrone when he cursed. That, she said was different because he was a child and was being disrespectful. Deek hated to hear women curse for no reason in casual conversations, the way Sondra did. She reminded him of that female civilian back in marine boot camp who supervised the issuing of gear at the receiving barracks. That woman stormed up and down a raised walkway fussing and cussing, spitting fire out of her mouth, berating the new recruits with every English equivalent of the word idiot, including that one, because some of the guys were taking too long and getting confused by her rapid-fire instructions. He realized now how much Sondra reminded him of this woman from his boot camp training days at Parris Island, which he realized now why he'd always been uncomfortable with Sondra.

When they first met at a singles bar four years ago, it was her brashness and determination that first attracted his attention. That body of hers didn't hurt any either he admitted. But after awhile Deek grew weary of the toughness and wondered what it would be like to spend time with someone a little less rough around the edges, someone a little more vulnerable, someone who needed him. Perhaps it was a bit sexist but Deek noticed he was beginning to admire women with qualities more like those his mother had—nurturing, soft, and refined. He knew those 'modern day', feminist types probably wouldn't appreciate his old fashion stereotyping, but it was how he felt these days. Deek wanted to be with a woman he could cherish and protect. Someone who would make him feel loved and needed, but who wouldn't be needy and who had clear goals and aspirations of her own and a passion for life—a woman who would not be ashamed to reveal her softness and femininity-someone like Doctor Renee Hayes. Deek had been trying to keep her out of his mind all evening but clearly it wasn't working.

He fantasized about what it would be like to make love to her. Being with a married woman would be safe. He wouldn't have to deal with that damn commitment issue. Deek knew he could not make a move in that direction without clear signals from her. Although, her signals were pretty clear in her office today. He still had to be careful, especially with shrinks. Deek realized it was more than sexual desire that drew him to Renee Hayes. He admired her intelligence, her calm feminine mannerisms. And there was a sense of vulnerability about her that attracted him. He still possessed the protective instincts towards his mother that his Dad had taught him and that had been further drilled into him during his three year stint in the marines—to protect and serve.

The doctor was a beautiful, mature woman who clearly needed to be treasured and protected. He sensed there was something missing in her life. No, Deek didn't think he'd miss Sondra much at all.

CHAPTER 5

▼

A hushed melody from a Bach concerto played softly in Renee's office. She unlocked a desk drawer and retrieved the spiral notebook that she used to record observations during sessions. Later she would transfer her notes to the patient's actual file. But right now the task of sorting through and organizing the mess that last night's burglar had left was too daunting a task, especially since she was currently without secretarial assistance. The actual files remained disorganized within the locked cabinet against the wall. She flipped open the notebook to the last entries made for her first appointment that day, Veda Simms.

<u>Case# 41, May 16. Private session with Veda Simms.</u> Psychosomatic reactions due to emotional stress often manifested in the form of headaches, fatigue, and sleep disorders. Patient experienced feelings of abandonment during childhood which fostered low self-esteem and emotional instability during adulthood. At the beginning of therapy, patient exhibited strong resistance to discussing her childhood, mainly wanting to only talk about her current relationship with her longtime companion, a Washington D. C. attorney from the firm where she is presently employed. Still, not showing signs of trust in therapy.

When Renee finished reading her notes, she couldn't help noticing there were quite a few similarities to her own life. Like Veda, Renee had felt abandoned as a child. For Renee, it was due to her mother's early death and her father's frequent absences. Veda's mother had been dead to her for many years, though the woman was still living alone in a small town in Virginia. Renee suspected the main thing they shared in common was the fear of getting older and regrets about not having experienced true love in their lives.

Despite the similarities, Renee believed that she was able to cope better than her patient. Veda had been referred to Dr. Renee as an outpatient from Washington Hospital Center's psychiatric ward just three months ago after she had swallowed half a bottle of sleeping pills. In Renee's professional opinion, Veda had only meant to draw attention to herself, not to end her life since she immediately dialed 911. Veda's suicide attempt was a classic plea for help.

Veda Simms sat in the empty waiting area outside her psychologist's office. She played with the unlit cigarette in her hand and tried to hide what she really felt like—a woman almost 40 and full of regrets, hanging on by a thread. She wanted to go outside where she could smoke. Underneath the 8 week-old, shoulder-length weave, Veda's naturally course hair only grew an inch from the nape of her neck, no matter how many hair growth vitamins she gobbled down. It was time to get her weave re-done or perhaps not. Maybe she would yank it out and say to hell with it. Veda wanted to wear her own hair in a natural, carefree style, but LaMarr liked long hair. The weave made her scalp itch, but she willed herself not to scratch it. That would be a sure give-away that her hair was fake. Not that her snooty doctor gave a damn.

Dr. Renee opened the door and invited Veda to take a seat in the large, cushioned chair across from her desk. Veda dropped her handbag on the couch and sat down in the chair, but did not give eye contact or respond when the doctor spoke. Several seconds of awkward silence filled the room. Instead of answering, Veda's bored gaze scanned the shelves of endless books and the wall full of framed certificates and degrees. Dr. Renee pointed to the micro recorder on her desk.

"Veda, do you mind if your session is recorded?"

"Let's not," said Veda and stiffened her back against the chair.

"As you wish. So, tell me Veda, why are you here?"

Veda stared at her therapist through coal-black eyes. "You know why I'm here. That 'so call doctor' in charge of the psych ward ordered it. If you ask me he's the crazy one. He should be in the cockoo's nest, not me."

"No one thinks you're crazy Veda. We don't use that word here."

Dr. Renee locked her fingers together and rested her hands on top of her desk. "You know what I'm talking about. Why did you try to kill yourself?"

Veda looked away. She glanced at her watch. Another 35 minutes to go.

Dr. Renee decided not to press it. The phone on her desk rang. She had forgotten to turn off the ringer before the session started. Renee glanced at the caller id display and noticed that it was Mrs. Addison, the social worker from HHS calling. Renee wondered if Mrs. Addison had reached Bill about the adoption and if he told her he wasn't interested. That would put an end to her chances of ever adopting a child. After the forth ring the phone stopped.

Renee briefly checked her notes from last week and forced herself to stay focused on the session. She didn't want to think about the possibility of Bill ruining everything for her.

"Last week you started to talk about your past relationship with your ex-husband and how that ended. Do you feel as though your needs are being met in your current relationship?" Dr. Renee asked.

Veda shifted in her seat. She placed an elbow on the arm of the chair and rested her chin on the back of her hand. The question had an easy answer, but not an easy solution. LaMarr Coleman was the real reason she felt so shitty these days. It hadn't always been like that. Veda told herself that things had long been over between her and Louis when she met LaMarr. She just hadn't ended the marriage yet. But when LaMarr walked into the law office where she worked as a legal aid, sporting a tailored, off-white linen suit against his ebony skin, and wearing a well-rehearsed, salesman's smile, said and did all the right things—she was doomed.

Veda lowered her hand from her chin and used it for emphasis when she tried to explain how she felt about LaMarr. "When me and LaMarr first started seeing each other 5 years ago, I thought to myself, this is a nice guy and he sure is fine …"

As she talked Veda didn't notice that Renee frequently glanced at the telephone and looked up at the clock on the wall. Veda kept on talking, "Here lately I seem to be the only one working on trying to maintain the relationship and fighting so hard to keep it going, while the other person couldn't give a crap. I never caught him in the act, but I suspect he's cheated on me. There's been too many times when he wasn't exactly where he said he was gonna be."

Veda shook her head. "Even if you don't wanna think something is wrong … nine times out of ten if your intuition keeps telling you something is wrong, it's probably true. Don't you think so, Doc?"

Renee tried hard to pay attention to what her patient was saying, but she caught herself simply looking through her in a catatonic stare. Perhaps I should excuse myself for a few minutes and go call Bill she thought. Let him know how important this adoption is to me.

Veda continued to explain, encouraged by a robotic nod every now and then from her therapist. She didn't notice that Dr. Renee had not bothered to take any notes. Veda described how they'd meet at LaMarr's place after work. In the beginning she tried to get home at a reasonable hour. Louis didn't say much but he had to suspect something was going on. Veda tried to convince herself that the breakup wasn't her fault. If Louis had been more interesting and more willing to change she wouldn't have left him. Though the truth about her feelings of self-reproach remained vivid in her own mind, Veda did not tell Dr. Renee that one day after cheating on Louis for over a month, she just walked out on him and her daughter Sherrelle, who was ten at the time. It was too late for a guilt trip now. LaMarr was all she had left. She would never reveal her true remorse to this woman seated across from her—one who had everything going for her, a loving husband, a beautiful home, money in the bank, no ungrateful kids to worry about. What the hell would Dr. Renee know about feeling lonely and worthless? Once again Veda glanced at the degrees on the wall. She took a deep breath and continued to talk in the hope that Dr. Renee could help her.

"It's like this Doc. A lot of women I see out here are afraid. Not of loneliness, but of being alone. So they settle. But I'm not saying that's me. I know what you're thinking," said Veda. "You're thinking, I'm in denial. You're wrong. LaMarr's the one for me. You gotta help me figure out how to get back what we once had. Show me where I went wrong. I gave up a lot to be with this man. We have a future together. I just can't let him get away after 5 years. Doc?"

Renee placed her hand on the telephone as she spoke. "I'm sorry, Veda. I'm going to have to cut our session a little short today. There're some personal matters I have to attend to right away."

Veda rose and snatched up her purse from the sofa. "Who's the patient here, me or you? You haven't heard one word I said. Why the hell am I paying you all this damn money? You need to sign those papers from HR and let my job know I ain't the one with the problem."

Veda stormed out of the office and slammed the front door before Dr. Renee could say anything.

Renee took a few minutes to compose herself before dialing Bill's office. When his voicemail came on she hung up. This wasn't something she could say in a recorded message. She picked up the phone again to try his cellular phone, but could not reach him that way either. She got up to change the music to a bluesy jazz soundtrack. Her five o'clock appointment was due in at any minute. Renee sat down to review her notes on Kenneth Blackwell while she waited for him to arrive. She was determined to stay focused and not zone out during her session with him. She found the jazz music to be a nice break from the classical music she usually played during her patients' counseling sessions. The 40's and 50's style music brought back images of her parents when they were in their prime and very much in love. Renee envied them. Although their time together had been brief, it was intense.

Renee glanced at the clock again and wished Kenneth would hurry and get there. She was anxious for this day to end. Renee began treating the young man two months ago at the request of his father. Kenneth was a shy, sensitive twenty-three year old senior at Georgetown University and the only son of Dr. Walter Blackwell, a prominent vascular cardiologist with a successful, private practice in Washington, D. C.

Renee learned through her sessions with Kenneth that Dr. Blackwell was also a functioning substance abuser and a control freak who over the years dominated his wife and two children. It was apparent that Dr. Blackwell believed in definite roles for everybody; starting with his wife and children, and expanding to men and women in general, blacks, whites, the haves, and have-nots. He put those closest to him in their own special little boxes and treated them according to the high standards he expected them to demonstrate.

Renee never actually met Dr. Blackwell but had spoken to him a few times over the telephone. Dr. Blackwell thoroughly checked out Renee's credentials prior to sending his son to her office for reparative therapy. He believed this treatment was the answer to helping his son lead a normal heterosexual life. Dr. Blackwell explained there were too many quacks in the mental health profession who planted misinformation in their patients' heads through false suggestions and told them that anything they wanted to do was perfectly all right.

After speaking with Dr. Blackwell, Renee's instincts told her to stay away. But the more she spoke to him, the more she realized that his son Kenneth needed her help if he was to survive his dysfunctional family environment and all the ignorance surrounding him. Kenneth demonstrated symptoms of chronic depression, insomnia, and stomach pains. Renee focused his treatment on these physical and psychological problems, as well as, his low self-esteem and feelings of anxiety. Renee glanced at the clock and saw that it was nearly 5:20. Kenneth was already twenty minutes late for his appointment. It looked like her patient wasn't going to show up after all today. She'd give it a few more minutes in case he got caught in traffic.

In their first private session, Renee assured Kenneth that contrary to what his father told him being gay is not an illness. She clarified that any type of conversion treatment he followed under her care would be a personal choice on his part and should not be taken as a professional recommendation from her. He would have to be the one to decide. After several weeks of consideration, Kenneth elected not to undergo the reparative treatment that his father had sent him to psychotherapy for.

Renee researched locations for Al-Anon family support groups in Kenneth's area and suggested that he urge his mother and older sister to join too. A few weeks later, Kenneth came back and told Dr. Renee that his mother was not interested and his older sister had been estranged from the family for over two years. He said his mother was simply too afraid to challenge his father. He said he remembered it had always been that way even as a child. Unfortunately, Renee found this to be a common occurrence among many women caught in abusive relationships.

Kenneth said his mother told him many times that she stayed with his father all those years for his sake and his sister's. But Renee knew from years of clinical study that exposing children to long-term mental and/or physical cruelty would have far reaching consequences throughout their entire lives. At twenty-three years old, Kenneth was a clear demonstration of this. Renee didn't know what else to do but listen to the young man's pain and offer ways to help him cope.

She heard someone enter the waiting area of her ground floor office. She figured it had to finally be Kenneth. Now, only twenty-five minutes remained in his session which wasn't enough time to accomplish much.

The footsteps sounded heavier than Kenneth's. Just as Renee got up to investigate, a tall, light-skinned middle-aged black man swung open her office door. His eyes narrowed closer together as he approached. Every muscle in his face looked tense and his fists were clinched at his side. Renee sensed that he was trying very hard to restrain his anger.

He stood well over six feet tall and took slow, robot-like steps as he moved closer to her. The fine, tailor-made suit complemented his svelte build. His features looked Romanesque—a thin-lipped mouth, an up-turned chin, and a large, straight-nose. His dark, slit-eyes glistened with coldness. The hair was jet black, waved and cropped fashionably short. To Renee he looked like a white man who had been dipped in cadmium yellow with a touch of burnt sienna added.

"May I help you?" asked Dr. Renee as she slowly sat back down.

"I am Dr. Walter Blackwell, Kenneth's father. We spoke by telephone a few months ago."

"Of course. Won't you please have a seat, Dr. Blackwell," she said, pointing to one of the floral, chintz wing back chairs that stood in front of her desk.

"No, thank you."

From the tone of his voice, Renee knew Dr. Blackwell was furious.

"Why are you encouraging my son to be gay?"

"Dr. Blackwell, I'm sorry if you're upset but I have no idea …"

"Of course you have no idea," he screamed angrily and pounded his fist on her desk, "I see now that you're just as incompetent as the rest of them."

"Dr. Blackwell, I realize you must face daily pressures and responsibilities as a surgeon so I'm willing to make certain allowances for your behavior," Renee responded in a soft, controlled voice and articulated every word carefully, "I wouldn't begin to try to tell you what is right or wrong for you to believe, but homosexuality is not considered a mental illness."

Renee flipped open the APA Manual and quoted directly from the marked text. "According to the American Psychological Association, … Homosexuality should not be considered or looked at as a mental illness, so there is no need to seek out a cure for something which does not need one." She paused before adding, "Perhaps, you should get help for yourself, Dr. Blackwell and let Kenneth lead his own life."

"What exactly are you trying to say?"

"Let me be frank, Doctor. You may have a serious chemical dependency that's effecting not only your life and your family's but could potentially endanger your patients as well. Unless you admit that fact to yourself, you'll never be able to solve it."

"Well, I'll be damned," Dr. Blackwell erupted in a voice so loud, the crystal bud vase on her desk vibrated.

"Who the hell do you think you are, trying to tell me how to run my life? I am a board certified vascular cardiologist, highly respected F.A.C.S. member, pulling in 5 million a year. You're nothing but a joke *Doctor* Hayes."

Renee detected his condescending tone as he emphasized the word 'Doctor.' Her hands shook in her lap under the desk and her heart beat rapidly from anger but she sat still and composed throughout the man's tirade. Her years of training as a psychologist taught her to remain calm when faced with irrational behavior and to speak in a steady and deliberate tone.

"Dr. Blackwell, it's obvious you're upset," said Renee. And possibly *drunk* she thought to herself as she continued, "I don't think it's a good time to discuss this now. Kenneth loves you very much. All he wants is for you to love him in return and accept him for who he is and not try to mold him into what you think is normal and acceptable."

"I intend to file a complaint with the District of Columbia Board of Psychology and have your license revoked."

"Do whatever you wish, Dr. Blackwell, but Kenneth has been advised according to APA guidelines as I just read to you," Renee lowered her voice almost to a whisper as she responded to his attack and kept her eyes fixed on him. "There is no scientific proof that reparative therapy works and could, in fact, be painful and traumatic. It could do Kenneth more harm than good." She paused while opening her desk. "Here, why don't you take this," Renee handed him a small, paperback book recommended by the APA advising parents of Gay children how to mend relationships and understand a grown child's alternate lifestyle. "I was planning to give it to your son this evening to share with you. I think it might be a first step to helping you to learn how to accept Kenneth as he is."

Dr. Blackwell snatched the book from her hand and glanced at the title. Then threw it on her desk and laughed so hard Renee winced.

"I see what's going on here now," he said glaring down at her, "It's obvious the faggots are taking over. Now, they even have the APA and incompetent fools like you on their side. You're not qualified to give out advice to anyone, *Doctor*."

He planted both palms on her desk and leaned forward right up to her face. Renee felt his brownish-hazel eyes pierce her soul as he spoke. "I know a great deal about you Dr. Hayes. You'd better stick to writing those useless self-help books of yours or perhaps try a radio talk show. But you should stay away from patients who need serious treatment." Dr. Blackwell shook his head. "You are in no position to dispense advice on how to raise children. You have no experience raising any yourself. Don't forget, I know all about you Dr. Hayes. And furthermore, I've read your book on keeping your mate satisfied. Perhaps we should ask your husband to validate that advice. What do you think he'd say, *Doctor*?"

Renee matched his stare without flinching but his hateful words stung deep. Her face muscles began to ache from the strain of trying to maintain a calm, dignified appearance. She did not intend to give this arrogant snob the satisfaction of destroying her self-discipline. She had learned all too well, beginning from early childhood, how to hide her anger, pain, and frustrations behind a false veil of illusion. Without uttering another word, she got up and held the office door open for him. She didn't want to risk speaking and have her voice crack.

On the way out the door, Dr. Blackwell turned around to face her,

"Kenneth won't be coming back tonight or any other night. I'll get him the help he needs from someone qualified to treat him. I'm sick of being told by some *expert* like you how to relate to my wife and kids."

Dr. Blackwell stormed out of the office, leaving Renee shaking and speechless. After he left, her head felt dizzy but the knots in her stomach slowly began to subside. She rested her forehead in her hand and stared ahead in front of her without looking at anything in particular. Dr. Blackwell was probably right, she didn't know how to solve anyone's problems; she didn't even know how to solve her own. All she ever wanted was to fit in, to feel needed and wanted by someone—a close friend, her husband, her parents, or even by a child of her own. She thought of how everyone important in her life pursued only their own selfish needs: Bill had his company and her father had his lifelong devotion to himself and his music. She didn't fit into anyone's plan. Time was running out. How many more years did she have left to find the right fit for her life? Renee didn't think she'd ever experience the type of 'all too brief' happiness that her parents shared.

When Renee calmed down enough to come back to her senses, the room appeared peaceful and quiet. As the music drifted through the empty stillness, Renee recognized another tune from the blues era. It was called 'Alone.' 'Alone' had been another favorite song of her parents. Listening to it when she was a little girl, she recalled that was exactly how she felt, completely alone—like now.

Renee heard a soft knock at the private door in her office that led to the house. She turned and saw Bill standing in the doorway of her office.

"Expecting any more patients this evening?"

Renee shook her head. Bill crossed the room and sat down on the couch.

"Mrs. Addison from Health & Human Services called me this afternoon. She said she met with you today about an adoption. Why didn't you tell me you were back on this kick?" asked Bill.

Renee didn't know how to answer him. She couldn't judge his mood. Was he angry with her? Was he trying to really understand? She rested her chin on clasped fingers and turned away from Bill's stare.

"Renee, I've told you how I feel about adopting at this stage in my life," he said, "Is this something you really want at forty-four?"

"I guess I don't know what I want anymore," she said, "All I know is this life I'm living isn't it."

"The social worker said adoption has to be a conscious decision and a loving choice for both of us, Renee. Otherwise, it's not fair to the child. It can't just be about what you want."

Renee remembered Mrs. Addison had emphasized the same thing to her and asked if she and Bill would be able to accept an adopted baby as if the child were their own biological offspring. Renee believed with all her heart that she could but she didn't know about her husband. She asked him, "What do you want?"

"Let's just see what happens at the meeting tomorrow with Mrs. Addison," said Bill, "She set it up for one o'clock in her office downtown. Can you meet me there then?"

Renee nodded but something made her doubt Bill's sincerity and her enthusiasm weakened. Or perhaps she was simply too tired to fight any longer for her happiness.

"Renee, I'm not against going through the steps to qualify if that's want you really want, but a child is a big commitment," he said, "By the way, did the police follow-up with you today like they said they would?"

Renee fought to restrain the yearnings of her starving heart as the memory of Detective Hamilton's image suddenly shot in front of her. She tried to sound casual.

"Yes. Some detective came by," she answered flatly, "He said there's not much to go on though."

"Well, I've got someone from ADT coming by to check out all our vulnerable points and install a security system by Wednesday," he said, "so you don't have to worry anymore. I'm getting the full package."

A sudden ringing noise startled them. Bill located the source of the ringing, a wireless telephone embedded between the sofa cushions. He handed her the phone.

"Must be yours. Mine's upstairs."

Renee noticed that a text message appeared on the phone's display panel. This was the first time she'd received a text message on her new digital cell phone that Bill had given her for her birthday. Renee frowned and reread the message to herself, 'Fried my motherboard! Pls Call.'

The message made no sense and she didn't recognize the caller's number. She was just about to ask Bill if he could make out the meaning of the message when she stopped and examined the phone more closely. While it resembled hers in size and color, she realized it was not her new digital PDA phone. It belonged to Detective Hamilton. He must have picked up the wrong one when he left that afternoon. Renee turned it off and quickly shoved it inside her front desk drawer.

"Aren't you going to return your call?"

"Later. It's not an emergency."

"Listen Hon, how about we go out to dinner and catch a late movie?" asked Bill, "I don't really have to go back to the warehouse tonight. I've only got one PC system to assemble and the client doesn't need it until sometime next week."

"Not tonight. I'm really tired and it's been a long day." She closed her patient's notebook and locked it inside the bottom drawer of her desk.

Bill nodded resigned and started to get up from the sofa. Then hesitated, "Renee?"

She briefly met his gaze. His eyes looked sad and defeated. His chin already cast a shadow from beard stubble. Except for the designer clothes he had on, Bill looked as wretched as a homeless person.

"I'm sorry about last night," he mumbled in a low voice.

"I suppose I didn't try that hard to wake you up," she said, "I know it was stupid to go downstairs alone when I heard noises."

"Yes, that too ... but I wasn't talking about the burglary."

Renee stared across the desk at him and wore a blank expression on her face.

"I'm sorry about how I acted when I got in last night. I know you didn't want to be with me. I just felt I needed you." Bill waited but when he received no comment from her he continued, "I should have considered your feelings. It'll never happen like that again."

Through his tired bloodshot eyes, Renee thought she detected a tear. She knew he wanted her forgiveness, wanted her to come over to him and wrap her arms around him, but she couldn't. Renee had forced herself to block out last night. How else was she to deal with it? After a few awkward moments of silence, Bill slowly got up from the sofa and left, gently closing the door behind him.

After Bill left, Renee's stomach tightened in knots. She listened to Bill's footsteps climb the stairs leading to the first floor of their house. When she no longer heard them, her thoughts turned to Deek. She now had a legitimate excuse for contacting him. Renee retrieved his phone from her desk drawer. She hadn't been able to get Deek out of her mind since they met that afternoon.

CHAPTER 6

▼

Bill's willingness to cooperate with the adoption suddenly held little interest for Renee. Now all she could think about was Deek. She took out the card he had given her and dialed his home number. The line was busy. Renee speculated that he was probably talking to one of his girlfriends and making plans for the evening. She had noticed, along with everything else about him that he was not married, or at least did not wear a ring. Renee felt foolish and tried to stop her fantasy thoughts, but it didn't appear to be working.

One of the basic premises in her psychotherapy approach involved helping patients gain control of their lives. During counseling, she urged her patients to dig deep and re-surface the truth in order to deal with it. This meant they first had to understand their subconscious desires. But in her own life she took just the opposite approach and hid from the truth. Renee tried to comprehend what unfulfilled needs had led to her desire for a virtual stranger.

Renee glanced at her watch. She was already five minutes late for her 6:30 hair appointment at Good Looks Salon. She rushed upstairs to quickly change out of the silk blouse and crepe pants and put on some comfortable chino slacks and a more casual top. While painting on her usual shade of ripened burgundy lipstick, she briefly thought about calling Cha-Cha before leaving. If another customer came in ahead of her and took her time slot, there'd be a very long wait. Renee decided to just go and take a chance that her beautician wouldn't be too busy this Thursday evening. Besides, waiting around for Cha-Cha to give her a touch-up and color, was better than sitting at home dwelling on her failures and thinking about being nothing but a childless, middle-age woman fighting to control her longings for a man who had to be more than ten years younger than she was.

Renee arrived at Good Looks Beauty Salon forty-five minutes late. By then, the shop was packed with women just getting in from work. At first she felt relieved when she saw Cha-Cha applying the finishing touches to a customer's hair. Her relief quickly vanished as soon as she realized another customer was already lined up to take her place.

One of the customers was flipping through the handfuls of beauty and self-help magazines that were scattered on top of a chrome and glass coffee table. Another customer had brought her two young children and tried to keep them entertained with crayons and coloring books. The young mother had an orange, black, and green kente-print scarf tied around her head.

The radio blasted nonstop music from a rhythm and blues station that Renee didn't recognize or care for. Voices rose in an attempt to compete with the noise from the hair dryers, the blaring music, TV, and people's casual conversations. Renee felt the hot, thick air swarming all around her. She held her breath in small spurts to block out the offensive odors of hair spray and heavy cologne. Renee felt out of place and wished she had remembered to bring her recent issue of American Psychologist. All she could do now was sit, wait, and listen to the noise and idle chitchat going on all around her.

The young mother with the two children struck up a conversation with a few other customers in the shop. They complained about their men troubles and the fact that they couldn't seem to keep one. Someone calling herself Tisha, who looked like she should know all about the subject of men, boldly interjected her opinions. The others stared at her with wide-eyed admiration. Tisha looked like she should be on a commercial for Wonder Bra. Her purple, tight-fitting jersey-knit dress didn't cover up much. She crossed her nutmeg brown legs and kicked the top one back and forth in a rapid motion, right in time with the loud music and smacking of her chewing gum.

"Honey, I ain't got much book learnin' but you don't learn about keepin' no man from a book, girl," said Tisha.

"Uh huh, you right about that," said the one with the children, nodding in agreement. The young mother swung around when she heard one of her kids wailing behind her. She grabbed her son and slapped him over the head.

"Give LaKeesha back that doll, boy and sit your ass down. Get on my damn nerves." She sucked her teeth and rolled her eyes at him. Then she turned back to her conversation with Tisha. The child popped back up out of his chair a second later but his mother didn't seem to notice.

"Yeah, girl. A man is just like an open book, honey. Flip to the first page and you got all you need to know."

Heads nodded up and down in agreement. "That's right, girl."

"Lemme put it to you like this. When your man get home …"

"If he get home," someone interrupted.

"Whatever," said Tisha, "Girl, you don't have on nothing but the stereo. He'll stay home. Trust me on that."

"Barbara! You next," Cha-Cha hollered out for her next customer over the women's laughter. The lady, who had been flipping through a Glamour magazine, jumped up and claimed Cha-Cha's chair.

Renee blocked out their bantering and watched the two children for awhile. The boy looked to be around four or five but talked no better than a two-year old. Renee cringed when she heard him open his mouth to try to speak. The girl was a toddler and looked to be no more than two or three years old. After a few minutes, one of the beauticians called their mother to the shampoo bowl. The young mother warned both kids to sit still and be quiet "or else," and pointed out where she'd be. Her useless warning lasted just long enough for her to get seated at the shampoo bowl. The children got out of their seats and ran around, jumped, screeched, and hollered, bit, and kicked each other from the moment their mother was out of sight. The little boy's mumbling and incoherent speech continued to bother Renee. It looked as though he barely opened his mouth when he spoke. A four-year-old should be able to speak better than that, thought Renee. She noticed the mother wasn't paying any attention to her children. Renee smiled and motioned with her finger to get the little boy to approach her.

"Come here for a minute, sweetheart," said Renee.

The child came over and stood in front of Renee. His little sister followed.

"How old are you?" asked Renee.

"Five," he mumbled.

His sister held up three fingers. "I free," she said. Renee smiled.

"Open your mouth for me, will you baby?" said Renee gently to the boy.

The young child obeyed and opened his mouth wide. He seemed to relish the attention and her soft voice. Renee was shocked and appalled by what she saw. The child had a mouth full of jagged, decayed baby teeth and one missing in the front. The three year old's teeth were also beginning to show signs of decay and neglect. Renee glared over at the mother who was laughing and talking rapidly with her beautician. She'd spend a small fortune to get her hair done but couldn't take her children to see a dentist? Renee was disgusted. She told the children to start brushing their teeth everyday and to ask their mother to take them to see the dentist right away. They both nodded their heads at the same time, then ran off to play again. Renee continued to fume. She had read enough parenting magazines and baby books to know that decay of a young child's primary teeth could later cause damage to their permanent teeth. She surmised that these kids must have been put to bed with a bottle stuck in their mouths too many times when they were babies instead of being held and fed correctly. Granted, their mother probably didn't realize that this would cause her children's teeth to decay, but ignorance was no excuse for letting it continue. You had to have a license for just about everything else but *any woman*, whether qualified to raise a child or not, could get pregnant. Any woman, but her. She knew she should get up and say something to that mother even at the risk of getting cursed out, but instead, Renee picked up some of the magazines on the coffee table and thumbed through them. They were all outdated and of no interest to her.

Twenty minutes passed. Cha-Cha put a customer under the dryer so her perm and color would hold better. She immediately began combing out and styling another customer's hair. Renee figured it would probably be another half-hour or so before it would be her turn. Renee watched as the young mother's beautician combed out the tangled, matted hair. She knew it would be several hours before that woman would be able to leave the salon with those children. It was already past their bedtime, if they even had anything like a regular bedtime.

Renee then thought about what Tisha and the young mother had said about keeping a man happy. Renee couldn't see herself trying any of their tips on Bill. All they seemed to worry about was keeping some trifling man happy.

Looking around her, she frowned at what she saw. Over the years the absentee owner had let the place rundown. A row of metal legged chairs with dingy yellow plastic seat covers lined one of the walls, facing the workstations. At the front of the shop windows were just big enough to let in faint bursts of light during the daytime. A plastic rubber plant with visible dust sat forlorn in the corner. Head-shots of models in outdated hairdos decorated paint chipped walls, now the color of oatmeal, that had once been painted daffodil yellow. Cha-cha had confided to Renee that she planned to one day buy the shop and give it a complete makeover. That day couldn't come soon enough for Renee. If only she didn't have to travel so far out of her own neighborhood to find a good beautician, but Cha-Cha was the best and Renee would follow her anywhere. Cha-Cha had been the one who had managed to transform Renee's once short, brittle hair into a healthy, shoulder-length mane. Her hair was now just as soft and lustrous as her mother's hair had naturally been.

Renee began to feel more nauseous from the mixture of strong colognes, stifling heat, and chemical hair processing odors that circulated throughout the unventilated room. When she couldn't stand the fumes or noise any longer, she approached Cha-Cha at her station and told her she would have to re-schedule for one day next week. Cha-Cha nodded and looked at her funny, but Renee didn't care. She had to get out of there. At the station right next to Cha-Cha's, she overheard the young mother with the rotten-teeth children ask her beautician about getting color.

"How much more to add some of that plum pudding color I like, Denise?"

Renee felt something tugging at her to turn around and speak to the mother about getting her children to a dentist. She would even be willing to take them herself and pay for it if the mother was not able to afford it. Renee also knew of several clinics that charged on a sliding scale. She stood there at Cha-Cha's station and silently rehearsed what she would say. Renee didn't notice her beautician's look of confusion until Cha-Cha called out to her again.

"Dr. Renee? You wanna make that appointment now or call me up later?"

"Pardon?" said Renee.

"Your appointment. You just said you had to re-schedule."

"Oh, Yes. I do. I'll call you tomorrow, Cha-Cha," said Renee, "I'm sorry I was late this evening."

"Too bad I couldn't fit you in. But you see it's a mess up in here. You okay?"

Renee nodded and turned to leave. She stopped suddenly in front of the children's mother.

"Excuse me, Miss?" said Renee.

The young mother stopped in mid-sentence and stared Renee up and down. Denise, her beautician, continued to fight with her customer's hair and wasn't paying Renee any attention. Denise's snarled expression told Renee she wasn't winning the battle.

"Yeah?" said the mother, staring stone faced at Renee. It felt like all noise in the shop had ceased. The look on the mother's face told Renee she had better mind her own business.

"You have lovely children," said Renee smiling, "Take good care of them. You really are blessed." Renee couldn't bring herself to say anything else and awkwardly dug into her wallet for one of her business cards. The mother glanced at the card that Renee handed her and read it aloud in a bored-sounding tone, "Renee Janette Hayes, Ph. D., psychology, contemporary psychotherapy and family counseling."

She handed the card back to Renee and said, "Thanks but no thanks."

The young mother immediately resumed her conversation with her beautician about getting the plum pudding hair color.

Renee left quickly. She felt the stares of a dozen pairs of eyes on her back as she walked out of the salon. Coming there had only made her feel more useless and unnecessary. The young mother had looked at Renee as if to say who the hell was she to tell her to take care of her children. She remembered Dr. Blackwell who had burst into her office earlier that day. His words rang out at her, "You're not qualified to give out advice to anyone, *Doctor.*" It was true; Renee didn't have any children of her own but what this young mother and Dr. Blackwell didn't know was that she knew a great deal about the wrong way. She had even experienced that herself. Her practice and volunteer work made her all too aware of too many instances of abuse and neglect that parents inflicted on their children everyday.

It was almost nine o'clock when Renee pulled into her driveway. Bill's Range Rover was not in the garage. When she got inside, everything looked neat and the rooms smelled fresh. On Thursday evenings, the housekeeper came and cleaned the house while she was at the beauty parlor. The fresh, airiness of the large rooms was a welcome change from the polluted, closed-in space she had just left. Renee quickly changed clothes and looked through her mail. She sat at her dressing table and reflected on how she had neglected Veda during her session today. Renee hoped this would not stand in the way of Veda receiving treatment. Who was this woman? How could Renee help her? Renee felt an obligation to be there for her patient and picked up the phone to call and apologize. She hoped Veda would agree to come back for the next appointment. When the answering machine came on Renee left a message, apologizing for being distracted today. She hoped her sincerity came through on the phone. That was all she could do now since the damage was done. If Veda did come back Renee knew she would have to start at the beginning to build trust. Renee went downstairs to fix dinner. She tossed a salad and thawed two steaks in the microwave. She prepared enough for Bill in case he showed up in time to have dinner with her. After setting the table and arranging the meal for serving, she poured herself a glass of wine and waited. She had no concept of passing time as she sipped the wine and listened to the music from a classical concertos CD. Her mind drifted back to her life's emptiness. Who would be there to share her successes and failures? Not her father. God only knew where he was. And certainly, not her husband Bill. He couldn't even get home for dinner on time. At 10:00, she poured another glass of white wine and ate alone.

It was eleven o'clock when she got out of a soothing, bubble bath and climbed into bed. But Renee was not sleepy. She grabbed a back issue of the APA Monitor from a huge stack on the floor next to her bed. Renee put on her reading glasses and tried to get absorbed in an article on 'Child Abuse and Repressed Memories.' She read the same paragraph over three times and was still not able to register the author's central point. Despite her efforts to distract herself with the article, her thoughts drifted back to Detective Hamilton. She knew it was too late to call him again to tell him about the mix-up with their wireless phones. He still hadn't responded to her earlier message. Although it was absurd and completely impossible, Renee wished Deek could be there with her now. She drifted into a light sleep with thoughts of him lying next to her.

CHAPTER 7

▼

The 'set to music' alarm went off at seven in the morning and a fast-paced tune pulsated through Veda's bedroom. The loud music didn't have to jolt her out of a deep, satisfying sleep because she was already wide-awake. Veda had been up since 8:30 the night before, trying to reach her boyfriend, LaMarr. Finally, after numerous unsuccessful attempts she stopped leaving messages and just hung up when his smooth recorded voice came on. She continued to call for several more hours. Because she was exhausted, she had drifted in and out of sleep, but she had not rested.

Veda sat up in bed and reached for the crumpled ball of paper on her nightstand. She smoothed out the wrinkled edges of the letter that had arrived yesterday from her ex-husband, Louis Simms. She re-read the note slowly and let each word sink in. Louis was only asking if their fifteen year-old daughter, Sherrelle, could come stay with her this weekend. To Veda he may as well have been asking for the moon. The letter said that Louis needed to drive his wife to Richmond because her mother was seriously ill. He didn't think it would be a good idea to take Sherrelle with them, not knowing what to expect once they got there. He wanted to drop off Sherrelle on their way down on Saturday and pick her up late Monday. Louis thought it would be a chance for mother and daughter to get reacquainted. Louis said he was sorry about the short notice but he discovered too late that Veda had her phone number changed so he had to write instead. He asked her to please call by Friday '*which would be today!*' thought Veda and let him know if Sherrelle could stay with her until Monday. He didn't want to leave their daughter alone in the house overnight.

More damn problems, thought Veda. As if she didn't already have enough of her own. An extended visit from her estranged daughter was the last thing Veda needed. She hadn't seen her daughter or her ex-husband in over a year even though they only lived an hour away in Baltimore. Having Sherrelle there would definitely cramp her style. Veda recalled the last time her daughter had come down for a visit. The two of them had a knock down, drag out fight over LaMarr. Sherrelle hated him and didn't want him around. Veda crushed the note within her fist and hurled it against the wall. Louis must have lost his damn mind. Why couldn't that simple wife of his drive to Richmond by herself? But she knew this is exactly what a loving, supportive husband would do for his wife, and Louis had always been that—even to her. But she had thrown that all away five years ago, had left her husband and her then ten year-old child, for LaMarr Coleman.

Just thinking about LaMarr excited her. He was like a shot of adrenaline. She pictured the smooth ebony skin tone of his bare arms and chest, glazed with perspiration after they made love. No golden glow, half-white complexion or pretty-boy features on him. No indeed! LaMarr was African Prince black. His look and attitude commanded attention. Always richly adorned in French or Italian tailored suits, custom monogrammed shirts, and Gucci or Ralph Lauren casual wear, LaMarr worked out and had a hard, muscle-toned body. He jogged and lifted weights despite a regular intake of unfiltered Pall Malls. Even after five years, Veda was still obsessed with him.

The morning sun forced its brilliant rays through Veda's bedroom window. Erykah Badu's music clashed with the outdoor symphony of 'caw caw' from a group of intruding crows. Between that damn letter and trying to come up with some good reason why LaMarr hadn't answered his telephone all night or returned any of her calls, Veda's stomach was in knots and her head ached. She got up slowly to get ready for work and felt more like someone pushing sixty rather than forty. She thought forty was bad enough considering where she was at this point in her life. Veda wished there was some magic pill that she could take to start her life over at twenty-one—only do it right this time. But the only magic pills she could get her hands on were the 20 milligrams of Prozac that Dr. Renee had given her for depression and insomnia. And those things weren't doing a damn bit of good since she wasn't taking them anymore because of the side effects. She got up to take a shower, hoping that would revive her.

Veda heard the telephone ringing as soon as she turned off the shower faucet. Before she could reach it though, the ringing stopped. She dialed her VoiceMail number immediately and keyed in her password, hoping it was LaMarr. But the caller wasn't LaMarr. It was only her therapist, Dr. Renee, who had called again to apologize for the other day and to confirm her appointment for 6:30 that evening. Veda knew she needed help. She had been feeling more lonely and depressed than ever since LaMarr seemed to be slipping away from her. The doctor sounded sincere. Veda decided she may as well show up for the appointment and give it another shot.

She dressed for work in slow motion. Small, dark puffy eyes stared back at her from the bathroom mirror as she applied very little make-up to her medium-brown complexion. Nothing but a quick swipe across the lips from a dull, cocoa-tinted shade. Veda had picked out the weave last night. It lay in a heap on the bedroom floor. Her own short hair was in desperate need of a stylish cut or at least a trim, but Veda didn't care how she looked and threw on a plain-looking, out-dated tan suit with the skirt an unfashionable length of two inches below the knee. She hadn't done laundry in a week and this was the only outfit that didn't need to go to the cleaners or need to be washed.

She wasn't one of those women who got a temporary lift from shopping for herself. Her wardrobe hadn't been updated in almost six years. The only shopping she still enjoyed was buying surprise gifts for LaMarr. She recalled the look on his face about a year ago when she presented him with a sculpture of a polished, black panther for his birthday. He had placed the reclining figure in front of his fireplace where its sleek, shiny body and fierce fangs glowed from the fire's flames in the wintertime. This one extravagant purchase brought her Visa card all the way to its limit and would probably take a good four years to pay off. She would never have spent that much money on herself, but just thinking of LaMarr's smile made her happy.

Now looking around her place, Veda sighed. She cared even less about decorating than she did about clothes. Old newspapers, Ebony, Jet, and Essence magazines cluttered one corner of the living room. A folded up sports section laid on the stained glass top coffee table. Water-starved plants with yellow, curled up leaves sat on a pastry cart by the window. A bamboo screen divided the living room from the dining room and clashed with the brown corduroy sofa and an unmatched floral covered chair. Veda didn't even bother to try to pick the place up before she left. She closed the door behind her, knowing that same chaos would be there to greet her at the end of the day when she returned.

It was a miserably hot and humid Friday morning, typical Washington D.C. summer weather. Veda was perspiring and out-of-breath by the time she stepped out of the Farragut North stop at the Metro station. She was already ten minutes late for her job at the law firm of Davis & Bookerman, where she worked as an office manager, but Veda didn't have the energy to rush. She arrived at the towering gray steel and glass building near K Street, N.W. and pushed through its heavy, double doors. The lobby receptionist at the large faux marble desk greeted her as usual, but Veda did not hear her and rushed right past to the elevators. She pushed the 'up' button several times and paced the floor as she waited. Veda stared at the numbers as they flashed before her in bold red digits. The elevator slowly descended towards the Lobby, 15 … 14 … 13. Two well-dressed white women walked up behind her to wait for the elevator and began to chat amongst themselves. Just then the bell rang and the elevator halted in front of them. Veda stepped on first and pressed fifteen. The women glanced at the number lit up for fifteen and kept talking. Veda found herself eavesdropping on the conversation between the two women. The women, one blonde and the other brunette, appeared to be law students from the nature of their conversation.

"Did you hear that Jonathan passed the Pennsylvania state bar last month?" asked the brunette.

"You're kidding right? Didn't he just barely make it out of AU last summer?" asked the blonde, "And besides, I thought he planned to practice here in Washington."

"He is and as a matter of fact he already landed a job at Klein, Cutler, and Norrison."

"No way, Fredricka. Just from passing an outside state's bar exam?"

"Courtney, everybody knows the D.C. bar is a bitch," said the one called Fredricka, "Nobody sits for it anymore. Why not get two licenses with one easy test? Me, I'm going for the Virginia bar when I finish up next year."

"You know what, Freddie? I'm not sure I even want to be a lawyer anymore," said the blonde, "It's all beginning to look like such a rat race."

"Yeah, well I guess some of us can live off Mommy and Daddy's money."

"Go to hell, Fredricka," said the blonde in a playful tone.

When the elevator reached the fifteenth floor, everyone got off. Veda followed behind the two law students. The brunette disappeared down the hall in the opposite direction but the blonde woman appeared to be heading towards the same law office where Veda worked. The blonde stopped at the heavy wooden door that read 'Davis & Bookerman Attorneys-at-Law,' then she entered and disappeared briskly down the carpeted hallway with legal brief in hand. Veda followed and sat down at her desk in the reception area at the front of the office. She had been out sick for the past two days, although she wasn't actually sick, just sick of being there. Now she wondered who this new blonde woman was and what changes had been made while she was out. She locked her purse away in the drawer and turned on the computer. She wore a clear sign on her barely made up face that said, 'Don't mess with me.'

"I dare that fat-ass Bookerman or that pocked face Davis or anybody else in here to say one damn word to me about being late this morning," mumbled Veda under her breath as she yanked open the bottom desk drawer, retrieved a stack of folders, and slammed them on top of her desk. From where she sat, she could see LaMarr's office and knew that he had not yet come in. She pulled open the front of her desk and took out a tube of mahogany-tinted cover-up crème from the makeup kit that she kept there for quick touchups. Veda dabbed concealer on the dark-circles under her eyes and applied a few swift strokes of eye-liner. She fought the urge to go straight back downstairs to smoke a cigarette. Ten minutes later, she was summoned.

"Veda, could you come in here please?" said Mr. Davis over the intercom. Veda got up from her desk and walked past LaMarr's office to the managing partner's office. Mr. Davis' door was open. He sat behind his large desk, pouring over stacks of law books as if searching for something. The young blonde woman from the elevator looked over his shoulder at the documents. Veda tapped softly on the door to get his attention.

"Ah, Veda. I'd like you to meet someone. Hope you're feeling better, by the way."

The blonde woman smiled in recognition and offered her hand to Veda.

"This is Courtney Hargreaves, Senator Hargreaves's daughter," he said with great relish and ceremony. Veda touched the tips of the woman's outstretched fingers then pulled her hand back quickly.

"Veda pretty much runs things around here," said Mr. Davis, "She's in charge of the girls up front, the bookkeeping, and our new A/R program as well."

"Veda, I want you to do everything you can to make Miss Hargreaves feel right at home with us. She's in her last year of law school at Georgetown University and we were lucky to get her to clerk for us this summer," he said still beaming.

Veda nodded and asked, "Is that all?" She folded both arms across her chest, and didn't even try to hide the snarl on her face.

"Well, yes for now. But I'll need you to show Miss Hargreaves, ..."

"Courtney," the blonde interjected, still wearing a stupid grin.

"Teach her how to use our computer system and where everything is," said Mr. Davis, "You've been to the vendor's training and we need you to pass that knowledge on down to the rest of the office." At that Veda raised her heavy-lidded eyes to the ceiling.

She slipped out of Mr. Davis' office and whispered, "*Shit*" under her breath, "*I should have kept my ass home again today.*" Before she could close the door behind her, Davis followed her out into the hallway and motioned her to the side.

"Listen, Veda," he whispered, "Courtney's father is not just an old friend of mine but he's also a very powerful man. He's been supplying our firm with private and government referrals for years. That translates into my job security as well as yours."

"I understand, Mr. Davis."

"And there's one more thing. Senator Hargreaves is on the judicial committee now and can appoint judges. A good word from him could mean a judgeship for me. You know I'd look out for you too." He winked.

"Don't worry Mr. Davis," said Veda in a monotone voice, "I'll do what I can to help."

"I knew I could count on you, Veda. After all, we go way back, don't we?"

Veda returned to her desk thoroughly pissed and revolted, especially about Davis' reminder that they go way back. She forced herself to block out those early years when she first went to work for him and the two of them had a hot thing going on for about six months, until she came to her senses.

Veda planted both elbows on her desk and rubbed her temples. She dreaded having to call Louis. Two whole days and nights with a child who hated her. Her ex-husband had said it might be a good time for her to get re-acquainted with Sherrelle. Veda still hadn't heard a single word from LaMarr in over twenty-four hours. And on top of all that, now she was supposed to spend her time training some hotsy-totsy, spoiled rich bitch from Georgetown University. As mad as Veda was at that moment, she still thought of LaMarr. If he wasn't floating face-down dead in the Potomac River right now then ... "If he dares stroll in here with another lame-ass story, I'm going to kill him myself," she mouthed to herself.

Veda tried to focus on her work. She had a 2 day backlog of work on her desk. No one else in the office had even thought about checking her inbox to help out while she was gone. Begrudgingly, she got busy with her work. Work was the only thing keeping her sane.

"Excuse me, Veda. Have you got a minute?" asked Courtney.

Veda had been absorbed in her work and had not heard the woman approach. Veda looked up into a pair of pale blue eyes and found Courtney Hargreaves standing over her desk.

"Yeah, what do you want?" Veda continued to stare at her monitor, and pecked rapidly on the keyboard, while Courtney waited patiently in front of her desk. Veda did not even try to hide her annoyance. She disliked Courtney and it didn't matter who her father was. It only made things worse that Courtney was tall and shapely, with long, silky hair the color of Jamaican sand. She wore a light shade of pink lipstick on her pinched lips. Her manicured nails were polished pink to match her lipstick and were adorned with butterflies in the center of each nail. She had on a light-gray skirt that reached 3 inches above the knee and a pale pink, silk blouse. Her shoes were matching gray, high-heel pumps. Veda didn't see how any judge would ever take Miss Legally Blonde seriously in a courtroom.

"I've been trying to get into FolderBolt," Courtney said, when it appeared Veda would not stop what she was doing to give her full attention, "but it keeps asking me for a password. Neither Lynn or Sheryl knows what the password is. I was hoping you could tell me."

"For what? You shouldn't need a password to get into your own work," said Veda still typing away on her keyboard as she spoke.

"Well, uh, I know, but Mr. Davis asked me to look up some legal references for the Sullivan case and update some of the files."

Veda stopped typing and glared up at Courtney.

"The Sullivan file? That's LaMarr Coleman's case. I'm supposed to be handling the legal aid work for him on that."

"I guess you'd better take it up with Mr. Davis when he gets back from court," Courtney grimaced. "I only know what he asked me to do." She appeared nervous, but determined.

Veda scribbled down the password and slid the slip of paper across her desk for Courtney to pick up, then immediately returned her attention back to the PC monitor. Courtney picked up the paper and walked back down the hallway to her office.

Veda decided she didn't give a shit if Davis wanted to give Courtney the Sullivan case to justify that brainless woman's job. Veda already had a boatload of other work to do as it was. Even though Veda was the office manager, the bulk of her duties were the same as the other two legal secretaries in the office. All three answered the telephone, typed contracts, conducted legal research, and made coffee throughout the day for the lawyers and clients. The only additional responsibility Veda had, was to deliver the checks received from accounts/receivable to the bank, deposit them, and keep detailed bookkeeping records. Veda couldn't understand why her four-year Business degree and office experience had landed her a job doing basically the same thing as these two half-wits in her office. Veda figured it was only a matter of time before Lynn, one of the other secretaries, took over the administrator functions of the new A/R System as well.

Veda became incensed every time she looked at where she was on the career ladder compared to Lynn Holte and Sheryl Ward. Sheryl Ward, was Mr. Bookerman's wife's sister's kid who barely finished high school with a C average. Neither one had Veda's qualifications or experience, but they still made almost as much money as she did. Though burning up inside, Veda chose to keep quiet. The little bit of dirt she had on Hilton Davis was wearing thin since just about all the attorneys in this town were crooked. What she had on Davis wouldn't even make the six o'clock news. She realized she was holding onto her job by a mere thread and couldn't afford to complain. She knew both Bookerman and Davis would love to replace her angry, black ass with another white secretary with a better attitude if given half a chance. She refused to give that to them. Veda got even more disgusted when she thought about all the times she caught Bookerman leering over Lynn's desk, his face puffy and red from trying to get a suntan, his mouth watering like a sick hound, and his blood-shot eyes begging to be noticed. It was George Bookerman who had convinced his partner, Hilton Davis, to hire Lynn over a score of highly-qualified, college-degree holding African American applicants who had also interviewed for the job. Bookerman championed for Lynn because he said she sounded professional over the telephone and handled clients well despite her lack of a college degree. She was bright and could learn quickly according to Bookerman—all code words for 'white' thought Veda. Besides Lynn's outstanding credentials, Bookerman added, she was recently divorced and had a young son to take care of. Veda figured Lynn had to be sleeping with Bookerman but she wasn't the least bit interested in these white folk's business. What really caught Veda's attention was that this girl, several years younger than her, without the years of experience or a degree to her credit, was immediately positioned on the fast-track and had her future success mapped out for her by George Bookerman. Veda had worked her ass off for four years at Hampton University to earn a college degree and had worked non-stop since high school. All that dedication and hard work meant nothing. She still got treated like the third fiddler in the back of the orchestra. Her two attractive, young, white co-workers used connections to get ahead. Now, here comes Miss Courtney Hargreaves with a powerful senator for a father to her credit. Veda realized she had better start going after what she wanted if she ever hoped to get out of this rut. She was so mad she couldn't concentrate on her work anymore and needed a cigarette break bad. Veda didn't know what was causing her blood to boil the most—LaMarr and his sorry antics or her own jealousy of Courtney Hargreaves, Sheryl Ward, and Lynn Holte. She was just about to go outside for a cigarette when her telephone rang. Veda picked it up before the second ring.

"Davis and Bookerman," she answered flatly and ended with a bored sigh.

"Hey Girl," said a light-hearted voice that Veda immediately recognized as her home girl, Natasha Gaines.

"Hey Natasha, what you been up to girl? Did ya'll go to June Bug's rehearsal dinner last Saturday?" asked Veda.

"Uh huh. Honey, that was a trip. I wished I had come up with some excuse and hung out with you and LaMarr at the Platinum instead."

"Oh yeah? How come?" Veda didn't bother to tell Natasha that LaMarr hadn't called or returned to her apartment at all last Saturday night or Sunday morning so she never made it to the nightclub.

"Well, let me put it to you this way. Ever since June Bug, I mean Junetta, 'cause that's what she prefers to be called now," she laughed, "Anyways, ever since some country doctor from Greensboro, Alabama proposed to her, she's been actin' like a damn fool. But her mama's worse than she is, chile. Do you know her mama called me yesterday morning? I'd just gotten back from church and had taken off my shoes to relax. I had me a box of KFC and biscuits waitin.' Well, honey, she calls and has the nerve to tell me to meet Junetta and the other girls in twenty minutes at Claire Dratch in Bethesda to try on my maid-of-honor dress."

Veda grunted an occasional, "umph, umph, umph" to show Natasha that she was still listening and sympathized with her predicament.

"Veda, you can't even imagine, girl! When I saw that dress I nearly fell out. It's some horrible, chartreuse, strapless number. The only use I'ma get outta that dress is if I decide to stand out on a street corner somewhere. But, honey, that aint't the worst of it. That dizzy broad's gone and hired four professional models to be June Bug's bridesmaids. She told Junetta it was a damn shame she didn't have no decent looking girlfriends, other than me of course, to be in her wedding. Said she wasn't about to pay that photographer all that damn money to take pictures of a buncha dressed up monkeys. The woman had the nerve to call Mabel too fat and Roberta too black. I don't know who the hell she thinks she is. Where does she come from anyway? That phony Bermuda accent has got to go."

"Go on, Natasha. You lyin." Veda had to laugh at that.

"Girl, I'm not making this mess up. You should've seen how she fell in Claire Dratch's, wearing a hat and gloves—ninety degrees outside now. Like she was on her way to high tea at Four Seasons. Just ordering us around like she's crazy or something. Girl, that woman needs professional help. I sure feel sorry for June Bug's daddy. I know he don't have no say in all this mess."

Veda sighed quietly into the telephone. She was only half listening to Natasha ramble on. Her mind was still on LaMarr. She glanced up at the clock over the doorway. It was almost noon. At that moment a strange-looking white man dressed in jeans and a T-shirt stumbled through the door and looked around. Wisps of blond hair peaked out from under his cap. Veda put Natasha on hold.

"Can I help you?"

"Yeah, where's Mr. Coleman? Me and him got business to discuss."

The man's cobalt-blue eyes stared down at Veda. He wore a snarled expression on his face. His eyes were not a clear, crystal blue like Courtney Hargreaves', but a deep dark blue, which appeared black and sinister as he squinted down at her. Veda had seen enough half-crazed, drugged-up dope fiends in her lifetime to recognize another one. She immediately pressed the button hidden under her desk to alert Security. Now the problem was just when would they decide to show up.

"I'm sorry sir but Mr. Coleman is in court right now," said Veda, lying easily in her most professional-sounding voice. The truth was she didn't know where LaMarr was. "Would you like to make an appointment?"

"Naw, I don't want no goddamn appointment. You jus tell'im Phebus come by. He knows where to find me."

The man left as abruptly as he had burst in. Veda let out a deep breath in relief. She remembered she still had Natasha on hold. Veda quickly got back to her phone conversation.

"Girl, you wouldn't believe what I have to put up with over here. They don't pay me enough for this shit," she said. She quickly told Natasha about her visitor.

"Tell me about it. Girl, I know what you mean," Natasha agreed.

Veda's alternate number rang indicating that an incoming call had rolled over to her other line. At first Veda thought she'd let it ring and let whoever it was leave a message but a split second later she realized it could be LaMarr calling.

"Let me put you on hold again for a sec, Natasha. I got a call coming in on the other line."

Veda pressed the hold button and clicked over to the alternate line while Natasha was in mid-sentence talking about what a good time she had at the BET Sound Stage restaurant the other night. She knew Natasha didn't mind holding. That girl didn't do no work anyway, Veda thought. She worked downtown for the government and emailed at least twenty messages a day filled with jokes, chain letters, and other nonsense.

"Davis and Bookerman," answered Veda hoping it was LaMarr calling.

"Hello, Veda. This is Dr. Renee Hayes. I wasn't sure if you got my message this morning or the one last night. I've been worried about you since our last meeting. Veda, I hope you will accept my apology. I ..."

"Forget about it, Doc," answered Veda, "I got your messages. I'm fine, I guess."

"That's good, Veda. But I'd still like to see you. Something happened at my home Wednesday night and it may or may not affect you. I'll be asking all of my patients a few questions, if you don't mind to see if we can shed some light on things. I'm sorry if I sound mysterious, but I'll explain later when I see you. Will you be keeping your 6:30 appointment this evening?"

"What happened, Dr. Renee?" Veda was curious.

"I think it's better if I explain in person. You remember there's a path leading to the entrance to my office at the rear of my house. I'll be expecting you at six-thirty this evening then?"

"Well, actually, if it can wait until next week, that'd be better for me," said Veda, "I just remembered I've got somebody coming in this evening."

"Sure. That's fine Veda. I'll see you next week. Good-bye."

Veda almost hoped Natasha had gotten tired of holding on and had hung up, but she was still on the line.

"Who was that—LaMarr?" asked Natasha.

"Nah. It was my shrink," said Veda, "She was calling to confirm my appointment, but I had to reschedule to next week."

"Girl, you must be kidding."

"No, I'm serious. Cha-cha recommended her, you know."

"Cha-cha? Then I know you crazy," said Natasha, "Look girl, if you got that much money to throw away, give me some of it,"

"Seriously, Natasha. I think this sister can help me."

"Well, she ain't done nothin' for Cha-cha. Honey, let me give you the 411 on that chick."

Just as Natasha was about to get into all the details on Cha-cha's business, LaMarr strolled through the door and walked straight past Veda's desk without saying a word.

"Girl, my man just walked in. I gotta go," Veda hung up the phone without letting Natasha finish her sentence. Veda sprung up from her desk and followed LaMarr to his office.

"Where the hell have you been?" she demanded.

"Business," snapped LaMarr and slammed the door to his office in her face.

Veda knew she would need that cigarette break now. She grabbed her purse and headed outside the building for a smoke. She'd give LaMarr fifteen minutes to get his day's agenda together then she was going to demand an explanation as to where he'd been all night.

When Veda returned upstairs to her desk, LaMarr's office door was still closed. She retrieved his unsigned expense reports to use as a pretense for interrupting him when his door was shut. Veda tapped gently on the door a few times then opened it without waiting for his permission to enter.

"What is it, Veda?" LaMarr said sternly.

Courtney Hargreaves was seated in a leather chair in front of his desk with a bunch of papers on her lap. Her well-shaped legs were crossed at the knee and showed a less than modest amount of thigh. Despite the cool, air-conditioned temperature in the office, Veda was hot. Courtney exhibited a quiet, unobtrusive demeanor as if she had something to hide. Veda immediately distrusted the bitch.

"Sorry, Mr. Coleman," said Veda, quickly recovering from her shock at finding Courtney there, "Mr. Bookerman needs your signature on these expense sheets right away."

LaMarr snatched the papers from Veda and scribbled his signature on each sheet. He tried to hide his annoyance at the interruption but she could tell he was pissed. Courtney studied the document in her lap and seemed not to notice LaMarr's anger. LaMarr shoved the expense sheets back into Veda's hand and immediately continued his discussion with Courtney. He leaned back and crossed one long leg over the other at the ankle. Veda stood frozen in place for a few seconds, watching LaMarr.

He had on shoes made of black, soft leather that shined meticulously. He wore a dark blue Armani suit and a colorful silk paisley tie with matching suspenders. The stylish haircut accentuated the soft, texture of his hair. Except for his mustache, all other facial hair was closely shaven, revealing a smooth, dark-brown complexion. He wore a large diamond-wrapped, black onyx ring on his right finger that Veda had never seen before. She smiled thinking how fine he was and looking around his office, she thought how everything about LaMarr reflected his exquisite taste. It was professionally decorated in black and burgundy leather furniture. Built-in, ceiling-to-floor bookcases lined the walls. Soft jazz music played in the background. A stark contrast to the open, bull-pen like atmosphere she worked in. If it hadn't been for her and her connections, LaMarr wouldn't be sitting behind that large mahogany desk right now.

And yet he still treated her like shit and got away with it; she got mad all over again.

"Well? Was there anything else you needed Veda?" asked LaMarr, finally looking away from Courtney's face and finding Veda still there.

Veda turned to leave but not before rolling her eyes at Courtney.

"Next time, knock, will you?" said LaMarr, "I am trying to have a meeting in here, for christsake."

As she closed the door, Veda looked back and noticed that LaMarr quickly turned his grin back on for Courtney. He smiled so broadly Veda could see nearly all of his straight, white teeth.

That simple bitch just sat there smiling and twirling her blond hair around her finger and tossing it out of her eye. Veda seethed with hatred for her new adversary. She wasn't about to let either one of them get away with pushing her aside. She'd been through too much with LaMarr to be thrown out like a pair of worn-out, old slippers. She'd show LaMarr that old slippers can still be more comfortable than a new pair.

CHAPTER 8

▼

Renee slid behind the wheel of her jade green Acura and checked the clock on the dashboard. It read 10:07 AM. Most of her neighbors had left for work hours ago. She inspected the bottom of her bag until she felt Deek's wireless telephone. She wanted to make sure she hadn't left behind the reason for her uninvited visit.

Renee sat frozen with both hands on the steering wheel, the key in the ignition, and the car in park. Did she really want to just show up at his house? This was perfectly innocent she told herself. After all, she'd left half a dozen messages since yesterday and he hadn't returned her calls. She knew she was lying to herself. The fantasies she had about him were too frequent and too explicit to be called innocent. She experienced a brief tightness in her chest just thinking about seeing Deek again. She thought of Bill and their fragile marriage. The last thing it needed was for her to fall for a man at least ten years younger than she was. Renee caught a glimpse of herself in the rearview mirror and stared at her reflection. *Who am I? To the outside world and even to the few people I might call friends, I'm educated, attractive, established—but, they can't see behind this mask.* Renee perceived what others didn't see—a lonely woman at the brink of a mid-life crisis, who has suddenly realized that she's never really been happy with her life. Meanwhile the clock skips forward each year towards midnight. And each year she is no closer to getting what she wants. There's not much time left before the clock's last chime. Renee pushed aside her fears of seeing Deek, stepped on the gas and sped out of the driveway. She pressed a button from inside her car to release the front security gates to the single exit and entry points of Foxhall Crescent Estates.

She checked the Mapquest directions at the next red light. Tension mounted as she realized she was getting close to his house. Renee was glad she had decided to clear her morning and afternoon calendar. Even better, Veda had rescheduled her evening appointment. Now Renee didn't have to try to focus on someone else's problems at all today. In less than 30 minutes she was standing on the front porch of Deek's house. Renee unbuttoned the bottom of her calf-length skirt well above the knee and smoothed out the wrinkles in her Moroccan-print tunic. Then she rang the bell. She felt sure she would get his attention in this flame stitched red, orange, and yellow outfit with bright turquoise and lime patterns interwoven throughout.

Even her earrings shouted for attention—large, gold-tone circles with turquoise-colored centers and multicolored drop-down shapes. She had brushed out her hair and decided to let it go free and natural. Her entire look was much different from the understated, conservative style she typically favored. Today she felt young, free, and sexy.

Renee was just about to ring again when the door opened. A kid of about fifteen or sixteen stood before her. He was slightly out of breath and wore Nike shorts and a sweat-drenched T-shirt with the sleeves cut out. His complexion was smooth and copper-colored with a thin row of fine fuzz above his lip. His hair was cropped short on top and shaved even closer on the sides. Droplets of sweat lined his forehead and trickled down his face. Staring back at her, his eyes looked dark and intense.

"My name is Dr. Renee Hayes. I'm looking for Detective Degas Hamilton," she said, "Does he live here?"

The young man didn't answer, but turned around and left with the door still ajar. Renee stood on the steps and waited.

After a few moments, Deek came to the door. The first thing that hit her was the intoxicating scent of his fragrance. Her heart raced from standing just a foot away. He was wearing a pair of faded blue jeans and a denim shirt that looked like it had gone through several washings. Both fit his well-toned, muscular body perfectly. A St. Christopher medal hung from his neck and gleamed in the sunlight.

"Hey, what a surprise," he said, smiling as he stepped aside for her to enter, "You look ... nice, Doc."

"Thanks, Detective. So do you," she said.

The house felt hotter inside than outdoors. The fan in the window made a lot of noise but hadn't cooled off the room.

"Sorry about the heat. I called someone this morning to come out and fix the air conditioner but they haven't shown up. So, Dr. Hayes, what brings you out this way so early in the morning?"

Renee retrieved the phone from her purse and handed it to him.

"You picked up mine by mistake yesterday afternoon. Here's yours."

He examined the phone, "So it is. Sorry about that, Doc. I've had yours turned off since yesterday but you should be able to retrieve all your calls. I just hope you didn't miss anything important." He turned his phone on and set it on the hall table, next to a pile of unopened mail.

"I doubt it," said Renee, "That is the number I give out to patients in case of emergency but I've been calling to follow up with them directly myself."

"That's good. Let me go get your phone. Be right back." He disappeared down the hall.

Renee had to admit that she found Deek difficult to resist and hoped he was attracted to her too. She wondered at how she could so easily change her affections, in less than twenty-four hours, from a man she had lived with for fourteen years to another she just met.

When Deek returned she couldn't come up with any excuse to linger so she thanked him and reluctantly headed towards the door.

"Look here, Doc, you came all this way, why not stay for awhile? Can I get you a coke or some ice tea?"

"No thank you, Detective Hamilton. I'm fine," she said and immediately regretted turning down the offer.

"You know, it wouldn't be against regulations for you to call me Deek," he said, smiling and for a few brief moments their eyes met.

"The same can be said for you," she smiled, "It wouldn't kill you to call me Renee."

"Nah, I'm just a poor city cop. You've got all the class and credentials."

Like many other people, Deek assumed Renee had led a privileged upbringing because she lived in an exclusive neighborhood, had medical training, and a Ph.D. degree in psychology.

"Let's go downstairs to my office. It's cooler in the basement," he said and led her to the door leading to the basement. Renee tried to appear calm, but her heart raced from excitement. He actually wanted her to stay! She followed him down the stairs.

Deek picked up the piles of papers and PC magazines that were stacked on a chair and motioned for Renee to sit down. His office was full of computer equipment. He had two PC's, a printer, a FAX, and a scanner that she could easily recognize. The television showed a baseball game in progress with the sound turned off while Reggae music played from one of his computers. Deek clicked his mouse, placed a disc in the CD-ROM of his computer and switched to a more soothing jazz selection.

"You might like this better," he said and turned the sound down on the speakers.

"Who was that you were listening to?" She leaned forward in the chair and rested an elbow on the arm of the chair. She realized that she exposed a hint of cleavage with her leaning gesture.

"Don't know. I pulled it off the web from liveconcerts.com."

"Oh," she said, "Sorry, I interrupted."

"Naw, I was really supposed to be searching for leads on a cold case I'm working on."

"A cold case?"

"Yeah. It's a homicide involving a credit card scam on the Net that's still unsolved after 18 months. If I can locate the security hole, I think it'll lead me to a suspect."

"Sounds reasonable," Renee said, with no idea what security hole was. Computers were not her thing, but she wanted to sound interested.

"I think so," said Deek, "My partner says using the Internet is a complete waste of time. But then, he's a fifty-seven year old dinosaur who's counting the days until his early retirement in December. So I'm pretty much on my own on this one."

Just then the telephone on his desk rang once, then abruptly stopped.

"Must be for Tyrone. I don't get to use my home phone anymore since he's been staying with me this summer."

"I guess that's why you never got any of my messages," she said, "Tyrone, I take it is the young man who answered the door?"

Deek nodded, "He's a good kid for the most part. A little hard-headed at times."

"Is he your son?" she asked.

"No, not exactly, but he looks at me like a father figure."

"Where're his parents?"

"His Mom works for the Department of Transportation downtown and also pulls the night shift at Safeway. She's raising Tyrone alone, along with his two little sisters. I try to help out whenever I can. She was glad to have him stay with me over the summer, said it would keep him out of trouble and away from those hoodlums in her neighborhood."

They heard a noise above that sounded like a stampede of elephants. Tyrone raced down the stairs and burst into Deek's study.

"Hey, Deek. That was A.C. He wants to know if I'm going to the Go-Go tonight at the rec center. Cool?"

Deek turned his attention to the boy, "I guess Desiree's going to be there, right?"

Tyrone shrugged his shoulders, smiled and started to blush, "How should I know? I don't care if she goes."

"And just how were you planning to get there?"

"Chauncey. He's the only one with a ride."

"Uh, I don't think so, Tyrone. You know your Mom doesn't like you going to those places."

"Man, she don't have to know." Tyrone screwed up his face and dug his hands in his pants pockets.

Deek gave Tyrone a stern look. Tyrone sighed heavily and threw up his hands.

"Why can't I go? They're gonna have police security. Nothin's gonna happen."

"I'm sorry, Tyrone. Not this time," said Deek, "I don't like the sound of it. You know there was a shooting over there last weekend."

"Man, there's a shooting every day," argued Tyrone.

"No can do buddy," Deek shook his head.

Tyrone muttered under his breath, "Shit, always messin' up my damn plans."

"I heard that Tyrone and I told you about using that kind of language. Your mother doesn't like it and neither do I. Did you put in your rubber bands?"

"No, I was eatin' something," said Tyrone.

"Well, you're not eating now are you? So put them back in."

Tyrone stomped back upstairs.

"Rubber bands?" Renee asked.

"Yeah, for his braces. I went ahead and took care of it for him this summer. I knew his mother couldn't afford dental work. Tyrone's a great looking kid. It'd be a shame to spoil it with bad teeth."

"You seem to care a lot about him. And he isn't even your child, is he?" she asked cautiously.

"Nope. Not biologically, anyway," he said, "But what difference does that make? Anyway, he's 16 and I'm only 28 myself. I would've had to start a bit early to be his daddy."

It was worse than she'd suspected. She was much more than ten years older than him. Renee thought about her desire for having a baby and wondered if her motives where as genuine as Deek's appeared to be—to simply provide love and shelter to a child who needed it.

The noise from a door slamming upstairs briefly startled Renee. In the next minute the office vibrated with loud Rap music coming from upstairs and drowned out the CD-ROM's soft jazz number. They both looked up at the ceiling. It seemed to pulsate from the continuous beat of Tyrone's gangster rap music. Deek glanced at his watch.

"It's almost eleven-thirty. Somehow I don't think we'll get much peace even down here," he said, "I don't wanna overstep my bounds Dr. Hayes, but can I take you out to lunch?"

"What?" She wasn't sure she had heard him right. He must have taken her surprise reaction for hesitation because he pressed on.

"I know this is short notice but I was thinking if you don't have plans for the day, how about taking a ride with me? It's a hell of a lot nicer outside than it is in here. Besides, there's someplace I'd like to take you." Deek felt inside the pocket of his jeans to insure he had his keys. Then, he stood up and held out his hand for her to join him. "You can leave your car parked outside. I'll bring you back here after lunch."

Renee stared into his sincere, dark eyes and only one answer came to mind, *yes*. There was nothing else she'd rather be doing than spending more time with him. She stood up and took his outstretched hand. "Thank you. I'd like that. What do you have in mind?"

"Trust me, you'll love it," he led the way back upstairs.

After Deek reiterated the ground rules for Tyrone, they left. As he drove Renee watched him out of the corner of her eye as his hand forcefully took hold of the gear-shift between them to change gears. He pressed a button on the CD player and jazz music came on. When she asked what was playing, he said it was an older tune he liked by Bony James called, '*Turning the Lights Down Low*.' His eyes left the road momentarily to smile at her. She looked away quickly, not wanting him to recognize the affect he was having on her. They barely knew each other, but Renee felt the chemistry between them intensify. She stared out the window in a dream-like state.

"You're awfully quiet over there, Doc," he said after several minutes of silence had passed, "You okay?"

"Sure. You still haven't said exactly where we're going, Detective. Is it a secret?"

He glanced over at her and smiled, "No secret. Don't worry Doc, I haven't kidnapped you. The restaurant's less than an hour away from the city." Deek explained he was taking her to a waterfront restaurant called the Yellow Fin at the Oak Grove Marina in Edgewater, Maryland. He had a friend who belonged to the Liberty Yacht Club and he kept his boat docked at the marina. He said the restaurant had a nice view of the South River that funneled into the Chesapeake Bay and it was just south of Annapolis. They drove a while longer and just as he said, in less than forty-five minutes they were in Edgewater. Renee had no idea that such a beautiful, serene setting was only an hour's drive away from D. C.

By 12:30 the sun had grown fierce. Renee and Deek sat at one of the tables outdoors and admired the spectacular view and tried to block out the muffled conversations of people around them. The heat furled over them like basting on a roasted turkey, but the reflection from the sun's fading rays against the rippling water was beautiful and produced a slight cooling breeze. They used the brief periods of silence to listen to the hushed waves and the chirped song of birds flying above them. In the distance they could see rows of boats moored along the floating docks. Renee was impressed with Deek's knowledge of boating. He pointed out the various types of vessels, the sailors, the "stinkpot" or powerboats, 24-foot sloops, racing yachts, and 28-foot Bayliners. He told her that some waterfront homeowners kept their yachts permanently moored and that their yachts had all the comforts of home, like floating Winnebagos with cook-tops, televisions, and bars inside. Others were used mainly for recreation. These yachters cruised up and down the East Coast liked they owned the District rivers and all 185 miles of the Chesapeake Bay.

When the food arrived, Renee noticed that, just as he promised, it was as luscious as their surroundings. They started with an appetizer of coconut shrimp. Deek ordered the Yellofin Crab Cakes with sautéed fresh baby spinach, and Renee chose the Stuffed Canadian Salmon, topped with Maryland-style Imperial crab and Chesapeake Mornay sauce. Afterwards, neither had room for dessert, but Deek convinced Renee to try the pear crumble anyway. She took a few mouth-watering bites before pushing the plate in front of him to finish. They sat for a long time after their table had been cleared, sipping on iced coffee and enjoying each other's company. Renee resisted the urge to slip her fingers within one of his large, callused hands as it rested on the table.

"So, tell me Detective Hamilton, who is this friend of yours with a yacht?" She folded her hands under her chin and looked into his eyes.

"He's more like a business acquaintance really. I knew Phil when we were both systems engineers at IBM. Only he went on to start his own software development company, grossing over 2 million in revenue a year. And me, I became a D. C. cop."

"Well, somebody has to stop criminals," she smiled.

"Phil's private slip is right down there on floating dock C," said Deek, pointing in the direction of the docks, "Wanna take a look inside the Sarina's Joy?"

"He's there now? Your friend?"

"Oh no, he's away on business at the moment but he owes me. I beta tested some new software for him last week so he gave me the keys to his yacht until he gets back in town tomorrow evening." Deek paused, "So how about it, Doc? Wanna check it out?" he smiled and stared into her eyes.

"Well, I ..."

Before she could answer, one of their telephones rang. They both checked and it turned out to be Renee's. She immediately recognized Bill's office number from the Caller ID display and did not answer it. The message waiting indicator flashed and she knew he had left a message on her VoiceMail. Renee glanced at her watch and saw that it was after 3 o'clock. It was only then that she remembered the 1 o'clock appointment with Bill and Mrs. Addison.

"I have to return this call in private. Excuse me," she said and suddenly got up from the table.

Renee looked for an isolated spot outside the café so she could call Bill and try to explain. She rehearsed in her head what she would say to him. She dialed quickly and hoped to get his VoiceMail greeting then she wouldn't have to lie to his face. But he picked up on the first ring. He had been sitting at his desk waiting for her call. Renee told him that an emergency came up with a patient and she wasn't able to call and cancel their appointment. Bill kept asking questions. He wanted to know where she was and when she'd be home but Renee dodged each one until he finally gave up. Before returning to the table, she tried to remove the guilty look from her face. She saw that Deek had already paid the waiter and left the tip on the table. He stood up when he saw her approach.

"Is everything all right?"

"Yes," she nodded, "but it's getting late. I should be getting back. Thank you for lunch, Deek. I really did enjoy it."

"Come on, Doc. It's just a little after three," he said and put his arm around her waist, "I promise to have you home by 7. Phil says he stocked the galley with champagne and caviar. You're not going to pass that up, are you?"

His dark eyes sparkled with a child-like playfulness. Renee felt her resistance weakening. She could feel him getting excited as he eased her body closer to his. He gently stroked the curve of her shoulders and back. There was no doubt in Renee's mind now as to what Deek's intentions were. But she didn't want to resist.

Deek offered his arm for Renee to hold onto as they walked slowly along the unsteady pier.

"I wouldn't mind having one of those," said Deek pointing out a speedboat. "And how about you, Doc? Do you like going out on the water?"

"No, I'm afraid that's not one of my passions," she said, holding onto him tightly. "When I was in college I almost drowned taking swimming lessons at the Y."

"So I take it you can't swim?" he said, giving her a look of surprise.

Renee shook her head, "No, and to be honest, I feel a little shaky just walking on this dock. I'm not too sure about boarding your friend's boat."

"C'mon, Doc. It'll be a piece of cake. I promise."

Renee stopped suddenly and looked up at him. "You've made quite a few promises today, Detective."

"That's right and you'll see I'm a man of my word," he smiled and squeezed her arm playfully.

Renee and Deek resumed their walk down the dock and savored the fresh, summer air. They looked from side to side and admired the various types of sail boats, powerboats and cabin cruisers that wobbled in the water. The wooden heals of Renee's sandals pinched into the fiberglass dock with each step. She had on city shoes and was not dressed properly for visiting a marina.

A seafarer dressed in summer whites and a maroon fez saluted them from the deck of his yacht. Deek returned the salute, "Afternoon, Captain." The older gentleman nodded back and took a sip of his Bloody Mary.

"Looks like the old goat's been drinking Bloody Mary's and Screwdrivers since he woke up this morning," laughed Deek as they walked past.

"Unfortunately, some of us have to work for a living." As they rounded the corner Deek pointed ahead, "There it is." Renee could tell he was excited by the boyish grin on his face.

At the end of the dock Renee could see the 60-foot Hatteras with its name, "Sarina's Joy" printed in bold, black letters across the stern. They walked down the narrow finger pier just off the dock and stood directly in front of Phil's yacht. Deek cupped both hands around his mouth and shouted out, "Anybody home?" No one answered him back.

"I thought you said your friend was out of town?"

"Yeah, but I want to make sure his wife and kids aren't using it today. They live in Reston and rarely come out to the marina but just let me check it out first. Be right back."

Deek jumped across the gangplank and landed on deck while Renee waited on the finger pier. He unlocked a side door leading to the pilothouse and then, disappeared from view. Moments later, she spotted him standing on deck high above her. He leaned over the railing and surveyed his surroundings.

"This is great," he smiled down at her, "Coming aboard, Doc?"

Renee shielded her eyes from the sun with one hand and looked up at him.

"I don't think so," she said and shook her head. Her face bore a measured look of caution as she planted her feet firmly on the platform.

Deek grabbed hold of the metal ladder and started to slowly descend. He leaned towards her and held out his hand. "Here, let me help you. First, hand me those shoes. They'll ruin the deck."

Renee removed her sandals and gave them to Deek. He reached out with his free hand to help her climb aboard. With his help, she carefully stepped across the gangplank. She was surprised to find herself standing on deck and not floating in the water.

Once on deck, Deek turned to her with a wide grin. "So, what do you say, Doc? Want me to launch her and take her out on the water for a little spin?"

When she displayed a look of skepticism, he explained it would be more private to anchor at Harness Creek, which was only about five minutes from the marina. "Harness Creek is so peaceful," he said, "It's just off the South River."

Renee gave him the thumbs up signal to proceed. Deek nodded and went to check the dock lines. He showed her how to untie the lines. Renee was surprised to discover she wasn't as inept as she thought, once he explained what to do. Deek started the engine and they were all set to launch. Renee sat on the bridge deck with him until they reached Harness Creek. Then, he anchored the boat and turned off the engine. He led her down the fiberglass stairwell to the lower helm. Renee picked up her shoes and followed him to the main salon, carefully watching each step. Windows, family photographs, and mementos filled the room. Deek pointed to a black leather couch covered with large white pillows and told her to make herself comfortable. She sank down on the soft leather. He said he'd be right back with something from the galley, the galley being a nautical term for the kitchen area. He withdrew and a few seconds later, she heard the faint sounds of Kenny G playing in the background from a CD player.

Deek returned with a silver tray of assorted cheeses, crackers, and pastries. He also carried two glasses, and a bottle of chilled wine. He sat down next to her. They toasted and began to drink. The scent of his cologne and the sips of wine began to take affect. The silence between them no longer felt awkward. She did not feel guilty about standing Bill up that afternoon. Renee did not push his hand away when she felt it rest casually on her knee. She felt the soft touch of his hand and was surprised at her sudden sense of freedom and lack of inhibitions.

Deek took the wine glass from her hand. He lifted her hand to his lips and kissed the inside of it with slow, lingering kisses. The hairs of his mustache tickled the inside of her hand. He nestled his warm lips to her ear and neck. Without warning, he kissed her passionately. Afterwards, he squeezed her hand gently and stared into her eyes, "You okay?" She nodded, yes. She could feel herself succumbing to the sound of his voice, his seductive smile, and good looks. Deek stood up and raised her from the couch. He led her three steps down to the lower deck, which contained the sleeping quarters. As soon as she stepped through the master bedroom door, Renee felt the soothing effects from its ethereal all-white color scheme. Two sconces hung over the headboard and bathed the room in soft amber. A white comforter lined with white lace and apricot satin pillows covered the queen-size bed. Being with Deek and enjoying his undivided attention felt like an escape from her loneliness, no matter how temporary. Tomorrow she'd face reality, she decided. Today, there was Deek.

The warmth from his body, which was pressed so near to her, flowed through to her insides as he held her close. She found his fragrance, his touch, and the wine all intoxicating. He pulled back the comforter. He lifted her into his arms and slowly lowered her down on the bed. She held on tight within his embrace and lingered over each slow and deliberate kiss. Deek placed his hand inside the front of her blouse and massaged and kissed her breasts until her nipples stiffened. She helped him unfasten and slip off her clothing and watched as he quickly stripped off his clothes and tossed them aside. Renee had time to think about what she was doing and could have easily said no at any point. But she didn't want to think at that moment; she only wanted to feel. She felt his tongue linger all over her body, in some places that had never been touched by Bill.

Outside, a fierce clap of thunder burst from the sky. A few seconds later, the sunlight from the porthole was replaced with dark gray skies. A torrent of rain hit against the window but Deek and Renee ignored it. The strength of his arms gave her comfort as the yacht rocked gently from the force of the wind and the storm outside. His warm, strong hands traveled up her thigh, across her stomach, and between her legs. His movements were slow and gentle. The waves hit against the yacht and swayed the boat in harmony with their rhythm. She followed his lead and explored his hard, muscular body in the same places that he touched her, the insides of his arms, legs, chest, and firm buttocks. It had been a long time since Renee remembered feeling this good.

Deek stopped to reach down and pick up his jeans off of the floor. He effort-lessly yanked a condom out of the back pants pocket. This made her trust him even more. He was no reckless lover. She hadn't even considered protection but then she hadn't planned for things to end up like this. Renee helped him put on the condom. The perspiration from his body mingled with hers. She felt his slow, gentle movements inside her and lost track of time. She heard herself whisper his name and may have mumbled that she loved him. Without understanding why, Renee felt she had become addicted to this man whom she had met only yester-day. She could still hear Aunt Clara's voice from the past resonant in her ear when she used to warn her that too much passion made a woman weak and need a man too much. To hell with Aunt Clara and her feeble warnings. Renee dis-missed her memories. She stayed nestled under him, locked within his arms until her pounding heart and rapid breathing returned to normal.

The day had turned into evening. It was not until hours later when lying across his chest and stroking the dint of his navel that Renee stopped to consider what she should do now. For the moment, all she wanted was to enjoy being with him. His dark, beautiful eyes were closed. Renee allowed her gaze to wander over every inch of his naked body. One arm rested next to his side and the other was wrapped tight around her waist. Renee watched as his smooth, hairless chest rose and fell with each breath. From there, her shameless scrutiny roamed downward over his sleeping body from the firm, flat stomach to the large, bulge protruding between his muscled thighs. The sheet covered him partially but she could still see with her mind's eye and the memory of how he felt was still vivid. Renee wanted to touch and taste him once again but he looked too peaceful and content to be disturbed.

Renee closed her eyes and snuggled closer to him. After awhile she felt him stirring. He kissed her briefly and then got up. She could hear him running water in the shower. She smiled and turned over on her side. Deek stood in the bath-room doorway and called for her to join him.

She saw that he had brought in a crystal vase filled with fresh flowers from the salon. They held each other and let the steaming water soothe their bodies with its tranquilizing effect. Renee closed her eyes, unaware of Deek's admiring stare.

It was almost ten when they left the yacht. The rain had stopped. The sky still looked gray and overcast and threatened to storm again. The air had turned breezy and now felt pleasant. The early evening showers had cleansed the air of the day's buildup of smog and heat, and washed over everything with a cool, sweet scent of honeysuckle.

CHAPTER 9

▼

"Veda, I need you to make these last minute changes to the Yamada contract," said Mr. Davis and pointed to some papers that sat on the edge of his cluttered desk, "and could you also confirm my airline reservations to New York on the 30th?"

"What airline reservations?" asked Veda.

"Oh that's right. Lynn must have made them for me. But since she's out today can you check on it? The National Women's Political Caucus is presenting me with the "Good Guy" award. I'm one of this year's recipients because of my strong support of women's issues."

Veda rolled her eyes, not caring if he saw her indifference. "All right, is that it?" said Veda, arms folded and wearing a scowl.

"No, one more thing. Get Courtney a reservation on the same flight. It'll be a good opportunity for her to do some networking." Mr. Davis checked his watch, and without looking at Veda fumbled with the papers on his desk as if searching for something.

Veda snatched the Yamada contract from the edge of the desk. She flipped through it and noticed that it was covered with red markings on every page. Veda shook her head and glared at Davis, but he had turned his attention to the law book that he had been searching for. It would take her all damn day to make these changes she thought. Veda cleared her throat before interrupting,

"Excuse me Mr. Davis. But did Mr. Coleman say exactly where he was going or what time he'd be back in the office?"

"He's preparing a witness for the Bowers trial coming up next week. Oh, and he also mentioned something about going with Courtney to a 'Meet & Greet' for

Senator Hargreaves later this evening. I doubt he'll be back in the office today. Anything I can help you with Veda?"

"No, thanks. It can wait."

She exited quickly to avoid Mr. Davis asking questions about her and LaMarr. She figured Mr. Davis already suspected they had more than a working relationship but LaMarr told her he wanted to keep things private between them. He said it was nobody's business what he did on his own time. But why the hell didn't LaMarr say anything about going to a 'Meet & Greet' for Senator Hargreaves? That was just like him to disappear early on a Friday before they had a chance to make plans. She was expecting her daughter to arrive tomorrow night and stay with her a few days. Her ex-husband said he planned to drop Sherrelle off at her place on his way down to Richmond. Tonight would be the only time she and LaMarr could be alone this weekend.

Veda returned to her desk, slammed the stack of papers down, and brought up the Yamada contract on her monitor. She already had a long list of unchecked 'To Do' items on her Day Planner. She jotted down a new item: Make airline reservations to NYC for C.H.

There was still that information to look up in Lexus/Nexis that she hadn't been able to get to all day. The blinking, red light on her telephone indicated that more telephone messages awaited her. And the last time she read her mail, there were over 27 e-mail messages still unopened. Veda wasn't about to check e-mail any more today. That was the one bad thing about getting an Internet connection. Every damn dog and his brother kept sending her junk she didn't give a shit about, and the rest were work related things that wanted immediate attention.

The day had been a complete 'time suck.' She had been tied up all morning teaching Sheryl how to use a new accounts/receivable program that Davis ordered installed on their LAN server. As the firm's office manager, it was Veda's job to make sure the support staff was up to speed on the new system. As far as Veda was concerned, Davis didn't pay her enough to put up with all the crap she had to do in that office.

Before she started to work, Veda tried LaMarr's home number just in case he had stopped by his home first to change. She knew LaMarr was very meticulous about his appearance. But, there was no answer. "Damn" she said under her breath. She typed rapidly on the keyboard without taking her eyes off the monitor and recalled the last time she had seen LaMarr. Veda had deliberately walked in on his closed-door meeting with Courtney Hargreaves that morning. She seriously doubted they were discussing the Sullivan case from the way she caught him staring at Miss Thing's legs. She had tried her best to keep an eye on what was going on with them but before she knew it, LaMarr and Courtney had left the office. She sighed and started to work, opening the Yamada Contract. After an hour of non-stop typing, Veda paused long enough to check the time. It was 3:49.

"Shit," she said to herself, "No telling when I'm a get the hell outta here."

Now Veda was glad that she had told Dr. Renee that lie about expecting company tonight and needing to reschedule her therapy to next week. She would never have been able to finish work in time to make a 6:30 session. Veda worked until 7, way after everyone had left. She finally got home around 7:30 and immediately stripped out of her tan suit and left it lying on the floor. She jumped in the shower and washed her hair. It was in bad shape and cried out for touchup and trim. Clumps of her hair had begun to break off from the weekly blow-drying, curling with hot electric irons, and wearing that weave. Veda hated the thought of spending half an hour wrapping her damaged split-ends around a dozen hard rollers, and then sitting under a hot hair dryer for another forty-five minutes. But she didn't think her weak hair could withstand much more abuse from blow-drying and electric curling.

Looking at her hair, Veda thought about her college days in the early eighties. At that time she was too involved in her studies to actively take part in political issues during the black consciousness movement, but the African-inspired look was back in style. Like millions of other black sisters during that time, Veda wore African garb, big jewelry, and proudly wore her hair natural. But now, despite the re-emergence of black consciousness and African culture, Veda couldn't see herself with hair in its own natural state or in braids.

Veda's struggle for acceptance wasn't because she worked downtown in a conservative law firm or felt constrained by the demands of what society said she should be. Dr. Renee had told her that her fears and loathing came from within. Still, it sure as hell didn't help to see MTV rap artists sing to light-skinned girls with hair straightened to the roots. Or black athletes and movie stars, court and marry white or almost-white women. Veda fought off the image of Courtney Hargreaves in LaMarr's office earlier that day.

She positioned a small mirror on the coffee table so she could watch her taping of Oprah's show as she began to set her wet hair on rollers. That's when she noticed an attractive, well-groomed sister on the cover of her latest issue of Ebony, lying on the table. The model's haircut framed her face and tapered at the neck in a carefree, natural styled wave. An air of confidence and sophistication radiated from her smile. Veda looked in the mirror at her own mass of dull, split-off, just barely chemically-straighten hair. Each attempt to comb out the wet tangles tore out another large clump. She stared again at the beautiful African-American sister on the cover. With that sharp cut, maybe she could look like that too. With her hair dripping wet and covered with Medusa coils, Veda gave up the battle and dialed her beautician.

"Is Cha-Cha there?" Veda asked.

"Hold on," said the woman who answered and then screamed in Veda's ear, "Cha-Cha! Phone!"

"Hello."

"Hey Girl, it's Veda."

"Hey Veda, how you doin' girl?"

"Honey, I can't even get a comb through this head. Can I *please* come in?"

Veda tried to sound as pitiful as she could. She knew Cha-Cha always got busiest after six during the week.

"Whatcha want done?" Cha-Cha asked as she smacked on a piece of chewing gum.

"Girl, I need a good cut. Somethin' stylish and natural looking. But no more strong chemicals, okay? I'll bring in a picture I saw on Ebony's cover page."

"Yeah, I know whatcha talkin' about. But look here Girl, your head ain't gon do what you want without some kinda mild relaxin'."

"Okay, Cha-Cha, you're the boss. Just do something with it. Please?" Veda was used to begging.

"Umhmm. Let me see." Veda heard Cha-Cha flipping through the pages of her appointment book. "I got a wash and curl comin' in at any minute, and I'm booked up 'til nine. If you can get your sorry behind on over here right now, I might be able to squeeze you in."

"Thanks, Cha-Cha. I'm already out the door."

"Umhmm. See you in a few ..."

Veda stuffed her damp, tangled hair inside a Washington Nationals cap and rushed out the door.

Twenty minutes later, she burst through the door of the salon and was happy to discover that Cha-Cha's eight o'clock had canceled. Veda plopped down and removed her baseball cap. Cha-Cha ran her fingers through Veda's thick, matted roots.

"Girl, you gon pay me for this. I hope you brought enough money, cause' it's gon' cost plenty for me to fix up this disaster," said Cha-Cha shaking her long hair extensions from side to side.

"Honey, don't you worry about that. I got the cash," said Veda, "Just make me look good 'cause I got plans for my man tonight."

"Umhmm, speakin' of Mr. Wonderful, did I tell you I ran into him last Saturday night at the Avenue?" said Cha-Cha as she rubbed huge globs of creamy relaxer through Veda's hair, "He was there hanging out with some skinny-looking dude. Looking like he was tryin' not to be seen."

"You sure, Cha-Cha? It couldn't have been last Saturday 'cause LaMarr said he had to work last weekend to get ready for a case on Monday."

"Well, honey, if you call sipping on Jack Daniels and Bloody Marys working, then I guess he was working real hard 'cause your man was still going strong when I left the club around two."

Veda felt a jolt of pain stab her heart, but she tried not to let her feelings show. Besides, Cha-Cha was always gossiping about somebody and usually didn't know what the hell she was talking about. Veda didn't want to get into this conversation with Cha-Cha. Now she regretted all the times she had sat in that chair and complained about the way LaMarr treated her.

"Honey, don't let me get started on your man," said Cha-Cha, "You take my advice girl, get out while you still have some pride left. How's your scalp doin'? Not startin' to burn is it?"

The only thing starting to burn on Veda was her anger. Her head could have been on fire and she wouldn't have felt a thing at that moment. What upset her the most was that she knew Cha-Cha was right about LaMarr, but she didn't want to face the truth.

Cha-Cha wiped the creamy relaxer off her fingers and directed Veda to the shampoo bowl.

"Is seeing Dr. Renee helping you?" asked Cha-Cha, "You know, she's one of my regulars too. Honey, Dr. Renee sure 'nuf straightened out my cousin, Leela. You remember, Leela, right?

Veda nodded and Cha-Cha continued, "Yeah, girl. Thanks to Dr. Renee, Leela finally got rid of that married man she been dealin' with for umpteen years. My girl went and got herself a new man, a new job, and a new attitude," she laughed. "And you know Dr. Renee got enough money to have one of them Capitol Hill hairdressers fix her hair but she still comes all the way uptown for me to do it," said Cha-Cha proudly as she rubbed the sweet-smelling shampoo into Veda's hair.

Veda kept silent. She didn't want to discuss her sessions with Dr. Renee, especially to Cha-Cha. Cha-Cha picked up on her mood.

"Shoot, girl, ain't no big thing going to a shrink nowadays. I been thinkin' about going to see her myself," said Cha-Cha.

"Say what?" smiled Veda. "Don't look like you need any help coping to me."

"Oh yes, I do too." Cha-Cha massaged Veda's temples and applied pressure to the right places to help relieve her tension.

"Naw," said Veda, "Looks to me like you even lost a few pounds, Cha-Cha. You look good girl. You been on a diet or something?"

"Uh huh, sure have," Cha-Cha stopped rubbing Veda's scalp and leaned down to whisper in Veda's ear, "The 'asshole boyfriend' diet."

"Go on, girl," laughed Veda.

"I ain't lying Veda. I can't eat when I'm depressed. When it comes to men, I am really losing, girl." Cha-Cha continued her endless chatter and kidding around for the next hour. For some reason it made Veda feel better.

While Cha-Cha applied the finishing touches, Veda studied her reflection in the mirror. She swiveled around in the chair and grinned. Cha-cha had given her a chic and natural, carefree style. She'd even added some reddish-brown highlights that livened up Veda's once dry, dull-looking hair. Veda dug into her purse and handed Cha-Cha ninety-five dollars and left the beauty shop transformed in both appearance and attitude.

Walking to her car, Veda thought of LaMarr. She hoped he would get home from his Meet and Greet in time to come over that night to see her makeover while the look was still fresh. On the way home, she decided to stop by the mall and pick up a sexy, black negligee from Victoria's Secret to complete her new look. Maybe Cha-Cha needed to see Dr. Renee, she smirked, but she didn't need any damn shrink to tell her how to keep her man.

CHAPTER 10

▼

It was thundering and raining by the time Veda left the mall and made it to her car. Every time she got her hair done, it rained. She could predict the weather just from going to the hairdresser. Veda looked up at her new image in the rear view mirror and smiled. The downpour had missed her.

Veda decided she didn't want to simply go home and hope that LaMarr showed up. Too many distractions out in the streets could keep him away from her. Although Cha-cha had just worked miracles on her drab appearance, Veda knew it was hard to compete with all the beautiful women he came in contact with on a regular basis—like the one in his office that morning, Miss Courtney Hargreaves, the Senator's daughter, she snorted.

Veda dug into the bottom of her bag until she found the duplicate key to LaMarr's apartment that she had copied one afternoon without his knowledge. She knew it would come in handy sooner or later. She made an abrupt U-turn in the middle of the deserted street and headed straight for LaMarr's place. She remembered LaMarr telling her that his apartment was a mess since his house-keeper quit several weeks ago. He'd be surprised when he got home and found a clean apartment and a sexy woman with a brand new look waiting for him.

Veda tried not to think about the times she had teased and laughed at her girl-friend, Natasha, for cleaning up after her no-good boyfriend. Veda had called Natasha a damn fool for fixing her man's meals, washing his drawers, and putting up with his abuse. Veda remembered shaking her head in disgust at Natasha. Back then she swore she'd never put up with that shit. But no more than two years later, it was Veda who had already put up with a whole lot more than Natasha ever did.

After knocking and getting no answer, she turned the key to LaMarr's apartment and walked in. She saw immediately that he had greatly underestimated the condition his apartment was in. It looked like he hadn't been spending too much time there at all. Veda began by hanging up clothes she found on the floor and tossed aside on chairs and on the bed. She retrieved dozens of shoes and placed them in neat rows inside the large walk-in closet. A compact washer and dryer sat tucked away in a closet off from the kitchen. Veda pulled some dingy-looking sheets from the unmade bed and threw them in the wash. Then, she sorted his dirty clothes in huge piles on the bedroom floor—sweat suits, socks, underwear, and piles of white shirts to be sent out for dry cleaning. "Just like Natasha," she said to herself. She pushed the thought aside and kept working.

Three hours had passed while she worked, before she realized she hadn't eaten anything since breakfast. Veda's head felt dizzy. She sat down at the dining room table and rested her forehead in her hand. Based on how bad she had found the bathrooms, Veda knew better than to look in the kitchen for any signs of edible food. Instead, she ordered an assortment of Chinese food to be delivered for herself and enough for LaMarr too in case he was hungry when he got in.

By the time the food arrived, Veda had already started to tackle the kitchen. She threw out everything in the refrigerator without even trying to guess what was still safe to eat. Not even a jar of water remained after she finished cleaning it.

It was now almost midnight. LaMarr's place looked immaculate and smelled fresh. Veda figured he would be coming home any minute and she didn't want to greet him smelling like sweat and Lysol. She rushed into the master bathroom and ran a tub full of hot, bubbling water. She doused the tub with her favorite scent and slipped in.

Veda closed her eyes and let the soothing steam envelop her body. How could LaMarr not appreciate her after all this? The tub was so relaxing that she lingered in and drifted off to sleep. Some time later, a sudden bolt of thunder woke her up. That's when she realized she'd been soaking in the tub for over an hour. A brief flash of lightening shot across the small bathroom window and it started to rain heavily. Veda jumped out of the tub. She hated being anywhere near water during a storm, and the water was cold by now.

Veda began to set the stage for LaMarr's arrival. She ignored the beating of the rain against the windows, and the occasional clap of thunder. She rubbed her body down with scented lotion and stepped into her new silky black nightgown. The gown clung to her body as she moved. Veda dimmed the lights and lit scented candles throughout the bedroom.

She slipped under the cool, clean sheets and anxiously listened for the sound of his key unlocking the front door. Veda expected to be awake when he arrived since it was difficult for her to get comfortable lying face down in the crook of her arm so as not to mess up her new hairdo. She had to forego rolling it up since she wanted to look sexy for LaMarr. The sight of her with rollers and a rag tied around her head would definitely kill the mood. Maybe she'd strip out of her nightgown and let him replace those outdated pictures of her he took four years ago with some new ones. He once told her it turned him on to sneak a look at nude photos of her during one of Davis's long, boring ass meetings.

Veda tallied up everything she had accomplished that day from scrubbing and disinfecting LaMarr's entire apartment, to washing and putting away all his clothes. She sported a hot, new look, and her body was perfumed all over and ready for his embrace. LaMarr had to realize he only needed her to be happy. They would linger in bed all Friday night and well into Saturday afternoon. Maybe they wouldn't even show up for work on Monday, Veda fantasized. LaMarr never worried about what time he arrived for work anyway and she knew how to call in and sound sick. Veda suspected he must have had even more dirt on Davis than she did because their firm's senior partner never complained about LaMarr's work habits. Veda suddenly remembered she had told Louis that Sherrelle could stay with her while he and his wife were in Richmond, so she thought, tonight would have to be the only night. She wished LaMarr would hurry up and get home.

While she waited, Veda continued her fantasy. More than anything she wanted to get married again and move away from the city. She wanted to go someplace far away from all the distractions pulling LaMarr's attention away from her. As the 'blissful couple' fantasy materialized in her thoughts, time ticked by and the rain continued. She longed to feel LaMarr's strong arms around her and taste his warm kisses, but exhausted from the washing, cleaning, working, and other mundane activities of the day, Veda struggled to fight off sleep. Despite her best efforts to stay awake and greet LaMarr when he walked through the door, she fell asleep. The sound of something crashing to the floor, woke her up. She sat straight up in bed and looked all around her in the darkened room.

"Who's there?" she called out, "LaMarr? That you?"

Raindrops thrashed against the window as the storm raged on outside. Must have been thunder Veda thought. Fully awake now, she figured she'd only drifted off for a few minutes. But when she turned to look at the clock, it glowed 2:45 AM. At that moment, the first question that sprung to her mind was where the hell was LaMarr? He should have been home hours ago.

Just as Veda reached for the telephone to try his office, a huge, hairy hand grabbed her around the throat. Her heartbeat quicken and she gasped for air, struggling against the big man's grip. Her assailant released her throat, snatched her arm and dragged her out of bed then swung her around. She pulled away from him and tried to run but fell against the wall. She looked out into the darkness and saw the silhouette of a huge man in front of her. As he moved closer into the glow of a lit candle, his image appeared. Small, dark, bloodshot eyes glared down at her. A purplish scar stretched across the left cheek of his dark, moon-shaped face. The nostrils from his lump of a nose flared out in anger like the smoking nostrils of a bronco bull. His full, colorless lips were outlined by a course-looking beard. When he spoke to her in a deep, throaty voice, the lips barely moved.

"Where's he at, Bitch?"

Veda trembled with fear and backed away from him. She shrugged her shoulders and shook her head in response to his question. At that the burly, muscled giant lunged at her. Veda tripped but got up in one quick movement and tried to run away again. He caught her by the shoulders before she could get away. His huge hands pinned her against the wall and he planted his ugly face right in front of hers. He was so close she could see the chipped, cigarette-stained teeth. The smell of his foul breath repulsed and made her dizzy.

The giant looked down at her and slowly surveyed her face and body. He shook his head and snarled in disgust.

"Umph, umph, umph. I feel sorry for the Counselor," he sneered, "and here I thought this brother was some big-time, ladies' man. All his good looks and fancy law degrees, you the best he can do? Damn, even my bitches finer than your pitiful ass."

He pushed Veda away in contempt. She landed on the floor and hit her back on the bed frame with such force, she felt the pain shoot up her spine.

"You tell pretty boy, Slade was here. And this ain't no damn social call. Tell that lame-ass chump, I want the rest of my goddamn money by Wednesday. All five g's. Wednesday, no later. You got that bitch?" Veda stared at him, speechless and unable to move.

As he turned to leave, she saw a silver toned stiletto sticking out of his back pocket. Its sharp, pointed edge glistened in the darkness. She knew that brute wouldn't need a weapon to destroy her if he wanted to. It seemed as if he'd already accomplished that with his words. Veda felt cold and frightened. She sat on the floor and rested her back against the bed for several minutes after she heard the front door slam shut. Finally, she got up, walked slowly into the living room and turned on a lamp. Broken pieces of a crystal vase were scattered on the black, marble dining room floor. That must have been the crashing sound that woke her up thought Veda. Obviously, that ugly brute didn't have any trouble picking the lock on LaMarr's front door to get in. She swept up the broken glass and threw it in the thrash. It was nearly 3:30 in the morning. Where the hell was LaMarr?

The rain had finally stopped. She didn't want to be in LaMarr's apartment anymore, not knowing who or what else might be looking for him. Veda got dressed quickly and drove back to her own place in the middle of the night. She thought about what that amazon had implied about her, that she wasn't pretty enough for a successful, good-looking player like LaMarr Coleman. She felt damaged, as if she'd finally heard the truth. Something uglier than sin itself had just confirmed it.

Though safely back in her own small apartment, Veda was still shaken and couldn't sleep. She got up and went to the bathroom and opened her medicine cabinet. She grabbed a bottle of Sominex sleeping tablets and shook the bottle. It was empty. Damnit. In a frenzy she searched the medicine cabinet for something that would help her sleep and get through this terrible night. Veda had to find a way to drown out the awful truth that tried to creep into the small shred of sanity she had left, the truth about LaMarr only using her, and the truth that LaMarr did not really love her. Veda admitted to herself that it hurt to know she couldn't ever find LaMarr when she needed him.

Veda opened the bottom cabinet of the bathroom sink and found a half-full bottle of Nyquil Liquid Cold Medicine. She didn't have a cold, but remembered how this stuff had really knocked her out the last time she had the flu. She poured out the dosage and gulped it all down, licking the inside of the plastic cup to get every drop.

She collapsed on her unmade bed and wrapped herself in the threadbare cotton/polyester sheets that looked like they had barely survived the years of repeated washings. Within minutes of sinking her weary head on the pillow, thanks to the Nyquil, all life's ugly realities were wiped out and replaced with a deep, nullifying sleep.

CHAPTER 11

▼

Early Saturday morning a fierce ray of sunlight intruded into Veda's bedroom window with a vengeance, snatching her out of her pain-free, Nyquil-induced sleep. She squinted her eyes shut and pulled the covers up over her head. But the sun continued to fire its translucent beam in her direction, keeping her awake. Veda laid in bed in a lifeless stupor for another hour. The effects of the Nyquil left her groggy. It was ten o'clock before she finally forced herself out of bed.

She made it to the bathroom and tried not to lift her head up to look into the mirror, but was compelled to take a hard look at herself. Her eyes, swollen and puffy from hours of crying. Her lips, cracked and colorless. Her skin looked dull and unhealthy. The sharp new $95 dollar hairdo, the one LaMarr hadn't even seen yet, was gone in less than a day. What she saw in the mirror was a pathetic, emotionally dependent woman. Her thoughts drifted to LaMarr. Where was he now and who the hell was he with? Could he still be with Courtney Hargreaves, his new legal assistant? She felt her heart beating faster and knew she had to think about something else. She flipped on the fan to vent out the steam and turned the shower on full blast. She let the heat sting her body momentarily like an electric shock then turned on a little cold water, but still kept the temperature as hot as she could stand it. The steam felt wonderful. Veda stood under the full force of hot water and steam for a good thirty minutes. After her shower, she put on a robe, lit a cigarette and settled down to a cup of instant black coffee. She sipped her coffee and flipped through the newspaper.

This was the second night in a row that LaMarr had been out all night. She was determined not to waste another weekend worrying about him and what he was doing. If she could spend her Friday evenings scrubbing and cleaning his filthy place while he was God knows where, doing God knows what, she could certainly clean up her own damn apartment. Besides, she needed to get the place straight before Louis showed up with Sherrelle later that evening. Veda thought about calling Natasha and suggesting that she come over for some pizza and a video after her daughter arrived. She looked in her wallet to see if there was anything left for pizza and a movie. She'd already spent a small fortune at Cha-Cha's last night for nothing. Surprisingly, there was still a twenty dollar bill left and some change in her wallet. She figured it might not be so bad for Sherrelle the first night with a referee around. Ever since the divorce, Veda had tried many times to get close to Sherrelle. She had suggested trips to the mall, the movies, and was even willing to take her to one of those annoying teeny-bopper concerts. But whenever she came within a few feet of her daughter, she felt the girl's disdain for her penetrate to the very bone. It was the worst feeling Veda had ever experienced, knowing that her only child loathed her. She shook the thought out of her head. Just as she opened to the paper's Style section, the doorbell rang.

"Now who the hell could that be," she said and got up to answer the door. Veda looked through the peephole and was surprised to see her ex-husband, Louis Simms, standing in the hallway. She wasn't expecting him until much later. It had been more than a year since she'd seen him. Even with the new beard and extra weight, his eyes were the same sad, puppy-dog eyes she fell for at seventeen.

Louis had on a too-tight, dark brown suit that looked like it was at least ten years old. In addition to the untrimmed mustache he always wore, his hair was now flecked with gray. When they were married, Veda complained about him not keeping his mustache trimmed and well groomed. Obviously, not much had changed in that department. What the hell, it didn't matter to her now. She was glad to see him just the same. Veda found it funny how little things seem to annoy people when they're first married but years later after a divorce, these same irritants don't seem so important anymore. Maybe it was just age that made people mellow out. Veda removed the deadbolt lock and let him in.

"How you been, Veda?" said Louis in his same slow-talking Virginia dialect.

He ambled forward taking big, clumsy steps and followed her inside. He had always been a big man and now he had the full jowls and lumpish belly of a man who hadn't missed many meals.

"I'm fine, thanks, Louis. You're looking mighty content yourself. Life must be treating you pretty good," she folded her arms and nodded.

"Yes, indeed. God's been good to me, praise the Lord," he said and looked upward, clasping his hands together and smiling. He hadn't lost much of his country accent since leaving the small, predominantly black town of Luthersville but Veda noticed his diction had improved over the years.

"I apologize for coming by this early without callin' but Ester's mama took a turn for the worse last night and we needed to get on the road this morning."

"Don't worry about it, Louis," she said and motioned him towards the kitchen, "I'm sorry about your mother-in-law. Guess you don't have time for a quick cup of coffee then. Is Sherrelle waiting outside in the car? You know I told you it's no problem for her to stay here."

Louis stood there as if he had something on his mind but couldn't find the words to say it.

"Louis, is Sherrelle with you?"

He hesitated for awhile, not meeting her eyes. "Well, matter of fact, Sherrelle wouldn't come. Flat out refused. Said if we made her come here she'd run away and hitchhike back home to Baltimore. She's staying with one of her girlfriend's family up the street from us. But it'll be fine, so don't you worry none. Here's the phone number over there if you want it." He handed her the number.

"I can't believe she wouldn't even spend a few days with her own mother," said Veda, looking away so he wouldn't see the hurt on her face. "Well, I appreciate you making the extra effort to stop by and tell me in person."

"Don't be too hard on her Veda. You know how young folks are these days. Got a mind of their own, you know."

Veda nodded. She tried to remain calm and not show her anger and disappointment.

"Well, I best be gettin' along. Ester's waitin' for me downstairs."

"Louis, what's the chance of me coming up to Baltimore to visit Sherrelle after you get back home?"

"Well, if it's up to me, 'course, I'd say sure Veda. You welcome anytime. But like I said, Sherrelle's got a mind of her own. Always did, you know. Maybe you could try calling her at that number first. See if she'll talk to you over the phone."

"So what you're saying is, she doesn't want to ever see me again?" The pitch in Veda's voice got higher and her eyes started to moisten. "I haven't seen my daughter in over a year and she still doesn't want to see me?" Veda almost never cried in front of people but she was on the verge of letting it loose now. Everything was coming down on her all at once. First, LaMarr and his lies, and now more rejection from Sherrelle. Veda tried to look away from Louis who she knew felt helpless and sorry for her.

"Me and Ester been readin' daily bible verses with her everyday, especially on forgiveness and how Jesus loves all his children even though we're not perfect and what not."

"Did she even read any of my letters?" asked Veda, "You know I still write and send her a little spending change from time to time."

"We used to beg Sherrelle to answer your letters but it didn't do no good. I can understand why you got tired of writin' regular and all, never gettin' anything back. Ester's got 'em put up in a box just in case she ever decides to go back and read 'em one day." Louis dug his hands in his pockets and stared at his shoes.

"Sounds like Ester's a nice woman."

"Yes indeed. She is that," said Louis and his eyes immediately brightened, "Been 'bout a year now that the Lord blessed me with my sweet Ester. I'm a lucky man. Always servin' the Lord, my Ester." Louis beamed with pride. Veda didn't say a word. She forgot her manners and didn't even congratulate him on his recent marriage. That's great Louis, she thought, just go ahead and make my day. Louis stopped talking about his wife and all her wonderful attributes when he noticed the sad look on Veda's face. Veda tried to tell herself she was happy for him. After all, he deserved it. She had made his life a living hell the whole time they were married. Why shouldn't he meet someone with whom he was more compatible? Veda knew she didn't want him then and she certainly didn't want him back now. So why begrudge the man some years of happiness just because her whole life was falling apart?

"What's Sherrelle doing with herself these days? Is she planning to go to college after high school? Does she have a boyfriend?" asked Veda.

"Don't know 'bout college. Says she wants to go to some kinda beauty school and fix up people's hair and what not. Anyway, she's a good girl, Veda. You'd be proud. As for boys, they call and come around sometime but she's pretty independent. I can't say she's interested in any one of 'em in particular though."

"Does she keep up with her school work?" asked Veda.

"Oh yeah, that's one hardworking young lady. Smart, just like her mama," said Louis with a smile, "and she's real fussy about her looks too. You know, that girl's been foolin' with her hair and her face in the mirror and what not ever since she was this big," Louis held up his hand to his waist.

"Now she's got all these long braids down her back. I think she calls 'em extensions," he said, "I don't know. Everyday, it's something different. Never satisfied with the same old look. Yes suh, she sure is one pretty chile. Looks just like you, Veda."

At that moment, Louis took out his wallet and showed Veda their daughter's recent school picture. Veda stared at the picture for a long time, not wanting to take her eyes off of it. Sherrelle had grown into a lovely girl, just like Louis said. She wore a white, button-down, tailored blouse and her chin rested casually on her hand. Her hair was cut in a short, stylish pageboy in the photo. Her eyes looked large and dreamy and the smile on her face was genuine. Her daughter looked happy and well adjusted. Veda handed the picture back to him, begrudgingly.

"You've done a fine job raising her, Louis."

"You keep it Veda," he said, giving it back to her.

"Thanks," Veda put the picture in her purse, "and thanks for not hating me. I only wish Sherrelle didn't."

"Hating you is something I could never do, Veda. I'm sure in time, God willin', Sherrelle will see it that way too." Louis bent down and kissed her good-by on the cheek, then held both her hands in his. He held on so tight, Veda felt the blood leaving her hands. She could tell he had been genuinely happy to see her. Veda didn't understand his capacity for forgiveness. Any other man would have hated her and probably sought revenge for what she had done to him, but not big, lovable, 'Teddy Bear' Louis. That's what everybody used to call him when they were kids back in Luthersville because he looked just like a teddy bear.

After Louis left, Veda sat alone in the kitchen and contemplated what a mess she had made of her life. Louis looked happy and definitely well fed. Even though he was a few years older than she was, Louis didn't have tired, swollen eyes from constant worry and lack of sleep. His smooth skin was wrinkle-free. Veda had lost weight over the past several months. But she didn't have the slender, well-toned body of someone who worked out to stay fit. She had the unhealthy, drawn-in look of someone too preoccupied with pain and anguish to take care of their health.

Was it any wonder that Sherrelle refused to see her, Veda asked herself. She'd never been a good role model for her daughter—even if you leave out the terrible things she had done to completely destroy any shred of respect and affection that Sherrelle might have felt for her. Veda admitted she didn't deserve her daughter's love. She had ignored Sherrelle throughout most of the girl's early years because she'd been too preoccupied with getting ahead at work and with her own selfish needs and desires. But Louis had been able to get past all that. He'd been hurt too when she left her family for LaMarr, perhaps even more so. No doubt about it, Veda considered herself to be a failure as a wife, and most definitely a failure as a mother. The only thing she had left to hold onto after her divorce from Louis was

LaMarr Coleman. Her obsession for LaMarr had cost her everything. Veda held the coffee cup to her lips and took a sip. It was cold and tasteless. She put the cup down and buried her face in both hands. She had no idea how she was going to get through the rest of the day.

CHAPTER 12

▼

Renee slipped into a pair of jeans, her worn-out Reebox, and a bright orange t-shirt. Susanna James, the 18-month old who Renee visited every Saturday, loved bright colors. Last week had been the baby's birthday. Renee had spent over an hour at the toy store looking for just the right birthday present to cheer up the sick baby. Despite a low-grade fever and poor appetite, Susanna smiled when presented with the soft and cuddly, red-furred 'Tickle Me Elmo' doll. Renee hoped Susanna would be up to an outing at McDonald's today but based on how the child looked last Saturday, she doubted it. Susanna's immune system was weakening and she could no longer fight off infections. Before she got really sick, Susanna had never tired of watching the other children run and play at the McDonald's fun center. Hours passed but her big brown eyes watched as kids climbed the tower all the way to the roof top then journeyed back down through the maze, again and again. Her chronic fatigue and small stature didn't permit her to climb the tower but just being a spectator seemed to thrill her. Renee could see the expression on Susanna's face liven up whenever she was around the laughter and excitement of other children.

Now, Susanna had full-blown AIDS. Her intravenous drug-using mother had carried the AIDS virus during pregnancy. Her mother abandoned her at infancy and her grandmother took on the responsibility of her care until she was about three weeks old. When her grandmother could no longer care for her she requested assistance from the D.C. Office of Public Health. A ward of the court since birth, Susanna was now slowly dying in a foster home. Many times Renee had attempted to bring Susanna home for the weekend to give the foster mother a respite. But Bill had practically gone berserk when she mentioned it again a few weeks ago.

Renee pulled her hair back in a ponytail that swung to her shoulders. She ran down the stairs with the energy of a teenager and was almost out the door when Bill appeared at the foyer entrance. They hadn't spoken since she'd gotten home after midnight last night. He was home when she got in, for a change. She couldn't tell for sure whether he believed the 'emergency-with-a-patient' story. Renee avoided any details, falling back on doctor-patient confidentially to shield her lies. Now, here he was again, standing at the bottom of the steps with that same accusing look on his face.

Deek had called this morning at seven and left a message on her digital phone. He wanted her to call as soon as she woke up. He assured her again that he would only call during the times she indicated and only on her business line. Deek's message said he didn't want to complicate her life but he wanted to see her again. The last part of his message talked about how beautiful and sexy she was and that he couldn't think of anything else but her all night. Renee had played the message over several times before finally erasing it. She didn't know enough about technology or trust it enough to believe that there wasn't some way Bill could retrieve her saved messages. Even though the sound of Deek's passion made her heart beat faster and her insides warm, she couldn't risk it. She didn't return the call that morning. Renee needed time to think about her life without any distractions. Being with Deek yesterday had already cost her a shot at getting Bill to at least sit down and discuss the pros and cons of adoption with a social worker. Renee couldn't allow this infatuation with Deek to get out of hand.

"Where you going?" Bill asked bluntly.

"It's Saturday. You know I do my volunteer work on Saturdays," she said and matched his frown with a smile.

"Oh, right," he said, "Listen, can you give me a lift to the dealership to pick up my Rover? It's at the service shop for maintenance."

Renee was relieved that's all he wanted to ask. She gladly complied even though it was out of her way. Bill sat sullen in the passenger's seat while Renee did all the talking. She gave him Susanna's complete history and told him she feared the baby didn't have much time left. As an ER nurse for many years before becoming a psychologist, she ran codes and administered injections. She was more than competent to care for an AIDS infected child and give her foster mother a break. But nothing Renee said seemed to elicit his sympathy.

"Bill, this is very important to me. I want to bring Susanna home this weekend," she said decidedly with both hands clutched to the steering wheel.

"Hell no. What I told you before still stands. Look Renee, you didn't even bother to show up yesterday afternoon for our meeting with Mrs. Addison. I was stretching it when I agreed to that. What the hell makes you think I'm going to allow an AIDS patient to stay in my home?" Bill folded his arms and sulked.

"I can't believe your ignorance, Bill. Susanna's not just an AIDS patient. She's a human being who needs love just like anybody else. How can you be so cruel?"

"What about my needs Renee?" he shouted, "When have you ever cared about that? Just stop the car and let me out. I'll walk."

"Don't be silly, Bill. It's too far to walk."

"Let me out, goddamn it. Now!"

Renee felt the car shake from his anger. She'd never seen Bill so out of control. His face looked contorted and his eyes turned a glistening red from what appeared to be tears. She suspected that his outburst was more a delayed reaction from her getting home late last night and less about Susanna, though that discussion probably didn't help. Renee stopped the car. Bill jumped out immediately and slammed the door. He walked briskly and kept his eyes focused straight ahead. He ignored her requests to get back in the car as she drove slowly alongside him for a few minutes. Renee glanced in her rearview mirror and saw that cars behind her were backing up on the single-lane street. She sped off and watched Bill from her mirror until he faded out of sight.

Shirley Ann Turner, Susanna's foster mother, greeted Renee with her usual wide smile and a hug. Shirley Ann had retired early at 59, after thirty years in the government. Now she took care of foster children full-time. All of her foster kids had been placed in adoption or returned to family members except for Susanna who had nowhere else to go. Gospel music played in the background from a radio left on in the kitchen. Renee responded to its uplifting tune and followed the sound and Shirley Ann straight to the kitchen where Shirley Ann was just about to prepare something for dinner. She said she always fixed her dinner in the morning. That way she'd have more time for Susanna throughout the day. Even though Renee typically listened to classical music, she enjoyed hearing Shirley Ann sing along with the radio while she cooked.

"I met Jesus in the morning,
when my day was at its best.
And now I know the secret,
learned from many a troubled way.
Just seek Him in the morning,
if you want Him through the Day."

Mementos of the Turner family's past were placed throughout the house. Renee sat down at the table and savored the scents of home cooked food, walls decorated with family photos, and doily-covered tables. The foyer led directly to a modest-size kitchen where a walnut oval table took up much of the space. Renee felt a sense of familiarity there. The Turner home was not far from where she grew up on Twentieth Street in NorthEast. Its layout was similar to her Aunt Clara's two-story house. Shirley Ann's husband, John, still got up every day at five and went to work for Amtrack as a train conductor. He worked long days and spent his Saturday mornings fishing or hanging out at the barbershop with his buddies. Shirley Ann didn't seem to mind. After forty years of marriage, obviously she was used to John's habits. Now, most of her time was devoted to the sick baby.

Renee lifted Susanna from her playpen and covered her plump cheeks with kisses. She knew they were soft and fat due to steroid treatments and the assortment of other medications she took daily; this was not the round, cherubic face of a healthy child. Her baby grin widened and she gave Renee a tight hug around her neck. It didn't take long for her to spot Renee's bright orange hoop earrings and begin to grab at them. Renee took off her earrings and gave them to Susanna to play with.

Shirley Ann asked Renee if she would watch the baby for a couple of hours while she ran some errands. Renee didn't mind missing all those screaming, active kids at McDonald's today. Surrounded by her toys and stuffed animals, Susanna looked happy to stay home also. Only one and a half years old, she was still too little to communicate much in words, but Renee could tell Susanna was loved and well cared for at her foster home.

As a medical professional, Renee knew the suffering and pain that was in store for the baby as her illness progressed. She felt grateful to Shirley Ann. Thanks to her, Susanna would experience a mother's love until her final sweet breath was taken. She admired this foster mother for her unselfish devotion but at the same time felt a tinge of envy. Shirley Ann had the courage to live her life exactly as she chose. She had told Renee that you have to deny your own selfish desires and wants in order to help others. That's where true happiness and satisfaction comes from when you can make a personal sacrifice. Shirley Ann and her husband had the means to vacation wherever they wanted, buy what they wanted, and indulge themselves. Their four children were all grown and successful. Shirley Ann said with the Lord's guidance, she had made her choice.

It was getting dark when Renee left Shirley Ann's. She closed the front gate and returned to her Acura. She spotted a familiar car parked behind hers. A man leaned against the passenger side door with his arms folded. The sun blocked his face but as she approached, Renee recognized him. "How did you know I'd be here?"

"You're on the D. C. Court's public record as a CASA advocate for Susanna James," smiled Deek, "Don't I even get a hello?"

"Yes, of course," said Renee and continued towards her car.

Deek held her arm and turned her towards him.

"I'm sorry, Doc but I had to think of something to get to know this beautiful, sensitive woman I'm falling in love with."

Renee turned her face away but he still had a firm grasp around her waist.

"Can we go somewhere and talk?" he asked.

"Today's not good for me, Deek." Renee tried to hide the tears that clouded her eyes.

"What's wrong, Renee?"

She laid her cheek against his chest and sobbed quietly. She told him about Susanna and how very ill she was. She confessed that she had wanted to bring the baby home with her today for the weekend but when she brought it up with Bill that morning, they had gotten into a terrible argument. So she hadn't bothered to discuss it with the foster mother. The last thing a sick baby needed was to be exposed to an adult's tension and turmoil.

"I feel like a fake," said Renee, "Like someone pretending to care and then only when it's convenient. I feel like I'm abandoning Susanna when she needs me most."

"Aren't you being a little hard on yourself?" he said and rubbed his hand against her cheek to wipe away a tear.

"You don't understand, Deek."

"Stay with the baby at my house for the weekend. I'll confiscate all Tyrone's CD's while you're both there. It'll be peaceful and quiet, I promise."

"More promises, Detective? You know I can't do that," she said, "Bill already suspects something is wrong. I can't keep lying to him. And I'm not ready to confess the truth either."

"I'm here for you, Renee," he said, pulling her to him, "You only have to decide what you want."

She untangled his arm from around her waist and stepped back. She tried to explain to Deek how being infertile made her feel like a failure. She didn't expect him to understand, being young and a man. There was nothing stopping him from marrying a healthy, young woman his own age and having children if he wanted to. Renee told him about what happened just two months ago when Brenda, her receptionist who was still out on maternity leave, had her baby. After visiting Brenda and her son at the hospital, she was overcome by a sudden feeling of emptiness and jealousy while driving home. She broke down crying and had to pull off the road. She told Deek how she had called Bill but he was teaching and couldn't or wouldn't come. She had cried for hours and had to wait on the side of the road until she could calm down enough to drive home.

Then Renee explained to Deek that she'd already missed her appointment with the HHS social worker because of her attraction to him, after working so hard for months to get Bill to even talk to someone about adoption. She confided to Deek that she didn't know what would take the emptiness away. She couldn't deny her feelings for him but she couldn't risk jeopardizing her marriage either. He was too young for her anyway. There was no future in a relationship with him. Deek looked stunned. He watched as Renee got in her car and drove off.

CHAPTER 13

▼

At 7:50 in the morning on Monday Veda walked into the darkened reception area of the law office of Davis & Bookerman Chartered. She thought no one was there until she noticed a thin beam of light coming from under the closed door of LaMarr's office. Veda swung the door open without knocking. The source of the light was a halogen dome lamp that stood in a far corner. It cast a natural glow across LaMarr's stunned face and the back of another man who sat facing him. LaMarr stood up when Veda entered. The other man turned around to see who had caused the interruption. LaMarr wore a rigid grin, attempting to hide his irritation, but it was clear to Veda that he didn't appreciate the intrusion. Veda, however, didn't care about irritating LaMarr that morning. She hadn't heard from him all weekend. She'd been threatened and humiliated by some thug on Friday night, pitied by her ex-husband and rejected by her daughter. The only thing she had to look forward to was a visit to her therapist later that evening at six. She hoped Dr. Renee could help stop her pain and make things right.

LaMarr's phony grin began to fade. She could tell he was trying to remain calm because of the visitor in his office. The man seated wore an expensive-looking dark blue suit. He looked to be late fifty-ish but had all his hair, black without a tinge of gray. His complexion looked pale against the amber glow of the darken office. He rose slowly from the leather chair and stood as tall as LaMarr. The smell of sweet tobacco overpowered even the strong fragrance of LaMarr's Lagerfeld. The client said he would conclude his business some other time and made a hasty retreat. LaMarr promised to contact him later that afternoon. He shut the door quietly as he left. LaMarr hadn't bothered to introduce him but had referred to him as Doctor so-and-so. Veda was too angry with LaMarr to catch the client's name.

The moment the door shut, fury clouded Veda's dark eyes. She placed one hand on her hip and pointed the other in his face. The echo from her voice filled the room. It was quiet outside his office so there was nothing to buffer her shouting.

"Where you been, LaMarr? I been calling your ass all weekend."

"Look, baby, calm down," LaMarr said, "somebody could walk in here any minute."

LaMarr grabbed Veda and wrapped his arms around her, "I guess I'm in deep shit, huh baby?"

Veda jerked back and pushed him away. "You're right about that," she said, "Where the hell were you all night last Friday? Some big, ugly dude came bustin' in your place and attacked me!"

"What big, ugly dude?"

"You know damn well who I'm talking about. Some Slate or Shade, or some damn Slave hoodlum, whoever the hell he was. He broke into your apartment in the middle of the night while I was there waiting for you to come home. Said he was looking for his money."

"Oh yeah," said LaMarr, "you must mean my main man, Slade. But what the hell were you doing there?"

"Don't try to turn this around on me. Your main man told me to tell you he wants his $5,000 by Wednesday or he's gonna kick your punk ass ..."

"Aw, baby, Slade ain't gonna hurt nobody. Slade works for me. I don't work for him. His bark is bigger than his bite. Besides, I'll get his money for him."

"Oh, yeah? And just how do you plan to do that? Is that why you're meeting secretly with so many new clients these days?"

"Nah. My client's son got into a little trouble over the weekend so he came to me for help. Said he heard I can fix things."

"Yeah, I know what the word is out on the streets about you LaMarr Coleman. D. C.'s own high-class fixer. But then, you only help people who can help you."

LaMarr smiled and eased his hand under her skirt and caressed her bare thigh. "Now baby, you know that's not true."

Veda glared at him out of the corner of her eye and pushed his hand away. He brought it right back. Veda couldn't stop her eyes from roving towards the bulge in front of his slacks. She knew he wanted her. Fool that she was she couldn't deny that she still wanted him too. Her heart and body wanted to believe in him.

She wanted to believe they could be happy together. Here was one fine specimen of a man who she thought could easily offer her all that and much more. All she had to do was forgive him. Again.

"That's where I was when you called this weekend, baby. Cashing in on a few favors to get Junior out of jail and all the charges dropped." He paused. "You believe me don't you?"

"I guess so. But what're you planning to do about your main man, Slade?"

LaMarr licked his lips, "Uh, you remember that little plan I told you about, right baby? About how we use those checks from that new A/R program?" LaMarr moved closer and rubbed her back.

"Oh, now, I get it. You expect me to get that money from the new check writing software," said Veda and shoved his hand away, "Figures."

"Damn girl. Now why you wanna be like that? Don't I have enough problems? I thought you were on my side, Veda." LaMarr frowned and sulked like a 2-year old.

"I am on your side, baby. You know that. But I'm just sick and tired of always having to save your butt," she said, "I can't understand why $65,000 a year ain't enough for you to live on. All you have to do is try putting some effort into being a halfway decent lawyer and forget about these moneymaking schemes of yours. Why the hell did you get that damn law degree, if all you planned to do was be a con man? Is this what I left Baltimore for? What I gave up my husband and daughter for?" Veda walked away from him and slouched in a chair with her arms folded under her breasts.

"Look, Veda, don't go blaming that shit on me. Remember, it was your idea to go back to your place. It's not my fault your daughter caught us."

"Just forget it LaMarr. Let's just drop it, okay."

"Fine by me," he said, "What happened back in Baltimore is in the past as far as I'm concerned." Veda watched as he moved towards his desk, sat down and flipped through his appointment book.

She got up and sat on the edge of his desk, leaning her body towards him. "LaMarr, why can't we just move away somewhere? Like San Diego, maybe. Somewhere nobody knows us and start all over?" said Veda, pleading with him, "There's nothing for me here or back in Baltimore any more. Baby, we don't need any more money to be happy." She reached out her hand to touch his face, but he jerked away and sprang up out of the chair, walking away from her.

"Speak for yourself Veda. Sixty-five thou a year ain't shit to me. That don't even cover my dry cleaning. Besides, it's not just about the money. I don't wanna be play actin' in front of no damn judge for the rest of my life, trying to save some fool I don't give a shit about. I got other plans and all my contacts are right here in D. C."

"What plans?"

"Don't worry about it, baby. I got it covered," LaMarr grabbed her waist and pulled her to him, "So how 'bout it, baby? Can you spot me enough to take care of Slade by Wednesday? I had his money for him yesterday but something came up and I needed to use it to make a quick business investment."

"LaMarr, you're full of shit," she said and struggled to free herself from his grip, "Anyway, what makes you think I got that kind of money lying around? You make a hell of a lot more than I do."

"Baby, don't you remember what you told me last week when you and Davis tried to complete a check run on those new A/R checks? You said two guys from IT were there all day trying to fix it, but the program still had a bug in it."

"So?" She folded her arms defiantly.

LaMarr seized both her hands and held them gently in his grasp. "So why can't you use those new checks to boost me a couple thousand dollars today from petty cash?"

Veda released herself and pushed him away with all the strength her small frame could muster.

"Negro, have you lost your damn mind? I see now I shoulda never showed you those checks in the first place."

"Now calm down baby. Like I told you before, this plan is foolproof," he said.

"I can't believe you have the nerve to hit on me again for that damn money. You really make me sick, you know that?" screamed Veda, "Why the hell can't you just go to work and make an honest living like everybody else? No, your ass is always got to be part of some damn scheme."

"You don't know what you're talking about Veda. I told you I had Slade's money but I needed to use it for a business investment. Besides, we're getting off the point here. Look, just like I told you before, the plan's simple, see. All you have to do is tell Davis that petty cash is running low and you need to replenish it. What's the minimum you're supposed to keep in petty case?"

"At least $8,000," she answered flatly.

"Okay. Then you just type up one of those checks for, say, $100 like you normally would. Go get Davis to sign it. Then come back to your desk and type a 5 in front of that 1. Those checks just have a place for you to type in the amount. There's no place to write it out in words like on a regular check, so it's simple, just like I said."

LaMarr gently stroked Veda's face as he continued his efforts to convince her. She felt a cold stone on her skin from the black onyx ring encased in diamonds that he wore on his right hand. Veda remembered seeing the ring for the first time on Friday morning. She wondered where it came from. Just as she was about to ask, he pulled her into his arms. At first his moist, soft lips barely touched hers, as if teasing her. Then he held her face and kissed her for what seemed like a long time to Veda. When their lips parted, she had to blink several times to refocus her vision. She felt weak and disoriented under his spell. But LaMarr quickly brought her back to reality when he continued right where he left off, begging for money.

"Then, you just go to the bank and cash the $5100. Put the hundred bucks in Petty Cash and give me the five thousand. It's perfect. The money won't even be missed."

"And what happens in two weeks when we get audited?" she asked.

"Baby, you said yourself how screwed up the accounts receivables are up in Rochester," said LaMarr, smiling, "The office is at least six months backlogged right now and they're still downsizing their staff. We both know that situation ain't changing no time soon. I'll have the money back in the firm's bank account before those fools get around to balancing the checkbook, if they ever do."

Veda shook her head. She was still skeptical.

"Baby, you know I love you," said LaMarr, "Why you making me beg like this? You know it's not my style to be beggin' and shit." LaMarr glanced down at his watch and appeared anxious.

"Well, I still don't like it. My ass'll be locked up messing around with you and your schemes. And how you gonna fix that, huh? What makes you think Mr. Davis is that damn stupid, anyway?"

"He was stupid enough to order those checks, wasn't he?" said LaMarr with a smirk on his face.

"Well, he and Mr. Bookerman thought it would save us time not having to write out the entire amounts by hand. Besides that check writing program came with the new A/R system he had installed."

"Whatever, baby. All I know is, the plan's foolproof," he grinned, "Anyway, so what if he does find out? You and I both know his ass ain't clean. He stole from his own client's escrow accounts when you worked for him back in Baltimore. I know he don't want that shit to come out … now that he's trying so hard to get himself appointed judge."

"I knew I shoulda kept my big mouth shut about Mr. Davis. That's probably the only thing still keeping me employed. And what got your sorry ass hired in the first place, don't forget."

"Look baby, are you saying you can't trust me?" LaMarr pointed to his chest and looked hurt, "I know that's privileged info."

"You damn right. I told you that shit in confidence," said Veda, shaking her finger at him, "When you caught me in a weak moment."

"Look here, all I have to do is hint to Davis that the Bar Counsel's Office might get an anonymous tip about his dippin' into client funds. No way he's gonna do nothing even if he suspects you. He's bent on getting that judgeship. He ain't about to let nothing stand in his way. Just the other day he and Booker-man told us that we all need to volunteer up to five percent of our billable hours to Pro Bono work."

"Sounds like a good idea," she said.

"Umph. The ABA started this "pro bono" challenge, mainly for the big guys. But Davis wants in so he can look good to Senator Hargreaves and the rest of those jerks on the judicial committee. Well, I ain't having no parts of it. I don't have time to give free legal services to no deadbeats and welfare recipients. Time is money," he said and tapped his watch. "And they better have some money if they wanna talk to me."

"For chrissakes, LaMarr, how can you say that? Money, money, money. That's all you care about. You've had advantages a lot of people haven't had. Most of these people are sick, poor, and elderly. Many with AIDS ... too sick to fight for their social security benefits. Well, if you ask me, I think it's a good idea, this pro bono stuff. Spend some of that wheelin' and dealin' time helping somebody else for a change. Just might keep your black ass out of trouble." Veda rolled her eyes at him.

"Look woman, I don't need you getting preachy on me. I got important things to do and I don't give a shit about Davis trying to profile so he can get his ass appointed judge."

He smiled at her and softened his voice. "Just think about what I said about getting that money for me, baby. It's real important to me. You know I wouldn't ask if I had any other options."

LaMarr held her close and nuzzled his warm lips to her ear.

Veda pushed his roving hands from her backside and jerked away. "Well, whatever that investment deal was for, it better not have nothing to do with drug dealing or gambling debts. And you better have it all back in petty cash before the audit. That is, if I decide to get the money for you, against my better judgment."

"I will baby, you know I will. And I already told you I spent Slade's money on a legitimate business deal. My returns have already been real sweet," said LaMarr with a thoughtful look on his face.

"Then why the hell are you strapped for cash?" she said, placing one hand on her hip and eyeing him suspiciously.

LaMarr cleared his throat. "Um, well, see, my assets aren't exactly liquid right now, baby. But don't worry, 'cause I got everything covered."

Veda didn't know what he was talking about and didn't care. She just wanted to make sure he understood not to play around with the firm's money.

"All I know is, if that money's not back where it's supposed to be in time for our audit, I'll kill your ass myself," she said, "Your boy Slade'll be the least of your problems." She saw he had already picked up his briefcase and started towards the door to leave.

"Where're you going now?" asked Veda, "It's not even 8:30 yet. You didn't really answer my question about where you were all weekend. And where the hell did that big ass ring come from?" She stood between him and the door with her arms folded.

"Sorry, babe. I gotta be in court early this morning," he said, "my docket number's up first. Be back this afternoon. Maybe, around two, I guess. If it's any later than that, I'll call you. Think about what I said okay? I really need you to do this little thing for me. Love you, babe." He barely finished these last words before the door to his office shut and he was gone.

Ten minutes later, Veda went outside the building and lit a cigarette. She puffed and exhaled slowly while thinking about the last five years of her life with LaMarr Coleman. She knew what kind of man she had fallen in love with, but she didn't want to give up her dream. It was easier to pretend. At 38 years old, she did not want to start over again. Besides, she had sacrificed a lot to be with LaMarr. She had hurt everybody she once loved and lost most of her pride in the process. A thread of hope that LaMarr would one day change kept her hanging on. She felt she had more to gain by explaining away his behavior than accepting the reality of it and losing everything she thought she had going for her in this relationship. Veda decided a long time ago, when she gave up on her marriage to Louis and gave up on being a mother to her daughter, Sherrelle, that she could not live without LaMarr Coleman. Just the thought of never hearing his deep voice or feeling his caress, put her body in a state of panic. When it got right down to it, she knew she would go along with whatever he asked of her.

Back at her desk, after her cigarette break, Veda spent the entire day worrying if Slade would keep his word and give LaMarr until Wednesday to come up with the money. She did a little filing, typed some, and then signed on to the new check writing system. She stared at the screen for several minutes until the system prompted her to press enter or get logged off automatically for security reasons.

Veda entered the secure information to generate a check. Even when the check printed out on her desk printer, she held it in her hands and thought carefully about what she was about to do. Then she got up slowly and walked down the hall to get one of a senior partner's signature. Everything went smoothly with the transaction just as LaMarr said it would. Both senior partners had signature authority. Since Mr. Davis was at the courthouse, Veda got Mr. Bookerman's signature of approval for one hundred dollars in petty cash.

Bookerman thought he was only authorizing $100 to replenish their petty cash fund but Veda placed the signed check back into the antique IBM Selectric typewriter stationed at a small work table next to her desk. It was now used exclusively for that purpose. She typed a 5 in front of the 100. She made it to the bank before they closed at two o'clock and cashed the $5,100 check. Veda replaced one hundred dollars in petty cash and kept the remaining five thousand dollars for LaMarr. After leaving the bank and returning to work it was impossible to concentrate on anything other than the wad of money she had hidden in her purse. She carried the purse with her everywhere, not even trusting a locked desk drawer since she knew both senior partners had keys. It was unlikely that they would go rummaging in her desk without cause, but at this point Veda was not thinking clearly. All she wanted was for the day to end, get in her car, and drive straight home, then call LaMarr so he could come get the stolen money so it would be out of her possession.

CHAPTER 14

▼

Veda's eyes roamed to avoid Dr. Renee's penetrating eyes and direct questions about her mother. That woman was the last person Veda wanted to think about. She glanced up at the ceiling, looked around the room at the floral chintz chairs, and peach leather couch in her therapist's office. Then she stared down at her rough hands and checked out the chipped wine red nail polish, wishing she had used clear polish instead. Who the hell had time for a weekly manicure? Veda's mind wandered as Dr. Renee sat cross-legged in a large burgundy leather chair in front of her. Knowing for a fact that her mother hated her from day one, Veda did not want to answer these damn questions about her childhood, about growing up in Luthersville, Virginia. Why did these shrinks always have to go there thought Veda.

Dr. Renee sat with her hands folded in her lap, looking intently at Veda. "What's bothering you this evening?" she asked.

Veda welcomed the chance to change the subject. For the first time she looked up as her tired bloodshot eyes met her therapist's velvet brown ones. "Doc, love's been rough on me," she said, shaking her head, "I always wanted that kind of forever love you see in the movies but it didn't happen that way. I know now if you want that kinda marriage you gotta work at it. I didn't do that with my first husband. I just want another chance."

"What would you do differently?" asked Dr. Renee.

Veda placed her elbow on the arm of the chair and rested her cheek in the palm of her hand, staring at nothing as her memory of first meeting Louis took shape. She saw through the filmy veil of time as if it had just been laundered yesterday. Veda was twenty-one years old when she married Louis Simms of Luthersville in Fauquier County. Louis had told her that he wanted lots of children, at least four or five. That following year, their daughter, Sherrelle, was born. Veda knew right away that just like her own mother she wasn't cut out for motherhood either. When she had to go into the hospital for a routine D & C procedure, she requested to have a tubal ligation performed as well to prevent her from ever getting pregnant again. She never told Louis.

Throughout their marriage Veda always felt that she and Sherrelle were her husband's number one priority. He was the type of man who would do anything for his family and people he loved. She really wasn't surprised when he hadn't shown any resentment towards her after the divorce. In this way Louis reminded Veda of her own father. Like Louis, her father had always been soft-spoken and easy-going and was the type to easily forgive and forget.

When Veda was growing up, Brother Thomas, as her Daddy was known back then, was held in the highest esteem right up there with the minister. Brother Thomas owned his own modest home, which stood on several acres of land. He had inherited the land from his father who had it passed down to him from his father. The only other folks who owned their own land in Luthersville were the White dairy farmers. Most folks were dirt poor and uneducated, but the kids had fun. To the children, Luthersville didn't seem like the hick town it really was. They had no concept of what a hick town was. They just enjoyed playing hopscotch, jump-rope, kick-the-can, and any number of made up outdoor games until the sun went down.

Veda had just graduated from Hampton Institute where she had attended on a special grant that their minister had recommended her for. She'd only been home a week when Louis Simms started showing up on her front porch. Louis declared that he had missed her terribly the last four years and decided he was going to marry her so she'd never get away from him again. Veda's parents loved Louis like a son. He knew he was well liked by her people but the day he stepped up on the porch where Veda's father sat smoking his pipe, he stammered through most of his words. After several minutes of hesitation, Louis worked up the nerve to ask Brother Thomas for Veda's hand in marriage then almost turned around and ran away. Brother Thomas quizzed him for over an hour about where they would live and what he was going to do to earn a living. Veda's Daddy went on and on about his daughter being smart and beautiful with a future in front of her. She deserved the best. Veda looked indifferent but Sister Lula Mae, her mother, raised her hands in joyful prayer.

Louis was excited when he revealed that he had landed a job in Baltimore with Southern Pacific Supply as a CDL truck driver delivering structural steel and building supplies. He said he had even found a pretty, little rowhouse for them to live in. Louis proudly pulled out two one-way greyhound bus tickets and three hundred dollars from his pocket. All he needed was their blessing and a trip up the road to the church to fetch the minister.

Brother Thomas finally relented. As soon as they heard the word yes, Veda and her mother began packing her bags. Sister Lula Mae found the white moire antique dress that she had worn and that had been handed down from her husband's family four generations past. She spot cleaned and pressed it for Veda.

Louis and Veda had a quick ceremony the following Saturday morning. Veda had never felt more beautiful in her life, wearing a wreath of orange blossoms and a Honiton lace veil that descended almost to the ground. Everyone from Luthersville attended. The churchwomen helped with the food. Louis's cousin, Otis, gathered flowers from his garden and arranged them throughout the church. It turned out to be a lovely country wedding.

Before the sun had set, Veda changed into a pair of worn-out jeans and cotton shirt. She and her new husband headed for the closest bus station, which was located several miles away in Fredricksburg, Virginia.

Almost right away things started out badly for them. Veda's first reaction was disappointment when getting off the bus in the East Baltimore section. It looked no better than where she had just left. Louis had painted a drastically different picture of the neighborhood that was now to be their new home. Dirty, foul-mouth urchins ran wild all over the streets. A fistfight broke out between two teenage girls. Louis and Veda crossed the street to avoid the conflict. Folks sat on their rowhouse porches and strained their necks to see what was going on. Trash, broken glass, and boarded up windows showed up everywhere. Only a few tiny trees that dotted the sidewalk curb had any greenery on them. The rest stood bent over dead or dying.

Louis took Veda's hand and led her up the steep, concrete steps of their rowhouse. He had already paid two months rent in advance. When he opened the screen door, he cut himself on the ripped out wire mesh screen. He licked the droplet of blood from his hand and unlocked the door with his other good hand. In the next instant, Veda found herself being lifted into his strong arms as he carried her across the threshold into the small foyer.

Veda tried to be cheerful but she knew Louis could see the displeasure in her face. He assured her this was only a start and they'd be moving to something better soon. She walked through the dark, narrow hallway that led straight into a tiny, closet-sized kitchen. The first room to the left of the hallway was the living room. Louis had rented some used furniture that was covered with stains, dust, and lumpy cushions. He said that too was only temporary and when they saved enough money they'd go pick out some real nice furniture at Marlo's. He was against charging and paying for things on credit.

Next to the living room was an open area for the dining room and it appeared to be only slightly larger than the kitchen. A card table and four folding chairs occupied most of the dining room space. Veda walked up the steep stairs that led to two small bedrooms and a filthy bathroom.

After a complete tour of her new home, Veda insisted they walk a few blocks to the corner store. She bought a large bag full of cleaning supplies, several cans of Raid, and a carton of cigarettes. They spent their honeymoon weekend on hands and knees scrubbing every inch of the entire house. Veda wasn't satisfied until she could smell the clean, fresh scent of Mr. Clean, Endust, and Lysol throughout every room.

The next morning Louis got up early and said he was going to look for part-time work in addition to his job with Southern Pacific. Louis was impressed with his wife's Business degree from Hampton and told her that with her skills she should be able to get a high-paying job before too long. Veda knew that Louis was doing the best he could, but she realized too late that her expectations were much higher than he could ever achieve.

Their marriage continued to be a big letdown to Veda. Not from anything obvious that she could point to, just a nagging, overwhelming feeling of boredom and profound disappointment that continued to plague her each day. And when their daughter, Sherrelle was born, things didn't improve. They got worse. Veda could not work up a maternal interest in the child. Louis was the one to get up for the baby's two o'clock, four o'clock, and six AM. feedings night after night. He was the one who stayed up whenever Sherrelle was sick. Veda watched Louis handle the role of caretaker so expertly that she slowly backed off from it, not even giving herself a chance to bond with her baby. Louis tried to coax her into feeding and holding the baby, but she would say she had work to do and would disappear in their bedroom for hours while Louis cuddled and played with their daughter. Louis felt confused and like most things he didn't understand, he ignored it, hoping it would go away or get better in time.

Veda stayed absorbed in herself and constantly focused on how miserable she felt. She compared Louis to the staff of white, professional, well-dressed attorneys at Richardson, Eades, & Williams, a Baltimore law firm where she worked as a secretary, answering the telephone, typing contracts, and making coffee in the mornings. This is where she first met Hilton Davis, her current boss, who was an associate attorney there at the time.

Veda wasn't tasked with doing any of the bookkeeping or legal aid work at Richardson, Eades, & Williams. Her Hampton Institute business degree had only landed her a job as a low-wage earning secretary. She asked for more responsibility and comparable pay but was constantly denied it or given some excuse that her performance was mediocre. The firm always brought in young law students to help out during the summers and busy spurts.

This incensed Veda but being the only black person in the office, she chose to keep quiet and simply perform the tasks that had been assigned. She couldn't afford to complain and risk losing her job. Louis didn't bring in enough money from both his regular and weekend jobs to cover all their expenses.

Veda had worked her ass off at Hampton for four years, and it wasn't getting her anywhere. What her Daddy had said turned out to be true: black folks had to do more and keep their skills sharp just to stay in the game. That's when Veda decided that she had to get more education than a four-year degree.

She'd go to law school at night and become a lawyer just like them. The only thing holding her back was time and money. She'd find the time if she could somehow get the money. Louis probably wouldn't like it but that was the least of her worries. She didn't have to worry about Sherrelle missing her because the baby never seemed to notice when Veda came home or left. She was already more attached to the babysitter than to her own mother.

Neither she nor Louis had extra money left over after the bills were paid to fund another college degree. The social programs that had helped low income minorities get an education when she first got into college had all but disappeared. Affirmative Action created during the civil rights era in the sixties was all but dead now. Veda knew if not for her minister's connections, she would never have gotten that scholarship to attend Hampton.

Not only did she hate her job but being married to Louis was boring at best. They never argued or fought. Louis was too low-key and gentle for that. But the worst part was she had no sexual interest in Louis whatsoever. On occasion she submitted to his appeals for sex just to relieve the boredom but she noticed his approaches had become more and more infrequent. Veda was glad because she wouldn't have to pretend to enjoy it any longer.

Louis worked hard and tried everything in his power to make her happy but it didn't seem to be enough. By the time their ten-year anniversary rolled around, Veda had an eight-year old daughter she couldn't relate to, a husband she was bored with, and a deadend job that she felt was far beneath her education and qualifications. She hated what her life had turned into.

One day Louis walked in tired, after his long hours of driving, but happy just to be home. Veda immediately presented him with a college handbook for the University of Maryland's Law School in Baltimore. She was surprised at how easy it was to convince him. All she had gotten out was I want ... and Louis told her to go for it.

They sat down at the kitchen table that night and worked out the expenses and logistics of everything. Louis said he could go back to working evenings like he had done when they were first married. He had noticed a sign that said Help Wanted for a short order cook at a diner nearby. Their credit was good because Louis always paid on time and usually with cash. He said they could get a student loan to make up what they didn't have in savings. This was important to Veda so he was willing to compromise on his 'cash only' policy.

Louis agreed to take on extra work everyday except Sundays. He always thought it was important that they continue to go to church and spend time together as a family on Sundays. He had obviously forgotten that Veda had long ago cut herself out of the Sunday family routine.

Louis said he'd be willing to go back to his part-time evening job if it meant she would be happy. The extra money he made added to a student loan would be just enough for her to take a few courses in the evenings. The only bad thing about the plan that Louis could see was Sherrelle would be alone on the evenings that Veda had class and he worked.

Even though she was only eight years old, Louis wanted to include Sherrelle in the family decision-making, especially when those decisions impacted her. He was kind and patient with her as he always was. He explained how important this was to her mother and that as a family they all had to pitch in and do their share whenever any of them needed something. He said he trusted Sherrelle to do the right thing on the evenings that she would be home alone. Sherrelle was old enough now to be on her own for a few hours in the evenings and Mrs Johnson next door would be keeping an eye on things. She'd be just a few steps away if Sherrelle needed anything. Louis presented a list of ground rules and posted them on the refrigerator. He made sure she knew exactly what was expected. Sherrelle shrugged her shoulders and seemed indifferent to the whole thing. Veda tried to read her daughter's thoughts, but had never been able to get close to Sherrelle, not even on a superficial level. She never looked at her mother once during the family council. Veda recalled her daughter's exact words that day, "Whatever you want Daddy is fine with me."

Then she quietly disappeared into her room. So much like her father thought Veda. Veda knew she didn't spend enough time with her daughter as it was, and now she wanted to get a law degree at night. For what? Veda didn't know exactly why. But she hoped it would drastically change her life in some way, bring passion and energy back or just give her a reason to want to get up in the mornings.

Louis had been the one to be involved with Sherrelle's school projects and activities. Veda always had some excuse for not attending the PTA meetings or parent/teacher conferences. Sherrelle was a good student Veda reasoned to herself and didn't need any intervention from her. But it was just a convenient excuse, an easy way out of her obligations as a parent. When Veda did make an effort to be encouraging and interested, Sherrelle saw right through her mother's facade. Now that Veda wanted to do something that excited her, Sherrelle didn't care. Veda got a taste of what it felt like to be ignored and neglected. She didn't like it but now her time and attention had to be focused on getting a law degree. She had no time to worry about Sherrelle and her moods.

Dr. Renee noticed that 45 minutes had passed.

"Veda, why did you want to talk about your past life with Louis and Sherrelle this evening?" asked Dr. Renee, "Your discussions are usually focused on your current relationship with LaMarr."

"I don't know," said Veda, staring down at her hands.

Veda couldn't answer her therapist's question but she sat still for a minute and thought about it. She'd been talking non-stop for forty-five minutes and had felt an overwhelming sense of loss and emptiness all day but didn't know why. The more she talked about Louis and the sacrifices he made for her and Sherrelle, the more she began to understand why he could still be so forgiving and loving no matter what pain she had dealt him. She was the one suffering more than Louis ever had or would. And she was the one who had been the most determined to seek out her own happiness no matter what the consequences. The consequences had been the loss of her daughter and a man who truly loved her with all his heart. But her ex-husband had discovered peace. And she still had not found it.

CHAPTER 15

▼

It was nearly 8 o'clock when Veda finally arrived home that evening after leaving Dr. Renee's office. She was beat after working late for the third day in a row. Just as she was about to put the key in her front door, she heard her telephone ringing from inside her apartment. She quickly unlocked the door, kicked off her shoes, and ran to the telephone, barely making it on the fourth ring.

"Yeah?" she answered out of breath.

"Sweet Pea, it's your Auntie Rose, baby."

Veda took a deep breath and realized that what had been a bad day just turned worse.

"How's my baby girl doin' up there in that crazy place ya'll like to call our nation's capital?" Veda could detect the sarcasm in her aunt's voice.

"Fine, Aunt Rose, and you?" Veda fumbled through her pocket book for her pack of cigarettes. When she couldn't feel them right away, she turned the purse upside down and dumped all the junk out on the coffee table. She reached for the pack of Newport Lights and lit a cigarette. She slumped down on the couch.

"Fair to middlin' chile. You know how it is when you gets to be my age. But I ain't complain', 'cause I'm still kickin', thank the Lord."

"How's mama?" asked Veda and blew out a puff of smoke.

"Well, ah, Sweet Pea, that's why I'm callin'. The ole girl's still on the battle-field but I'm afraid she's jus 'bout ready to lose the war."

"Exactly what do you mean, Aunt Rose?" Veda crushed out her cigarette in the ash tray and massaged her temples with her free hand, bracing herself for the worse.

"Look a here, chile, all I'm tryin' to say is this … now I know you and your mama ain't seen eye to eye over these years on the 'count of you leavin' a good man like Louis Simms and runnin' off with that fancy pants hustler. But even though she say she done disowned you for good, bein' your auntie and all, I felt like it was my duty tuh …"

"Just please get to the point, Aunt Rose, for chrissakes." Veda felt her chest tighten as her patience began to slip.

"Well, Sweet Pea, lemme put it to you this way, if you wanna make up and say your farewells to your ole mama before she passes on to glory, then you better get on down here chile."

Veda asked her aunt why hadn't she called sooner. Aunt Rose explained that she never did like those damn answering machines. Now, Veda knew who had been calling her for the past week and hanging up without leaving a message. She wasted another thirty minutes listening to Aunt Rose give her a detailed account of every facet of her mother's illness. Aunt Rose recounted the time her mama could barely walk when her hands and feet had swollen up from rheumatoid arthritis. Then she went on to detail her mama's stroke last year—how she had found Veda's mother unable to speak or move and how her eyes had wandered and rolled in the back of her head, unable to focus. "That's right, baby chile," said Aunt Rose, "but yet again the good Lord saw fit to spare Lula Mae from the stroke that ole Devil laid on her. But honey, I think this is it." Aunt Rose lowered her voice to almost a whisper, "Your mama ain't got much time left." Aunt Rose told Veda that her mother was coughing up blood. She could barely catch her breath and her fever hadn't broken. The doctor said she had pneumonia and her body was too old and tired to fight it. Just as Veda was about to say good-bye and thank her aunt for calling to let her know, Aunt Rose branched off into the minor and major ailments of the rest of Luthersville's sick and shut-in.

An hour later, after finally hanging up the phone, Veda headed straight for her medicine cabinet and gobbled down three extra-strength Tylenols. The call from Aunt Rose gave her a splitting headache and brought back too many emotional memories of when she had to rush back home for her father's funeral five years ago. She had not been back to Luthersville since. Although she occasionally made the dutiful telephone calls, her conversations with her mother were always brief, never lasting more than five minutes. Once Veda had succumb to pangs of guilt and had even invited her for a visit to Washington, D.C., but thankfully, her mother refused the invitation. Veda had let out a loud sigh of relief and didn't much care if her mother heard it. Over the years she hadn't found the time or the inclination to return to Luthersville and Aunt Rose's melodramatics concerning her mother's impending death posed no exception. And yet, listening to Aunt Rose made her head throb.

She turned on the television but after several minutes of staring at it, all she heard was noise; she couldn't concentrate on the program. She got up and went to the kitchen and looked in the refrigerator. There was nothing to heat up and she didn't feel like cooking. Even though she hadn't eaten since that morning she still didn't have an appetite. Veda closed the refrigerator and went to her bedroom to lie down. She stretched out on her back fully clothed and stared up at the ceiling. Veda was so deep in thought, she almost didn't hear the doorbell ringing. She got up and opened the door and found Courtney Hargreaves from the office standing there.

"What the hell do you want?" said Veda, rubbing one eye. She had too many other things on her mind right now to think about work or to try to be polite. She assumed Davis had sent his flunky to dump more work on her.

"Can I come in? I'd like to talk to you about LaMarr. I apologize for the intrusion but I couldn't speak freely at the office." Courtney hugged her shoulder bag close to her body and appeared nervous, yet her blue eyes stared with determination at Veda.

Veda kept a stone face but stepped aside to let Courtney enter. Since she wasn't there about work, Veda was curious as to what she wanted. She stood before the pretty young law student with both arms crossed under her breasts and waited as Courtney struggled to find the right words.

"I know that you and LaMarr are close, Veda," said Courtney, "despite his efforts to conceal it."

Veda looked at Courtney in disbelief but kept her mouth clamped shut for the moment. The nerve of this bitch coming here and talking to her about her relationship with LaMarr she thought.

"I hope you'll believe me when I say I've come here with good intentions, not to hurt you," she said, "but there're private things about LaMarr that you don't know."

"And you do?" said Veda sarcastically, "I've been with LaMarr for five years. I ain't about to throw all that away because of you. You just a little white bread diversion for him, that's all."

Courtney opened her mouth wide, but was unable to speak at first. The chill in Veda's voice had caused her to step back; she tried to explain. "You're wrong Veda. It's not like that," said Courtney almost in a whisper, "I'm not after LaMarr romantically and he isn't interested in me. But he also isn't interested in you, so take my advice and stay away from him or you're gonna get hurt." Courtney continued to edge closer to the door as Veda advanced towards her.

"Why the hell do you care?" snarled Veda, only an inch away from her face.

Courtney stuttered and reached for the door knob as she spoke. "Well, because ... because I think it's important for women to support one another, don't you? Stay true to the sisterhood, you know what I mean Veda—look out for each other, one sister to another. I ... I just thought I had to come and tell you the truth before ..."

"You're a damn liar!" shouted Veda, "Get the hell outta my house, bitch. As far as I recall you wasn't at my mama's dinner table growing up. I don't have no sisters."

Before Courtney could grab the door knob, Veda unleashed her anger on the startled young woman and snatched a handful of Courtney's blond hair, shaking her head back and forth. The handbag slipped from her shoulders. Courtney managed to push herself free and reached for her purse with one hand and juggled the door handle with the other, frantically trying to open the door. When Veda pushed her she tripped backwards and almost fell.

"I'ma kick your bony ass," said Veda. The look on Veda's face indicated she was ready for some more. Veda breathed rapidly and her eyes narrowed into fierce slits of anger. She positioned her feet and fists in a fighting stance. Courtney held up her hand in defense and turned her face away.

"Stop," she sobbed, "If you'll just let me explain. I can prove it."

Veda froze. She felt Courtney's words pierce her heart as if she had been hit with a stun gun. She didn't want to listen to any more of this. Veda pushed her out of the door into the hallway and slammed the door shut. Courtney heard the double locks and chains being latched into place and slowly limped out of the apartment building.

To Courtney, Veda was acting like some crazed, wounded animal ready to strike anything in her path. Courtney couldn't believe this was the type of person Davis & Bookerman hired as their office manager. This woman's true crude and violent nature had unfolded in plain view. No one in the office would ever believe her if she told them what had just happened. From where she came from professional, civilized people did not behave like that. She had only wanted to spare Veda the hurt and pain she knew was in store for her when she learned the truth about LaMarr but she realized that Veda would never listen. Courtney knew she had to stay away from her. She had no idea what the street-side version of Veda was capable of doing.

Veda was still panting and staring at her crazed-looking image in the mirror for several minutes after Courtney left. She reached for the comb on her dresser and fixed her hair. Despite telling herself that she didn't care about what Aunt Rose had said on the phone, Veda felt conflicted. Without meaning to she had taken out the brunt of her frustrations on that simple-minded girl who had the nerve to come to her house with some bullshit. Well, it served her dumb ass right thought Veda. She should have known better than to try to come between a determined Black woman and her man. Beside, Veda didn't trust Courtney. She could have been trying to spread some lies to break them up. Veda didn't want to hear anything she had to say. And she didn't want to hear what Aunt Rose had to say either. Dr. Renee always wanted to talk about her childhood, but Veda resisted. She wondered if this was the reason she wasn't progressing in her therapy sessions. Maybe there were some things that she had pushed aside for too long and needed to bring out. Veda dialed Dr. Renee's number and left a message on her voicemail, requesting an emergency meeting tomorrow as soon as she could see her. Maybe it was time to finally face her demons.

The following morning at 9, Veda sat in Dr. Renee's office. She had left a message for Mr. Davis that she wouldn't be in to work until 10:30. This time when Dr. Renee asked about her mother Veda reached back into her memory and told what it had been like growing up with Lula Mae for a mother.

"Growing up all I ever heard from Mama was, '*You ain't no good. The devil got too much of a hold on you.*' Or even worse, as soon as I was about to walk out the door she'd spin me around by my shoulders and get right up in my face. '*You bet not be lettin' dem old nasty boys mix up they milk in your honey pot, girl. Don't be bringin' me nothin' to take care of. I got my hands full with you.*' It took me a little while to figure out what she was talking about because I wasn't as frisky as she thought I was. Mama used to say I talked back and had a sassy mouth, but I knew better than to say anything directly to her face. At first I'd call myself being slick and would whisper under my breath, but I soon figured out that mama had good ears and was just pretending to be hard of hearing when Aunt Rose came by. The truth was Mama could hear a fly crawling on the wall. After I got boxed in the head with her fist a couple of times, I soon learned to keep my damn mouth shut when she told me to do something I didn't wanna do. Mama was always saying how she tried to teach me right from wrong but I was determined to choose wrong over right. Eventually I gave up trying to please her."

Veda sighed. "What's the point of going back home now, Doc? I know it may be cold-hearted to say this, but her dying is not gonna change a thing. It's too late to fix anything between me and my mama now."

Veda saw that Dr. Renee was not going to give her advice, and in fact sat there in total silence while Veda let the flood gates open and kept talking, nonstop. Veda described her last trip back home, 5 years ago when her daddy got sick. She had approached her father's bedside and tried to avoid her mother's disapproving glare. His withered faced looked like he could have been a hundred years old. Veda's mother wept at her husband's side. She blamed her only daughter for his deterioration. Veda sat down next to her father and knew she had been a complete disappointment to her parents. It was written all over her father's face as he looked up at her through dark, sunken eyes.

She held her father's hand and said she was sorry for all the disappointments and heartache she had caused her family. She knew he had been devastated when she walked out on Louis and took up with LaMarr Coleman. The white-haired, feeble head nodded his forgiveness. The last words he uttered just before closing his eyes and going home to Jesus was 'I love you, daughter.'

When he died, Veda felt numb from the pain but no tears flowed from her eyes. This too, her mother took as a sign of wickedness in her. Sitting across from Dr. Renee, Veda clasped the back of her neck and stretched to relieve the tension before speaking, "Dr. Renee, I kid you not, from the way Mama shot me an evil look after Daddy died … if looks were bullets I would have been stone dead." Veda told Dr. Renee that her mother said it was the shame and grief over what Veda had done to Louis and Sherrelle that finally killed her father. But now her mother was too old, sickly and feeble to hurt Veda anymore. What more harm could she do now? Veda pictured the once energetic and defiant young woman who raised her and recalled those early days of mistreatment and abuse under her tirades.

Veda briefly closed her eyes and leaned back on the couch, remembering what it was like in Luthersville when she was thirteen years old. Her mama, known to the town as Sister Lula Mae Thomas, dealt out many a harsh word and heavy hand. Even today her words still rang sharp in Veda' ears like it was just yesterday and she was only thirteen. In her mind, she could hear her mother's voice as loud, annoying and shrill as those test fire alarms that went off in her building and always seemed to take forever for security to turn off.

"Get your lazy behind up out'a dat bed, girl. You know you got tuh feed dem chickens 'for you leave," said Mama, slapping me on my backside with as much force as her skinny hand could muster.

"Get on up girl 'for you be late tuh Rev'ren lessons. Uh 'portant man like dat got better things tuh do den waitin' on you girl."

I couldn't feel Mama's blows because I kept the quilt that Aunt Rose had made me pulled up over my head. The last thing I wanted to do was trudge a mile up the road through six inches of snow to Pastor's house to study the bible and all those other boring subjects he droned on and on about, especially, since Sister Charlotta wasn't there any more. Sister Charlotta had been the minister's wife until she died of Tuberculosis. She was the prettiest and nicest person that had ever come through Luthersville. And she was young too, not even 17. She was more like a best friend than an adult figurehead. I remember she had dark brown hair past her shoulders and her skin was the color of fresh honey. She had delicate, pretty features, and a nice figure that those old bats from the Baptist Mothers Committee were jealous of because when they sat their wide hips down on the church pews they took up enough space for 2 or 3 people.

When Sister Charlotta was alive, I liked going to Pastor's house during the winter months for my lessons. She was like the big sister I never had. She seemed too young and full of life to be the wife of a minister who was almost forty years old at the time of their marriage. According to church gossip Pastor had met her one summer when he attended a convention in Richmond. The church elders and other busybodies complained that Sister Charlotta was much too young to be the First Lady of the Church. But Pastor didn't pay them any mind and I didn't either. I didn't care what anybody said about the pastor's wife because I loved her dearly. She treated me better than my own mama ever did.

That morning not even the smell of bacon cooking or the sizzling of fried eggs in the iron skillet could entice me out of my warm feather bed at five-thirty in the morning to go to Bible lessons when it was still dark outside.

Wintertime had always been my favorite time of year because we couldn't get to school on account of the snow. All that fun snowboarding and snowball fights out in the fields with the other kids stopped for me when mama went and ruined everything with those damn school lessons and bible studies at the pastor's house. The other kids would be out sleigh-riding and having snowball fights after they finished their morning chores. All the kids I knew including Louis Simms, his eight younger siblings, and even his cousin, Otis, who they say was borderline retarded, would be out having fun in the snow. In the beginning I tried to petition Daddy for help but he never interfered in Mama's decisions especially where I was concerned. He believed she knew best when it came to raising young girls into respectable ladies. His job was putting food on the table and a roof over our heads. He said that's just what he was good at so he would not cross over into Mama's territory, dealing with me.

During the worst of the winter months, parents in Luthersville didn't bother sending their children to the public schools in Warrenton, Virginia. There was no transportation and they found it too inconvenient to drive them and pick the children up themselves. Many parents didn't know any better so didn't make the effort to see to it that their children got an education. All the other children in my hometown got off easy in the wintertime, except me, Sister Lula Mae's girl as the older folks called me. Mama said she didn't want her only child to grow up unskilled and uneducated. She wanted the best possible advantages for her daughter, so she said. Anybody that didn't really know her would think she was sincere, but I knew better. Mama just wanted to get me out of her hair when I couldn't go to school. So that's when she apparently got the bright idea of sending me to Reverend Beecham's place for private tutoring lessons during the winter months when no school bus would venture out to pick us up.

Reverend Henry Beecham was a graduate of the Richmond Theological Seminary and regarded as learned and well-traveled by the entire congregation. I began my studies under his tutelage when I was only ten years old. Mama told the pastor that just because she herself was ignorant and unrefined, did not mean that her only child had to be. When the pastor appeared skeptical about the idea, Mama reminded him that she had already paid more than her share of Sunday fried chicken dinners with homemade biscuits and he owed her.

I turned and shifted my weight in the warm bed and sank further into the feather-filled mattress. This time I wasn't going to get up the first time Mama called. Before my winter study sessions began, I couldn't wait for the first chill when it was time to pull out the feather beds from the cedar-scented, storage closet. Aunt Rose saved certain feathers from chickens, geese, and all kinds of birds. The townsfolk would also bring Aunt Rose more feathers to add to her stockpile. Practically everyone in Luthersville owned one of Aunt Rose's feather beds because when I was growing up no one had heat except for the warmth from their ovens and fireplaces. But they didn't really need a heating system with Aunt Rose's feather beds. Folks would lay their feather bed on top of the flat spring and regular mattress in the wintertime. It was the closest thing to heaven that you could find in Luthersville, falling down into those soft, warm, down feathers.

Just as I was about to drift off to sleep again, I heard Mama slam my schoolbooks on the kitchen table—at least I think that's what I heard because I was still snuggled under my blankets. But then she marched into my room and snatched me from my sweet thoughts.

"Is you defyin' me girl?" Mama hollered.

I opened one eye and saw her standing in front of me with one hand on her hip and the other holding a large, iron skillet.

"No, ma'am," I said, throwing the covers back and jumping out of bed.

Mama stormed back into the kitchen to fix Daddy's breakfast. After she left I pulled off my flannel nightgown. I caught my reflection in the mirror and turned to study my budding breasts. I had just turned 13 and for the first time I was aware of them and wondered when Mama would take me to get a bra. Standing naked in front of the mirror I felt embarrassed about my blossoming womanhood. Most of the other children I hung out with still looked and acted like little kids, even Otis, who was 16 years old but short and still very immature for his age.

I had always suspected that something was wrong with Otis. All the other kids teased him because he had a lazy eye and you never really knew when he was looking at you or someone else. The kids called Otis the 'One-eyed Cyclops.' Me and his cousin, Louis Simms, were his only friends and protectors from the other children's cruelty. I really felt sorry for Otis. Kids could be mean sometimes.

The weight of the snow dragged Veda's feet down and left deep footprints in the snow as she headed for bible lessons at the pastor's house. Finally Veda saw the steeple of the church up ahead and knew she was close to Reverend Beecham's house, just beyond St. Paul's A.M.E. Church. Since his wife's death last year, he lived there alone.

One of the few good memories Veda retained about growing up in Luthersville was of the times she spent with the minister's wife, Sister Charlotta. Veda smiled when she recalled the times that Sister Charlotta had patiently combed out the tangles in her hair after her lessons with the pastor were over. She'd braid it into thick, course plaits and tie different color ribbons on each end. She was always buying bows and ribbons or some other trinket for Veda whenever she went into town to pick up her husband's favorite Chaptain Black tobacco. Occasionally, she'd bring back a yard or two of cotton fabric and whip up a new dress for Veda in one day. There was no end to Sister Charlotta's talents and loving ways.

One of the most precious gifts Veda ever received from Sister Charlotta was a musical jewelry box. It had a delicate figure of a ballerina perched on top with arms raised above her head and one leg lifted high in the air and the other on pointed toes. When opened, it played a soft, sweet melody of 'Claire de Lune.' Veda treasured that gift more than any other. Some days they'd bake bread, pies, or cookies in the early afternoons. The smell of fresh baked bread or pastries in the oven filled the house with appetizing aromas. Veda felt safe and loved in this peaceful refuge with Sister Charlotta. The Reverend would always disappear into his musty-smelling study to work on his sermons and left the giggling, young females to their own devices.

Veda was more devastated than anyone when Sister Charlotta suddenly got sick and died. She immediately wanted to quit her studies but her mother wouldn't hear of it. She'd seen the remarkable improvement in Veda since she started her lessons and attributed her daughter's growing self-confidence and interest in learning to the good Reverend's teaching. Veda knew it had nothing to do with him. It was the daily dose of unconditional love and attention she received from Sister Charlotta that boosted her confidence and made her eager to learn. All that ended without warning when Sister Charlotta suddenly died.

Veda didn't realize that she had been talking to Dr. Renee for 45 minutes about her childhood until Dr. Renee told her that their time was up. This was the first session where she had really opened up to her therapist in counseling. The distant memory of Sister Charlotta caused her to smile, remembering the sweet young woman who had loved her like a mother should. As Veda recalled those long ago days, she had to be honest with herself and admit that she had been just as bad a mother to her own daughter, Sherrelle, as her mother had been to her. Going home to Luthersville or even thinking about it always brought back painful childhood memories that she had fought to suppress throughout her adult life. There was no way she was going back to Luthersville even if Aunt Rose did insist her mother's condition was critical and there wasn't much time left. As far as Veda was concerned it was too late.

CHAPTER 16

▼

It was late Tuesday night. Renee and Bill hadn't spoken a word to each other since Saturday morning when Bill had blown up at her suggestion to bring Susanna home for a few days. Bill didn't even attempt to understand how important this was to her. Renee threw down the APA Monitor she had been trying to read for the past hour. It was now close to midnight and Bill hadn't called all day or given her any indication that he'd be late getting home.

No matter how hard she tried to concentrate on the article, nothing wiped away the memory of many other nights just like this one when she sat up late in bed, read her journals, and waited for Bill to come home. It was too late to call people but out of desperation she began to ring up some of Bill's colleagues and business associates and anyone else who she thought had an inkling of where he might be. No one could give her any information. Feeling useless and alone after having drifted in and out of sleep while trying to come up with a plan, Renee now knew what she would do.

She crawled out of bed, still drowsy from lack of sleep, and took a quick shower. The shower and a cup of instant coffee woke her up. By 1:30 AM. she was fully dressed and nearly all packed. She neatly laid the last outfit on top of the mound of folded clothing and pressed down to force her suitcase shut. It helped to keep busy doing simple things like rechecking to make sure she had everything she'd need for the next several weeks. But Renee knew she was just killing time in hopes of catching Bill before she left. She wanted to explain why she had to leave home and stay at Shirley Ann's for awhile. Shirley Ann had given her an open invitation to come stay with them ever since Susanna's condition began to deteriorate. All it took was a phone call to let Shirley Ann know she'd be there later that day.

Renee had been in daily contact with Susanna's foster mother since Saturday. The baby was in the late-stage of the disease and getting worse by the minute. Susanna needed her and it was obvious that her husband didn't, no matter what he said. Renee knew that caring for Susanna around-the-clock would be hard work and demanding. She recalled Shirley Ann's words when she said that true fulfillment comes from being able to make a personal sacrifice for others.

Renee's mind raced over all the details. She could make arrangements for her less severe patients to see another therapist over the next several weeks. She would only see the more emotionally dependent patients and fit them into forty-five minute evening sessions. Her mentor from college, Dr. Helen Stone, rented office space in a medical building close by Shirley Ann's house. Renee didn't think Helen would mind letting her borrow the office temporarily a few nights a week once she explained the circumstances. This way she'd be just five minutes away if anything happened to Susanna while she was counseling a patient.

By the time she was ready to leave, Bill had still not come home. Renee sat down at her vanity table and wrote him a letter telling him where she'd be and that she couldn't say when she'd be back home. She had never left before under these circumstances and didn't know what effect it would have on their already strained marriage. She felt just as insecure as some of her patients and couldn't stop thinking about the possibility that Bill didn't really love her at all. Her father certainly never believed Bill loved her the way a man should. Perhaps there was someone else in his life. Renee experienced a sudden tightness in her chest. Then right away assured herself that he was not involved with another woman. A wife always knows these things. Her instincts told her that Bill was just driven to succeed in his own business because he was competing with her success. Ego and his determination to outdo her kept him away nights not another woman. But what if she were wrong? Bill was not home most nights and when he was home, he rarely talked to her. If not sitting in front of his computer, eyes locked on the screen and fingers pounding across the keyboard, he'd be slouched on the coach watching an HBO sports event—football, basketball, tennis or golf—whatever sport was in season. Her husband hadn't shown much genuine interest in her in a long while.

Renee placed the note on his pillow. She grabbed her suitcase and left. She wasn't surprised to find Shirley Ann still wide-awake when she called from her cell phone to say she was on her way. Between the two of them, they could share the load of Susanna's care. This was definitely the right thing to do. Renee wanted to cherish each moment with this precious child who'd been dealt a rotten hand. For now, Renee put her uncertain future with Bill and her own selfish desires for Deek, on hold.

When Renee pulled in front of Shirley Ann's house, she saw a light coming through the front window. Shirley Ann was waiting for her.

"How's Susanna?" asked Renee, cautiously.

The older woman's slumped over shoulders and the downcast look in her eyes gave Renee the answer. Shirley Ann said she already administered the baby's 2 AM. medication and had left her asleep in her crib. She showed Renee to the guestroom and told her she would tend to Susanna the rest of the night and for her to get some sleep.

Shirley Ann switched on a lamp sitting atop a small dressing table by the door. The fragrance of rose petals immediately filled the room.

"Smells nice," said Renee, looking around.

"A little trick I learned from my sister," explained Shirley Ann, pointing to a crystal perfume decanter, "Dab a little cologne on your light bulbs every now and then. When you turn on the light, the scent comes out."

Renee put down her suitcase and smiled, "I'll have to remember that." The light flickered periodically indicating that the bulb was about to go out soon. Shirley Ann said she'd replace the bulb first thing in the morning, that no one had used that guestroom in quite awhile.

After she left, Renee took in her new surroundings. The light was dull but better than pitch darkness. Her bedroom at home was massive and ornate. This room felt small and cozy. Its pale pink walls were bathed in a warm glow from the flickering lamp. Renee felt the tenseness in her neck and shoulders slowly ease up. In the center of the room, stood a 19th-century iron and brass, four-poster bed with a Star of Bethlehem quilt laid neatly across it. Directly over the bed, a wood-framed picture of Jesus hung on the wall. His hands were clasped in prayer while his eyes gazed piously upward. A black leather-bound bible with gold lettering rested on the nightstand. Next to it stood an old wedding picture of John Turner and Shirley Ann who looked to be no more than twenty-one in the photo. The dresser was cluttered with personal effects all belonging to a woman—a silk and taffeta evening purse, boxed and loose pieces of jewelry, silver buttons, a powder box, and crystal perfume bottles. An array of antique-framed family pictures surrounded a pewter teapot, its matching cup and saucer, and brass candlesticks. One of the larger photos looked like the Turners' son in graduation cap and gown. He wore the same broad smile he'd inherited from his mother.

Renee noticed that Shirley Ann had stamped a bit of herself throughout their home. It reflected exactly who she was. Not the latest design trends or some decorator's personal taste. You could tell a great deal about Shirley Ann and the home she kept for her family just by being there. In contrast, Renee thought her own home projected nothing real about herself. Suddenly, she felt relieved not to be within its huge, cold walls. A crystal clock indicated the time was now 2:35 AM. Renee knew she had better take Shirley Ann's advice and get some sleep. Tomorrow would probably be a long and difficult day, both emotionally and physically.

After only a few hours of sleep, Renee woke to the noise of an alarm going off and a baby crying. She followed the distant sound of soft lullaby music to Susanna's room. The little nursery had been set up to promote calm and relaxation. At the recommendation of Susanna's doctors, lights remained dimmed, and calming music played in the background. A teddy bear border outlined walls painted in a muted shade of yellow. No one was inside the room. Renee saw signs that this room had once belonged to Shirley Ann's youngest daughter, now grown and married. She noticed a quilt that Shirley Ann had made years ago lay folded at the edge of a twin sized bed. Shirley Ann had once told Renee that quilting had been one of her favorite hobbies when her children were young. It was apparent to Renee that the handmade quilt had been meticulously pieced together from dozens of tiny fabric remnants. The once brilliant arrangement of colors were now faded from constant washing over the years. A chocolate-colored doll she made for her daughter's third birthday sat perched against a pillow. After years of being dragged around and loved by a three year old, one of its pigtails and a large, button-sized eye was missing. Not surprisingly, it was also one of Susanna's favorite toys. As Renee was about to turn and leave the room she spotted the baby's soiled sheets that had been stripped off the crib and lay in a pile by the door, along with brownish-stained baby clothes.

Renee found Shirley Ann in the bathroom bathing Susanna. The older woman looked like she hadn't slept much, if at all. Fly-away wisps of gray-streaked hair fell across her face, and her eyes looked tired and heavy-lidded. She told Renee that Susanna had developed diarrhea in the last few hours. She'd started her on kaopectate and hoped she'd take some juice and eat a high-protein breakfast of turkey sausage and scrambled eggs later. Though Susanna still showed a temperature of 104°F, Shirley Ann expected the fever to go down since she'd received medication regularly around the clock all night. Renee glanced at the listless baby that could now barely sit up in the tub without being held. Her once beautiful golden-brown complexion had red undertones. Renee thought she detected a strain in her breathing. As a registered nurse who had spent years in hospital emergency rooms, Renee did not share the foster mother's optimism, but kept her opinion to her herself. She knelt down in front of the tub to help Shirley Ann, aware that her stomach knotted and cheeks burned from the effort to keep from crying; she had to maintain a strong front for Shirley Ann.

Shirley Ann had a receptacle for used latex gloves and boxes of clean disposal ones in the bathroom and in Susanna's room. Renee donned a pair of gloves and took over for Shirley Ann. She told her to go call Susanna's nurse to schedule a home visit for that day, that the baby needed to be examined thoroughly as soon as possible. Then she instructed her to go straight to bed and get some rest. She could find everything she needed to take care of Susanna. Shirley Ann was too exhausted to protest.

Renee lifted the baby out of the tub and gently patted her dry. Susanna's large brown eyes focused on Renee's smiling face and familiar voice. Their eyes locked into each other's and maintained eye contact while Renee changed her diaper and dressed her. Renee discarded the dirty gloves in the receptacle. She gave the baby her pacifier and laid her down in the crib while she wiped off the changing table with a disinfectant solution of one part bleach and ten parts hot water. Susanna's gaze followed Renee's every move throughout the room. Her muscles had felt weak to Renee and she looked anemic. Staring at her was probably the only activity she could muster enough energy for, Renee thought. Renee kept turning back to peak at her through the crib slats. Each soaked up the other's love with their eyes. Once everything was clean and straightened out, Renee carried Susanna downstairs and deposited her in the playpen in the kitchen while she prepared breakfast. Her thoughts drifted to Bill and what he must be thinking. Surely by now he had seen her note. Yet, he had made no attempt to get in touch with her. Knowing Bill he was somewhere sulking and would not be the first one to show signs of weakness by contacting her. He'd wait until she gained control of her senses and came running back home. She thought she knew her husband well enough to guess what his response to her leaving the comforts of a privileged home life to care for a sick child would be. She would admit she was wrong and that he was right, that the whole terrible ordeal had been too much for her just as he warned her it would.

The shrill ringing of an alarm startled Renee until she remembered this was the cue to give Susanna her anti-retroviral medication of zidovudine drops or

AZT. She carefully dispensed the correct number of drops into the baby's reluctant mouth. It had to be taken on an empty stomach so Renee had difficulty coaxing her into finishing the complete dosage. She knew there was nothing to camouflage the bitter taste. Susanna cried loudly. Renee tried to comfort and settle her down, before feeding her breakfast, but by then the baby had lost all interest in putting anything else into her mouth except the pacifier. Over Susanna's screams, the telephone rang. Renee gave her the pacifier just long enough to answer the phone since Shirley Ann was trying to sleep and John had long since left for work.

"Hello, Turner residence," answered Renee.

"Yeah, Doc. It's me, Deek. Look, don't get mad but I called your house this morning when I hadn't heard back from you. I spoke to your husband."

"You spoke to Bill? What did he say?"

"I identified myself as Sergeant Hamilton and said I needed to reach you to ask you some questions about the burglary last Wednesday night. He told me where you were staying and gave me this number."

"I see," said Renee calmly, "so what's the question you wanted to ask me?"

"When can I see you again? I miss you, Renee."

Renee tried to explain what was going on but in the middle of telling him about Susanna and how Bill had reacted, she broke down and sobbed into the telephone.

"Let me stop by for a little while after work this evening. Maybe I can do something to help you out with the child."

"No, I don't think that's a good idea, Deek. Susanna's very ill. Her doctor reported her CD4 plus T-cell count dropped below 200 yesterday. A normal T-cell count is about 1,000. She's not getting better."

"I'm sorry, Renee," he said, "I don't understand what you mean about T-cells dropping but it sounds like all this could be a tremendous strain on you."

"Now you sound like Bill. Don't you understand I have to do this for both Susanna and for myself?" said Renee, surprised at the irritation in her voice. She glanced over at Susanna while massaging her forehead with her free hand to help ease the tension.

"Please help me understand," he said, "I assure you I'm nothing at all like your husband. Can I stop by for just an hour? Say around eight o'clock?"

Renee sighed. "Okay, Deek but I don't know how I'll explain your visit to Shirley Ann."

"I'm a friend and I want to help. That's not an explanation, it's the truth."

"Thanks, Deek. I'll see you later tonight then. I have to go now."

"You can count on it."

Renee hung up the phone even more confused about the direction in which her life was heading. She picked up the baby from the high chair and held her close. Afterwards, she was able to get Susanna to accept a few bites of eggs and to drink all her juice. They played patty-cake and peek-a-boo until Susanna's eyes began to droop from sleepiness. Renee took her back upstairs to the nursery and laid her in the crib. While Susanna napped, Renee rested on the twin bed in the nursery. She closed her eyes, but despite her weariness she couldn't sleep.

CHAPTER 17

▼

Renee directed Veda to a comfortable seat in Helen's office where Veda collapsed into the chair and removed her sunglasses. Her eyes were red and swollen. Veda had never cried during her therapy sessions but Dr. Renee sensed she was on the verge of breaking down now. She had sounded extremely troubled on the telephone that morning. Renee switched on the tape recorder and pressed start. She spoke into the recorder to give a brief preface to the session, "*Six PM, August 10. Dr. Renee Hayes. Private session with Veda Simms in the office of a colleague, Dr. Helen Stone.*"

Renee began by asking Veda a few simple questions. She wanted to put her patient at ease and create a relaxed, non-threatening environment. "How have you been feeling, Veda?"

Veda avoided Dr. Renee's intense gaze by studying the degrees and certificates hanging on the wall and did not answer. The framed credential directly above Dr. Renee's head indicated that her associate, Dr. Helen Stone, had received an M.D. degree with a specialization in mental health from Georgetown University in 1982. Veda fidgeted with her hands. She wanted a cigarette. In her rush to beat the traffic, she'd left work early and missed her late afternoon cigarette break. When Dr. Renee repeated her question, Veda replied.

"Tired. Sort of down in the dumps, I guess. Not much appetite," answered Veda, finally.

"Can you pinpoint what's wrong?" asked Renee.

The pitch in Veda's voice got higher as she spoke. Veda had appeared to be teetering on the brink of self-destruction ever since she started to feel her future with LaMarr Coleman begin to crumble. That's why Renee agreed to schedule an emergency appointment with her even though she herself felt completely drained from caring for Susanna all day.

"How does that make you feel Veda?" asked Renee.

Veda explained to her therapist that everything seemed to be coming down on her all at once—her unresolved feelings about her mother, LaMarr's lies, and rejection from her teen-aged daughter. Dr. Renee noticed that Veda's hands shook, and that her nails were ragged and raw from chewed up hangnails. Nerves, thought Renee. She asked her patient had she been taking the antidepressant medication. Veda admitted that she hadn't taken it on a regular basis for several weeks now.

"I dunno, Dr. Renee. I get this feeling that I can't trust my boyfriend anymore. And the type of person I am, if I lose trust in somebody I slowly begin to lose respect, know what I mean?"

"What has he done to make you think you can't trust him?"

"It's more like what he hasn't done." To that statement Dr. Renee raised her eyebrows, and Veda went on to explain. "In the beginning it was just about sex, like a good time thing. But after 5 years and all I put into this relationship, it changed for me. I wanted something more permanent. But it seems like the more I try to get a commitment from him the more he backs off. LaMarr doesn't give a damn about me and I'm tired of begging for his love."

"You know Dr. Renee, this morning when I woke up I asked myself what I would honestly do if LaMarr finally did ask me to marry him. And you know what I'd say?" Without waiting for a reply Veda continued. She sat up straight and stuck out her chin defiantly. "I'd say, Hell No. I'm not putting myself through that."

Veda continued to explain. "And you know why? LaMarr's nothing but a self-serving, egomaniac who's only concerned about himself. The longer I stay involved with him the longer I'm gonna need therapy."

"How do you plan to proceed from here now that you recognize the truth?" asked Renee.

After several moments of silence and a blank stare from Veda, Renee repeated the question. She wanted to prompt Veda to see herself ending a destructive relationship. Instead Veda sank down in her chair, her resolve shattered like a window that had just had a brick thrown through it. It was one thing to recognize the truth, but another thing altogether to accept it. Veda was still not ready to accept it.

"Let me ask you this Veda. Many women don't think about this, but do you actually sit down and think about the qualities in a man that you want and that you would want to live with and be with you as you both grow older? Because it's great when you're young. Like you said, he was fun and it was all about the sex in the beginning. But once you turn 50 and beyond … is this man really what you want as a life-long companion, Veda? Be honest with yourself."

Veda wore her pain on her face. Her eyelids drooped and her languid eyes stared out at nothing in particular. Renee surmised she was deep in thought. Dr. Renee leaned across the desk and asked Veda if she had been thinking about another suicide attempt. Veda admitted to her psychologist that recently she'd been thinking along those lines. She admitted that this time she wouldn't call 911 to rescue her. After all, who would care? What did she have worthwhile to live for? Veda said she could think of just three people in her life who had honestly loved her, Louis Simms, her father, and Sister Charlotta. Louis, she had recklessly thrown away, like last night's garbage. Her father had died five years ago, soon after she left Louis for LaMarr. Sherrelle, the only child she had brought into this world, couldn't stand the sight of her, but Veda knew why. Had she ever been a loving mother to Sherrelle? Had she ever given time and attention to her child? Not from day one. Veda had always been jealous of the devotion Louis showered on their baby daughter from the very beginning and so she had neglected Sherrelle. She'd been too involved with her own personal goals and ambitions to think about anybody else.

As her patient spoke Renee recalled Shirley Ann's words and saw how Veda's life proved a testimony to the wise older woman's message that you have to be willing to sacrifice your own selfish desires and wants in order to achieve true happiness and peace in life. And only God can show you the way if you're willing to listen and follow his guidance Shirley Ann had said.

Veda told Renee that she had given up the only two people in the world who possessed the capacity to love her unconditionally, her husband and her newborn child. She had thrown it all away for a one-sided affair with a man who had consistently used her over the last several years. She felt like she was being punished with no pardon in sight. In the beginning of her relationship with LaMarr, her hopes and dreams had been for them to spend their days as lovers, friends, and soulmates, but the reality had always been something different. Veda always found herself as an accomplice to some scheme, a part of a plan to satisfy a singular goal of LaMarr's.

She had finally begun to see the light, and now she hated LaMarr Coleman, as well as herself. It was too late to get back what she had lost. At thirty-eight years old Veda didn't think she'd ever find love or even deserved it. Dr. Renee feared that something else more destructive than LaMarr was at the root of Veda's self-loathing and she was determined to get to the bottom of it.

Renee urged Veda to relate the events of a disturbing dream she had last night that began with memories of her father's funeral five years ago. Earlier yesterday, Veda said she had been driving home and heard a familiar song on the radio that she hadn't heard in many years. It caused her to grip the steering wheel and tense up until the song was over. The song was the 1973 Motown hit by Marvin Gaye, 'Let's Get It On.' Veda didn't know why the song troubled her so much until she heard it again in the dream she had.

There was a dark man in Veda's dream who had attended her father's funeral. At first his face was just a shadow in her mind until his face gradually emerged like the developing images on a Polaroid snapshot. All her ugly childhood memories accompanied the recollection of him.

"My father's funeral took place on a hot afternoon in July, the day after he died. For the past several weeks, everybody knew he would soon meet his maker, so most of the arrangements had already been set."

"Everybody filed into St. Paul's to pay their final respects. The church was packed. Everyone had loved and admired Brother Thomas. That's what they called my Daddy. I squeezed in between two strangers sitting on a crowded back pew rather than sit up front with Mama and my other immediate family members."

"Why didn't you sit with your family?" asked Dr. Renee.

"Because I knew they all hated me and I didn't wanna hear their damn mouth," she said in a brisk voice.

Veda went on to describe the church, using her arms for gesturing and becoming more animated as she spoke. She told Renee that the heat and lack of ventilation made the closeness in the small, wood framed church, unbearable. The whirling fans and crying babies drowned out the sound of the aging minister's voice as he performed at the pulpit. Veda glanced at the serene elderly faces of the choir behind the minister and let her gaze rest upon the open coffin of her father, laid out in his Sunday best for the last time. Veda opened the funeral program that the two women next to her were using as a makeshift fan and read it silently.

Brother Richard Thomas, the eldest of four children was born February 14, 1920 to the late Augustus and Cora Thomas in Luthersville, Virginia. He was united in Holy Matrimony to Miss Lula Mae Jenkins in 1940. To their union, one child was born, Veda Lucille. Brother Thomas was a faithful and diligent member of St. Paul's African Methodist Episcopal Church until his health failed.

The church membership bestowed upon him the distinguished honor of deacon. Like his devoted wife, Sister Lula Mae, Brother Thomas was an active missionary and always inspired young and old to get saved.

He leaves to mourn his passing: his wife, Lula Mae Thomas, (1) one daughter, Veda Lucille Simms of Washington, D.C., a sister and two brothers: Rose Marshall, Harold and Andrew Thomas; and a host of other relatives and friends.

Veda closed the program and glanced at those seated around her. Several pairs of evil eyes beamed at her from all directions throughout the service. She could tell that she was being watched. Except for her Aunt Rose, there was not a friendly face in the crowd. Even her Uncle Harold and Uncle Andy barely gave her a welcoming smile. Veda knew just what it felt like to be the black sheep in the family, not that she blamed them. She had severed ties with her family years ago. During the summer of 1980 when she was twenty-one years old—right after marrying Louis Simms, Veda left Luthersville for good. Now, the breakup of her marriage to Louis helped fan the gossip about her and another man.

Veda shifted in her seat and continued her story. "At first I had wanted to ask LaMarr to come home with me for moral support. But after I saw so many ugly faces glaring at me, I was glad I didn't ask him to come down there. LaMarr would have fit in their backwoods town like a Nubian prince at a hog slaughtering. They had all heard the whole story by now since knowing other folk's business was a full-time occupation for them. They knew how I'd left what they called a good, hard working man and my eight year old baby for a big city lawyer." She watched for Dr. Renee's reaction and when her therapist nodded for her to continue she told what happened next at the funeral.

From her seat in the back pews Veda glanced up at the huge white cross hanging just above Reverend Henry Beecham's head. Her eye's moved cautiously downward to the minister's leathery-smooth, brown face. His arms rose up high in the air towards the cross for added emphasis and his strong voice bellowed throughout the church. The bounce in his step was still youthful and full of energy despite his advancing years. He easily kept pace with the jubilant choir behind him. Her father's funeral had not been sad but just another opportunity for Luthersville churchgoers to praise the Lord and get happy.

The aroma of ham, cornbread, fresh greens, fried corn and okra, and sweet potato pies worked its way up from the church basement. Veda heard several "Amens" and sighs of relief when the minister finally said the Benediction. The choir was still singing <u>What A Mighty God We Serve</u> as everyone filed out of the church. Not everyone followed the Reverend out to the cemetery in back of the church. Most folks went straight down to the basement to get a head start on the food line, but Veda went to the cemetery. She was the last one to leave the cemetery. Now alone, she allowed a tear to escape, but quickly wiped it away. She hadn't cried much during the service nor when the Reverend gave the word to lower the coffin into the freshly dug up dirt. She didn't notice when the minister walked up behind her.

"Sorry about your Daddy, Sistuh Veda. "You know how much I respected Brother Thomas." He paused and flashed a grin, "You sure lookin' mighty fine, young lady. Yes indeed. Must be doin' all right for yourself in D.C."

Veda turned around slowly and found him grinning at her. The stench from his pipe-smoking breath got stronger by the minute.

"Don't have to thank me though, Sistuh Veda," he said, "But the Good Lord knows, if it wasn't for your ole Reverend here, you'd still be one of them 'Dis, Dat, and Dem' country hicks we still got runnin' around here." Reverend Beecham went on bragging about all he had done to contribute to her success and education while Veda stared at him in silence. She saw his mouth move but couldn't hear a word he said. As he spoke, her thoughts drifted back to another time—when she was just thirteen and he was a much younger version of the aging minister who appeared before her now.

"Go on Veda," urged Dr. Renee, "tell me what happened when you were thirteen."

Minutes elapsed without a word from Veda but Renee waited patiently. Renee nodded reassuringly for Veda to continue. Finally, she continued telling the story, and Dr. Renee listened.

"At thirteen years old, I realized that Reverend Beecham was not the brilliant scholar and educator he professed to be. For one thing, he never could answer any of my questions. He explained things in vague, sketchy generalities and unclear metaphors. The minister's wife, dear Sister Charlotta, had not finished grade school but her common sense reasoning made more sense than anything the Pastor had to say."

"I remember how Reverend turned into an angry tyrant whenever his wife interrupted him or offered another explanation to something he said. He told Sister Carlotta that he was not going to be contradicted by an uneducated female. He said he was the one who had graduated from seminary school and she hadn't even finished high school with her dumb self."

"Mama thought highly of Reverend just like everyone else in St. Paul's congregation. Mama would've never believed anything unfavorable about him. I knew this and decided to keep my opinions about our minister's shortcomings to myself."

"One day soon after Sister Charlotta had died, Reverend was sitting at his kitchen table, slurping his tea when I arrived for my wintertime lessons. He offered to make me some hot cocoa before we began and I accepted. The whole while I could feel his red beady eyes looking at me, every time I looked up from taking a sip of my cocoa, there he was—staring. I flipped open my math book to where we left off the day before. I figured the sooner we got started with the lesson, the sooner it would be over. But he wasn't making any movements to get out his teaching materials."

"So I asked him … Do I have to take my lessons today Rev'ren? 'Cause all my friends gon be out sleigh riding today." Renee was startled when Veda switched to a childlike voice, but she didn't interrupt as Veda continued to relive the past.

"Rev'ren didn't answer but he kept his eyes pinned on me. I waited patiently for his permission to leave just like Mama had taught me. After slurping another spoonful of tea, he grinned and patted my hand. I thought this meant I could leave so I jumped up from my chair and bolted for the door. All I could think about was going sleigh riding with my friends."

"Rev'ren shot up from the table and grabbed my arm. 'Hold on, girl, Not so fast' he said. He was right up in my face so I could see the stains on his teeth from the pipe he always smoked."

"That's when he explained his intentions. He went over to the table and slammed my math book shut and said, 'Sistuh Veda, instead of math, I think we'll begin with a history lesson today. Lord willing, chile, I might be able to teach you a thing or two.'"

"I didn't know what he meant but I was disappointed when I realized he wasn't going to let me skip my lessons and go sleighing. Besides, I hated history even more than math."

"I didn't say anything but I was confused. The routine had always been to start out with math first, then reading, and spelling. We'd always end with scripture readings from the Bible. Rev'ren told me that mastering those subjects would give me all the tools I needed to be self-taught in anything else I ever wanted to know about. But that day, he diverted from the normal curriculum and began telling me about things that happened a long time ago during slavery times." Veda told Dr. Renee what happened with Reverend Beecham when she was 13, exactly as she now remembered it. She said he sat down and directed her to sit in the chair right next to him. Then he launched into his 'history' lesson.

"Sistuh Veda, let me tell you a little story about my great-grandmama, Olimpia Dupres. She was born a slave in the Creole district of New Orleans. Mama Dupres was just about your age when she was sold away from her mama and the rest of her family to a Mississippi tobacco planter for the sole purpose of breeding. It turned out she was lucky though 'cause her mama had taught her a few Creole tricks to fool the master."

Reverend gave a sly wink and got up from the table and opened a cabinet under the kitchen sink, "Now I'm gon pass along some of my great-grandmama's old tricks to you, chile," he said still smiling.

He grabbed a handful of tiny jars filled with herbs and spices and placed them on the table. Veda said she watched him measure out a little cayenne pepper and some other spices that she didn't recognize. He dumped the mixture into a large bottle that was already filled with a clear liquid.

"This here's an old Creole prevention passed down from my great-grandmama's mama all the way down to my mama. I must have watched her fix up this concoction so many times that one day I asked her what it was," he said and watched Veda as he shook the bottle, "and you know what my mama said?"

Veda shook her head.

"Well, Mama said and I quote … *Ain't gon be droppin' no more nappy-head pickaninnies like you boy to be gettin' on my damn nerves.*"

Veda's eyes widened. She didn't understand a word he said but figured it had to be something for grown-ups to worry about. She didn't know why he was telling this story to her.

"You know I been watching you, don't you girl? Yes Indeed. Appears to me you starting to bud like a sun gold tulip in spring. Old Reverend knows more than you think I do about what's going on, Sistuh Veda. Um hum, sure nuf do," continued Reverend, "Yes Indeed. You be about ready to start your journey into womanhood by now."

"Huh?" Veda gave him a blank stare.

"Don't tell me your mama didn't tell you nothin' at all about the birds and the bees," he said and looked at her in surprise.

"Girl, you know what I'm talking about. A sweet little thing like you. Don't try to act like you and that big, ole fool, Louis ain't been testing out what a man and a woman do to please each other."

Veda stood up and started to slowly back away from him. His outstretched hand offered her the bottle containing the substance he had just concocted. He told her to swallow a large dose of it for protection.

"Here you go, Sistah. Just hold your nose and gulp it all down quick and you won't even taste it."

Her nose was instantly repelled by the strong, pungent smell of the devil's brew that he offered her.

"What is it?" cried Veda in a frightened voice.

"Nothing but plain camphor doused with cayenne and some Cajun spices to knock out the smell and taste, is all. Here girl, drink it up. I ain't got all damn day. I promise it won't hurt you none."

"But what I need to drink this for?"

"Lawd, lawd, lawd chile, I already done told you that. Wasn't you listenin'? Now don't you be acting up on me girl."

He unbuckled his belt and walked towards her taking slow, cautious steps like he would corner a scared rabbit that he planned to cook for supper. That's how Veda pictured herself, as his Sunday supper. She knew he planned to beat her with his belt, the way her mama did whenever she didn't do what she was told right away.

"Please, Rev'ren. Don't beat me," cried Veda as her eyes filled with tears, "I don't wanna drink that ole, nasty-smellin' stuff." She continued to ease backwards away from him and stopped only when her back bumped against a wall.

Reverend laughed out loud, displaying all his stained, crooked teeth.

"Beat you? Girl, I wasn't planning to do no such thing," he said, "I only want to show you what a real woman needs to know to get along in life."

"Well, I ain't no woman," she shouted, "and Sister Charlotta told me how to take care of myself when the bleedin' come. I don't need you to show me nothin'. She say don't let no boy touch me. She say she love me and I was pretty and a good girl. If any boy try to touch me I was to run and get her and she'd give him a lickin' herself no matter what his mama say."

"Well, I ain't no boy and Sister Charlotta ain't here no more," he said, "You're mama begged me to teach you and that's just what I'm about to do, girl."

Veda found his grin disgusting. She was scared but held her ground and argued back at him even though her mama had told her to be respectful towards your elders. But Sister Charlotta had taught her to respect herself first and warned her not to let anybody take advantage of her. Veda cried out at Reverend, "It don't matter, boy or grown man. Sister Charlotta said don't let <u>nobody</u> touch me. Even if it's somebody in my own family. Nobody has a right to hurt me. Not even you Rev'ren. She would get 'em all locked up if they even tried anything."

"Like I said before, your precious Sister Charlotta ain't here no more to do nothin' about it. Now, we can do things the hard way or the easy way."

Veda tried to run towards the front door, but he blocked her path and grabbed her by the shoulders.

"Listen here, girl, you don't want me to have to tell your mama I can't teach you no more. I might have to tell her how I saw you getting fresh in them bushes with Louis and his brothers—that you ain't the good little girl she claimed you was. That the devil done got a hold of you and I got to wash my hands of it, ... wantin' no parts of that ole devil myself, you understand."

"That's a lie," she screamed, "I didn't do no such'a ..."

"You not sassin' me now are you, girl? You calling Reverend a liar? Just who you think your mama's likely to believe? Me or you?"

Veda stopped struggling and considered what he had just said. She knew her mama would believe the Reverend, of course. She'd think Veda was just trying to get out of her wintertime lessons again.

She recalled her mama's reaction when she found out that her period had started. She accused her of messing around with boys and that's why it had started so early. Veda hadn't known anything about a monthly period prior to it starting up. When she asked Sister Charlotta what was happening to her, she sat Veda down and explained the importance of it. Her mama's reaction had been much different.

"Don't bring me no 'ilegitmite babies in ma house if you know what's good for you, girl."

Her mama laid a thick, leather belt on the table and ran her bony finger along the entire length of it.

"You see this here belt, girl? This belt got your name on it. Don't you know, I brought you in this here world and I can take you out. You bed not be bringin' me no bastard gran chillins' in dis here house. The sooner you get married and settled down the better, with your fresh tail self."

Veda had stared down at the floor while her mama ranted and raved. She was afraid to utter a sound, much less ask any questions about why she had suddenly started bleeding from her private area.

She knew she would get a good whipping and anything else her mama could think to heap on her if Reverend told any kind of story at all about her. With a child's mind and without her protector, Sister Charlotta, Veda didn't know what else to do. She snatched the bottle from the table, held her nose, and gulped it down.

Reverend smiled. He explained to her that each month just before her bleeding started and right after it stopped, she had to drink a dose of this special mixture. There'd never be any babies to worry about and no one would ever know a thing.

He switched on the radio to the only R&B station that they could get in Luthersville. Marvin Gaye's current hit song, 'Let's Get It On' was playing. That day Veda didn't learn anything about math, reading, spelling or history from Reverend Beecham.

Once or twice a week or whenever he felt like it, they began the lessons in his bedroom in the rear of the house. Veda focused at the rotating fan on the bedroom ceiling and blocked out what was happening to her. He conducted her lessons on the same four-poster bed he had once shared with her sweet beloved friend and pretend mother, Sister Charlotta. At those times Veda felt like the Devil had gotten hold of her body and soul, and he grinned at her with crooked, tobacco-stained teeth.

Veda covered her face with her hands and sobbed. This time she couldn't fight the tears. Dr. Renee's own eyes watered, but she blinked several times to prevent herself from crying. She handed Veda the box of tissues that sat on her desk. Renee's heart raced and she found it hard to breath, but she needed to stay strong and in control of her emotions. She glanced at the clock and saw that they had gone five minutes past time but she knew she couldn't leave her patient like this.

"Veda, did this really happen or was it just a dream?" asked Dr. Renee.

"It really happened and I dreamt about it for the first time last night. Ever since my aunt called from Luthersville to tell me my mother was dying, I've dreaded the thought of going back there and facing him again. I didn't know why until the dream brought it all back," said Veda, "I've never told this to anyone, Dr. Renee."

"It's good you brought it out in the open Veda. Now the healing process can begin."

"No, you don't understand, Doctor," said Veda through her sobs, "I never made him stop. It went on until I left for college."

"You were just a child, Veda. It wasn't your fault," said Renee in a sympathetic voice, "you mustn't blame yourself." Renee instructed Veda to resume her medication tomorrow evening and gave her a mild sedative to help her sleep that night. She told her to call anytime she needed to talk before her next appointment. Renee didn't think she could feel any worse after watching Susanna suffer all day but she was wrong. Despite her professional training to stay detached during therapy, Veda's revelation had affected her.

After Veda had gone, Renee updated Veda's file with her notes. She now realized that her patient was emotionally scarred because of a depraved individual disguised as a spiritual leader and teacher. She surmised that the abuse Veda experienced in childhood was a major factor causing her clinical depression, along with a combination of other psychological factors that caused stress—the loss of her relationship with her husband and daughter, and now with LaMarr Coleman. Renee diagnosed that Veda suffered from disassociation as well as depression. During her years of sexual abuse, her body was there but her mind went elsewhere. Now that her memories had started to come back Renee would be able to help her work through those painful memories and gently ease her out of a disassociated mental state that subconsciously affected her daily life, her self-esteem and her decisions. Focusing on Veda's diagnosis and treatment helped Renee to calm down and resort to her clinical training of maintaining a professional distance. She could not let her patient's emotional turmoil become her own or she would be no good to anybody. Despite this, she couldn't help feeling drained and heavy hearted from today's session. She didn't think she could return to Shirley Ann's and face Susanna again until she had a few moments to get herself together.

CHAPTER 18

▼

Renee laid her head on the desk in Dr. Stone's office. Her eyes felt filmy from her tears. She didn't hear Deek step quietly into the office. He gently lifted her chin.

"Mrs. Turner said she expected you home by now," he said, "I came over to walk you back."

"How's Susanna?" said Renee and quickly wiped away the signs of crying from her face.

"I didn't see her but Mrs. Turner said she's been sleeping peacefully for the past hour or so."

"Good. I'd better get back before she wakes up."

"I'm sorry if I'm too early. I couldn't wait until eight to see you." Deek pulled up a chair and sat down opposite her. He leaned over the desk and stroked her arm. "I miss you Renee."

His deep voice held a tranquilizing power over her that she didn't want to resist. When Renee got up and came from behind the desk, he rose and drew her to him. She felt the strength of his arms pull her close. She took a tissue from the box sitting on the edge of the desk and dabbed her eyes gently. Deek held his arms around her waist.

"Let me take away your pain for a little while, Doc."

"I wish it were that simple. And that's all I'd have to do."

"It can be," he said and looked down into her eyes, close enough for their lips to barely touch, "just that simple." Deek caressed her face and neck.

Renee blocked out the guilt. She blocked out her feelings of failure as a wife for not being able to connect emotionally with Bill. She blocked out all the stored up pain and frustration she felt at seeing people less fortunate than herself suffer.

She blocked out Veda's pain. Her wounds were far from healed, but the moment she tasted his warm, wet tongue intertwined in hers; everything else but him disappeared. She not only succumbed to his kiss, but prolonged it. Her heart and body could no longer deny her feelings for him. He kissed the tip of her chin then let his tongue travel down her neck. It settled within the hollow at the base of her neck where he covered that tiny space with a rapid succession of delicious kisses. Renee felt her black, silk blouse cling to her breasts as his tongue slid further downward, moistening the silken fabric and warming her entire body. While his tongue explored, she fumbled with the button on his pants and cursed her ineptness for not being able to quickly unbutton them. She gave up on the button and unzipped his slacks. Then boldly slipped her hand inside the pant's zipper and squeezed his hot, throbbing flesh.

Deek grabbed the front of her blouse and yanked it open as several tiny buttons popped off. They stripped frantically and dropped to the velvety pearl-colored carpet on the floor. Wet tongues and glistening sweat moistened their bodies.

Renee felt his penis grow larger and harden next to her naked skin. She caressed his shoulders and outlined the bulging biceps of his upper arms. The pleasure was almost unbearable when the tip of his penis found her opening and thrust within. Her body answered for her as she arched her pelvis against him. She wrapped her arms around his shoulders and welcomed him into the already warm, moist opening between her legs. Renee felt free and uninhibited, shielded from the effects of what anyone else thought or said about her. She moaned his name in utter delight and the pleasure lingered for longer than she thought possible. Afterwards, he collapsed his full weight on her breasts and panted heavily from exhaustion. Renee stroked his back with one hand and with the other slipped her fingers through the soft, short waves of his hair.

CHAPTER 19

▼

"You no-good son-of-a-bitch," Veda shouted.

She brushed passed LaMarr, bursting into his apartment before he had a chance to close the door.

"Look Veda, I'm on my way out. What're you doing here this late? You been drinking or something?"

"Hell no, I ain't been drinking," she said and glared up at him, "Where's that five thousand dollars I gave you several days ago? I was a fool to let you talk me into stealing that money out of petty cash," said Veda, with one hand on her hip and the other pointed at his face.

LaMarr turned his back to her and headed towards his bedroom. He ignored her request to return the money.

"Don't walk away from me when I'm talkin' to you, damnit," she said, following him into the bedroom. She grabbed his elbow and tried to force him to acknowledge her, "Ever since I gave you that money, you've been avoiding me."

"What the hell do you want from me Veda?" LaMarr jerked his arm away from her and straightened the gold lamé lapels on his black silk robe.

Veda planted her feet in front of him, her body only inches away as she looked at him through eyes enflamed in anger. "What the hell do you think I want?" Her voice ripped through the apartment walls, and her chest heaved above folded arms. "I want honesty. Trust. A commitment, goddamnit. I gave up a lot to be with your sorry black ass."

"Ah, shit," said LaMarr, waving her off with his hand, "Here we go again with that same 'ole broken record." He stepped aside and started for the bathroom, but Veda raised her outstretched arm and cut off his exit again.

"You damn straight this is the same broken song. I already wasted five good years on you and what the hell do I have to show for it? Some bitch showing up at my place telling me that I ain't got a snowball's chance in hell of making a future with you."

LaMarr's look of indifference suddenly changed, and she detected something she rarely saw on his face—fear. The corners of his mouth drooped and his eyes quivered—his normal arrogance shaken.

"What ... What're you talking about Veda?" he asked cautiously in a timid-sounding voice that seemed to crack.

"Courtney Hargreaves stopped by my apartment the other night. Claimed she had something important to tell me about you that she couldn't discuss in the office."

Veda hesitated, observing him closely while she let her words sink in. Maybe he'd give himself away and confess that he'd been sleeping with Courtney all this time she thought.

"Oh yeah?" Without looking at her, LaMarr walked over to his dresser and nervously picked up a pack of cigarettes, shook one free and lit it. He then calmly took a long puff before he spoke, still attempting to hide the edginess in his voice, "and what did she have to say about me?"

"Do you think I was gonna stand there and listen to her damn lies?" said Veda, her voice rising. "I trust her even less than I trust you. But just tell me one thing, LaMarr. Are you fucking her?" Just the thought of Courtney Hargreaves made Veda seethe with hatred and jealousy. She couldn't figure out what her man saw in that stupid white bitch. Always twirling her damn hair and tossing it out of her eyes. Lost in her thoughts, she did not notice LaMarr's instance switch back to his air of hostility and confidence until he spoke to her in a condescending tone.

"Look Veda, you knew what I was when we met back in Baltimore. So what makes you think we're in some goddamn Disney movie and you're Cinderella? I ain't that dude on the white horse."

"I'm not tryin' to be no damn Cinderella," she shouted, "All I want is something back after giving you five fuckin' years of my life and thinking we had a future together."

"If you're talking about marriage, you can forget about it, baby. The woman I marry ain't been born yet and her mama's dead." LaMarr brushed past Veda and headed for the bathroom, leaving her standing there, "Now if you don't mind, I gotta get dressed. I'm sure you can find your way to the door."

Veda's eyes burned from her salty tears. She lunged at his back and caught him off guard. LaMarr stumbled and almost fell over but grasped the arm of a chair to balance himself. She climbed on his back and dug her raggedy fingernails into his cheek.

"Ow, Bitch. What the hell's wrong with you?" LaMarr pushed her hands away and rubbed the side of his face.

Veda balled up her tiny fist and swung her arm back. She was about to land a punch to the other side of his face but he grabbed her wrist. Veda watched his expression change from boredom to wrath. His mouth was set in a rigid line. Every muscle in his face looked taut. His eyes were knitted together in a fierce frown, and the red-veined sockets of his eyes were barely visible against the trans-fixed stare from his large black irises. LaMarr had finally lost his composure. He used both hands to hold her down.

"You better calm your ass down before I get mad," he said, tightly squeezing her wrist.

Veda ignored his warning. She was too angry to calm down. She jerked up her knee and was about to thrust it into his groin. He jumped back just in time and grabbed her by the arms and threw her on the bed. The force of his muscular body kept her pinned down. He huddled over her. He frowned into her face and she stared up at him through red, teary eyes.

"Don't you ever try that again, you hear me?" he shouted.

Veda didn't answer. She tried to pull his strong, rigid body away but she could not budge him. She found herself in emotional turmoil, hating and loving him at the same time. Not knowing what else to do, she planted a swift slap across his face. She knew it stung because his cheek turned dark red.

LaMarr raised his hand in the air, his entire body shook while he held her down with the other hand. He took a few deep breaths to try to calm down, then slowly lowered his hand. "You're trying my patience, woman. Get the hell outta here before you get seriously hurt."

LaMarr released her hands and lifted his body off hers. Before he could get too far, she grabbed hold of his neck and pulled him back. He jerked away angrily.

"I said for you to leave now! And don't forget to lock the front door behind you." He stood over her and twisted his mouth in disdain, then tightened the gold belt on his robe as a final gesture.

LaMarr disappeared in the bathroom and closed the door. She heard the running of shower water at full blast. She lay across his bed, her heart aching and her stomach burning in knots. She wanted to tear out of there, wanted to walk away from him forever, but she didn't have the strength. She felt weak, completely worthless and ashamed.

CHAPTER 20

▼

A week had passed. She'd last seen LaMarr on Wednesday night. It was now the following Tuesday morning. LaMarr had still not returned the $5,000 to the firm's petty cash fund and the Price Waterhouse audit was now only a few days away. Veda laid in her bed wide-awake at three o'clock in the morning. Panic gripped at her lungs and thoughts of despair raced through her mind. She had pleaded with LaMarr numerous times but he still showed no signs of returning the money. She even threatened to write a letter to Mr. Davis, confessing the embezzlement and claiming it was LaMarr's idea, but he had laughed in her face. He said he'd just deny having anything to do with that cockamamie scheme. It would be her word against his and who would believe her? Veda believed him. Over the past couple of days it had become very clear to Veda that she no longer had a chance of sharing a future with LaMarr. It wasn't always like that. Veda closed her eyes and thought back to the time when they had first moved in together, when LaMarr was the man she wanted and needed, when he was actually vulnerable to her. She remembered coming home from work one evening and finding their apartment in almost total darkness except for a light coming from the bedroom.

Veda opened the bedroom door and stepped into a darkened room lit only by candles. She detected the soothing sounds of a love ballad playing in the background. The small table next to the bed was set for two. A bottle of Dom Pérignon chilled in a bucket of ice on the table next to two fluted champagne glasses. A bed of vibrant red showed through sheer white canopy drapes that hung from the bedposts. Veda approached the bed and could smell the sweet aroma of roses.

A crystal vase containing a single red rose sat atop her white wicker trunk at the foot of the bed, where she stored the handmade quilts that Aunt Rose had given her when she first left Luthersville after marrying Louis. Veda swung open the sheer canopy from the bed that had not been there when she left for work that morning. This explained the reason that he missed work that day. Her mouth flew open when she saw their four-poster bed covered with layers of red rose petals. At that moment LaMarr entered the bedroom, carrying two dome-covered plates on a tray and wearing the black silk pajamas she gave him for his birthday. It was the first time she had seen him wearing them. He placed the tray on the table. His smile embraced her.

"What's that, baby?" asked Veda pointing to the tray.

"Omelets. I hope you're hungry, honey," he winked.

"For dinner?" she asked.

"Well, that's about the only thing I trusted myself to cook," he laughed and held out his hand for her to join him at the table. They ate, sipped champagne, and spoke only with their eyes. The omelets were surprisingly very good, though his omelets were more like scrambled eggs with chopped onions, peppers, and sausage. Still, Veda had never known LaMarr to prepare anything in the kitchen before, other than sandwiches. She wondered what other talents he had tucked away and smiled at him, seductively.

When they finished eating, he cleared away the dishes then disappeared into the bathroom, carrying a small covered plate with him. Veda heard the tub being filled with water. When she peeked in LaMarr invited her into a tub full of steamy rich suds. She quickly removed her clothes and tossed them aside on the floor. He broke off a handful of pastel-tinted sweet peas from a glass vase and dropped the petals into the tub of foamy water. Veda sniffed their sweet fragrance and sank into the tub. LaMarr sat on the bathtub ledge. He squeezed the sponge and let the soapy, warm water trickle down her back.

"Why don't you join me, baby?" Veda smiled at him playfully, "The water's nice and warm."

LaMarr took off his pajamas and carefully maneuvered his tall, lean frame into the tub and sat down opposite her. They drank champagne and languished in the tub. LaMarr reached over to the dessert plate sitting on the ledge and fed her tinted meringue morsels and fondant-frosted petits fours that he had picked up from the gourmet bakery that afternoon.

After their bath, Veda slipped into a white satiny soft gown that clung to her curves as she moved. LaMarr stood still and stared at her for several moments. Then, he quickly whisked away most of the rose petals from the bed and pulling her to him, gently lowered her down. He slipped the strap of her gown from her shoulders and began covering her neck with kisses. In no time, the nightgown was off.

LaMarr poured droplets of champagne between the crevices of her breast and on top of both nipples. He licked the rich-tasting champagne from each one and felt her nipples stiffen. He traced the flow of champagne with his tongue and gently licked off every drop. Veda tingled all over from his touch. She admired his firm, muscular body and traced it with her fingertips. She felt his heartbeat quicken and his muscles tighten as their lovemaking intensified. Afterwards, she felt a longing for him and the security that comes from feeling truly loved by someone. LaMarr wrapped his arms around her and she fell asleep snuggled in his arms.

Veda's eyes snapped open as she returned to the reality that faced her now. That memory of her and LaMarr was a lifetime ago. Today, she felt devastated. Her obsessive love for LaMarr that had grown over five long years turned into intense hatred in just a few short days. She no longer wanted LaMarr, but she had to have that money back. She couldn't lose her job over him and Lord knows she couldn't do time. Veda knew she'd have to show him she meant business.

She sat up in bed and clutched at the covers as an idea began to take shape in her mind. The Sullivan takeover! For the last several days everybody in the office had been talking about the ongoing court battles during Sullivan Investment Corp's management buyout of a local communications internet company. The partners were impressed with LaMarr's shrewd handling of the negotiations. The firm stood to make close to a million dollars if LaMarr successfully navigated the deal in his client's favor.

Veda jumped out of bed. "I'ma get this sucka," she said aloud with a new gleam in her eyes. She didn't even bother to take out her hairpins or change out of the Chinese red silk pajamas she had on. She glanced out her bedroom window and saw that it was drizzling outside. She threw on a London Fog raincoat and pushed a large floppy hat down over her head.

She inhaled several deep breaths and let each one out slowly to try to calm down the way Dr. Renee had taught her in therapy. That didn't work. She still felt tense and full of anger as she drove. Nothing could steady her nerves, not the lull from her windshield wipers or the solitude of the wet, deserted streets at three thirty in the morning. Even though it was the middle of August, the night air felt brisk from the rain. She turned the heat to its lowest setting. Soon the warmth from the heating vents embraced her and she began to feel a little better. Despite the rain, Veda drove about ten miles per hour past the speed limit. Every five minutes she considered turning around and going back home, but didn't. She knew what she had to do now.

Traffic lights flashed yellow at an intersection up ahead. She slowed down and stopped just as the light changed to red. As she sat at the stoplight, Veda heard the echo of Rap lyrics long before her rearview mirror caught the reflection of an emerald-green, late-model Chrysler LeBaron. The LeBaron screeched to a sudden halt in the lane next to her. Two young black males sat in the front seat and three more were crowded in the back. The driver wore a dark hooded sweatshirt. The one in the passenger seat had his head shaven. His eyes gleamed and his grin widened when he turned around and caught Veda looking at him. She quickly faced the road ahead and willed the red light green. Veda watched them out of the corner of her eye. She could only make out dark silhouettes of the three teenagers seated in the back. They rocked their shoulders and bopped their heads to the loud music.

She recalled hearing about a scam on the news recently whereby criminals rear ended a driver's car on purpose to force them out of the car. Then they robbed the victim, stole their car, and in some cases shot them in cold blood. Her muscles began to tense up as she watched the young men singing and bouncing in their car. She pressed the lock button to automatically lock all her doors. While waiting for the light to change, she watched as the LeBaron eased past her. She saw the driver toss a dark object out the window. The object hit the wet pavement with a loud clank. Before the light turned green, the LeBaron sped off and left her range of view within seconds. Veda wondered if they had thrown out a weapon. Suppose someone found it? Perhaps even a child. She felt frightened and glanced around first before unlocking her doors. Then she stepped out of the car to see what the driver had thrown away.

She stared at the gun lying on the ground and thought how no place was safe nowadays. The image of that ugly thug who broke into LaMarr's apartment almost two weeks ago came clearly into focus. That gun might come in handy she thought if she ever found herself in danger again. Veda looked around to see if anyone was watching, then picked up the gun and stuffed it deep inside her purse. She stayed alert and on guard as she drove through the city beneath a dreary night sky that periodically rumbled from distant bursts of thunder. Ten minutes later she parked in front of the deserted office building where she worked and used her night passkey to get it.

As she rode up the elevator, she mentally went over her plan to break into LaMarr's account and mess with the Sullivan files so he would lose the account. As careless as LaMarr was about security, she would try something as simple as his birth date or his name to get in if he had already changed the password like he was supposed to do every 10 days. She sat down at her desk and booted up the computer, then logged in using the old password just for the hell of it. Veda beamed when she discovered that LaMarr and Courtney hadn't bothered to change the password to the Sullivan case files. This would be easier than she thought since she didn't even have to figure out a new password. Veda was able to easily access all the documents pertaining to LaMarr's case for the Sullivan Investment Corp's takeover. She put her plan into motion and quickly changed vital information that would sabotage the negotiations, which were due to conclude at that morning's nine o'clock hearing. LaMarr was in for a big surprise and she'd let him know just how much power she had to ruin his life if he didn't return the money. Five years of being a fool for him hadn't been a total waste after all. He'd taught her how to be cold and ruthless in order to get what she wanted, and how to screw others before they screwed you. She was feeling pleased with herself. She printed out the revised court papers. She knew she would find the folder marked 'Sullivan' stacked neatly on his desk. He kept papers that he needed for court the next day conveniently nearby. Veda switched her copies with the papers Courtney had prepared for the case, then she headed back home to get some sleep. In the morning, she'd call in sick and stay clear of the line of fire when LaMarr realized what had happened. She'd call him up later that morning and tell him to have the money in her hands tomorrow before the two o'clock deadline on 'next day' deposits. Then she might or might not give him the correct figures to fix the problem with the Sullivan account. She would decide that later. Veda smiled the entire way back home, pleased with herself. It had taken her only thirty minutes to screw up his life whereas he had taken five years to destroy hers. But she was ready to fight back now and would do whatever it took to get back in control and mend her self-esteem. The emotionally-dependent, love-obsessed fool was dead. The strong, competent, 'kick-ass' sister she once knew was back in the saddle. That night she stayed awake gloating.

"Hey, girl. You up?" said Veda between blowing out a thin puff of cigarette smoke.

"Veda? Are you crazy? Girl it's only six o'clock," yawned Natasha through the telephone, "I got another half-hour to sleep."

"Girl, you ain't gonna believe what I just did Natasha. You know that money I took out of petty cash for LaMarr?" She squashed her cigarette out in an ashtray beside her bed and pushed her knees up under her chin like she used to do when she was a teenager.

"You mean the money that's gon get your ass put in jail 'cause His Highness ain't about to get up off no money, especially not to save your ass. I don't mean to talk about your man but …"

"Girl, please! He ain't my man no more. I'm a get that money back today."

Veda filled Natasha in on what she had done, and told how she had changed all the information on the contracts that LaMarr had drawn up for his client. "Hey Girl, why don't you call in sick too. Come on over here and help me. I need somebody to calm my nerves so I can be ready to phone LaMarr when he gets outta court at eleven."

"Well, I guess I could call in sick," said Natasha, "since I do have cramps. Besides, I ain't got nothin' to do at work today, except play Solitaire and read my new paperback," she yawned, "I should be there about nine. Want me to stop at McDonald's and get us some breakfast?"

The word cramps had distracted Veda. She was silent, lost in her own thoughts.

"Veda? Girl, you still there?"

"What did you just say Natasha?" Veda rubbed her temples and her voice went from lively to somber.

Natasha sighed, "I said do you want me to bring some food from McDonald's on my way over there? Do you want …"

"No, not that. About cramps. Girl, I just realized I don't remember the last time I had my period. Hold on." She left Natasha in mid sentence.

Veda dropped the receiver and jumped up from the bed. She retrieved the calendar from the kitchen wall and nervously flipped back through the months. She spotted the red x marked on her calendar two months ago. Hell, she thought. I can't be pregnant. Veda picked up the telephone receiver.

"Natasha, I'm late, girl!" She half shouted.

"Damn Veda. Your shit just goes from bad to worse. Guess I better pick up a kit too," said Natasha, "Umph, umph, umph. Pregnant and in jail."

"Girl, please. I can't be pregnant. You know I had my tubes tied right after Sherrelle was born."

"I don't know, Veda, you remember my girl, LaKeeta? She ended up pregnant after she got her tubes tied. She went back to the clinic and kicked that doctor's ass too. She said they tried to tell her the procedure wasn't 100 percent effective. Only abstinence is a sure thing."

"Hell, after all these years. I don't believe it."

"Well, I'm no doctor but they say it's possible."

"Damn. Damn. Damn," said Veda, shaking her head.

"Girl, that's some messed up shit. Guess you can't fall no harder. Your ass is already on the floor."

"Hold up Natasha. Maybe I can use this pregnancy to my advantage," smiled Veda to herself, "Never mind about that pregnancy kit for now, but bring some food. I'll put on a fresh pot of coffee. See you in a few." Veda hung up the phone and rushed to get dressed.

She felt nervous and excited at the same time. Now she couldn't wait to call him. If she were in fact pregnant she could make LaMarr pay for a long time—make his life a living hell and the court system would help her do it. These days the system didn't put up with Deadbeat Dads and what other kind of a father could LaMarr be, she thought. She might even be able to get him locked up, knowing what a selfish, cheapskate tightwad he really was.

When Natasha walked through the door a few hours later, she found Veda sitting on the living room couch with her legs stretched out on top the table, smoking a cigarette, sipping a cup of coffee, and watching TV. Natasha dropped the McDonald's bag on the coffee table.

"Girl, you look like shit. You must be pregnant."

Veda glanced away from the TV for a second and gave her friend a wicked look. A spattering of freckles was easily visible on Natasha's cream-colored complexion, mixed with only a hint of cocoa. Veda saw that Natasha's smile was genuine, stretched across her pretty face. Her auburn-tinted extensions were pulled back into a ponytail.

"There's a pot of strong coffee in the kitchen," said Veda, deep in thought.

Natasha swayed across the room in a pair of tight-fitting stretch jeans. Veda looked at Natasha and rolled her eyes upward. That's Natasha, thought Veda as she shook her head at her friend. That girl sure thinks she's all that. Natasha poured herself a cup of coffee and talked to Veda from the kitchen.

"Girl, I been thinking. Maybe you better not mess with that crazy-ass LaMarr. I hear he's into some pretty wild shit."

"What're you talking about?" Veda looked away from the TV and gave Natasha her full attention.

"Well, you know how folks like to gossip. And I don't have any proof but they say LaMarr may have paid somebody to off this dude a couple of weeks ago. Personally, I don't know nothing about it." Natasha came back into the kitchen and dug through the bag for her sausage and egg McMuffin. The food smelled good but Veda realized she wasn't hungry. Her stomach felt tied up in knots.

"Girl, maybe you should just go to Mr. Davis and spell it all out. Just tell him you had some money problems and you'll pay everything back in installments," said Natasha between bites, "You've been working there a long time. He might not even press charges if you tell him you're pregnant. Just be up front with him and present it like that. That's what I'd do, girl. Lord knows I wouldn't mess with no LaMarr Coleman if I was you."

"You expect me to just lay down and play dead?" shouted Veda, "Hell no. I already lost too damn much because of LaMarr. He's gonna pay me back that money and he's gonna pay it back before the audit on Monday. I'm not letting him get away with nothin'." Veda got up from the couch and started pacing back and forth. She checked the clock and saw that it was almost time to make that call to LaMarr's office.

"Girl, just what are you going to do if he tells Davis that you sabotaged his case this morning? Veda you're just not thinking straight. This pressure is getting to you, Babe. Now, I told you what you need to do."

Veda's eyes darted frantically as she tried to mentally lay out all her options.

"And what happens if he still refuses to pay the money back?" asked Natasha. She took out the other sausage-egg McMuffin, "You not gonna eat this?"

When Veda shook her head no, Natasha took a big bite into the sandwich. Veda watched her friend gulp down the other sandwich and wash it down with orange juice and coffee.

"Umm umm, that sure was good. I was starving, girl."

"That's it," said Veda suddenly and raced into the kitchen, "I got something that'll fix his ass if he don't wanna act right. Hump, bet' not mess with me."

Natasha followed Veda into the kitchen. Veda searched the cabinet under her kitchen sink and pushed aside cleaning containers and disinfectants until she found what she had been looking for. Veda smiled as she held up a box of D-Con Ready Mixed Bait kit for killing mice and rats.

"Girl, have you lost your damn mind?" said Natasha in complete shock, "You can't be thinking what I think you thinking."

"All I got to say is, he better do the right thing." Veda read the instructions on the back of the box and ignored Natasha.

"You have really lost it, that's all I got to say," said Natasha with one hand on her hip and shaking her head.

"Well, I'm not gonna kill the fool," said Veda, briefly looking up from the box, "especially not until he gives me back my damn money." Veda studied the warning label then held the box out to show Natasha who was still looking at her as if she had lost her mind. "See Natasha, I only need to slip enough in his food to make him sick. Then he'll realize just how far I might go if I have to."

"Honey, that shrink of yours ain't doing you a damn bit of good," said Natasha, "'cause you've gone completely crazy." Natasha rinsed out her cup and placed it in the sink. She sat down at the kitchen table and rested her cheek in her hand. She flipped through the pages of an outdated fashion magazine, realizing it was no use arguing with Veda.

Both women sat in silence by the telephone for the next five minutes until the clock turned eleven. Just as Veda was about to pick up the telephone to call the office, the phone rang. Veda and Natasha looked at each other. After the third ring, Veda picked it up.

"Yeah," she said into the receiver.

"Bitch, what the hell's the matter with you?"

Natasha heard the screams coming through the phone. She knew it was LaMarr. Veda took a deep breath and tried to sound in control. She had already rehearsed exactly what she would say.

"Just have the money in my hands by noon tomorrow," she said calmly and with authority, "That gives me plenty of time to make a deposit to the firm's petty cash fund before two. Everything'll be straight when I hand over the books to the auditors on Monday."

"Look here, 'cause I'm only going to say this once, Veda," he whispered into the phone. His calmness frightened her more than his yelling when he spoke. "Don't try to fuck with me bitch. You're lucky I was able to turn things around this morning. The shareholders at Sullivan got a nice piece of change and I made the firm look good."

"Look baby, I'm sorry about messing up your files but you left me no choice," said Veda, taking a different tactic. He had thrown her off-guard and things weren't turning out the way she expected. She decided to take a softer approach. Veda searched for the right words to disarm him. "We don't have to be at each other's throats. Baby, we've been together more than five years. Why do things have to end like this between us?" Veda tried to fight back the tears but her emotions resisted her efforts and the sobs broke through. "Baby, I have something important to tell you," she said through her tears, "LaMarr, I think I'm pregnant. I can't go to jail." Veda held her breath and waited for his reaction. After a few seconds he broke the silence.

"How do I know it's mine? I don't even remember the last time I was with you," he said in a nasty sarcastic tone.

Veda felt her face grow hot from anger. "I can't believe you could say that to me, after all I've done for you," she screamed and shot straight up out of the chair. Veda was so angry she wanted to rip the phone out the wall.

"Well, if you are pregnant, my advice is you better go someplace and get that shit scraped or sucked out. And while you're at it, you better get yourself a good lawyer." LaMarr hung up abruptly in her ear before she had a chance to say anything else.

Veda heard the phone go dead. She couldn't believe he hung up on her. She collapsed on the chair and sobbed into Natasha's arms.

"I told you, girl. That man ain't shit. You better go talk to Mr. Davis before Monday, like I said. I don't see no other way out of this mess," said Natasha, comforting Veda with gentle pats on her back.

"Well I do," said Veda. She jumped up and grabbed the box of rat poison that she had left on the table. She shook the box of poison at Natasha, "And like I said, I'm gonna make that joker pay."

CHAPTER 21

▼

Natasha's co-worker, Delilah D'Arcy, wanted to make sure she had all the facts right before facing Veda's ex-boyfriend, the notorious LaMarr D. Coleman. Delilah sat on the Metro and slowly re-read the phony letter that Veda had typed up on professional-looking letterhead. Veda told her this is what they would use to trick LaMarr.

Universal Trust Home Mortgage
P.O. Box 742, Tampa, Florida 33631

Ms. Delilah D'Arcy
1220 Larson Street, SE
Washington, D. C. 20019

RE: UTHM No.—448902 NOTICE OF INTENT TO FORECLOSE

Dear Mortgagor:

This letter is to notify you that your account has been forwarded to our attorney for immediate initiation of foreclosure proceedings.

Once a loan has gone into foreclosure, nothing but FULL REINSTATE-MENT in CERTIFIED FUNDS will be accepted, including all late fees and attorney's fees and costs.

You will be notified as to the date the property needs to be vacated if this loan is not brought current prior to the sale date which is scheduled to take place at public auction in thirty days. The amount due to bring your loan current and avoid the sale of your property at public auction is $10,072.89.

Please direct any questions you may have to our attorney at Walcott & Benson who is handling the foreclosure. The address and telephone number appear below.

Sincerely,

Ms. Gloria Atkins, Foreclosure Department.

The letter certainly looked authentic to Delilah. Except for the recipient's name, Veda had copied the entire foreclosure letter word for word from one of her firm's client files.

Delilah was glad the letter was only a fake and that she wouldn't really be tossed out on the streets in thirty days. At twenty-three years old, she still lived at home with her parents and didn't have to worry about paying a mortgage, although, things had been getting tense at home since she dropped out of college and took a temporary receptionist job at CityWide Insurance Company downtown. Her father had issued new threats again last month about what would happen if she didn't straighten up her act. But he had issued that same threat too many times for her to take it seriously. Her father had her whole life mapped out in his mind. For starters, she was to check into a new six-month drug treatment program and begin attending church. Then he wanted her to finish out her last year of college and do something meaningful with her life. More than anything Delilah knew he wanted her to be someone he could be proud of instead of someone he saw as a disgrace to the family name.

Delilah had quit college and got a job in order to feed her worsening drug habit. She hated the school he had insisted that she attend—Georgetown University, and had been failing anyway. She'd never live up to her older sister Rachael's accomplishments as a doctor, so why bother. Delilah told herself working at that minimum-wage job would only be a temporary nuisance until the trust fund that her grandmother left her kicked in when she turned twenty-five.

Last night at Veda Simms's place, over several bottles of Zinfandel and Chinese carryout, Veda and Natasha had meticulously gone over the plan. The first step was for Delilah to take the foreclosure letter to LaMarr's office and seek his legal advice. Veda had promised Delilah a hundred bucks to go through with this plan, as a way of getting back at her ex-boyfriend. Delilah figured she could always use a little extra cash so she agreed to do it.

As soon as Veda met Natasha's co-worker, Veda couldn't believe the things Natasha had said about her. Delilah was striking, with thickly lashed sea-green eyes, long brown hair tinted with henna, and a body any woman would kill for. And as if that weren't enough, Delilah had been blessed with a flawless honey brown complexion. Veda hated her the moment she laid eyes on her, despite Natasha's claims, but she could overlook her own jealousy to get what she wanted. Veda realized that Delilah was the only person who could pull this thing off. For one, LaMarr had never before seen Delilah. And two, she was a knock-out. LaMarr fancied himself as a ladies' man and had a weakness for beautiful women. Veda knew that he wouldn't be able to resist Delilah. And it would be the ultimate insult if he happened to discover the truth about Delilah. It was obvious to Veda that, her relationship with LaMarr was now over. Nothing could breathe life back into that corpse. Veda felt she had nothing more to lose. Her intent was to show LaMarr that she meant business. It would be a huge mistake on his part not to take her seriously this time.

Veda had suggested that Delilah wear something sexy to get his attention right away, so Delilah decided on a short, form-fitting red knit dress with spaghetti straps and matching bolero jacket. Sheer, black stockings covered her shapely legs. She had no problems walking in black, ankle-strapped stiletto heels. After all, she'd had plenty of practice playing dress-up in her Mama's clothes from the time she was five years old until she turned 13. She wore her hair down and it fell in soft waves almost to the middle of her back. Delilah felt the stares from several men on the train. She knew she looked good.

The conductor announced over the intercom that the train had reached Farragut North, her stop. She pushed past the other commuters to get off.

A tall, handsome, well-dressed man with a coffee cup in his hand greeted her just as she entered the law office of Davis & Bookerman. Delilah figured he had to be LaMarr Coleman from the description Veda had given her.

"Can I help you, Miss?" he asked in a smooth, deep voice.

"I think I need a lawyer," said Delilah.

"Well, you found one," he said, extending his hand out to her. "LaMarr D. Coleman, *Esquire* at your service." He smiled so broadly she could see nearly all of his straight, white teeth, then LaMarr led her to his office.

She was immediately impressed with his sense of style and taste from the designer clothes he had on to the professionally-decorated office. He invited her to have a seat while he sat at his desk and leaned forward, giving her his full attention. "So, how can I help you Miss...?"

"Delilah D'Arcy." She reached into her purse and pulled out the phony foreclosure letter. Delilah managed a few fake tears to add some drama to her performance. This act should be worth more than a hundred bucks, she figured. Thoughts of what she'd probably do once she got her hands on that money began to torment her. Delilah forced herself to stay focused on LaMarr and carry out Veda's plan. She dabbed at her cheek until she was sure he noticed her distress.

After briefly scanning her letter, LaMarr Coleman handed it back to her. "I sure can't see a sister as fine as you in a homeless shelter," he said and shook his head, "Do you have anything of value that you could use as collateral Miss D'Arcy?"

"Mr. Coleman, I work as a temp for an insurance company here in D. C.," explained Delilah, "I'm not even a permanent employee so I don't get benefits or job security. I could be replaced any time by another temp or an agency with better rates. So in answer to your question, ... No, I don't have anything of value."

LaMarr smiled. "Don't worry, Delilah ... do you mind if I call you Delilah," he said, "I can still take care of your problems."

"How?" she asked.

"Let me worry about that. I've got contacts all over this city, and from New York to Miami."

"Maybe I shouldn't have come here. I don't know what I was thinking," she said and got up from the chair, like she was about to leave, "I can't even pay your retainer fee, Mr. Coleman. Much less your legal expenses."

"LaMarr. Call me LaMarr. And please sit back down," he said, motioning with his hand, "Delilah, have you ever heard of pro bono work?"

She shook her head no.

"Well, it's Italian and it means, 'for the good' of others. So you don't have to pay me one red cent. It would be my pleasure to help you out as part of my pro bono work."

"Thanks, Mr. Coleman, but I don't think so. I'm sure you'd be expecting me to pay you back in some way." Veda had told her to play hard to get. She had said LaMarr thrived on a challenge.

LaMarr stroked his mustache with a single well-manicured finger.

"You know Delilah, you look familiar. Have we ever met?" asked LaMarr, leaning forward in his chair.

Delilah studied his face for a moment. He was using a common pick-up line but now that he mentioned it, he did seem familiar to her as well but she couldn't place where or when she might have met him. Probably, at a nightclub she thought.

"I don't think so, Mr. Coleman" she said, and decided to stick to Veda's script.

"Hmm, I wonder," said LaMarr. He narrowed his eyes and gazed at her with a pensive smile. Delilah felt naked and exposed under his inspection.

"Wonder what?"

"If you'd consider modeling for *Ebony Silk*. One of my business associates publishes the magazine. It's classy and full of nothing but beautiful black sisters like yourself. You'd be perfect for *Ebony Silk*."

"Are the models nude?"

"Semi. But like I said, it's a very tasteful publication. And who knows, it might open some doors. The pay ain't bad either," he grinned, "Think about it, Delilah."

"Yeah, okay, I'll think about it."

LaMarr smiled and leaned closer to her. "Did I tell you, you look breathtaking in red," he whispered, "but I guess you hear that all the time."

Delilah felt herself falling under his seductive spell and almost forgot what she was supposed to do next. She got up and started towards the door. "I'd better leave, Mr. Coleman. I shouldn't be wasting your time like this."

LaMarr sprang up from his chair and grabbed the door handle before she could reach it. Veda was right. This 'playing hard to get' routine works, she thought, suppressing a smile.

"I meant what I said, Delilah. I can turn this thing around with your mortgage company. I know a few people at Walcott & Benson. And you don't have to pay me anything."

Now for the good part, Delilah got ready. All of a sudden she let her feet give away from under her. She anticipated he would catch her just in time and he did. LaMarr held her up in his strong arms.

"I'm sorry," said Delilah, in a feigned weak voice, "I've been too upset to eat after opening that letter yesterday. Looks like it's starting to catch up with me."

"Well, we can certainly do something about that too," he said, "I know a place that has an excellent champagne brunch. It's not too far from here, called La Maison de Marcel."

So far everything had worked out just as Veda predicted it would.

LaMarr led her downstairs to the parking garage to get his car. He held her hand in his and walked with a confident, superior attitude, ignoring clerks and staff people who she figured he probably regarded as of no importance to him. As they approached the car, LaMarr removed the automatic lock release from his jacket and clicked the button to unlock the doors to his black Lexus Coupe. When he smoothed the hairs of his mustache and flashed a smile at her, Delilah wanted to melt in his arms. He was good-looking, dressed sharp, and had a fine ride. She had to keep reminding herself that she was only there to do this job for Veda and get paid.

The noontime city traffic was backed up as usual and barely moved. LaMarr reached under his seat and grabbed a bag of what looked like marijuana. He placed a square of paper on his thigh, and filled it with marijuana. Then he rolled, twisted and licked the ends to keep them together. Veda had said LaMarr was a risk-taker but this was just plain stupid, she thought. It was in the middle of the day, and he didn't really know her. Suppose she had been an undercover cop? What would he have done then? Once the fumes started to drift throughout the car, Delilah felt her body begin to tingle at the mere possibility of getting high. A little voice inside her head told her to demand that he stop the car and let her out. But another little voice, the stronger one, urged her to stay.

LaMarr took a long, deep puff before passing it to Delilah. She took two puffs and passed it back. She could see why Veda said LaMarr Coleman was a man who took risks. It was broad daylight and they were in the middle of city traffic, smoking a blunt. In D. C., a cop could pull up along side them at any moment. The danger thrilled her. She knew it was a crazy thing to do but LaMarr didn't seem the least bit concerned. The effects of the blunt suddenly hit her. She felt lighthearted and completely uninhibited.

Just that morning, she had promised her mother that she'd go to a Narcotics Anonymous meeting this morning with her sponsor, but that probably wouldn't happen now. Her father always said drugs were like an elevator that only went down. He told her she could get off at any floor without hitting bottom. Delilah hadn't hit the ground floor yet. Her parents were always there to bail her out of trouble. They had already spent thousands of dollars on treatment programs but nothing helped. Years ago her Dad wanted to try tough love tactics, but her mother wouldn't let him. Mama told him that she wouldn't be able to stand putting her baby out in the streets to fend for herself. She said there were too many wolves out there in the streets, but what Mama didn't understand was that the wolf was right there, inside of her. Delilah knew she had free room and board and getting her hands on drugs was easy to enable her habit. She wasn't ready to get off the elevator no matter how many times her mother cried and pleaded, and her father threatened to disown her and throw her out. Delilah wanted that feeling she got from getting high. That feeling that made all the pain from life's disappointments and her inability to be what everybody expected, melt away. Smoking that blunt had been a big mistake. Now, all Delilah could think about was getting a hit. She wanted to hurry up and get this stupid ass scheme over with so she could get her hundred bucks from Veda. Delilah didn't think of herself as a junkie because she didn't shoot up and she went to work everyday. Well, almost everyday. Since she worked for a temp agency, she was never at one place too long. She'd managed to hold it together for several months but now the pressure to be "perfect" was beginning to wear her down. One day she'd get off the elevator and quit but not right now.

LaMarr glanced at Delilah, then turned his attention back to the road as he spoke, "You act like you're somewhere miles away over there, beautiful lady. Weed makes most women I know act silly as shit. They can't stop running their damn mouth, but not you, I see."

"Guess I still got a lot on my mind. With the house thing and all," she lied.

"Look baby, you don't have to sweat that. Just take that damn letter and rip it up. I'll have everything all fixed for you by tomorrow," he grinned.

LaMarr pulled into the circular driveway of a row of late eighteen century townhouses and dropped his car keys in the valet's hand. The entire cluster of four-story townhouses had been renovated a few years ago and converted into a historic hotel and restaurant. The uniformed doorman held open the entranceway's stately double doors for them to enter. Delilah looked around in awe. She was impressed. LaMarr offered her his elbow as he escorted her inside.

CHAPTER 22

▼

As they walked through the long emerald-green carpeted foyer LaMarr pointed out the objects as if he were a museum curator. He identified a popular Rembrandt reproduction and a well-known work by 19th-century French impressionist Edgar Degas called <u>The Dancing Class</u> that featured a group of tutu-clad ballerinas. Oval-shaped porcelain-framed mirrors hung on the foyer walls and shared alternating wall space with reproductions of Renaissance paintings by Botticelli, Raphael, and da Vinci while violin music played in the background. Delilah felt regal and held her head high as she glided by onlookers, trying to appear unfazed by her surroundings when in fact she had never been anywhere this elegant in her life. Floor-length champagne-colored silk taffeta draperies with ruffle-trimmed swags framed all the windows. The entrance that led to the main dining area had *Trompe l'oeil* detailing painted on the doors. They entered the dining room and Delilah sat down on a Regency sofa upholstered in pale green silk while LaMarr went to speak to the maître d.' She glanced up at the 20-foot ceilings supported by marbleized columns and noticed that there was a balcony area that accommodated additional seating, but all the tables appeared to be occupied. LaMarr returned and sat across from her in an elaborately carved Gothic-period armchair while they waited for their table. "It won't be long now," he smiled, "I gave the maître d' an extra incentive to find us a table." Before their conversation even got started, Delilah excused herself and instead of going to the ladies room as she said, she looked for somewhere private to call Veda. She spotted a darken nook near the rest rooms and took out her cell phone. Delilah called Veda and Natasha, as planned, to let them know where LaMarr had taken her.

Veda said they would be there in less than thirty minutes. Delilah hurried back to the lounge before LaMarr became suspicious.

The main dining room's decor was richly decorated with nineteenth century flair. An antique baby grand piano stood in the far left corner of the massive room. An 1820 Palladian-style mahogany bookcase had been placed at the opposite end of the room. Statues of Greek goddesses stood in strategic locations, and French screens served as room dividers to create a cozy, secluded atmosphere in some areas of the dining room. All the furniture still displayed their original antique finish. Bouquets of fresh cut flowers adorned every accent table that lined the room. Based on the reproduction paintings, antique French tapestries, and gilt-framed mirrors that covered the walls, Delilah could only imagine what the hotel's bedroom suites upstairs must be like.

"This place is like a mansion," said Delilah, scanning her surroundings.

"I knew you'd like it, baby," he said, smiling, "Just wait until you see the rest of the hotel."

They waited less than fifteen minutes before a hostess came to escort them to their table. The hostess led them through a narrow passageway that was embellished with foliage and climbing white roses. It looked like they were moving to yet another building. Delilah was speechless; everything was so beautiful. This section of the hotel housed the very romantic and elegant French restaurant called La Maison de Marcel.

In La Maison de Marcel, the hotel's smaller dining room, each table was tucked away in its own secluded hideaway. The burning flame of a single candle on each table illuminated their faces. Tables and chairs were cloaked in mauve brocade fabric. White drapes of raw silk billowed from ceiling to the floor. A wall-sized mural, depicting a landscape overlooking the Seine River in Paris, added a surrealistic touch to the room. Delilah heard classical piano music playing. She figured it was low so it would not impede the guests' intimate conversations.

LaMarr and Delilah's table held a crystal vase of white hyacinths, coral-tinted sweet peas, and snow-white daffodils as its centerpiece. Delilah thought his cologne blended in nicely with the floral arrangement's naturally mild, pleasant scent. LaMarr reached across the table and kissed her full, crimson lips.

"Where're you from, Delilah?" asked LaMarr, staring into her sea-green eyes.

"Right here in Washington, D. C."

"Really?" he flinched in surprise, "You look foreign. Where're your people from?"

"I'm actually a mixture of African, French, and Native American, if that's what you're asking."

"Aha, so that's were that unique beauty of yours comes from—a gift from 3 continents."

After a few minutes had passed, LaMarr glanced at his watch then looked around impatiently for someone to serve them. One waiter walked back and forth between a few tables. But no one approached their table.

"What the hell's his damn problem," said LaMarr as he glared at the waiter without taking his eyes off the man, "I know damn well that asshole sees me sitting over here."

LaMarr momentarily turned his attention back to Delilah. She felt her muscles tighten in anger at his crude remark about the waiter. This was not the type of place to start acting up, she thought. She hoped he didn't notice the sudden change of expression on her face. Delilah looked across the room and spotted Veda and Natasha being seated a few tables away from them. They both were dressed in dark conservative business suits, wide-brimmed hats and dark sunglasses. The two of them looked like complete idiots she thought, as she tried not to laugh. She began to make small talk with LaMarr in an attempt to distract him from noticing their waiter's neglect. It was useless. She was discovering that the worst thing somebody could do was to ignore LaMarr Coleman.

"If that bastard's not over here in the next ten seconds, I'm a get up from this goddamn table and yank his ass over here," said LaMarr between gritted teeth.

"Good afternoon, Monsieur and Madame," said the waiter with a slight accent, "My name is Guilliame and I will be your waiter. Our specials for today are ..."

"Skip all that bullshit," snapped LaMarr and waved his hand.

"Will you be selecting from the champagne buffet or would you care to see the menu?" asked the waiter.

"I think I'll just have the champagne buffet" Delilah chimed in first.

"Of course, Madame. And you Monsieur? Will you need more time to decide?"

"No. We've had more than enough time to decide, sitting here for the last twenty minutes. Just bring me a couple of Bloody Marys," ordered LaMarr, "and make 'em strong."

"I'm afraid the bar is not yet open, Monsieur," explained the waiter nervously, "Our bartender is not due to arrive until three today."

"Say what?" LaMarr cocked his head to the side and squinted his eyes at the waiter; "All this fancy shit in here and nobody can throw together a Bloody Mary? Damn." He looked at Delilah, "Can you believe that shit?"

"Maybe we're a bit early for alcoholic beverages," offered Delilah in a whispered voice.

"Then why the hell are they serving a goddamn champagne brunch?" yelled LaMarr.

A few heads turned to look over in their direction. His voice carried like an echo throughout the small dining area. Delilah was embarrassed, but for some reason an unexplained fear of LaMarr kept her from openly criticizing his rude behavior. He seemed to be able to instantaneously transform himself from the civilized, Dr. Jekyll to the raging lunatic, Mr. Hyde.

"Very well, Monsieur. I will see what we can do," said the waiter and hurried off. After a short while, the waiter returned and told LaMarr that someone would fix his Bloody Mary directly. He slipped away immediately before any more comments or criticisms reached his ears.

"Asshole," said LaMarr, shaking his head.

Delilah didn't want to make matters worse by commenting further on the situation so she remained quiet. She knew Veda couldn't make her move until the waiter brought LaMarr his drink. Delilah wished this ordeal was over and she had the hundred bucks in her hand. All she could think about now was going to her familiar spot and getting a quick blast of coke.

Without warning LaMarr leaned across the table and kissed her again gently on the lips. "I feel better now," he said and turned from Mr. Hyde back to Dr. Jykell.

Most of his conversation centered on himself and on making money. Delilah tried hard to seem interested but she had only one thing on her mind. Still, she attempted to carry on a conversation with him.

"I just don't understand how you do it, LaMarr. I could never be a trial lawyer," she said, "How can you defend somebody you know for a fact is guilty?"

"That's how the American justice system works, baby. If we have to we'd let ten guilty men go free rather than risk imprisoning one innocent man. Anyway, Davis & Bookerman's clients aren't ax murders or child-molesters. We handle white-collar crimes like business disputes, embezzlements, a divorce now and then—light shit like that. But I got other plans for my future. I ain't gonna be carrying no damn briefcase forever. I got some serious plans to make me a whole bunch of Benjamins."

The waiter crept back with a fluted glass of champagne for her, an assortment of delicacies that looked too fancy to eat, and two tall Bloody Marys with a wilted piece of celery stuck inside. Delilah smiled at the waiter and said thank you, hoping LaMarr would follow suite and do likewise or at least, keep his mouth shut. The waiter moved away as quickly and quietly as he had appeared. LaMarr took a sip of his drink, then slammed it down on the table.

"This shit is weak as water. I bet the goddamn dishwasher made it."

Delilah glared over at Veda and wondered just when she was going to make that bogus telephone call to get him to leave the table. LaMarr had already polished off one drink and had started working on the other one. Delilah still nursed her champagne. She was sick and tired of this obnoxious, ill-tempered man. It was beginning to look like Veda should have paid her double just to sit through a meal with this arrogant son-of-a-bitch. Delilah noticed he didn't take his eyes off her for more than a few seconds at a time. She knew exactly what was on his mind. When LaMarr suggested that he go out to the front desk and reserve one of the hotel's suites upstairs, there was no doubt about his intentions. After witnessing his volatile temper, Delilah didn't want to risk upsetting him so she just nodded yes. Anyway, Veda was supposed to make her move before anything serious developed. She didn't want him to insist that they leave before Veda had a chance to complete her plan. LaMarr got up from the table, promising to be right back. He said he would get them the best room in the hotel so they could enjoy a little privacy.

Delilah's eyes followed him as he walked out towards the passageway leading back out to the hotel lobby. He walked with his back straight and his head held high and displayed a confident, superior attitude. Living in the nation's capital, Delilah knew that attitude full well. She found it was the norm rather than the exception among the typical crop of political and professional men in Washington, D.C. As soon as LaMarr was out of sight, Delilah motioned for Veda and Natasha to hurry over.

"How's it going girl?" asked Veda as she leaned over and whispered to Delilah, while keeping her eyes on the door.

"How the hell do you think?" snapped Delilah and tapped her red manicured fingernails on the table, "Let's get this over with, Veda. Where's my damn money?"

Veda counted out five crisp twenty-dollar bills and slipped them to Delilah under the table. She looked around quickly then retrieved a pill bottle from her purse. She had filled it with rat poison. Veda dumped the entire contents into LaMarr's half-empty glass and stirred it a few times with the celery stick.

"You sure that stuff won't kill him?" asked Natasha, with concern, "I'm not trying to be no accomplice and end up in jail."

"Nah girl, but he should feel the pain though."

"I hope so 'cause this brother's out there right now getting us a room. And I definitely ain't about to give him no nukey," said Delilah.

"No chance of that, girlfriend. Two minutes after he drinks this, you'll be dialing 911 for his sorry ass."

Veda told Delilah they'd be waiting outside the building to make sure everything went down as planned. Veda and Natasha quickly disappeared. The next thing Delilah knew LaMarr had slipped back into his seat and had dropped a key on the table.

"I got us a whole suite, baby," he said, grinning, "just like I said I would."

He motioned for the waiter to come to their table. The waiter immediately stopped what he was doing for another customer and rushed right over. "Yes, Monsieur," he said.

"We're leaving, Gill or whatever the hell your name is. I'd like the check now."

Guilliame hurried off to tally up their total.

"I'm not quite finished my champagne and I haven't even started on these delicious-looking strawberries," she said, trying to prolong the meal.

"Forget that," he snapped, "We can order room service."

"Aren't you going to finish your drink, LaMarr?" said Delilah sweetly. Underneath her calm demeanor her heart pounded. Veda had said the rat poison would work fast, but suppose Veda didn't know what the hell she was talking about, Delilah worried. She did not want to go upstairs with him.

"Oh, yeah," he picked up the Bloody Mary and drank it all down in one long, steady gulp.

Guilliame returned and laid the check on the table next to LaMarr. LaMarr took out a fifty-dollar bill and threw the money on the table in front of the waiter. When they left, Delilah could tell from the expression of relief on Guilliame's face that the tip didn't compensate for LaMarr's disrespectful behavior.

Delilah walked out of the restaurant with LaMarr, watching him closely. She hoped something would happen to incapacitate him before they got upstairs to the room. But he appeared full of energy and there was even a bounce in his step. Damn that Veda and her stupid ass plan. Delilah felt trapped and afraid. The only thing she could do now was play this out.

They rode the elevator to the third floor royal suite in silence. She felt his breath at the back of her neck as he stood close behind her and held on tightly to her arm. Although, she couldn't see him, she felt LaMarr's eyes peering down on her.

As soon as they entered the suite, LaMarr pulled her into his arms and kissed her despite her obvious attempts to be released from his firm grasp. He ignored it when she tried to turn her face away from his lips. He abruptly grabbed her face and held it while he kissed her hard on the lips. Delilah pulled free and jumped back away from him.

"Stop it LaMarr. What the hell are you doing?" She pushed him away with both hands.

He laughed, then picked her up and threw her on the bed. Without saying a word, he climbed on top of her. He covered her face with kisses and pulled frantically at her clothes, trying to remove them.

CHAPTER 23

▼

Natasha caught a cab and returned home as soon as she and Veda left the restaurant. She didn't want to be anywhere near that place when the ambulance came for LaMarr. Veda stood outside the hotel and waited for Delilah. She couldn't shake the feeling that something had gone wrong. She figured she'd better go back inside and check it out. The doorman held the door open for her. Veda sailed past the lobby and walked briskly back to the restaurant. She quickly surveyed the darkened dining area but saw no sign of LaMarr and Delilah. Veda raced back to the hotel lobby. She stepped up to the bony, wisp of a figure behind the front desk marked room reservations and offered a forced smile.

"Excuse me, sir but I'm meeting my husband. Could you please tell me which room LaMarr Coleman checked into?"

The desk attendant flashed a yellow-stained grin at Veda and reviewed his screen monitor to check reservations. "We show your husband has the royal suite on the 3rd floor. Would you like me to ring him for you, Mrs. Coleman?"

"No, thank you. That won't be necessary. He's expecting me," said Veda sweetly and walked swiftly towards the elevators.

"I said let go of me," shouted Delilah and jumped up from the bed.

"You can't be this naïve. Girl, why do you think I brought you up here? Just to check out the view?"

"Well, you got it all wrong, Mister, if you think I'm just some cheap thrill you can hop into bed with."

"Hold up, Miss Black American Princess. I don't know what makes you think you're so high and mighty," said LaMarr, "I can get ten more just like you anytime I want."

"Good. Then don't let me stop you," she said and tried to move towards the door, "Go right ahead."

LaMarr grabbed her arm and pushed her back down on the bed.

"Sit down, Bitch. I'll tell you when you can leave."

Delilah stood still, too afraid to move. He reached into his jacket to retrieve a pack of cigarettes and lit a Pall Mall. Just then, they heard a soft knock on the door.

"Hotel Security. Is everything all right in there?" asked a man with a pleasant-sounding voice from behind the door.

"Get lost," barked LaMarr.

Delilah heard the hotel security guard's footsteps fade away. She decided to try a gentler approach in reasoning with LaMarr. Her big sister, Rachael, had always told her you can get more bees with honey than vinegar, although, LaMarr was acting more like a viper than a bee. She took a deep breath to relax and let the muscles in her face soften.

"Look LaMarr, I don't know you and you sure as hell don't know me. Don't you think we should slow things up a bit and get to know each other better first?"

"Baby, I've seen your legs. That's all I need to know," he drew in his cigarette then slowly exhaled.

He sat down on a mahogany cane-seat sofa and patted the space next to him as a gesture for her to sit down.

Delilah stood motionless. She didn't understand why it was taking so long for that rat poison to take effect. Maybe all those Bloody Marys had canceled out the toxins. Whatever the reason, she knew she was in trouble because he didn't appear to be showing any signs of weakening.

LaMarr puffed on his cigarette. All the while not taking his eyes off her. He crushed the cigarette out in an ashtray on a nearby table then got up and walked casually towards the bed. He stood in front of her with his hand outstretched. Delilah refused to take it. She felt his dark penetrating eyes scrutinizing her entire body.

All of a sudden, he pushed her flat on the bed and held her down. When she screamed he tried to muffle her screams with one hand while pinning her down with the other. Delilah bit the inside of his hand. He let go just long enough to plant a swift slap across the side of her face. Temporarily free of his sweaty hand over her mouth, she screamed as loud as she could.

Then a succession of heavy thuds banged against the door. It sounded like someone trying to kick the door in. Delilah hoped security had returned to rescue her this time. Veda had picked the lock and when she turned the knob the door flew open. It wasn't hotel security who stood at the doorway brandishing a silver toned knife. It was Veda Simms. Veda walked up to LaMarr and pointed the glistening edge of the knife at him. Between gritted teeth, she spoke calmly, but her dark eyes squinted together and revealed her rage.

"You slimy bastard. Move away from that bed."

LaMarr stood up slowly. He glanced back and forth from Delilah to Veda with an amused smirk on his face.

"And who are you supposed to be? The bodyguard?" said LaMarr, and burst out laughing.

He didn't appear threatened by Veda despite the weapon in her hand. He came towards her.

"I believe the young lady told you she wanted to leave. Is that right, Delilah?" asked Veda still watching LaMarr's every move.

Delilah nodded and leaped off the bed. She held one of the straps to her dress together that had broken loose during her struggle with LaMarr. She eased towards the door, and clutched her bolero tight across her bosom.

"Delilah, you better stick with me, babe," he said, "Now I can help you. Veda, on the other hand, can't do shit. She can't even help herself."

"Delilah doesn't need your help. I typed up that foreclosure letter and paid her to bring it to you. I knew she'd get your attention. You fell right into the trap. Just like the rat you are."

"What the hell are you talking about?" said LaMarr still grinning, "You bitches are too much." He still didn't take either of them seriously.

"This is what I'm talking about ...," said Veda.

She reached into her purse and held up the label that she had cut out of the empty box of D-Con rat poisoning and had tucked in her purse as proof.

"What the hell is that?" he said, wearing a smirk on his face.

Veda hurled the cardboard label at him so he could take a closer look. "It's the warning label from the box of rat poison that I put in your Bloody Mary. The drink you gulped down in one swallow. When you stepped out the restaurant to get this room reservation, I dumped it in your drink."

"You crazy Bitch," shouted LaMarr.

In one swift motion, he grabbed Veda's wrist. The knife dropped to the floor. "Run, Delilah?" Veda shouted. Delilah ran out the door. Veda grabbed him by his shirt and tripped him to the floor with her leg. He looked up at her in surprise, then sprang up and grabbed for her. Veda jumped out of the way to avoid his grasp. She lifted her skirt above her hip and retrieved a gun from inside her pantyhose. She held the gun at LaMarr with both hands and gave him a look that needed no further explanation.

"I'm gonna give you a similar warning like the one you gave me. Go find yourself a good doctor. And take that warning label with you. They'll need to know all the shit that's in it so they can treat your sorry ass."

"You're lying. You wouldn't have the nerve to do that to me. I don't feel a thing."

"I have the nerve to do that and much more if you don't show up at the bank tomorrow at one with that five thousand dollars. I gotta turn the firm's books over to the auditor from Price Waterhouse by ten o'clock Monday morning. As you can see, I'm a desperate woman and this is your last warning."

"You're just bluffing," he said and waved her off.

But as he spoke those words he suddenly felt dizzy. He rested his forehead in his hand and leaned his body against a table. LaMarr looked up at her in disbelief. She matched his angry gaze with her own look of disdain. She tucked the gun back in its hiding place under her pantyhose then retrieved her knife from the floor and buried it deep inside her purse.

"Call 911," he pleaded in a strained, slurred voice, "I think I'm about to throw up."

Veda took her time getting to the telephone on the nightstand to dial emergency. She told the dispatch operator where they were and what he had ingested. When the dispatcher began asking too many personal questions about her, Veda abruptly hung up.

"When the ambulance gets here, make sure you show them that label," she pointed to it lying on the floor. "Unfortunately, you didn't swallow enough to kill your ass but you definitely won't be going out tonight," said Veda as she opened the door to leave.

"You can't just leave me here like this, Veda," he begged, clutching his gut and doubling over in pain.

"The ambulance is on its way. Just make sure you have that money by one tomorrow."

"How ... how the hell am I supposed to do that ... in the hospital?" he said between gasps.

"Like you always say, you got contacts. Figure it out," said Veda. "You'll live, but the next time you might not be so lucky. Your ass might just end up in the morgue."

She walked out and closed the door behind her. Veda knew the amount she gave him wasn't lethal because she had looked up the dosage on the internet, but she hung around the lobby just the same until the ambulance showed up which turned out to be about five minutes later.

LaMarr laid motionless on the stretcher as the EMS attendants hoisted him up in the ambulance. Veda found out from one of the attendants that they were headed for Georgetown University Hospital.

Several hours later, she called the Emergency Room at Georgetown to inquire about his status. The nurse on duty said Mr. Coleman was stable and would be released that evening. Veda thought about calling his room to reinforce her threat then decided against it. She was sure he got the message this time.

CHAPTER 24

▼

Day turned into night again and again, but Renee had no concept of time passing for several days after finding out that Baby Susanna had died in her sleep. As a former emergency room nurse she expected this to happen, but somehow the depth of her grief surprised her. The home nurse told her the baby succumbed due to infection caused by pneumocystic carinii pneumonia or PCP, a common complication of babies infected with HIV/AIDS. Renee got angry all over again that Susanna's HIV-positive mother still walked the streets free of symptoms, probably shooting up and still having unprotected sex, while Susanna lay dead from a disease she got from her mother's drug-infested lifestyle.

Being in the mental health profession Renee was familiar with all the stages of grief recognition and resolution, yet that awareness did not insulate her from experiencing the loss of someone she had grown to love. On the ride to the funeral at Mount Olivet Cemetery in Northeast, oak and beech trees lined each side of the dirt-pebbled road that led to the cemetery grounds, where Baby Susanna was to be buried. Renee sat between Shirley Ann and her husband, John in the back seat of the funeral director's black town car. They rode in silence. Renee stared out the window as they passed endless rows of headstones embedded in lush, green pastures. Nothing, not even the lovely, tranquil setting could erase the pain of being there.

The funeral director led the way to the burial site, followed by Shirley Ann's minister. John held onto his wife's arm. Renee's heels sank into the grass as she trailed closely behind Shirley Ann and John. They were a small and somber procession that moved in slow motion. Her shoulders slumped forward and her feet dragged as if she were carrying a fifty-pound backpack. Tears seeped into her eyes.

The tombstones reached out from the ground as if defying the living to cross over their sacred grounds while the procession of mourners climbed a steep hill to their final destination. The site was marked by a mound of fresh dirt next to an open child-sized grave.

The sun peered through the clouds and softly touched Renee's face. At least a beautiful morning beckoned Susanna's soul into heaven, thought Renee. At least the baby who had suffered for most of her eighteen months on earth would finally know peace. That thought comforted Renee but she could not yet look at the tiny white coffin that she had picked out for her. The coffin was still raised above the ground, waiting to be lowered. Renee bowed her head and closed her eyes while the minister prayed that Susanna's soul be delivered unto Almighty God. Shirley Ann held onto John, and sobbed. Renee wished she had someone to hold onto, but there was no one to lean on. She sobbed softly into her white handkerchief that was now stained with tears and makeup smudges.

At the end of the funeral, Renee laid her bouquet of white roses on top of the coffin. She dried her eyes and followed the small group of mourners. The funeral director did not give the order to lower the coffin until they had all left.

Renee felt like she was in a daze as she stumbled pass an endless sea of grave-stones back to the roadside. She hadn't seen him at first because she was looking down, but she recognized Deek's familiar fragrance before she felt his presence next to her.

"How are you Renee?" he said in a low comforting voice that embraced her with its gentle tone.

She looked up and experienced a moment of joy but couldn't speak.

"Are you okay? I was worried about you." he asked again, and took her hand. She just wanted to hear his voice. If Deek had been a late night radio announcer on a soulful station, his voice could lull his listeners into falling in love with him just from hearing his voice. Deek took her shivering body in his arms and gently pressed her head against his chest. Renee muttered that she was okay. Then an outburst of tears betrayed her. Despite her remorse for not being there for Susanna at the end, the closeness of Deek's muscular body felt too good to let go. Renee closed her eyes and leaned her check against his shoulder, but couldn't wipe away the memory of returning to Shirley Ann's house just three days ago and being told that Susanna was dead. That had been right after making love to Deek on the floor of Helen Stone's office. Ever since the baby's death, guilt and sadness consumed Renee. She had taken a leave of absence for a few days. She wasn't eating or sleeping well. She increased her days for volunteering at Children's Hospital and spent all her time with the 'at risk' preemies or the critically ill children. If it meant she'd return home each day emotionally spent in order to hold a baby for twenty minutes that otherwise would not get held, then she would do it. Seeing so many sick and poor children without medical insurance and without someone there everyday to love them made her feel helpless and depressed. She felt there was too much misery and injustice in the world for one person to make a difference.

If only she had stayed home with Susanna, Renee thought. She suspected the baby had not been breathing well earlier that day, which is why she told Shirley Ann to ask the home nurse to come examine her. If only she had returned to Shirley Ann's instead of making love to Deek maybe she could have seen signs that the baby was in distress, maybe she could have prevented this.

Deek had tried to comfort her that night. Tried to convince her that it wasn't her fault. Susanna was terminally ill and there was nothing she could have done to change the fact that she was going to die anyway. What a cruel thing to say, Renee had lashed out at him. Now, here he was at the cemetery, back for more, but she couldn't be angry at him, she was too sad. She continued to cry into his shoulders. As her released tears began to calm her, she felt better. She didn't blame him or herself anymore. As each day went by, Renee came to accept the tragedy of Susanna's life and death.

"Let me drive you home," said Deek after she had regained her composure.

"Thanks. That would be nice." When he gently squeezed her hand, she leaned into his arm and let his strength give her support.

"Have you eaten anything today?" he asked, "Looks like you've lost a few pounds."

"Well, if so, I don't think it'll hurt me," she smiled.

"It's good to see you smile, Doc. So how about it? Can I take you to lunch?"

"Sure, I'd like that. And Deek?" she turned and glanced up into his eyes, "thanks for coming today."

"I wasn't sure if I should. I thought your husband might be here with you."

"He offered to come," said Renee quickly in Bill's defense, "but I told him not to."

"Here's my car. So what are you in the mood for? Seafood, Thai, Italian, Chinese or just plain old American?"

"Whatever you like, Deek. Why don't you surprise me?"

"Then I know just the place," he said.

Shirley Ann and John were waiting for her by the car. Renee told them that her friend Deek was taking her home. She hugged Shirley Ann good-bye and promised to call tomorrow.

Deek and Renee drove through the city and not more than thirty minutes later crossed the Memorial Bridge into Arlington, Virginia. Deek took Renee to his favorite little Vietnamese restaurant in Arlington called Queen Bee. It was safely tucked away on a side street that no one would notice except by recommendation from its loyal patrons. Soft lighting bathed the red painted walls and black lacquer accent pieces. A rock water fountain and a large statue of Buddha dressed the entranceway. The tiny pink-clothed tables were adorned only with silk flowers in a simple vase, and tables were packed close together. The restaurant's major attraction was due to its outstanding cuisine and excellent service, not its décor Deek explained.

Even without having a reservation, their order arrived quickly. They spent most of the meal in silence. Deek didn't press her for conversation, which she was grateful for. Renee only dabbed at her food, though it was delicious. Finally, he broke the silence. "When do you think you'll be going back to work?" asked Deek after finishing off the last of the Spring Rolls.

Renee looked down at her plate and pushed the food around without eating. "That's a good question. I was planning to contact some of my more critical patients later in the week. I'm scheduled to go see Helen first thing Monday morning to get an update on their status."

"Oh yeah, that's your colleague who's been covering for you. Dr. Stone, right?"

"Umhum," Renee nodded. "I really appreciate her taking over for me these past few days. I don't think I could have dealt with listening to anyone's problems."

"I think it'll be good for you to start seeing your patients again," said Deek.

"Yes, I suppose you're right. I do need something else to think about."

"So I take it you have to get right back home today?" he said.

"I should, but thanks for bringing me here, Deek," said Renee and held his hand across the table, "I needed it."

"You're welcome, Doc. I needed it too. Look, are you going to be all right?" he asked. He lifted her chin gently to make eye contact with her. "You've barely eaten a thing."

"Sure. It's my job to help other people cope, remember."

"I know but it doesn't always work that way, Doc. It's common knowledge that shrinks don't usually follow their own advice."

"All right, Detective Hamilton," smiled Renee playfully, "You're treading on dangerous ground now."

"Then I'd better quit. The last thing I want to do is offend a beautiful lady."

"Thanks, for your concern. I'll just have to take one day at a time and let go of what's not important. I still have my special memories to cherish. I only had her for a little while but every moment counted. Those times Susanna and I spent together when I knew she felt loved and happy will always remain with me. That's what I'll think about when I think of her, not her suffering or her illness."

"I understand," said Deek.

"It's just that ..." Renee shook her head without continuing and looked away.

"What is it?" At first Renee didn't want to talk about how losing Susanna had reminded her of other losses in her life, but finally she revealed how much she had missed her father's presence in her life. She told Deek all about LeRoy Curtis and how she hadn't seen or heard from him in over two years. She had no idea where her father was or if he were even alive. As she stared out, she noticed some-one seated several tables away that looked familiar. The young man resembled a former patient of hers named Kenneth Blackwell, whose domineering father had abruptly ended his son's therapy sessions because he disagreed with Renee's coun-seling. Renee sighed. Another troubled soul that she could not help. Kenneth sat across from a well-dressed gentleman wearing a dark Brooks Brothers suit. Renee noticed that Kenneth's lunch companion gulped down one cocktail after another and appeared to monopolize the conversation while Kenneth sat with his lips pressed shut, his delicate hands folded meekly in his lap, and wearing a pained expression on his face.

"Are you okay?" asked Deek, turning to glance in the direction where Renee stared. She looked away from Kenneth and met Deek's worried expression with a forced smile. "It's nothing. I thought I saw someone I knew. It doesn't matter."

When the waiter returned, Deek paid the check and escorted Renee out the door. During the ride home he wanted to say something to make her feel better, but he didn't know what to say. She stared out the window in silence, unaware that he frequently looked over at her, feeling helpless just as she had felt. He hoped that just his being there would be enough.

CHAPTER 25

▼

It was almost midnight. Bill poured himself a cognac and retreated to the study with his laptop. He hadn't seen Renee all day, which was fine with him. The one thing he didn't want to think about right now was her. Bill liked working in his study. Surrounded by walls filled with ancient classics, artwork, and the smell of leather and freshly polished mahogany, seemed to focus his mind. But, despite his best effort to prevent it, his thoughts drifted back to Renee. That morning he had found a dozen long-stem red roses in a porcelain vase in her office. He'd looked around for a card and found shredded remains stashed in her trash basket, the pieces too tiny for him to repair. Each time he called on her private line, he was greeted by her voice mail recording. He also noticed that she had been going out a lot more recently without telling him where. Bill had begun to suspect his wife of having an affair. He wondered if her desire to adopt a baby with him had vanished along with their marriage. Perhaps she had found something else she wanted more.

He clinched his hand in a tight fist. His heart pounded fiercely inside his chest. He swallowed the cognac and slammed the glass down on the antique English desk. Fortunately, the glass was made of heavy lead crystal and didn't break. He considered sleeping in the study and avoiding the climb up the spiraling staircase to their bedroom. He was afraid of facing the possibility that she might not be in their bed. Suppose she wasn't curled up under the covers, pretending to be asleep like she usually was when he got in late? How could he brace himself for cold, empty sheets?

He thought about confronting Renee with his suspicions, but he knew it would destroy their marriage if his suspicions were confirmed, and he wasn't sure he wanted that. All he could do now was wait and hope she came to her senses soon or, better yet, that maybe he was wrong about her.

Bill realized he'd been staring at the same e-mail message from his manager for ten minutes and hadn't typed a response yet. His manager wanted him to teach a five-day networking class in Atlanta next week. The regular instructor had some emergency come up and wouldn't be able to go. Forget him, Bill thought. He had no intentions of going to Atlanta when his marriage was falling apart at home. Without sending a reply, he shutdown his laptop and headed upstairs to bed. He wanted to make love to Renee, not just physically but he wanted to be there for her emotionally as well. But he knew he couldn't make love to her without knowing whether or not she'd be thinking about her lover. For now, he'd settle for just finding her upstairs.

Renee had dozed off while reading "Child Abuse and Repressed Memories," an article from a recent issue of *Modern Psychiatry Journal*. After Veda's revelation more than a week ago about the abuse she experienced in childhood, Renee understood the reason for her patient's low self-esteem. She hoped to teach Veda new ways of altering the distorted thought patterns that had taken shape during her childhood. Veda had refused to see Dr. Stone while Renee was on leave of absence, but Renee planned to resume her therapy sessions with Veda that Thursday.

She had dropped the journal on the floor and quickly turned off the reading light when she heard Bill's heavy, labored footsteps climb the stairs. Renee edged her body away from Bill's side of the bed and faced the wall with her eyes closed. She listened to his familiar nighttime ritual of taking a quick shower and brushing his teeth. When Bill got into bed, both he and Renee lay on their own side of the bed, at the farthest opposite ends and listened to each other's tense breathing. Two more adults could have easily fit between them, with room to spare, on the king size bed. A tear trickled down Renee's cheek and landed on the rim of her lip. The sudden beeping of her pager startled her.

Bill remained motionless. He tried to mimic the sounds of heavy snoring so that Renee would think he was fast asleep. Was that him paging her? Bill thought.

Renee got up and retrieved the pager from her handbag. She glanced at the telephone number displayed on her pager but didn't recognize it. She hurried out of the bedroom to return the call from her basement office and was grateful to this unknown caller who had given her an excuse to leave an apathetic marriage bed. On the way to her office, Renee recalled what her father had once said about the long and steady pull of the mule. She felt like she didn't have the strength or the desire to pull that mule along any further. Her father's feeble words of wisdom meant nothing to her now. She didn't see much of him when she was growing up and probably would never see him again now that she was grown. Once during a therapy session, Veda had accused her of being out of touch with her patients because she already had it all. Veda couldn't accept the notion that having money didn't automatically make people happy. Renee unlocked the door to her basement office, flipped on the desk lamp, and punched in the telephone number displayed on her pager. After several rings, someone answered the telephone.

"Yes?" whispered the unknown voice cautiously on the other end.

"This is Dr. Renee Hayes. Did someone just page me?"

"Dr. Renee, ... it's, ... it's me." The woman calling managed to stammer out the words between sobs and sniffles.

"Who?" asked Renee, not recognizing the distraught sounding voice on the other end of the telephone, "Who is this? Hello? Are you still there?" Renee held on for several minutes without receiving a coherent response from the caller. Only frantic sobbing could be heard.

"Yeah, I'm here. This is Veda Simms. Dr. Renee, ... something terrible's happened."

"What? Veda, where are you?"

"Dr. Renee, I don't know what to do," said Veda, "I tried to reach you all last week. I still didn't have the money and the audit's on Monday. I just wanted to ... I mean ..."

"What're you talking about Veda?" asked Dr. Renee, "Are you all right?"

Veda seemed to be on the verge of hysteria. Renee couldn't calm her down enough to find out exactly what the problem was. Renee sensed something was terribly wrong.

"Veda, calm down and give me your address. I'll be right over. You just stay put until I get there." Renee was worried that Veda might try to harm herself. She had already lost Susanna. She couldn't take a chance at losing anyone else in her care.

Her promise to be right there seemed to reassure her patient. Renee scribbled down the address at Madison Towers and grabbed her mini recorder and the taped recordings of Veda's therapy sessions to review on the way. She ran back upstairs to her bedroom and in no time she was dressed and out the door.

CHAPTER 26

▼

Renee's patient had pleaded with her to come help—said she needed her right away. Veda had once been suicidal. Driven by the desperation in Veda's voice and her own professional ethics as a psychologist, Renee felt she had no choice but to come to Madison Towers, apartment unit 620 in the middle of the night. When Renee arrived and entered apartment 620 instead of finding Veda inside, all she found was the stench of death. As Renee inched forward towards an open bedroom door and looked inside, there sprawled on the bed was the body of a naked man, seemingly dead. His lifeless eyes stared out at her. She checked his vitals without expecting to find any sign of life. But the worse discovery was yet to come when she lifted the blood-soaked hand towel that partially covered him at the waist. His genitals had been severed and burned. She ran in horror out of apartment 620 with her own silent screams echoing in her ears. She didn't bother to wait for the elevator, and ran down six flights of stairs and burst through the rear door that opened into the ground floor lobby.

Renee ran up to the sleeping guard and shook his arm vigorously until he woke up.

"What the ... what's going on?" the guard looked up and rubbed his eyes. He became alert only when he saw the panic in Renee's face.

"Call ... call the police," she gasped, out of breath, "There's a man upstairs ... in 620 ... he's been murdered."

Instead of making a move to place the call, he stared at her chest. Renee followed his gaze to a bloodstain on her pearl-white, silk blouse. She hugged her jacket over her chest to hide the stain.

"Call now!" she yelled and rushed towards the front door.

"Hey lady," he hollered after her, "You better stay put. The police'll wanna talk to you, ya'know."

Renee stopped and waited until she saw him dial 911.

"Yeah, this is night security at Madison Towers. Some lady claims there's a stiff in apartment 620. That's right. Just off Massachusetts Avenue, in Northwest. Fine, I'll be here." The guard hung up.

"Hey, where you goin'?" The guard called after Renee, but she kept walking briskly towards the door. She had to get some fresh air or she would throw up.

Once outside, she searched the surrounding area for Veda, but her patient had apparently fled the scene. Renee's head pounded from a tension headache. It felt like a team of cleat-wearing football players trampling around inside her head. She returned to her car and turned the ignition on just long enough to activate the automatic button to slide her window down. She took in a deep breath of fresh air and savored the cool summer night. Last night's storm had brought a brief respite from the usual hot and stagnant Washington, D. C. weather. She glanced down and noticed the tape recorder lying on the front passenger seat and quickly locked it inside her glove compartment. Renee closed her eyes and tried to wipe away the sight of the dead man whoever he was. But she couldn't get the mental image of him out of her mind. She opened her eyes and glanced at her watch and saw that it was almost 1:15 in the morning. Suddenly, she realized she hadn't called Bill to let him know what happened. She dialed Bill on the car phone and waited several rings. Finally, his sleepy voice answered. Despite the tension in her marriage the knots in her stomach finally began to subside when she heard his voice that connected her to home.

Bill asked where she was but as soon as she started to answer, the shrill screaming of sirens drowned out her voice. Up ahead, several police cars and an ambulance approached. All she could manage to convey through the noise was that one of her patients was in trouble but she was all right and would call back later.

A half dozen police cruisers pulled up to the circular curb in front of the Madison Towers condominium complex. The once quiet night turned into chaos. Noises from radio dispatch and voices talking in unison filled the air. Just as Renee got out of her car, a midnight blue Ford Crown Victoria with a siren perched on the dashboard screeched to a halt, just barely missing her. A balding, sepia toned man about 5'9", heavy-set, and wearing a rumpled, light-gray suit stumbled out of the passenger side of the car. The detective on the driver's side leaped out after his much shorter, middle-aged partner. Renee saw that the other detective was Deek.

"Who the hell are you lady?" asked the older man while devouring a Big Mac. He smelled like french fries and grilled meat. The memory of the smell she had just left came back and she couldn't answer. Renee thought she was going to be sick right in front of them.

"Dr. Renee Hayes. I'm a psychologist."

"Yeah? Sorta like a shrink, huh. Well, I'm the lead homicide detective. Lieutenant Melvin Bradford."

He unbuttoned his jacket, revealing a dingy blue shirt clinched over his belly. He reached into the breast pocket of his jacket and briefly flashed his badge.

"And this here's my partner, Detective Sergeant Degas Hamilton."

Renee noticed signs of fatigue in Deek's face as he spoke, "Dr. Hayes and I met several weeks ago when I was on the B&E case." He spotted the blood stains on her blouse, but didn't say anything. He wanted to take her aside and find out what was going on, but his partner would probably get suspicious. The last thing he needed was for his senior partner to find out just how close he and the doctor really were. He knew Bradford would take him off the case if he felt there was the slightest chance of conflict of interest. Deek wanted to be on this case so he could protect Renee as much as possible.

"Uh huh," Bradford nodded and finished gulping down the last remains of his greasy burger. "You the one that called?" he asked Renee.

"No, the security guard called. I discovered the body though. It's up in apartment 620."

He took out a piece of gum and popped it in his mouth.

"All right. Come on, Deek. Let's go see what we got," Bradford looked back at Renee, "Better stick around for awhile, Dr. Hayes. We'll need a statement from you."

Deek gave Renee a reassuring glance, but realized it was not the right time to exchange words. He followed his partner to the crime scene. Renee watched as Detectives Bradford and Hamilton led a caravan of police officers into the building. At that moment the medical examiner got out of a black van marked CORONER across the side. He walked briskly to catch up with Deek and Detective Bradford. Renee followed behind, maintaining a safe distance to avoid getting in the way.

By the time she reached the lobby, Detective Bradford was questioning the security guard. "Who's the victim?" he asked.

The security guard checked the complex's resident directory for apartment 620.

"All it says here is L. D. Coleman, Detective," answered the guard.

Renee's suspicions were confirmed. Veda's longtime lover, LaMarr Coleman, had been murdered and Veda had called her from his apartment less than an hour ago. Renee heard the guard whisper something to Bradford. They all turned and looked directly at her. Renee wondered what the guard had just told the police about her.

Renee stood transfixed and waited for the lead homicide detective to summons her. Instead, he turned away and proceeded towards the elevator. She thought about remaining downstairs in the lobby, but something pressed her onward and she found herself following the investigative squad back up to the victim's apartment. She knew there was no way she'd get pass the yellow crime tape, yet she felt an uncontrollable force pulling her back to the scene of carnage.

CHAPTER 27

▼

Renee went back up to the 6th floor and found teams of officers banging on doors and waking up residents to ask them if they had heard or seen anything. Renee tried to blend in with other curious onlookers who had peeped out into the hallway, some with night cream smeared faces, wearing bathrobes and jumbo rollers and others who had just arrived home only to find their apartment building in chaos. The noise from the police radios continued to echo in the background, as some of the officers used their portable radios to converse with dispatch. The place swarmed with police officers and all kinds of hectic activity.

The victim's front door stood wide open, but the apartment was sealed off with yellow crime tape. A team of uniformed officers waved onlookers away. Renee stepped in front of an officer blocking the yellow taped entrance.

"I'm Dr. Hayes," she said in an authoritative voice, "I need to get inside to speak to Detective Hamilton."

"You with the medical examiner?"

"No, I'm a psychologist. I discovered the body. The detectives told me they needed my statement."

"Sorry Dr. Hayes. No civilians allowed inside the crime scene while evidence is being collected. They'll come get you when they're ready for you. You'll have to wait outside the taped area, ma'am."

Renee tried to peep inside the doorway but couldn't see much except people moving about. TV camera crews and reporters had just arrived to further add to the confusion. The guard turned his attention to the media crew. Coming from inside the apartment, Detective Melvin Bradford's bellowing voice could be heard above the noise.

"Keep those people back, McNeil," yelled Bradford, "We're trying to conduct an investigation in here for christsake." Renee found herself being pushed back with the others.

When the police photographer arrived, the officer lifted the tape for her to enter. The photographer stepped inside the large foyer and immediately began snapping pictures of the crime scene. Renee edged her way back to the front. From her position close to the open door, she could see some of what was happening. She periodically caught sight of Deek but he was too involved in his work to notice that she had positioned herself as close to the entrance as she could get to be able to make eye contact with him.

"You're late, Sloan," Bradford snapped at the photographer.

The photographer ignored him and moved in for a close-up shot of the bloodstains on the carpet that Renee had noticed just before she discovered Coleman's body. After the photographer moved on to another area, Deek hunched over the floor with a razor blade and carefully cut out a small piece of bloodstained carpet. He placed the sample in a plastic evidence bag and sealed it. When he stood up, he saw Renee standing by the door.

Deek tried to figure out what her blank stare revealed. Fear? Guilt? Concern? He wanted to take her in his arms and demand to know what the hell she was doing at this man's apartment in the middle of the night, but he had to remain calm. Just stay focused on your job, he thought and don't draw any conclusions until we're ready to take her statement.

Renee didn't know what to think when she caught Deek staring at her from across the room. When he noticed her watching him, he immediately turned his attention to a group of police officers nearby. To, Renee, it felt like he was ignoring her.

Deek flipped open his wireless notebook-sized laptop, accessed the police station's crime files remotely through his computer's built-in modem, and keyed information directly into the main computer. Bradford shook his head and jotted down his own notes in a small, black memo pad that he retrieved from his coat pocket. Deek assigned a case number of 75 for the investigation, and entered the date and time the crime had been called in. Seventy-five homicide cases amounted to a hell of a lot of unsolved open murders for his squad's caseload he thought. He checked e-mail while several uniformed officers dusted the furniture and surface areas for fingerprints. After the dusting powder had sat for the required time, they covered all the surfaces with lifting tape. Then they transferred the tape onto white index cards, where it retained the developed prints.

"Make sure you people comb every inch of this place once these guys finish dusting," Deek told another team of officers, "We don't want the killer getting off because of sloppy police work. Collect any clues, no matter how trivial. Get anything that might reveal what happened here tonight."

"Yes, Sergeant," they all chimed in unison.

Deek worked closely with his senior partner, Mel Bradford, to look for traces left by the killer. He helped Bradford supervise every detail to make sure none of the officers missed any vital clues or did anything improper to destroy evidence. Officers crawled on their hands and knees, searched under furniture, inside drawers, and just about any place a killer might inadvertently leave a clue. Deek knew that the moments or hours after a murder were critical for being able to find the best evidence. Whenever something looked promising or suspicious, he recorded its description into an evidence database he had created on the computer. Then the evidence was dropped into a bag or envelope and labeled, all ready for processing at the crime lab.

Once they were satisfied that the rest of the evidence would be properly collected by the uniformed officers, the two detectives entered the bedroom where the medical examiner had been examining the victim. The medical examiner held a microphone to his lips and spoke into a recorder to note his findings. The victim's hands were bound and covered in clear, plastic bags.

Deek surveyed the bedroom. He walked over to the nightstand and carefully eyed a bottle of prescription pills, a pack of unfiltered Pall Malls, and a gold lighter with the initials LDC embossed in fancy lettering. He slipped on a pair of gloves and picked up the pill bottle. He flipped open his laptop that was still logged on and typed in the name of the medication, phytonadione, the date it was prescribed, and the physician's name, Dr. Raj Singh at Georgetown Hospital. Deek called out to some of the officers in the next room.

"Hey, how come nobody's been in here to start bagging this stuff?"

"Where the hell is that idiot Kane?" asked Bradford looking around, "I told him and his three stooges ten minutes ago to search this bedroom."

"I sent him out to bother the neighbors. He's trying to find out who the victim knew," Deek replied.

"Look Hamilton, who's running this doggone show, me or you?"

"Sorry, Mel. I'll get Vance and a couple of guys to bring some bags in here."

Deek left the room for a moment and returned with Officer Vance and two other police officers. While out in the front room he took a quick look through the open doorway for Renee but didn't see her. The crew donned latex gloves and crawled on the bedroom floor searching for anything they could find.

"Somebody sure messed this guy up pretty good," said Bradford and shook his head, "I guess it wasn't good enough just to waste him. So whaddaya got for me this time, Norman?" Bradford asked the medical examiner.

"Well, looks like the victim was hit with a round from a 32mm. I'd say, based on his deep rectal temperature, the approximate time of death was about 11:45 PM," said the medical examiner, "but you'll have to wait for the autopsy for an exact time. Then, I'll have a liver temperature to go on. I'll do the hand swabbings too when I get him back to the morgue."

"Then the cause of death was gunshot wound to the abdomen?" said Deek.

"Yup. Point-blank range. Two shots. Here's one of the 32mm caliber bullets to add to your collection, Mel," said the examiner.

Wearing latex gloves, the medical examiner held out the bullet. Bradford took a handkerchief from his pocket and grasped the bullet with the handkerchief, without letting it touch his fingers.

"Most likely from a Browning or a Davies," Deek said, eyeing it carefully. "Hey, can somebody get me a bag for this thing?" he shouted to one of the officers.

One of the officers who had been searching under the bed, scrambled to his feet. He held open an evidence bag so that Bradford could drop the bullet inside. The officer took the bag from Bradford and labeled it.

"What about that shit?" asked Bradford, pointing to Coleman's dismembered, shriveled up penis.

"Appears to have been severed with a sharp, surgical instrument. Then doused with nail polish remover, a highly flammable substance," said the examiner, "and ignited after the poor slob was already quite dead."

"Why the hell would somebody do all that?"

"Damn if I know. Isn't that one of your job descriptions, Mel, figuring out the whys and what fors?"

"Don't be such a smartass, Norman," said Bradford as he reached into his pocket for his Maalox tablets. He popped two into his mouth. The medical examiner placed the victim's organ in a specimen container to send to the lab. Then he started to put away his supplies.

"Mel, I've done all I can do here tonight," he said and picked up his case, "I'm going to have the body moved to the morgue now. You can stop by tomorrow afternoon for the final results." The medical examiner instructed his medics to bag the body. One of the medics wheeled a stretcher next to the bed. A dark green body bag sat on top of the stretcher, unzipped and waiting for Coleman's lifeless body. The assistants lifted up the victim's body and shoved it into the open body bag.

"Ashes to ashes, dust to dust," said Bradford in a cool, apathetic voice as the medical assistants wheeled Coleman's body away. Bradford narrowed his eyebrows together, wrinkled his forehead, and scratched the whiskers on his unshaven chin. "Man, I wanna close this thing within the next 24 hours. Gotta get my clearance rate back up before I go out this year," reflected Bradford, "But that prosecutor's a real tight ass bitch. We better have us some solid evidence before we try to get her attention. Deek? You listening to me, man?"

Deek walked over to the window without answering and bent open one of the venetian blinds. He saw Coleman's body being loaded into the Coroner's black van parked out front of the building. He knew the van was headed straight to the morgue. Deek wondered if Renee was still waiting outside the apartment.

"So whatcha think, Bill Gates?" said Bradford to his junior partner.

"Looks like we can definitely rule out robbery," answered Deek, "Coleman still had on his gold monogrammed id bracelet and a big ass diamond ring on his finger."

"Well, that took a lot of genius, Sherlock," teased Bradford, then looked thoughtful, "You think it could've been some kinda drug dispute?"

"Nah. There's no sign of drugs or drug paraphernalia. But that doesn't rule out some other type of drug-related activity like money laundering."

"Could've been a jealous lover," Bradford added, "or an enraged husband if lover boy here was messing around with somebody else's old lady."

Deek coughed nervously without commenting. He couldn't get that one question out of his mind, … why was Renee there? He caught Bradford scrutinizing him and quickly turned away.

Deek opened a large walk-in closet, revealing a wardrobe of French and Italian suits, custom shirts, and several rows of shoes. The closet walls were also lined with a rich collection of color coordinated casual clothes by Gucci and Ralph Lauren.

"Looks like Coleman was a real ladies' man, all right," said Bradford.

Deek pulled out a large, wicker hamper from the closet and dumped the dirty clothes out on the floor. He picked up a woman's lime green silk scarf and examined it closely. It looked familiar. Someone's initials were stitched in the corner. RH. Then he recognized the scarf as one Renee had on the day he took her to Phil's yacht. The scarf had visible bloodstains on it. Deek threw it back in the heap of dirty clothing and moved quickly to the black marble dresser where he pulled open several drawers and rummaged threw its contents. Bradford had been watching him. He lifted the scarf from the heap.

"Know anybody with initials, RH?" he asked and stored it in an evidence bag, "Didn't that shrink who found the body say her name was Renee Hayes?"

"Check this out, man," said Deek pointing to the opposite end of the room, "a goddamn fireplace in the bedroom. Must be nice to have a little spare change, huh? I can't see how this brother could afford to be livin' uptown like royalty and buying all this shit on an associate attorney's salary. Musta been doin' a little moonlighting on the side and a deal turned sour on him," said Deek, "Yeah, one of his enemies probably smoked him. Rolled him up like a blunt and smoked him. What you think, man?"

"I'll tell you what I think," said Bradford as he pointed to the bloodstained scarf, "Looks like we disagree on the motive. Considering the fucked up state we found this brother, my money's on a jealous broad as our murderer."

A plain-clothes young detective, Sergeant Thaddeus Kane, the newest addition to Bradford's squad, stood patiently at the doorway and waited until Deek and Mel stopped talking. Bradford noticed him standing by the door and acknowledged him.

"Whatcha got Kane?"

"No one saw or heard anything, sir."

"Damn. Anybody find a weapon?"

"Not yet, sir."

"Figures. What else you got?"

"Not much. No sign of a struggle or forced entry. I'll bring in the evidence bags for you to look at, sir" said Sergeant Kane.

"You sure those guys checked out every nook and cranny—stairwells, the hall-way, outside, everywhere?"

"Yes, Lieutenant."

Bradford picked up Coleman's wallet from the dresser and took out the driver's license.

"Send somebody out to the parking lot to search the victim's vehicle. Look for a black Lexus Coupe. License Number Larry David Charlie 701. And check his answering machine messages too."

"Yes, sir," said Kane and rushed out to follow orders.

"Asshole," whispered Bradford under his breath after the young detective had left, "Tell me something, why would anybody name a kid Thaddeus?"

"Lay off, Mel," said Deek, "the kid's all right and he's learning fast. Besides, my grandmother didn't do me no favors by naming me Degas."

"Yeah, man. You're right about that," agreed Bradford, "Degas is a fucked up name too. But I still don't see why I had to get stuck with this nitwit on my squad when I'm trying to go out in December with a clean record. I'm telling you, man, that Kane is a jinx. Just because his old man's in good with the chief, they give him a shot on my homicide unit. I'd rather have my eighty year-old mother on the squad. Don't you remember his last blunder on that drug bust? Made the lead detective look like a complete fool."

"He's okay, Mel," said Deek, "You can't blame him for all last year's screwups, you know."

"All I know is somebody up there hates my guts," said Bradford, pointing upwards. "Seventy-five unsolved cases last year," moaned Bradford, shaking his head, "I look like a goddamn rookie myself."

"Yeah, it's a real treat for all of us working with your ass, Mel."

"Don't be a wise-guy, Young Blood. And don't think I didn't notice how you avoided my question about the lady Doc and that scarf you pulled out the hamper. We still don't know why the hell she came over here tonight. Kane, get the Doc in here."

Renee noticed a young detective of average height and thin-build walking towards her. He said that Lieutenant Melvin Bradford wanted to ask her a few questions. Renee followed the detective inside the apartment to the living room.

Lieutenant Bradford motioned for her to sit down then sank his heavy frame in a nearby white leather chair.

"This here's Sergeant Thaddeus Kane. Rookie to the homicide squad."

Sgt. Kane had a youthful, clean-shaven face. What little facial hair there was, blended in completely with his cafe-au-lait complexion. He positioned his black spiral notebook on his lap, in preparation to take down Renee's statement. He glanced at her through dark, hazel colored eyes and waited patiently for her to begin.

"Where's Detective Hamilton?" asked Renee.

"He's where he's supposed to be," Bradford smiled.

"Now, let's begin with you, Dr. Hayes. What's your story, exactly? You can start by telling me why you came here to Mr. Coleman's apartment tonight?"

"Detective Bradford, am I a suspect?"

"Everybody's a suspect until the case is closed," he snapped, "Do you have a problem with one of my officers checking your vehicle?"

"No, of course not. It's the green Acura parked out front. I have nothing to hide."

"Good. McNeil?" he yelled out to an officer standing by the doorway. The officer approached. "Yes, Lieutenant?"

"Go check out that green Acura parked next to mine."

"Is it open?" he turned to Renee.

"No. But the unlock key combination is 4317."

"Check it out, will ya McNeil?"

"Sure thing, Lieutenant." McNeil abruptly left. Just then Deek came out of a back room and spoke to Bradford.

"I've gone over all the evidence bags and the inventory's ready to be sent downtown to the evidence room," said Deek.

"Good. I'll go down there later and check it out myself. Might see something you missed," smiled Bradford, "What's that?" he said, pointing to papers in Deek's hand.

"Some legal papers from Coleman's briefcase," said Deek and handed Bradford the stack of papers.

"Here, Kane," said Bradford and dumped the papers in Kane's lap, "Write down all the names and addresses of Coleman's clients. Contact friends, lovers, and acquaintances. Everybody'll have to be checked out. We'll run'em all through records when we get back to headquarters." Sgt. Kane nodded and began studying the papers to look for the information.

"Here you go, Pint," said Deek and handed Kane a printout and a flash drive, "I already copied over Coleman's client data file and some of his email from his PC in the study. How 'bout checking out those names for us right now, Buddy."

"Right, Deek. I'm on it," said Kane and rushed out the door.

Deek then sat down across from Renee and opened his laptop computer.

Bradford asked her again what was she doing at Coleman's place. Renee hesitated. Anything she said would incriminate her patient. Renee wanted a chance to speak to Veda before revealing that she was at LaMarr's apartment before he was killed.

"I asked you a question, Dr. Hayes," said Bradford. He leaned forward and stared directly in her face. "If you can't answer me here, we can go down to the First District substation." Renee looked at Deek. Lieutenant Bradford shot an angry glance at both of them.

"Is there something goin' on here that I should know about?"

Deek shook his head. Now was not the time for him to confess his involvement with Renee. He wanted to learn the truth just as bad as his partner did but he knew Mel was out for blood. All Mel wanted was to wrap things up and tie a neat, little bow around it for Chief Riley. A suspect, any suspect would do. He already made it clear that he thought the killer was a jealous female.

"Was Mr. Coleman a patient of yours?" asked Detective Bradford.

"No. He was not."

"Did you know the victim?"

"Not exactly."

"Then why *exactly* did you come to Mr. Coleman's apartment tonight?"

Detective Bradford would not let up. It was obvious to Renee that he was trying to hold back his anger. Renee didn't know how much longer she could keep Veda's name out of this. She knew Veda didn't do it. Or at least she believed she couldn't have done something so grisly and horrific. But this detective would never believe that. If she could just speak to Deek alone, she could explain what happened.

"Well, I came here because … Actually, I was concerned about …"

"Who, what, when? You'd better start cooperating with this investigation Dr. Hayes," said Detective Bradford, "It's late and my patience is running thin."

"Okay. The truth is I was responding to an emergency call from my pager number."

"From who?" he asked and opened his mouth wide to yawn. He sounded bored as well as irritated. His brown eyes looked bloodshot and heavy-lidded.

"Don't you mean, from whom?" corrected Renee.

Bradford jumped up from the chair and pounded the palm of his big hand on an end table. The sound was muffled by the smooth white marble surface, but his anger was unmistakably loud and clear. He moved forward until his face was only inches from hers.

"Goddamn it, lady. It's almost three in the morning. I'm tired and hungry. I been constipated for three days. We got a dead body, no weapon, no eyewitnesses, no motive, and maybe only one suspect. You! So you'd better start talkin' fast or you're gonna be hit with a 1st degree and facing 30 years to life."

Bradford's breath smelled like fried, greasy meat and stale cigarettes. Renee leaned back, as far as she could, to get away from him without losing her balance.

"Look, Mel. Why don't you let me take over here?" said Deek.

"Not a chance, Bill Gates. You just keep typing in her statement, such as it is."

"Okay, Dr. Hayes, let's start over," said Bradford and glanced down at his notepad, "The guard downstairs says he saw you go up the elevator at around 11:00 PM. Time of death was estimated to be about 11:45. The call came into dispatch at 1:10 AM. That would give you plenty of time to argue with Coleman, kill him, and report the murder. Then hang around to see what we find. That's my version, what's yours?" Detective Bradford smiled, took out a piece of gum and started chewing on it.

"I arrived here at 12:55 not 11:00, Detective. That guard was asleep the entire time until I came downstairs and woke him. He didn't see a thing. I told him to call the police. Why would I wait in a dead man's apartment for over an hour, doing nothing? Why would I do that if I had killed Mr. Coleman? And why would I ask the guard to phone the police?"

"Murderers do it all the time. They think it might eliminate them as a suspect. Maybe you hung around to try and figure out how you could get away with it, who knows. So, where were you at 11:45, Doctor?"

"I was home in bed with my husband, Bill. We were asleep or at least he was."

"I see. So your alibi is your husband who was asleep, right? Okay, say I buy that. And let's assume the guard was wrong about what time you got here. You say you and your husband were in bed asleep at 11:45. That still doesn't explain what the hell you were doing here at 12:55."

Renee didn't respond. Detective Bradford opened the lapels of her jacket. He pointed to the bloodstains on her white silk blouse.

"So, tell me, Dr. Hayes, who the hell paged you and why did you come here tonight?"

Renee jerked her jacket loose from his grip.

"Answering that question, Detective, would violate doctor-patient confidentiality. Circumstances led me to discover Mr. Coleman's body. I had no motive to kill him. I did what any good citizen would do. I reported a crime. May I go now?"

Bradford burst out laughing. He addressed his comments to Deek who now appeared visibly concerned. "Deek, looks like Dr. Hayes here is ignorant of our American Justice System. I think we better take her to the precinct and acquaint her with it."

"Uh look, Lieutenant, you don't really think she killed Coleman, do you?" asked Deek, "Let's get real, Mel. What prosecutor would take a case as weak as this one? We really don't have any evidence against her. And like she said, where's the motive?"

Bradford narrowed his eyes and glared at Deek, "That's for me and you to find out, partner."

Detective Bradford got up and went into the room where Deek had been reviewing the evidence. He returned with two clear plastic evidence bags. Inside one was the lime green silk scarf that Deek had found in the dirty clothes hamper. The other bag contained a false fingernail tip painted with gold-flecked polish. The label on the bag said exhibit number 108 false nail left hand and indicated that it had been found behind the bedpost. Lieutenant Bradford held up the bag that contained the false nail tip to Renee's eye level.

"Hold out your left hand," he ordered. Her nails where polished in a clear, neutral tint and filed down short.

"Loose a nail?" he asked.

"Of course not. I don't wear false nails," snapped Renee.

With glove protected hands, Lieutenant Bradford removed the scarf from the other evidence bag. He showed Renee the initials and bloodstains on the scarf.

"Is this your scarf, Dr. Hayes?"

"Yes, it is but I don't know what it's doing here. I left it hung over my jacket at home, in my office closet."

"Look," said Lieutenant Bradford, "I'm going out to the kitchen to get a slab of that chocolate cake I saw in the fridge earlier. By the time I get back, you'd better be ready to start talkin'. No more bullshit, you hear?" Just then, Officer McNeil returned.

"Bad news, Sir. We finished searching the victim's car," said McNeil, "Nothing worthwhile. And we didn't find anything inside the doctor's car either. Except we couldn't get into the glove compartment because it has a different unlock passcode."

Lieutenant Bradford turned around to face Renee. "Well," he yelled, "What's the goddamn passcode to the glove compartment?"

"I can't tell you that," said Renee, "The glove compartment contains confidential patient information which I'm not at liberty to divulge."

"Dr. Hayes, just who the hell are you protecting? If you don't tell me what you know about this homicide case, I'm gonna charge you as co-conspirator, as well as, an aider and abettor to the 1st degree murder of LaMarr Coleman, after the fact."

"Detective Bradford, I don't know anything about this homicide," said Renee, "I'm sorry but I can't willingly violate my patient's privacy and allow you access to my confidential files."

"That's it," yelled Bradford, "McNeil, get downstairs and impound this suspect's vehicle as evidence. And get a search warrant for her car. I wanna see what's in that glove compartment. We're making an arrest."

Deek stepped in front of Bradford and towered over him. His voice was deep and serious. His eyes narrowed and his forehead pinched together in a frown as he stared down at his senior partner. "Mel, you know this is ridiculous. Why don't you go home and get some rest. I'll take Dr. Hayes's statement tonight. I know I can get her to cooperate."

"The hell you will," shouted Bradford, "Do I look like an idiot? I can see you got a thing for her. If you hadn't been with me all night on the midnight shift, I'd be interrogating your ass right now too. You'd better back off, Young Blood, and let me do my fuckin' job or I'll have you thrown off this case."

"I'll back off and let you do your fuckin' job when you start doing it," yelled Deek, "All you're interested in is breakin' Jack Densen's record when you retire. You don't give a damn who gets arrested."

"Look man, I know what I'm doin'," said Bradford in a calmer tone, "I'm a give her a taste of what'll happen if she keeps playin' this fuckin' charade with me."

"You're full of shit, Mel." Deek stormed out the room in disgust.

Bradford grabbed Renee's elbow and twisted it behind her back. He held both her hands tight with only one of his big, sweaty palms. He took out a set of handcuffs from his back pocket with his free hand. He clamped the handcuffs on her and pushed her face against the wall. He stood behind her, only inches away. The foul smell of his breath and his deep breathing sickened her.

"Doctor Renee Hayes, you're being charged with 1st degree murder. You have the right to remain silent. Anything you say can and will be held against you in a court of law. Understand? You have the right to an attorney and to have an attorney present during questioning ..."

Bradford treated her like a common criminal. She didn't hear the rest and didn't utter a single word of protest. Her mouth felt dry. She licked her lips and took a deep swallow of her own saliva. Renee couldn't believe this was happening to her. She thought she heard herself scream out loud but realized the scream only existed in her mind. Her mouth flew open but nothing came out. A group of onlookers peered out of their doorways as Detective Bradford dragged her down the hallway in handcuffs.

CHAPTER 28

▼

Renee rode in the back seat of a police car driven by a young cop who tried to make small talk. According to the name printed on his uniform, he was Officer Bobby Sherman. Officer Sherman said Lieutenant Bradford must be in a foul mood about something to treat her like this. Renee was too upset to speak and rode in silence. Still in handcuffs, she barely managed to keep her balance on the hard plastic seats. She shivered and clasped her knees together to try to keep warm. Even though it was pitch black outside, her eyes remained shut. Tears dribbled down her cheeks. She was being treated like a murderer and there was nothing anyone could do about it, not even Deek.

Officer Sherman drove through the garage entrance of D.C. Police headquarters at 300 Indiana Avenue, N.W. He helped Renee out of the vehicle. When she was able to stand upright she tried to appeal to him. "Officer, can you please remove these handcuffs?" said Renee, holding out her clasped wrists, "I assure you I'm no threat."

Officer Sherman looked at her, then hesitated for a moment. "What the hell," he said, retrieving the keys from his belt and unlocking her cuffs. "You don't look like no dangerous criminal to me. Bradford likes to play these head games. You musta done something to really piss him off."

"Thank you," said Renee, rubbing her sore wrists. Officer Sherman held onto her elbow and led her through a dark, dingy tunnel leading to the receiving area. He was tall and Renee had to take quick steps to keep up with his long strides. Before they reached the receiving area, Officer Sherman received a call on his police wireless handset. After completing the call, he took her in the opposite direction, still holding onto to her arm. "C'mon. Looks like you're getting a reprieve from the jail cell tonight, Dr. Hayes," said Officer Sherman. "That was the Lieutenant. He wants me to bring you right upstairs for questioning. Word of advice, Doctor—don't make him mad."

They rode the elevator to the third floor and entered a large processing room. Renee was exhausted but the glaring bright lights overhead kept her alert. Although it was 4 o'clock in the morning, the room was packed with officers. They laughed and joked amongst themselves as they moved leisurely about the room. Desks lined the walls on both sides. Several columns of ugly, gray, metal file cabinets stood against one wall from floor to ceiling.

Renee noticed Detective Bradford hunched over his desk, absorbed in paperwork. Officer Sherman stopped in front of his desk. Bradford looked up.

"Thanks, Sherman. I'll take it from here."

After exchanging a few brief words with Bradford about another case, the officer left. Renee sensed a strong odor of onions and spices. The source of the aroma lay spread out on his cluttered desk amidst stacks of paperwork and forms. Three jumbo hot dogs smothered with chopped onions and spicy-brown mustard, a large bag of potato chips, and a box of chocolate chip cookies. She waited. Finally, he pointed to a chair next to his desk without looking up from his paperwork. Renee sat uncomfortably in the straight-back, wooden chair. Bradford picked up one of the hot dogs and devoured it in about two bites. The mustard oozed out and dripped between his fingers and onto his paperwork. He licked his fingers then wiped the drops of mustard from the papers, leaving a putrid-looking, yellow stain. He shoveled a handful of chips into his mouth, then took a large bite from the second hot dog.

Renee didn't understand how he could eat after what they'd seen at Coleman's place that night. But it obviously, hadn't affected the detective's appetite. He wolfed down the meal as if it were just an appetizer.

"How the hell can you eat hot dogs and chips for breakfast, Mel?" asked a pregnant female officer on desk duty sitting nearby.

"This ain't breakfast. This is just a snack," he said.

"Then you must have a big appetite," she said, and shook her head, "I thought I was bad."

"Yeah, I got a big appetite all right and I like food too," he winked at her then took in another mouthful of his hot dog. After he had finished eating and belching, Bradford laid out a stack of forms in front of him. He wrote the victim's name, LaMarr Coleman, across the top front tab of a brown folder. Renee watched him fill out the first form in triplicate. He filled in the date, time, and the victim's address. He entered 31 under victim's age, Black for his race, and male for victim's sex.

"Deek wants me to put all this shit on a computer. Says we can look up stuff quicker. Not me. I'm stickin' to what I know works," said Bradford. When he finished the first set of forms, he laid them aside and took out another set. For a brief moment her eyes met his. She turned away abruptly and stared down at her lap.

"You ready to cooperate?" he asked her.

"Why can't Detective Hamilton question me?"

"Well, he ain't here at the moment and we don't have 'til fuckin' Christmas to solve this thing," yelled Bradford.

"Full Name?" He positioned his pen on the form.

"Detective, I'd like to make a telephone call. I couldn't reach my husband earlier," said Renee, "I think I have rights to make a phone call, don't I?"

"You'll get your phone call when I'm good and ready, goddamn it! I'm in charge here. Name?" He shouted.

"Renee Janette Hayes," she answered flatly. Bradford started to scribble her name on the form without looking up.

"How you spell that?"

"Which part?" she asked.

"All of it," he said. Renee slowly spelled out her entire name.

"Social Security Number?"

Renee slowly recited the numbers. "Detective, is all this really necessary?"

"We can put an end to this whole goddamn ordeal, Dr. Hayes," he said, "all you gotta do is tell me what I wanna know." She looked away from him without saying a word. "Have it your way then … age?" he asked and stared at her with weary-looking eyes.

"Forty-four." she answered.

"Height?"

"5 feet, 4 inches."

"Weight?"

"Why do you need all this information? I haven't done anything wrong?"

"Weight?" he repeated.

"About one thirty-five, I think."

He stopped and allowed his gaze to scrutinize her body up and down. Then he scribbled on the form.

"Looks more like a one fifty to me," he said with a smirk on his face. Who was he to criticize someone else's weight, she thought. His gut spilled out over his belt as he hunched over the desk. "Don't get me wrong," continued Bradford wearing a lurid grin, "I like my women round, not square. One fifty looks just fine on you to me." Considering the crude qualities he had displayed so far, Renee was not surprised that he would take such liberties with her now.

"Yeah, like I always say," he grinned, "don't nobody want a bone but a dog. I bet Deek agrees with me on that too, huh. Hair color ... dark brown, right?"

Renee nodded.

"Eyes?" he said while inching closer across the desk and peering into her face to figure out her eye color.

"They're brown. Isn't that obvious?" she answered flatly and leaned her body away from him.

"Yeah, they match your hair real nice."

"Detective, can we just get on with this?" she said and hoped he could pick up on the annoyance in her tone of voice. He didn't get it or didn't care because he made several more remarks filled with sexual overtones.

Suddenly, a young, attractive woman in handcuffs bustled in the room flanked by Deek and an arresting officer. Deek held a firm grip on her arm. Detective Bradford temporarily halted his questioning. He sat there with his mouth hanging open and stared at the shapely young woman with long, dark brown hair and greenish eyes. A leopard-printed, mini skirt pinched her curvy hips as she walked. She wore a matching jacket with a black, lace teddy underneath and sheer black stockings. A gold, heart-shaped pendant fell from her neck, and was almost lost between the crevice of her exposed cleavage. Renee felt a sting of jealousy and irritation at Deek. Why had he abandoned her ordeal to handle this pretty, young woman's problems?

Deek stood in front of the doorway while the arresting officer filled him in. The entire time the accused fired off obscenities at both of them, which they ignored. The officer told Deek that he and his partner spotted this individual walking up and down Park Road in NorthWest in front of Bluridge Heights Apartments. The officer said they were automatically suspicious of anyone caught cruising a known drug zone like Park Road. They decided to watch her, hoping she'd lead them to her connection and a bigger bust. The arresting officer said they watched from a short distance and saw her lure her bait, ... some guy in an '89, maroon, Dodge Shadow. When they saw an exchange take place, they arrested the young lady and her bait, a Jason Phebus, for using, buying, and distributing illegal drugs. The guy was also charged with a D.U.I. and carrying a concealed weapon.

"What kind of evidence did you find on him?" asked Deek, referring to the young lady's bait, Jason Phebus.

The arresting officer described some of the drug paraphernalia they found in Jason Phebus' car. An empty Coca-Cola can with a hole burnt in the flat end. He said an indentation punctured in the can's cylinder was used to hold the crack.

"And we found a ten piece in the dude's vehicle. He was pretty wasted by the time we showed up," said the arresting officer, "By the way, we also found a stack of file folders stashed in the backseat."

"Oh yeah? I'd like to talk to Mr. Phebus when you're done with him. Where's he at now?" said Deek, looking around the room.

"He's chilling out in the holding cell downstairs. My partner just finished processing him. Looks like he violated his probation on top of trying to pick up this doped up hooker here."

"Hey, man, who the hell you calling a hooker?" shouted the young woman.

"Pull a report on Jason Phebus for me, will you John?" asked Deek and gave him a pat on the shoulder. "And let me see those folders you found on him ASAP."

"Sure thing, Sergeant. Can you watch the prisoner for a sec?" said John, "I'll go get my partner to come up and start the paperwork. I'll dig up those file folders and Phebus's criminal activity report for you right away."

"Thanks, John. I'll handle things here for you until you get back."

"Just try to control yourself, Sergeant," teased John while motioning his head towards the accused. "She's a hottie."

Deek thought about the break in at Renee's place several weeks ago where patient data files were stolen. He wondered if Jason Phebus could be the same guy. Deek held on tight to his prisoner's arm.

"Hey man, what is your damn problem?" she shouted and attempted to jerk her elbow free of Deek's grasp, "Get your filthy hands off me." The prisoner was argumentative and did not hide her annoyance at being detained from her purpose of getting a hit and who knows what else. Deek grabbed hold of her again. He led her to his desk and stopped briefly when he saw Renee being questioned by Bradford. No longer in handcuffs, the young woman turned suddenly while Deek was momentarily distracted by Renee and snatched away from him. She started to run out of the room but Deek caught her by the shoulder. They struggled. She was strong and in good shape but Deek managed to wrestle her to the floor.

"Look," said Deek, "make it easy on yourself and stop fighting me."

John and his partner walked in and found Deek holding down their prisoner with her face pressed to the floor. Deek rose immediately and helped her up off the floor.

"I told you to try to control yourself," laughed John and nudged his partner.

"You both go to hell. Take your goddamn prisoner," said Deek as he brushed the dust off his pants legs, "Where're those files?"

John handed Deek the information he requested. Deek watched as John handcuffed the feisty young woman and led her to his desk at the end of the hall for processing. John ordered her to sit down. She crossed her legs and assumed a defiant expression. Deek shook his head and focused his attention on the files that John had given him. After studying the files for several minutes, he approached Bradford and once again offered to take over Renee's questioning.

"Fine. I need to go to the john and take a cigarette break. Let's see how far you get 'til I get back." Bradford disappeared down the hallway.

It was difficult for Renee and Deek to concentrate on their own conversation because several desks down from them, John's prisoner argued loudly with him.

"Look man, I didn't do nothin'," she tossed her long hair to one side, "that skinny, little asshole ratted me out. I wasn't tryin' to get high. He asked me for directions and I tried to help him. That's it."

"Yeah, right, Princess," said the officer, "I just bet you tried to help him, all right."

"Look, man. Can you get rid of these damn handcuffs? They're too tight and they're bruising my wrists," she complained.

"Only, if you promise to behave yourself," said the officer as he got up to unlock the handcuffs. She rubbed her wrists and tried to stimulate the blood flow.

"Now then, let's start with your real name," said John and settled back down into his chair, "You told my partner your name is Peaches. Now we know that can't be right. So what is the full name on your birth certificate not your a.k.a.?"

"Didn't you stupid cops just finish running me through your freakin' records? You didn't find no jacket on me, did you? 'Cause I'm clean."

"You're right, we didn't find any criminal record for the alias you gave us. Now we'd like to run a check on you. So what's the name Mommy dearest gave her precious little girl, huh?"

"Don't you cops got nothin' better to do than harass innocent people? Why you guys gotta hassle me? Like I told that other dimwit, I didn't do nothin'"

"What's your address then, *Miss* Peaches?"

"When can I go home?"

"And where might that be, ... Home?"

The prisoner avoided the officer's questions. She kicked her crossed leg, back and forth, in front of the officer's face. One high-heeled shoe dangled loosely from her toes. She rubbed her nylon-covered knee in a continuous, circular motion and squinted her green eyes at him in anger. She noticed the officer's gaze fell on her shapely legs then traveled down to her gold stiletto shoes. She tapped a well-manicured nail, painted gold to match her shoes, on the desk in annoyance. John's mouth fell open as he watched her seductive motions.

"I wanna call my lawyer," she demanded.

"Okay, Princess, I got time."

The officer retrieved the telephone directory from a side drawer and slammed it on top of his desk.

"What's your attorney's name? I'll even look up the number for you."

"You think I don't have a lawyer. Well, I do," she yelled at the officer and shoved the telephone book aside, "His name is LaMarr D. Colman. He's with Davis & Bookerman in Washington, D. C. But he's probably at home at this hour."

Not only had Renee and Deek heard the name LaMarr D. Coleman loud and clear, but so had Detective Bradford who had just returned from his cigarette break. Deek sprung up from his chair and approached John's desk.

"What did you just say about LaMarr Coleman?" Deek asked John's prisoner.

"You knew Coleman?" demanded Bradford next, "When did you see him last?"

The prisoner's eyes darted from Bradford to Deek. Not sure which one to answer. "What's going on here?" she asked.

"I'm sorry to tell you but LaMarr Coleman was murdered last night. If you have any information that could help this investigation, I'd appreciate your cooperation. We might be able to ease up on your drug charges in that case," promised Lieutenant Bradford.

"What's your real name, Peaches?" John asked again. This time she answered, wearing a look of shock and disbelief at what she'd just heard. "Deliah D'Arcy. My name's Deliah D'Arcy."

Lieutenant Bradford told Delilah's arresting officer that his homicide case took priority over a prostitution or drug bust. Now that Bradford had someone willing to talk, he turned Renee's questioning over to Deek without protest. The two detectives planned to get together and compare notes after the interrogations.

Deek escorted Renee to a private Interview room. While Bradford led Delilah to another Interview room at the end of the corridor to question her. Delilah told Detective Bradford everything she knew about Veda Simms and LaMarr Coleman in exchange for dropping the charges against her. She revealed Veda's attempt to poison LaMarr and admitted her part in it. Delilah said Veda was desperate because of an audit due on Monday. Veda had stolen $5,000 from their firm's petty cash fund at LaMarr's request and later he refused to pay it back. When Bradford asked her why she had befriended LaMarr after the poison attempt, she admitted they had later formed a mutually beneficial arrangement. He provided her with drugs and she became his informant on the streets. After nearly an hour of questioning, Bradford released Delilah back to her arresting officer's custody. The police dropped all charges. With her consent, they arranged for her to be transported to Montgomery General Hospital for detox. Delilah still insisted that her folks not be contacted.

Renee tried to answer Deek's questions truthfully without volunteering any additional information about her patient. She told him how she came to be at LaMarr Coleman's apartment last night. But she still didn't have an explanation for how her scarf landed in his laundry basket or how bloodstains got on it.

When Detective Bradford entered the interrogation room where Deek was still questioning Renee, she could tell from the expression on his face that he was pleased with the information he had obtained from Delilah D'Arcy. "Looks like things are finally beginning to fall into place," he said, looking sleepy-eyed but smiling. Bradford motioned to Deek that he wanted to speak to him privately. They both left the interrogation room without saying anything to Renee. Bradford was out in the hallway talking to Deek for about ten minutes, and Renee figured he was telling Deek what he had learned from questioning Miss D'Arcy.

When the door opened again, only Bradford walked through. He sat down at the long, narrow table and placed his notebook in front of him. Just then Deek returned and handed Bradford a file folder-size box, then immediately left the interrogation room. Lieutenant Bradford placed the box on the table, lifted the lid and removed several file folders. Renee recognized her patient files. The labels on the tabs indicated the files belonged to Veda Simms. She figured the police must have apprehended the burglar who had stolen her patient records.

"Detective, if that's what I think it is, you have to return those files to me immediately," she said, "Any information contained in those files is strictly confidential."

Renee tried to deter him from reading the files by claiming that the information about her patient could not be submitted as evidence in court. Bradford ignored her protests and began quickly reviewing each file. Suddenly, she reached for the folder and tried to snatch it out of his hand but he pushed her hand away. Renee matched his angry glare with her own stern look. She was even more annoyed at Deek for giving her files to his partner.

"Look, Detective Bradford, I want my files back. You have no right to hold on to my property."

"It's evidence."

"I'm warning you, Detective. Those files are protected under doctor-patient privilege and without a court order you have no authority to keep them."

"That's bullshit. What's the matter, Doctor, afraid of a malpractice suit?" said Bradford wearing a smirk on his face.

"No, I'm not concerned about being sued. I'm concerned that you don't have the necessary training to accurately evaluate my notes."

"Why don't you just let me worry about that," said Bradford.

Renee realized it was no use trying to get Detective Bradford's assurance that the information Deek acquired by capturing the burglar would not be submitted as evidence.

Bradford grew weary of her interruptions and evasiveness. He began to read her notes out loud. He started with her introductory remarks and was glad her handwriting was legible.

"The patient arrived at her session hysterical and in tears. She said she had made a terrible mistake and didn't know how to get out of it. I asked Veda what was causing her to feel so anxious and threatened. She said she couldn't tell me because she was too ashamed of what she had done. I told her that it was not my role as a psychologist to judge others but to help them cope with their fears and anxieties. Eventually, she confessed ..." Bradford looked up at Renee and smiled before continuing. "She confessed to trying to get back at her lover by poisoning him." He read through several more of Veda's patient records before he was satisfied that he had enough to confirm his suspicions.

Renee searched Detective Bradford's face for a reaction. He gave none. He bent over a notepad and wrote down his own notes that were too illegible for her to read upside down from across the table. He stared at the scribbled notes on his notepad. His head rested between his cupped hands and both elbows were planted on the table just barely keeping his head from collapsing. He wrinkled his forehead in deep concentration. The clock on the wall indicated it was 5:30 Sunday morning.

Renee wished she had her wireless phone with her so she could try Bill again. The last time she had been able to get through to him was around one o'clock, just before the police arrived at Mr. Coleman's apartment. That was over four hours ago. Her forehead throbbed and face felt clammy. What if Bill had suffered another angina attack? She worried. Last year, he had experienced a mild attack that fortunately turned out to be only pain from angina and not an actual heart attack. Nonetheless, it had frightened them both. Bill's doctor instructed him to take it easy, reduce his workload, exercise a little more, and go on a low-fat, reduced-sodium diet. The only part of the doctor's advice that Bill even attempted to follow was to increase his tennis game. Luckily, since then there hadn't been any other episodes. But Renee still couldn't figure out why he didn't answer when she tried to call him again at four in the morning. Perhaps he had been in the bathroom and didn't hear the telephone, but he should have gotten her message. She knew she had to get home as soon as possible. Renee looked up at Lieutenant Bradford and noticed that his eyes were shut. She shook his arm gently. His head bounced upright and his eyes popped open like a jack-in-the-box. He looked around from side to side, somewhat disoriented.

"Detective Bradford, it's after 5:30 in the morning," said Renee, glancing briefly at the clock, "And I'm worried about my husband. I've cooperated with you all I can. Please, may I go home now?"

She prayed there was a soft spot somewhere in this despicable creature. Bradford tried to form a genuine smile, something, Renee knew he found difficult to do.

"Let me go check on Detective Hamilton's progress with questioning your burglar. If he's almost done, I'll see if he can drive you home. I'm a little too beat or I'd take you myself."

The last thing Renee wanted was to be in the same car with Detective Degas Hamilton. He had betrayed her by reading her private notes without her permission, then handing them over to his partner to pillage through. She didn't think she could ever trust him again.

"If I'm free to go, why can't I just take my own car?"

"Sorry, it's already been impounded and signed in as evidence in this homicide investigation. It'd take me hours to undo all that paperwork and get it back."

"You can't be serious," she said.

"I'll have all that cleared up by tomorrow. Promise. You can come by the station and pick up your car then."

Renee threw up her hands in disbelief.

"Sorry, Doctor Hayes, but you shouldn't have acted so unreasonable back there. I guess I did go a little overboard but you did piss me off."

"I pissed you off?" She said, trying to remain calm.

Renee took a few deep breaths and silently counted from one to ten. Bradford looked genuinely sorry. Fatigue appeared to mellow him into an almost tolerable person.

"Don't worry," said Bradford with a sarcastic smirk on his face, "We'll see to it that you get safely back home to good ole Bill. But don't leave town without letting us know."

He reached into his pants pocket, took out a roll of breath mints, and popped several into his mouth. He held out the roll to offer her one, but she shook her head no. Deek and Sergeant Thaddeus Kane returned just as Bradford was about to leave.

"Get anything out of Mr. Phebus?" asked Bradford.

"Yeah. He talked pretty good all right to get himself out of trouble," said Deek, "says that LaMarr Coleman paid him to break into Dr. Hayes's office and steal all the patient records for Veda Simms. Phebus doesn't know why. But I can guess. Coleman was probably worried about what this Veda Simms was telling her shrink about him."

"I intend to question this guy Phebus myself the first chance I get," said Bradford, "But right now, all I wanna do is go home and crash for a few hours."

"Me too. I've had enough for one night. I'll meet up with you guys at the crime scene around noon. If that's okay with you, buddy," said Deek and gently slapped Bradford on the back.

"Sounds like a plan. Hey, Bill Gates you mind running the good Doctor home for me first?"

"No problem," said Deek. He detected a look of displeasure on Renee's face but she didn't protest when he held the double doors open for her.

As they walked down the hallway towards the main exit, Renee stopped in the ladies room. The police detectives' voices carried through the bathroom door and Renee listened to their discussion about the case.

"Is it just my opinion or do you fellas agree we've got enough evidence for the D.A. to get a little excited about," said Lieutenant Bradford.

"Maybe, but only a little," said Deek, "First off, there was no sign of a struggle or forced entry. So we're probably talkin' about somebody Coleman knew. To be honest, all we really got is a shitload of circumstantial evidence and an unsubstantiated accusation from a crackhead."

"What about the string of messages from Veda Simms that we found on Coleman's answering machine just hours before he was murdered?" asked Kane. "Wouldn't we consider her our prime suspect right now?"

"Maybe, maybe not," said Deek, "True, we found out she was at the scene of the crime the night Coleman was murdered. Looked like she also had motive and opportunity. But we still need that murder weapon pointing directly to her. Only then would we have ourselves an open and shut case. Besides, there're some other questions still bothering me."

"You're right, Hamilton," said Kane, "A murder weapon with her prints on it would definitely clinch it all right."

"Yeah, wouldn't that be nice," offered Bradford, "Then I could go notify the D.A.'s office to file charges, get me an arrest warrant, and go home to Jim Beam on ice. Another one off the books. But with or without a murder weapon, Veda Simms is still our most likely suspect," said Bradford. "Kane, go ahead and put out an APB on her. We need to haul her ass in here for questioning. Let's see if she can produce an alibi during the time of the murder."

"Right, Lieutenant."

Renee opened the door and the detectives fell silent.

Sergeant Kane and Lieutenant Bradford branched off into different directions in the parking lot. Deek handed Renee her patient files and asked if she wished to press charges against Jason Phebus. Renee told him yes, even though all the files had been returned to her she still worried about client confidentiality. A serious crime had been committed and she intended to see it through, but she preferred to go through someone else to submit the claim. She didn't want to talk to Deek about it anymore. There were too many other things on her mind right now and her patient was one of them. "It looks like you and your band of buddies have already made up your minds against Veda," said Renee with an edgy tone in her voice.

"Bradford and Kane are not my buddies. They're homicide detectives doing their job, just like me," he said with a twinge of irritation in his own voice. Then he sighed. "I'm sorry Renee. I guess we're all tired. Let me just take you home."

Deek opened the door on the passenger side of his car and Renee slid in the front seat. She hugged her thin, linen jacket tightly across her chest and folded her arms to keep warm. Deek turned on the heat to take the chill off the crisp, early morning air.

"Too bad all you cops seem to be interested in is closing this case," said Renee and glared at Deek, "You and Detective Bradford could care less about finding out the truth."

"Do you really know this woman, Renee? How can you be so sure she didn't waste this guy? She did feed him rat poison, didn't she?"

Renee knew she couldn't be 100 percent certain of Veda's actions. She refrained from making any more comments about the case and rode alongside Deek in silence. He sang along with a hit R&B tune playing on the radio to hide the silence and try to ease the tension between them. It didn't work. Renee felt her muscles stiffen. She kept her mouth clamped shut so tight her jaw began to hurt. She felt like she didn't mean anything to him. Just a temporary distraction and now it was back to business as usual. Suddenly, Renee felt his warm hand on her thigh. She turned and met his brief gaze as he took his eyes off the road for a few seconds to look at her. The longing in his eyes spoke before he did.

"I've missed you, Renee" he said. "You don't have to go home. I can take you back to my place. Tyrone's spending the night with one of his buddies. After I called home earlier and told him it would be a late night at the station, I gave him permission to stay with his buddy just a few doors down. I know the people and he's fine, so we'd be alone at my place tonight."

Renee looked down at her lap without answering. She didn't want to admit to him how badly she did in fact want to go home with him and wake up the next morning in his arms. But that was not possible or practical right now. She would have to be sensible. She glanced at the strong contour of his handsome unshaven face and tried to sound believable. "I can't. I want to go home, Deek. I'm exhausted and I haven't heard from Bill all night. He never returned my calls. I have to ... find out if everything's all right."

"I understand. But can you tell me one thing, Renee? Why did you marry him? You deserve so much more."

She folded her arms and rested her chin in the palm of her hand, staring thoughtfully out the window before answering him. "When I first met Bill he was different then. He wasn't as cold and aloof as he acts now. I thought we'd be happy, have kids and settle down like a real family. That was something I never had growing up and I wanted it for my own children."

"I thought you told me Bill doesn't want children," Deek said cautiously, not wanting to upset her again.

"I know." She sighed. "To be honest when I look back he was never really as enthused about the idea as I was, but I thought after the baby came he would fall in love with it once it became something real to him. I know what you're thinking. It's crazy for a trained psychologist to believe she can change another person. Of course I knew this logically, but emotionally I wanted to believe it would be different for Bill and me."

There was a few seconds of silence before she continued. "After my last miscarriage, he completely rejected the idea of trying to have children again. He said he didn't want to see me go through another loss. But I suspect it was more like he never wanted to be a Daddy in the first place. I didn't want to see the truth when I married him."

Renee didn't notice that while she was talking Deek had pulled over and stopped the car alongside a deserted curb. The streets were quiet. They were alone. The only sounds came from their gentle breathing and the muffled music playing at low volume on the radio. With the car stopped, he leaned closer and slipped his hand in hers. Renee twisted her body towards him and he adjusted his long legs so that he sat closer to her. "I didn't mean to snap at you earlier," she said. "It's okay. I'm sorry too," he said.

Renee felt his warm lips on hers while the radio played. When their lips parted, he looked at her through dark vibrant eyes and spoke in a serious tone. "Renee, I just want the chance to make you happy."

Renee squeezed his hand. "No one can do that Deek—no one, but me." She drew in his hand tighter, not letting go. "Once I find out how." Renee's face turned solemn and she stared straight ahead. "I understand now that you can't look to someone else to fulfill you. Then resent it when they can't be what you want them to be."

Deek tilted her chin towards him. "Are you talking about your husband?"

"I guess I'm referring to everything in life, including you."

"You know what your problem is, Doc? You think too much." He held her face as they kissed for what seemed like a long time. Their tongues touched and lips joined, first with a burst of quick pecks and then a more lingering caress. She felt a wave of heat ignite her body. She touched his thigh and gently stroked his growing hardness and knew his moans came from both pleasure and pain.

CHAPTER 29

▼

Veda turned to check behind her then quickly unlocked her front door. Roaming the streets all night hadn't helped. It was now 8 o'clock on Sunday morning. She was tired and hungry and hoped the police wouldn't be there waiting for her when she got home. As soon as she stepped through the door, she saw Natasha sitting on the living room couch with her legs stretched out on the coffee table, smoking a cigarette, and watching TV.

"Girl, how'd you get in here? That door was locked."

"Honey, picking locks ain't no big deal," said Natasha, "Jerome taught me how."

"Yeah, and where's he at now? Up in Lorton if I'm not mistaken."

"The question is where have you been? I been here all night waiting for you, girl. When you didn't return my calls I got worried. Sorry, about bustin' in your place, but I thought you were in here stone cold dead or somethin'."

"Don't worry about it," said Veda, collapsing into a chair, "Any more coffee left?"

"There's a pot on in the kitchen. Sit down, rest. I'll get you some," said Natasha.

Natasha returned with a coffee mug and a doughnut and set them on the table.

"Veda, please tell me my instincts are wrong and that you didn't go to LaMarr's last night after I begged you not to? 'Cause I'm getting some pretty strong vibes telling me you did ..."

Veda got up quickly and went into the bathroom. She placed a hot, wet wash-cloth over her eyes that were red and puffy from lack of sleep and hours of crying.

Suddenly, a news bulletin interrupted the regular television show. Veda stood frozen in front of the bathroom door and listened closely to the commentator.

"… to recap this morning's headlines, D. C. Police are investigating the brutal slaying of a thirty-one year old Washington attorney whose body was found late last night and reported by a psychologist who had been treating the victim's girl-friend. Police later discovered that the girlfriend, Veda Simms, had been at the victim's apartment last night and fled the scene of the crime. The name of the victim is being held pending notification of relatives. Several neighbors questioned last night said they did not hear any shots fired or see anything unusual. The murder weapon has still not been recovered. Veda Simms is wanted by the police for questioning. An All Points Bulletin has been put out over dispatch to locate her. If you see this woman contact the police immediately at the number shown on the bottom of your screen."

A photo of Veda stayed plastered on the television during the entire news report. Natasha appeared at the bathroom door. Veda answered her friend's shocked expression without waiting to be asked the question.

"Girl, don't be stupid. You know I didn't kill him."

"I believe you Veda, but my opinion doesn't count. Look at it from the cops' point of view, you were at his place last night even though I told you not to go there. We both know you had good reason to kill him, and the cops'll know it too if they don't already. I'm sure they got your shrink to talk. And just last week you tried to poison the man with some D-Con rat bait …"

"Scare him. That's all, Natasha. Not poison him to death," said Veda, "Okay, it was a dumb idea, but I was desperate at the time."

"Why don't you call your doctor? Lord knows what she must be thinking by now. Who knows, maybe she can help you."

"Yeah, okay but right now we gotta get out of here for awhile before they catch us," said Veda.

"Us?"

"Oh, it's like that, huh? We're only tight when things are cool," said Veda with a look of panic on her face, "How long you think it's gonna be before they start knocking on my door?"

Natasha stared back at her. Veda was right. She couldn't abandon her friend now. She had to help Veda get away for awhile, but where and how? Veda waited for Natasha's answer.

"Well?"

"Okay, you can hold up for awhile at my place," said Natasha, "Come on, I'll help you get some things together. The longer we sit around here, the riskier it gets."

"What about your roommate?"

"KaLeese? She's cool."

"By the way, how much money do you have on you?" asked Veda.

"About fifty bucks."

"That's all? I can't get too far on fifty bucks."

"Well, how much do you have?"

"Girl, I'm broke."

"Okay then," said Natasha, "Beggar's can't be choosy, can they?"

"Let's just get you packed. Maybe KaLeese will have some cash you can borrow."

They packed quickly.

"We're in this shit together, girl," said Natasha, "LaMarr wasn't nothing but a dog. Anybody he knew could've blown his ass away."

Veda pressed down to force the suitcase shut. It bulged at the seams and could barely be lifted by either of them.

"Girl, this ain't gonna work," said Natasha, "You gotta leave some of this mess behind."

Veda retrieved her duffel bag from the hall closet and repacked just the bare essentials. She threw in an open box of Tampax into the bag.

"I see you finally got your period," said Natasha, pointing to the box of tampons, "That's good, 'cause I didn't wanna have to be raising your baby while you're in jail."

"I'm glad you got my back, girlfriend," Veda said sarcastically and rolled her eyes, "Yeah, but you're right. At least that's one problem I don't have."

"Hurry up, Veda. Let's get the hell outta here," ordered Natasha, "You can call that shrink of yours after we get to my place."

Veda left the rest of her things scattered all over the floor. Just as they were leaving, the telephone rang. Veda hesitated before reaching for the receiver. Natasha shook her head no, then grabbed hold of Veda's elbow and gave her a quick shove out the door.

They spotted a cab within minutes of leaving the house. Veda stepped off the curb and blew a piercing whistle with two fingers. The cab screeched to a halt and they climbed in the back seat.

"Where to ladies?"

"Minnesota and Benning, North East. And make it fast," said Natasha.

They nervously peeped through the back window to see if anyone was following. Veda's fear and despair grew stronger by the minute. She saw the cab driver looking at her in his rear view mirror.

"The next time I hit the streets, I'm a be incog-*negro*," whispered Veda.

Once Natasha saw they were getting close, she directed the cab driver to the red brick duplex that she and KaLeese rented. Natasha paid the carfare and they quickly hopped out of the taxi. They heard music coming from the apartment through the closed door.

"Girl, get your butt in here," KaLeese pulled Veda inside the door, "They been talkin' about you on the news all morning."

Right away, Veda felt comfortable in her friend's modest, sparsely furnished home that she'd visited many times before. All three women worked full-time, yet they lived from one paycheck to the next. Even Veda, the only one with a four-year college degree, struggled to keep her finances out of the red.

KaLeese was all dressed to go out. She had created an elaborately styled, upsweep hairdo by attaching layers of extensions to her hair. Her two-piece, tangerine-colored suit hugged the curves around her body and complimented her dark brown complexion. The hem on her skirt reached four inches above her knee and she wore a pair of high-heel, black, patent leather sandals with a matching handbag. A pair of gold chandelier earrings dangled from her ears and touched her shoulders. Her toes were painted tangerine orange to match her outfit.

"Honey, where in the world do you think you're going dressed like that on a Sunday morning?" Natasha asked her roommate.

"Where you think I'm going? The same place I been going every Sunday since that fine, new preacher showed up. To church, of course."

"To church? Dressed like that?"

"Damn straight and ya'll 'bout to make me late."

"Don't you even wanna hear what I been through?" asked Veda with a hurt look on her face.

"Girl, you can tell me about it later. Right now I better get on down to that church before those desperados from the Worship Committee get their hooks into that fine chocolate-brown Pastor Holland before I do, girl."

KaLeese took one last look at herself in the hall mirror and dabbed on some more tangerine lipstick. She moistened her fingertip with spit and smoothed out her eyeliner. Then she puckered her lips and blew herself a kiss in the mirror. "Gorgeous," she said, smiling at her reflection. Veda and Natasha shook their heads and gave KaLeese a look of annoyance.

"Hmph," said Natasha, with hand on hip, "This Pastor Holland must be something else to get you, the biggest sinner I know, to get up early every Sunday morning to go hear him preach."

"Girl, I ain't listening to his preachin'," said KaLeese with a wave of her bejeweled hand, "I'm looking at those straight white teeth, that smooth dark skin and that sexy smile he got. I'm so glad old wrinkled-up Reverend Porter finally retired. Our new spiritual Sheppard is young, hip and would ya'll believe it, he even wears his hair in dreds? Ya'll just gon have to come to church one Sunday and see for yourself."

"You mean, this Pastor Holland is not married?" asked Natasha, sarcastically.

KaLeese grabbed her purse from the table and did a swift model's pivot before answering. "Not yet girl, but give me time." She gave her roommate a wink and headed towards the front door. "By the way, there's plenty of food in the fridge, and the TV's fixed," said KaLeese on her way out. "Oh and I got a bottle of Cordon Negro stashed under the kitchen cupboards. Ya'll know whatever I got is yours. But don't expect me back before three. And if I get lucky, I might not be back at all tonight. Later, sistahs," KaLeese flashed a big grin and was gone in less than two seconds.

"Damn," said Veda, "I forgot to ask her for a loan. Wonder what time is it?" Veda went into the kitchen to check the clock on the wall. It was ten minutes before 10 o'clock.

"Girl, I'm a have to do something quick or my ass is going to jail."

"Well, you sure can't hide out here for too long. This area is infested with drugs, thugs, and cops," said Natasha.

Veda collapsed on the sofa. She really didn't want to get Dr. Renee involved in all this. But there was no one else to turn to. If Dr. Renee lied to the police about having talked to her or seen her, she could be arrested as an accomplice. She figured the police had probably already questioned Dr. Renee about her relationship with LaMarr. But how much did her therapist tell them?

"Veda? Girl, snap out of it," Natasha stood over her with both hands on her hips.

"If only I had listened to you and stayed away from LaMarr's place," said Veda under her breath.

"Look here, the whole damn bucket of milk is spilt and you're still asking how to get it back," said Natasha, "we ain't got time to worry about what coulda, woulda, shoulda."

Veda nodded in agreement.

"Look, Veda, if you expect me to trust you, you've got to be straight up with me, okay? What happened when you went to LaMarr's place last night?"

"Okay, okay. The truth is I only wanted to scare him with the gun."

"What gun? No you didn't have a gun, Veda!" shouted Natasha, throwing up her hands in disbelief.

"You remember about a week ago when I drove to my office at three in the morning to break into LaMarr's big case and mess up his contract papers. Well, that night I saw a group of kids throw a gun out of their car window so I took it for protection. Just in case."

"Girl, that was one of the stupidest things you've ever done. Did it ever occur to you that gun could have been involved in a crime? Why do you think those hoodlums threw the damn thing away?"

"I was too upset about the audit and getting that money back to think clearly, Natasha. I'm the office manager in charge of the books and all LaMarr had to do was deny knowing anything about the missing funds," Veda said, "Anyway, when I went to LaMarr's place I only meant to threatened him with the gun. I could tell he was telling me the truth when he said he didn't have the money. He was still weak from the medicine he was taking to clean the toxins out his system. I told him I was sorry about the rat poison. He wasn't angry anymore. When I left his apartment that first time LaMarr was alive, I swear."

Veda explained to Natasha that at that point she was desperate to come up with the $5,000. The only thing to do was swallow her pride and drive all the way to Luthersville to ask her Aunt Rose for the money. Aunt Rose managed her mother's finances. She knew her mother had been hoarding every penny she got from her Daddy's retirement and insurance since he died. She'd have that much tucked away and then some.

Aunt Rose had called several days ago and said her mother was recovering from her illness. Veda suspected that her aunt had probably exaggerated the seriousness of the illness in the first place just to get her down there and try to convince her to reconcile with her mother, but getting that five thousand dollars was the only good reason to go back home to Luthersville. Veda told Natasha that after driving for over an hour she turned the car around and headed back to her apartment. The thought of having to listen to her mother's mouth wasn't worth it. Veda knew all she would hear over and over was "I told you you'd never amount to nothing if you left a good man like Louis Simms for that lowlife creep. All he'd ever do for you was bring you down. Now you come crawling back here looking for sympathy and five thousand dollars. What God joins together let no man tear asunder. The devil has got a hold of you Veda Lucille Thomas and I wash my hands of it." Veda decided it would be easier to face the auditors than to face that.

After she got to her apartment she suddenly remembered leaving the gun on LaMarr's bedroom dresser. She knew it had her fingerprints on it and she had to get it back. When she arrived at his place after midnight that same night to get her gun back, she found LaMarr dead. His body had been mutilated. She covered him up and called Dr. Renee. As proud as LaMarr was, she knew he wouldn't want to be found like that. For a fleeting moment, the image of LaMarr appeared in her mind—sprawled out naked on his bed, an oozing gunshot wound in his gut, and his penis burnt and completely cut off.

Veda said she became frightened. The gun wasn't where she had left it, and she was too scared to look for it. She didn't know if the killer was still there hiding somewhere or if he or she would come back. In a panic, she fled. Later, she thought about how it would look to other people, especially to the police. After all, she did come to his place and threaten him with a gun and then ran away from the crime scene. Everyone would believe she did it. So she drove around and around, trying to think of what she should do.

"That's the absolute truth, Natasha," said Veda, exhausted.

"Girl, you better call that doctor and tell her exactly what happened last night. Get her to help you find out who killed LaMarr."

CHAPTER 30

▼

After Deek dropped her off at home, Renee climbed the stairs, still in a daze. Her legs moved as if on autopilot. When she opened her bedroom door, she found Bill sitting up in bed, and he appeared to be working on his laptop computer. He immediately turned it off when she entered. He arched his back straight against the headboard and folded his arms under his chest. Before she could say anything, he stared at her through hard, cold eyes and demanded in a firm voice, "Who the hell is D. E. Hamilton?"

Renee looked stunned, but didn't answer. How could he know about Deek she wondered? Bill repeated the question. Without looking at him Renee quickly stripped out of her clothes, slipped on her robe and disappeared into the bathroom and locked the door. She drew a bath of steamy hot water, as hot as she could stand it and stepped in. She planned to lie there until the water turned cool, perhaps then he would grow tired and fall asleep she hoped. She was too exhausted to deal with a confrontation with Bill after the ordeal she had just been through all night. After soaking in the tub for an hour, she got out and tapped her body dry with a towel and put on her nightgown. Renee didn't turn on the light, but felt her way through the darkened bedroom and eased herself gently into bed. She turned to the opposite side, facing away from Bill and hoped he was asleep, but he wasn't. He switched on the lamp from his nightstand and grabbed her by the shoulders to turn her around to face him. "I wanna know right now what the hell's going on!"

Renee moved away from him and pulled the comforter up to her shoulders. "I don't know what you're talking about. I tried to call you several times. I had an emergency with a patient. My patient needed me and in fact I'm just getting home from the police station. You can call the First District precinct if you don't believe me. Anyway, where were you last night when I called?" This time her voice sounded suspicious and indignant.

"Where was I?" he yelled, pointing at his chest. "I was out looking for you, goddamnit. Just tell me one thing, Renee," he said as he jerked open the night-stand top drawer and retrieved a telephone summary sheet, "Who is this person that's been calling you and that you've been calling?" He held up the detail pages of her phone bill, and showed her row after row of incoming and outgoing calls made to and from her wireless telephone to the same phone number.

"How did you get that?" she frowned. Bill explained how easy it was to request a detailed listing of the calls on her phone since they shared a family account that happened to be listed in his name. "Not only do I have this D. E. Hamilton's phone number, I also have his home address. So unless you want me to get up right now and go pay this joker a visit, you'd better start talking."

Renee turned away and avoided his eyes. "All right," she whispered. She got out of bed and sat down on one of their matching gilt chairs that had been uphol-stered in emerald green velvet. She stared ahead at the floral-design glass light fix-ture that hung on the wall. Slowly Renee revealed to Bill who Deek was and how they had met several months ago. She tried not to look at his face as she spoke. She admitted that her feelings for Deek had grown unexpectedly and that now she found herself attracted to him. She told Bill that she was confused right now and didn't understand what was happening to her. She did not admit that they had already slept together, but she didn't have to say it. Bill knew.

He jumped up from the bed and paced the floor, breathing heavily as he walked back and forth in short, clomping movements. She approached him, but he pushed her away. His face looked vacant and contorted. She noticed that his eyes were bloodshot and when she tried to get him to talk to her about his feel-ings he only gave her an empty stare. A thousand thoughts raced through his mind. No matter how hard he tried, he couldn't erase the image of his wife with another man. He wiped his eyes quickly with the back of his hand and silently cursed himself for revealing his torment. Bill felt her hand on his. "What're you going to do?" she said.

"What do you think?" he snapped, jerking his hand away, "I'ma find him and then I'ma kick his ass!"

She grabbed his elbow, "Bill, this is between us, no one else. We have to deal with the problems in our marriage. It has nothing to do with him. It's between you and me."

"No, Renee, you made sure it wasn't just between you and me," he sneered.

"Let's talk about this," she begged, "I'm sorry I hurt you. I didn't plan for this to happen. I just don't know what I want in my life right now."

"When you find out, let me know." He snatched his robe from across the bed, swung it over his arm and walked out of their bedroom, banging shut the door behind him. She heard his footsteps going down the stairs and soon after she heard the door to his office swing open and then abruptly slam shut.

The next day, Sunday afternoon after too little sleep, Renee got up and dressed quickly. Bill had already left the house. She considered calling him, but thought it better to give him some time to cool off. She hoped he wouldn't follow through on his threat to confront Deek. She called a cab and rushed back to the crime scene where she knew she would find Deek. At her urging the cab driver drove at record-breaking speeds and it wasn't long before the taxi swung around the circular driveway of LaMarr Coleman's apartment building. Renee paid the fare and returned to the victim's apartment in search of Deek and his partner, Detective Mel Bradford.

The front door had a crisscross yellow tape barrier, but she found the door ajar just enough to see inside. She hoped she would spot Deek and could catch his attention. She heard voices and movement coming from inside the apartment. She stepped over the tape and pulled the door open wider without being noticed. After a few minutes, one of the officers saw her standing by the door.

"You'll have to leave, ma'am. This is a crime scene."

"Sorry, Officer. I'm Doctor Renee Hayes. I'm looking for Detectives Hamilton and Bradford. I have some new information about the case to give them."

"Stay right there. Let me check." He disappeared briefly then returned.

"Sergeant Hamilton's not here at the moment," said the officer, "But Lieutenant Bradford's in the study. He'll see you now."

Detective Bradford sat at a desk reading papers from Coleman's file cabinet when Renee entered. He looked tired, but his weak smile appeared genuine.

"Get your car back, Dr. Hayes?" he asked, "I made sure everything was taken care of before I left last night."

"Not yet. I took a taxi here. Thank you anyway," said Renee, "I thought you were going straight home last night to get some sleep."

"Naw. Too wired up," he said, "Besides, I gotta put this case to bed before I can relax. The chief's really been breathing down my neck."

"By the way, we didn't get any answer at your patient's apartment this morning. Seems she may have skipped town. That certainty doesn't help her credibility. And when you add in your incriminating notes from her files ... sounds to me like we got ourselves a pretty solid suspect."

"Your equation doesn't add up, Detective. I know this woman. She's not the cold-blooded killer you're trying to make her out to be."

"Yeah, well, why don't you let me determine that. Do you have any idea where we might find her?"

"No, I do not."

"I get the feeling you know more than you're sayin' Dr. Hayes," said Bradford, "I hope you know you could get your license revoked if you're withholding evidence or obstructing justice in any way. You're not withholding any information are you?"

"Of course not. As a matter of fact, I came here to give you some information that might help your investigation."

"I'm all ears, Doctor. Shoot."

"I think I know who may have killed LaMarr Coleman," said Renee.

"Yeah? What a coincidence! I think I do too. Now, all I gotta do is bring her in so I can prove it."

"If you're willing to listen to another possibility, I remembered something important last night."

"Yeah? What important information is that?"

Renee told Detective Bradford what happened about a month ago, when Veda told her she had encountered a dangerous man who broke into LaMarr's apartment while she was there alone. The man had been looking for Coleman. The events Veda described came back to Renee in fleeting moments. All she could remember was that a man had come after LaMarr Coleman looking for a large sum of money that Coleman apparently owed him. Renee thought it was possible this man could be Coleman's killer.

"Veda said she believed that if LaMarr didn't pay the $5,000 he owed, that man would have no doubt killed him. That's why she took the money from her firm's account and gave it to LaMarr," said Renee, "But what if he used the money Veda gave him for something else and didn't pay the debt?"

"Yeah, okay and do you have a name or an ID for this character?"

"It took me awhile to dig it up from my notes. I must have missed it before, but Veda said he called himself Slade."

"Slade, huh? Wait, don't tell me," said Bradford and placed a chubby finger to his lips, "Is this Slade a bad-ass, ugly dude about 6'6"? Big, muscular, with a scar on the left side of his face about so long?" Bradford held up his hands about four inches apart.

He had described Slade to the letter based on Veda's description. Renee stood there with her mouth open, unable to speak while Bradford continued.

"Malik Brown, a.k.a. Slade, a known banker and drug-runner for a crew leader named Julio Garcia."

"Vice squad caught Slade holding a couple of kees last week. He's been locked up and awaiting trial since then. So much for your killer, Doctor. I think you better leave the police work to us." Detective Bradford's stomach began to rumble from hunger pains. "Damn, it's two o'clock already? I could use a little snack," he said, rubbing his plump belly. Bradford got up from behind the desk and headed straight for the kitchen with Renee following behind him.

"That's all you came here to tell me?" he asked as he opened the refrigerator and peered inside, "Sure you don't have any idea where your patient is hiding out?" He found the refrigerator practically empty, except for a bottle of champagne, a small tub of imported Brie cheese, and a carton of milk. "Shit, this guy must've eaten out all the damn time," said Bradford. "Kane?" he hollered out past the kitchen into the living room. Kane appeared at the kitchen entrance.

"Yes, Lieutenant?"

"Where the hell is that chocolate cake that was in the fridge last night?"

"Oh, I asked Reyes to take it around to all the Safeways in the area and try to find out if anyone served a customer who ordered a birthday cake for Coleman. The cake box label we found in the trash had Saturday's date on it. So whoever ordered it, delivered it to him on his birthday ... the day he was murdered," said Sergeant Kane.

"That's fine, Sergeant," he sighed. "Is Deek back yet from talking to Hilton Davis?"

"Not yet, sir."

"Let me know when he gets back. Good work, Kane. Carry on."

Kane grinned and returned to his search, glad that he had taken an appropriate action that had pleased his superior.

"Even when he does something right, it ends up pissing me off," said Bradford shaking his head, "Now what the hell am I supposed to eat? Damnit, I had my mouth all set for that chocolate cake." He started opening the cupboards and banging them shut. No doubt looking for something to eat, rather than searching for any additional evidence thought Renee.

"Detective, how can you come into a murdered man's house and casually rummage through his kitchen to look for food? You seem to be more concerned about what's for lunch than finding out who killed LaMarr Coleman," said Renee with an obvious tinge of annoyance in her tone.

"Like I said, I already know who killed him." He opened the doors to the pantry. It was also scarce. Only a few cereal and cracker boxes remained on the shelves. Bradford picked up a box of Honey Nut Cheerios and shook it. He took down a large, metal mixing bowl from the cupboard and emptied the entire box of cereal into the bowl. Renee watched as he dumped several spoonfuls of sugar over the already pre-sweetened cereal. Apparently, he was not worried about excess sugar consumption she thought. Then he grabbed the milk from the refrigerator and poured milk over it and proceeded to shovel a huge spoonful into his mouth.

"Go ahead, Doc," he said while chewing a mouth-full of Cheerios, "tell me your theory since we obviously have a different opinion on things."

Before his next swallow, Bradford suddenly spit out the partially chewed cereal into his bowl. After having consumed several mouthfuls at once, he had finally tasted it. "This stuff tastes like shit," he said.

He dumped the cereal out into the sink and turned on the garbage disposal. Bradford lifted the carton of milk up to his nose. "No wonder. The damn milk is sour."

"Damn," he said and poured the milk down the drain, "What's the matter with that son-of-a-bitch Coleman ... leaving sour milk in his frig."

"Yes, it really is a shame he didn't make it to the grocery store before you came over to investigate his homicide," said Renee.

"Guess I'll just have to eat it with water," said Bradford, "Had to eat cereal with water all the time when I was a kid. Didn't taste too bad."

He retrieved the bowl from the sink, rinsed it out and added a little water to it. Then he took down an open box of Cocoa Puffs from the shelf and shook it gently.

"Hum, feels heavy. Hot damn, a brand new box," he said with a grin on his face.

He poured the Cocoa Puffs into the bowl. As he poured, little round chocolate balls fell into the bowl, and all over the table, followed by the clank of a heavy object as it hit the bowl's hard metallic surface. Cocoa puffs and splashes of water darted out on the table and onto the floor in all directions.

"Hey, guess what? Looks like I found the prize! Kane, get in here," he yelled out into the other room.

Bradford pulled a ballpoint pin from his pocket, slipped it through the trigger guard and carefully lifted the pistol out of the bowl. He grinned broadly and examined what he hoped to be the murder weapon.

Sergeant Kane appeared at the kitchen entrance.

"You called, Lieutenant?"

Bradford held up the gun.

"Is that the murder weapon?" asked Kane.

"I'm banking on it," said Bradford, "Looks like a Davis P-32 semiautomatic. If it matches the bullet removed from Coleman, we got our murder weapon."

Lieutenant Bradford slipped the gun inside a plastic bag.

"What do we do now, Lieutenant?" asked Kane.

"Take it to FIU. They can check for fingerprints and let us know if the bullet that killed Coleman matches this weapon. If it matches, a trace should lead us right to the owner."

At that moment Deek burst in, slightly out of breath.

"What the hell's the matter with you?" asked Lieutenant Bradford.

"Nothing. Took the stairs," Deek answered between short breaths, "for exercise. No time to go jogging." Lieutenant Bradford shook his head. Deek tapped his senior partner's protruding gut. "You ought to try it sometimes, Mel," he said, "How do you expect to keep up with the criminals out there?"

"I'll leave the chasin' to you, Young Blood."

"Where're you going with that, Pint?" asked Deek, referring to Sergeant Kane who held the bag with the gun inside.

"Down to the District Building to the Firearms Identification Unit," said Kane.

Bradford called out to Sergeant Kane as he was leaving. "Tell 'em to put a rush on it. If it turns out to be our murder weapon, go on and take it down to the National Tracing Center in Landover and get ATF to put an urgent trace on it. Not routine, urgent, else it'll take too damn long to find out anything. Got that?"

"Yes sir, Lieutenant."

"Looks like I missed all the fun," said Deek.

"Sure did. We should know who the weapon belongs to and whose fingerprints are on it within eight hours if we're lucky," he said with a satisfied grin, and rubbing the palms of his hands together. "Think I'll swing by Jimmy's for a Seafood Combo," said Bradford, patting his belly, "I need to get me some real food. Hey," he yelled out into the main room, "somebody get in here and clean up this mess." Bradford turned to Renee. "I'm going out for lunch, but I can drop you off at the station first so you can pick up your car, if you want."

"I'll take care of that, Lieutenant," offered Deek, "I can meet up with you later at Jimmy's and fill you in on what I found out from Hilton Davis this morning."

"Sure," Bradford waved his arm as if to dismiss him, "And I also wanna hear more details of what went on yesterday with Jason Phebus. Just don't be all damn day. I eat fast. Besides, in another day or so, I should be able to make an arrest and close this goddamn case for good."

Bradford's signs of frustration and anger from the day before had disappeared now that he assumed he had found the murder weapon.

"Thank you for the ride," said Renee to Deek after the Lieutenant left.

"My pleasure," smiled Deek.

Renee wasn't sure if she should tell him about Bill and what he knew. At first she had planned to tell him, but the more she thought about it, the more afraid she became if Deek decided to retaliate against her husband. She prayed that everything would blow over, but in the back of her mind she knew the flames of anger still simmered inside Bill and his anger would not easily burn itself out. She would have to be strong and put some distance between her and Deek. At least she needed time to figure out if she really wanted things to work out between her and Bill. It would be difficult to stay away from Deek. She told herself it was because Veda needed her to stay involved in the case, but Renee knew it would be far more difficult to stay away from him for other reasons. Deek walked alongside her with both hands tucked inside his pockets, shoulders drawn back, and head lifted high as he strolled out to the parking lot. Like Bradford, Deek appeared pleased with where the investigation was headed.

"Deek, I really think you and Detective Bradford are wrong about Veda."

"Sorry, Doc. I guess we just don't see eye-to-eye on this one."

"You and your partner don't seem interested in following any other leads," she said, "You're bent on trying to prove my patient's guilt and nothing else."

"Not true, Doc. I just came back from questioning Coleman's boss and he had some very interesting insights on Veda Simms."

"What did he say?"

"It's official police business and I'm not at liberty to discuss that with you."

"But it's okay for you and Detective Bradford to violate my patient's right to privacy and jeopardize my reputation as a psychologist even after being told repeatedly that a patient's records are confidential."

"Your patient is a murder suspect. That changes everything in my book."

"Fine. I see how it works," she said, "Deek, I thought we could trust each other."

"You seem to forget, Renee, I'm investigating a homicide and your patient is a suspect."

After that the silence between them thickened. Deek dropped her off at the front door of the police station. Before he could come to a complete stop, she jumped out of the car and slammed the car door shut.

"I'll call you," he said.

"I think not, Detective." She walked away quickly and headed for the front door of the police station, knowing his eyes followed her.

Deek drove around the parking lot in the back of Jimmy's Soul Food joint but Mel's car was not there. He headed for 46th Street in SE, hoping to find his partner at home. Deek knocked on the door several times but there was no answer. When he looked through the window, he saw Bradford stretched out asleep on a tattered sofa with the telephone close by on top the coffee table. Deek tried knocking on the window but that didn't wake him either. Bradford lived alone since his wife had left him last summer. Deek dialed Bradford's number on his cell phone. After several rings, his sleepy voice answered, "Yeah."

"I've been outside banging on your door for ten minutes, Man," said Deek, "Unlock the goddamn door."

When Deek walked into the living room, he found Mel lying on the couch, staring at the ceiling, his eyes glazed and expressionless. A bottle and an almost empty glass of whisky sat on the table next to the telephone.

"Thought you were going to Jimmy's to get some lunch."

"I needed this more," he said, pointing to the glass of whisky on the table, "Turns out today's my anniversary. Me and Mamie would've made twenty-five years today if she hadn't left me. Can't say as I blame her though."

"Sorry, Man."

"How's things with you and the lady doctor?" said Bradford, sitting up so he could catch Deek's reaction, "Must be hard when you gotta wait your turn."

"Mind your own fuckin' business, Mel. I'm here to go over this goddamn case."

"Look Young Blood, just take my advice. Stay away from married women. You'll end up gettin' yourself hurt. Either by her or her husband."

"For chrissakes, Mel, I don't wanna talk about this right now," said Deek.

"Aw right, Man," said Bradford and picked up his drink. Deek shook his head to decline Bradford's offer to get him one.

"So, you get anything outta that lawyer, Hilton Davis?"

"Quite a bit. It helped that I had already broken into Coleman's deleted e-mail that was still stored on his PC's hard drive. When I showed Davis this, he spilled his guts all right. Nobody's hands are clean. It looks like everybody in that place had something on somebody." Deek handed Bradford a printout of personal e-mail that Coleman thought he had safely deleted.

"You did what?" said Bradford and reached for a pack of cigarettes from the table. He took out one then put it back. "I almost forgot you don't like cigarette smoke. So, you say you broke into Coleman's private mail, huh? Is that legal?" asked Bradford.

Deek sighed and massaged his temple before answering. "Mel, you're going to have to stop running from technology and accept it. You know we took Coleman's computer as evidence. That includes everything on his hard drive. Let me explain." Deek leaned forward and took on the countenance of a patient teacher. He pointed to the printout in Bradford's hand. "I found those e-mails that had already been deleted, but many people, including you, don't understand that when files are deleted from a computer those files remain on the hard drive until they're overwritten by another file or program. To get them back, all you have to do is run a data recovery utility program to change the status of the deleted file to un-deleted so that the file can be read. Understand?"

Deek didn't notice that Bradford had let the printout slip from his hand. Nor, did Deek acknowledge that his partner's slumberous eyes stared vacantly as if looking into empty space. Instead of slowing down, Deek spoke more rapidly and his dark eyes grew more animated as he explained how technology can be used in crime solving. Bradford picked up his glass and polished off the last drop of whiskey in one swallow and then poured another drink as Deek continued talking.

"There's something else Mel that the average person doesn't know. Copies of every e-mail you send are stored on one or more mail servers by your internet service provider or ISP as it's called. E-mails are not like regular mail!" Deek gestured with his hands to emphasize the point. "An ISP saves copies of e-mails in the form of backup files regularly and they keep these backups for a long period of time. Thousands of cases are being solved these days because copies of e-mails and related communications are obtained from ISP's via search warrants." Deek stopped talking long enough to clear his throat, then continued. "It gets worse—since 911 many government agencies are running software programs that examine all e-mail messages sent over the internet looking for key words and phrases that might be related to terrorist activities …"

Suddenly, Mel plunked the drink down on the glass tabletop loud enough to get his young partner's attention, while Deek was in mid sentence. "What's the gist of it, Deek? You know, I don't feel like hearing all this shit right now, Man!"

"You're right," said Deek and clasped his hands together under his chin. He gave Bradford a weak smile. "Mel, I'm sorry, man. I know you didn't want all of that information when you asked the question. Guess I get carried away sometimes. Sorry."

Deek summarized what Coleman's recovered e-mails meant to their investigation. It appeared that several e-mail messages clearly revealed a possible motive for Hilton Davis to murder LaMarr Coleman. Coleman had proof that Davis had embezzled over ten thousand dollars from an elderly client's escrow account five years ago in Baltimore and got away with it because the client died and his only benefactor was not knowledgeable enough to question the records.

"So what happened when you showed this stuff to Davis?" asked Bradford.

"He sang like a canary as they say and handed over a lot of dirt he had tucked away on Veda Simms. That gives Miss Simms just as much motive as Davis had. So the question is, who's lucky enough to have an alibi?"

CHAPTER 31

▼

Deek returned to the processing room on the third floor and sat at his cluttered desk. He loosened his neck tie and turned on the tape recorder to listen to Jason Phebus' deposition that he had taken last night. While he stared at the time line laid out before him and attempted to connect the dots, his memory played out the scene that occurred when he questioned Phebus in the interrogation room last night.

The man sitting across the table from Deek in the interrogation room wore a black, cowboy hat cocked low over his forehead that almost hid his cobalt-blue eyes. Deek ordered him to remove the hat. One of his ears was pierced with a gold earring. He worn a pair of scruffy boots, a black T-shirt, and faded jeans. When asked, Jason Phebus gave his age as thirty-three. The four-day old whiskers and stringy, blond hair that fell to his shoulders, made him look unkempt and even older than 33.

"It says here you just got out on probation after serving five years for manslaughter, Mr. Phebus. From what I read about that case you should have gotten murder one."

"Somethin' snapped in me when my older brother got killed almost at the end of his two-year hitch in Nam," said Phebus with a wild-eyed look on his face, "I was only ten years old at the time. I ain't been right since. Sometimes when I look in the mirror, I see my brother, Jeff's face instead of mine. I know what I done was wrong, Detective, and I paid for it."

"I'm sorry about your brother, Mr. Phebus, but that doesn't justify bludgeon-ing your girlfriend to death. And neither does being strung out on LSD and Angel Dust, in my book. Be glad I wasn't on that jury."

There was no reaction from the prisoner so Deek continued.

"Your attorney got the sentence reduced because of some lame argument that you weren't responsible for your actions. Well, that won't happen for you here today, Mr. Phebus. You violated your probation. We got you on a D.U.I., carry-ing a concealed weapon, and drug possession. Any one of those charges would be enough to send you straight back to the pen."

"Whatcha want from me, Detective?" said Phebus in a meek voice.

Deek had given him enough incentive to cooperate and asked if he would mind having his statement recorded. Phebus agreed.

Deek spoke into the recorder; "This is the deposition of Mr. Jason Phebus. He's appearing without counsel."

Phebus confessed that nearly three weeks ago the junior attorney from his defense team paid him to break into Dr. Hayes's office and steal all the patient files on Veda Simms. He swore he didn't know why. The attorney who hired him to steal the files was the now deceased, LaMarr Coleman. Although Mr. Hilton Davis, the senior partner, did most of the talking during his trial, Coleman did all the legwork. Phebus told Deek he felt like he owed his former attorney for help-ing to get him only five years instead of life without parole. But later when he asked Coleman to pay him the $300 he had promised to pay for obtaining Veda's records, Coleman said the files were useless to him. At first Coleman had refused to pay for the job, but finally he gave Phebus the money and told him to destroy the files. Phebus said he forgot they were stashed under the seat of his car until the police stopped him.

"Where were you last night between ten and midnight?"

"Just out driving," answered Phebus into the recorder.

"Driving where? Out looking for a hit?"

"Nowhere. I got sleepy so I pulled over and fell asleep?"

"Anybody see you?"

"I dunno. Don't think so."

"How well did you know the deceased, LaMarr Coleman?"

Phebus shrugged his shoulder, "I dunno. As good as anybody facing a murder rap knows his lawyer, I guess."

"Did you *snap* like you did 5 years ago and this time murder LaMarr Cole-man?"

Phebus looked down at his calloused hands and mumbled a reply.

"Please, speak into the recorder, Mr. Phebus. Did you kill LaMarr Coleman?"

"No, I did not," Phebus shouted. "I ain't murdered nobody. That's exactly what I told them police when they asked me the same damn questions."

"At least not in the last five years that we know of," said Deek, "That'll be all Mr. Phebus. Thank you for your cooperation."

Deek looked up from his paperwork when he saw Lieutenant Bradford approach and pull up a chair alongside his desk. Bradford placed an extra cup of coffee on the desk for Deek, and they both listened to Jason Phebus's recorded statement from the beginning.

"Do you believe him?" asked Deek.

"No alibi," said Bradford.

"No motive either that we know of," said Deek, "unless somebody paid him to hit Coleman. He's already proven he can be motivated by money to commit a crime."

"Good point. You didn't promise that asshole anything, did you?" said Bradford.

"Hell no. I gave him back to Vice for now," said Deek, "I know where to find him if I need him."

Deek put in that morning's tape-recorded interview with Hilton Davis next. "Now listen to this." Deek started out the interview by informing Davis that the police caught the burglar who stole Veda Simms' patient files. The burglar, Jason Phebus, said he was paid by Coleman to break in and steal all Veda's records. As it turned out Veda had revealed some incriminating information about Davis in one of her therapy sessions, but Davis claimed that whatever Veda said about him was a lie, and no one could produce any proof to show otherwise. It would have ended there if Deek hadn't pulled out an email correspondence sent to Davis by Coleman, clearly indicating that Coleman had been blackmailing him. Davis finally admitted that last month Coleman found out about one of his now deceased client's escrow accounts, probably from Veda. She had worked for him in Baltimore and was the only one who knew about the embezzlement. Davis said the only way to stop the blackmail was to find some dirt on Coleman to even the score and convince him to back off. But he didn't kill LaMarr Coleman or have him killed.

"Mr. Davis, … sure you didn't have LaMarr Coleman killed and make it look like Veda Simms did it?" asked Deek, "That way, you'd take care of both problems at the same time. You said no one else knew about the embezzlement."

"I'm no murderer, Sergeant Hamilton. I'm willing to take a lie detector test, if necessary. My plan was to squeeze Coleman the same way he was squeezing me since I couldn't very well fire him."

Davis explained that Senator Hargreaves was a longtime friend of his and had promised to support his upcoming appointment to judgeship. Davis said he even got the Senator's daughter, Courtney, a summer job clerking at the law firm. He could not afford to lose Senator Hargreaves' respect and his support. He had to keep the knowledge of his embezzlement from getting out. And he couldn't fire Coleman because of the damaging information he had on him.

Davis said five years ago he and Coleman plea-bargained Jason's first degree murder charge to a reduced sentence. When Coleman discovered Jason was out on probation, he apparently asked him to steal Veda Simms's patient records as a favor. Although Coleman assumed nobody knew about their office affair everybody knew. They also knew that Coleman was cheating on her every chance he got. The list of people that wanted Coleman dead was long. When Deek questioned Hilton Davis about his whereabouts on the night of the murder, Davis said he and Courtney were in New York for an awards ceremony that Friday before the murder. He was receiving an award and thought it would be a good opportunity for Courtney to go and do some networking. Courtney took the red-eye back that Friday night but he spent the entire weekend with his family in Long Island. Davis said he kept an apartment downtown near the office and stayed there during the week. Typically, he returned home to New York on weekends. He didn't get back to Washington until late Sunday night.

Davis told Deek that LaMarr was well known on the streets as a high profile fixer for rich clientele. He was virtually untouchable in court because so many people owned him favors. People did favors for him and he returned the favors.

"Was Coleman into drugs or drug dealing to your knowledge?" asked Deek.

"I have no evidence of that," answered Mr. Davis, "Look Detective, all I wanted was a little dirt on Coleman to stop the blackmailing. I didn't kill him but I'm glad somebody else did."

"Do you think Veda could have murdered LaMarr Coleman?"

"I don't know what Veda is capable of. But I can assure you there're many people happy about his death, including myself. Why not try the Metropolitan D. C. White Pages? Almost anybody could have killed that son-of-a-bitch."

Deek turned off the recorder.

"Courtney Hargreaves is another one I intend to follow up with," said Deek to his partner, "See if she had motive and opportunity."

"Yeah, but we still need proof. Hopefully, Kane'll show up soon with prints and a trace on that gun. Go ahead and waste your time on those other leads if you want to Deek, but I'm still bettin' on our girl, Veda Simms as the murderer."

Deek sighed and glanced at his watch. There was no use arguing with Bradford. "I'd better be shoving off," he said, getting up from his desk. "I'll call you if anything else turns up. Tyrone's got his flight class this afternoon. It'll be good to get my mind off this damn case for awhile."

Bradford shoved the papers into the Coleman case folder and also rose from his chair. "Is that the summer flying program you mentioned getting Tyrone into a few weeks ago?" asked Bradford with the case file in his hand. "What's it called again?"

Deek nodded. "Yeah, it's called the Youth in Aviation Program. It's an 8-week summer flight program sponsored by the Black Aviation Employees at FAA and the Tuskegee Airmen organization. You know about the Tuskegee Airmen from World War II, don't you Mel?"

"Yeah, I heard of 'em. A long time ago the Army did this experiment to see if Blacks could learn to fly airplanes. The Army didn't think these guys were smart enough or brave enough to pull it off, but they excelled with flying colors, so to speak. Something like that, right?"

"Yeah, something like that. I can see you keep up with your history," said Deek, as he shutdown his laptop and unplugged the adapter from the wall. "During World War II as a U. S. Army Air Corps experiment, the Tuskegee Airmen were trained in Tuskegee, Alabama as black fighter pilots, navigators, bombardiers, mechanics and many other support roles. They didn't get their just dues from the U. S. government until sixty years later. Sponsoring this youth flight program is another way for them to give back. As for Tyrone, you know the problems we had keeping him out of trouble last summer. Well, a couple of weeks ago I saw an announcement about a career day being held at Potomac Airport to introduce kids to flying. I thought Tyrone would get a kick out of seeing the planes take off and land, never figuring how excited he would be to actually learn to fly himself."

Bradford folded his arms and gave Deek a doubtful look. "You sure this thing isn't really about you? I know how you're always talking about getting your pilot's license. Hell if I know why. It's bad enough being out there on that boat, but no, being on the Atlantic Ocean's not dangerous enough for you is it, Young Blood? Now you gotta go 30,000 feet up in the air! Not me, buddy. I'm a keep my fat ass on solid ground. So, I guess the kid liked it, huh?"

"Are you kidding?" said Deek, as he packed his laptop inside the case. "Tyrone loved it! When we saw some of the young men from last summer's program flying solos in front of other kids and their families, I'm not gonna lie to you Mel, we were both very impressed."

"How much did you have to shell out on the kid this time?" asked Bradford, frowning.

Deek positioned the laptop case's strap across his shoulder and picked up his keys from the desk and stuffed them inside his pocket. "Mel, you just don't get it. It's not about the money. But as it turns out, the program is free to candidates that get accepted. They only take 10 kids at a time and Tyrone was one of them. The only out-of-pocket expense for me was paying for his physical that the FAA requires and buying a few extra books for the ground school training. Everything else is provided for by The East Coast Chapter of Tuskegee Airmen."

"And you didn't get any flak from his Mama? Or was she glad to have somebody else take over her responsibilities as usual?"

"That's not fair. The woman works two jobs. She's alone and has younger children at home to support. Tyrone's real Dad hasn't been around since he was a baby. If I can help her keep him out of trouble, I will. Of course, I had to get his Mom's permission on the release form, but she's just as excited as I am to see Tyrone participate in something worthwhile."

Bradford waved his partner off and headed towards his own desk. "Okay, Mother Theresa. Go ahead and save the world if you want to. Me, I got enough to worry about just trying to save myself. As soon as we catch up with that Simms woman and lock her up, that'll be one less thing I have to deal with. I'm certainly not about to go lookin' for more things to do. But you go ahead Young Blood and knock yourself out."

Deek headed for the elevator. He realized that he would be the only one investigating any other leads on the Coleman case. Mel Bradford just didn't give a damn. His partner had pretty much made up his mind that Veda Simms was guilty. Anything else would have taken too much effort on Bradford's part. Though Renee was probably still angry, she wouldn't be able to say that about him, he thought. But for right now, he decided to enjoy his afternoon with Tyrone and not worry about the murder investigation. After having completed his ground school studies last week, Tyrone was probably home studying for his first important test later that afternoon. If he passed he'd be ready to begin his flight lessons. Deek was nervous and excited for Tyrone all at the same time. What Deek hadn't told anyone was that right after Tyrone had received his acceptance letter into the youth flight program, Deek had made some inquiries into what it would take to get his own pilot's license. He had recently joined the Cloud Club for adults and would soon be taking private weekend flying lessons. Deek wanted to surprise Tyrone when the time was right. He figured that one day they could fly together. The thought of experiencing complete peace while soaring through the clouds was something to look forward to. He needed as many outlets as he could find to drive away the daily stress and frustration that comes with being a D. C. homicide detective.

CHAPTER 32

▼

Veda kept getting a recorded message saying that the phone had been temporarily disconnected. "Girl, when's the last time y'all paid the damn phone bill?"

Natasha realized that the phone company must have cut off her telephone again. She'd have to wait until Thursday when she got paid to give them a money order. "What are we supposed to do now?" said Natasha.

"Guess you'll just have to go to her office. See if she'll come here. Between the two of us we should be able to scrounge up enough for your bus fare and a metro ride."

"And say what? You need to tell her what happened yourself, Veda." Natasha suggested they look around for some type of disguise to change into.

"Let's start in KaLeese's room. That girl's got all kinds of stuff."

They rummaged through KaLeese's closet and dresser drawers, found an assortment of dresses, pants, tops, and suits, and laid them all across the bed. Natasha held up a metallic, body-skimming, mini-dress and a fire engine red, strapless outfit in each hand.

"What about one of these?"

"My goal is to avoid attention, Natasha. What I really need is a wig."

Natasha reached on top of the closet and brought down KaLeese's two wigs. One looked like a 'Proud Mary' Tina Turner wig. It had straight, shiny black hair that came almost to the waist. The other was a short, honey blonde one. Veda tried each of them on. The blond wig framed her brown face with head-hugging wisps of short, golden tresses.

"You look like one of those soccer Moms living out in Potomac or Bethesda/ Chevy Chase," laughed Natasha.

"Ex-*Cuse* me," said Veda, putting a heavy emphasis on the 'cuse' part, but she chose the long, black wig and a black jumpsuit. She clamped her fake hair into a ponytail. She accentuated her lips and eyes with excess makeup and used black eyeliner to plant a fake mole above her lip.

"Come on, Tina." Natasha laughed, "We don't have all day."

Veda rolled her eyes at Natasha. She carefully inspected her transformation in the full-length mirror. She slid her hands down over her figure to outline her shape. Not bad for thirty-eight she told herself.

"Okay, I'm almost ready."

"*Almost* ready? What else do you need to do?"

Veda walked into the kitchen and pulled open the silverware drawer. She felt around for the switchblade that she knew Natasha and KaLeese kept there for protection.

"This," said Veda and retrieved the knife from the drawer. She rolled up one of the pants legs on her jumpsuit and secured the knife firmly under the ankle strap of her sandals, then pulled down the pants leg to hide it.

"Now, I'm ready," said Veda.

They crossed Benning Road and approached a large mural painted on a stone wall. The mural displayed the multi-colored faces of famous black people. Veda and Natasha competed to see how many faces they could identify.

"If I ever have a kid, I'm a make sure he knows his history," said Natasha.

"Well, I hope you won't be the one teaching him," teased Veda, then quickly regretted her remark. Who was she to criticize? Just what had she ever taught her own daughter? Veda knew she had done a piss-poor job of raising Sherrelle and it was no joking matter. The bus stop up ahead was only a block from McDonald's. The smell of french fries and crispy chicken strips reached their nostrils before they even got there. Natasha offered to run in and get them something to eat while Veda waited outside.

While Veda stood in front of the McDonald's, a youth who looked to be no more than 16 talked loudly on his cell phone, oblivious to her look of irritation. From the gist of his conversation, Veda could tell he was talking to his girlfriend or someone he wanted to be his girlfriend. Two of what Veda surmised were his "boys" came out of the McDonalds with bags of food. They stood by their friend on the phone and conversed amongst themselves while they waited for him to finish his phone call. Natasha appeared through the door, carrying two McDonald's bags. One of the homeboys stopped talking and pointed to Natasha. Damn, Veda thought. She had warned Natasha not to wear that metallic outfit.

She was only attracting a bunch of under-aged hoodlums. That girl was always trying to be too cute. Both teens moved in closer to Natasha. They approached her with a slow, definite rhythm to their step. The one who had noticed her first kept his chin pointed upwards, as one arm swung freely by his side. The other hand remained hidden in the pocket of his baggy, cut-off trousers.

"Hey baby," said the first young thug to Natasha, "Wanna come home with me?"

Natasha ignored them and sat down with Veda at one of the outside tables. By this time, their buddy on the cell phone had hung up. He looked around and saw his friends then grinned while sliding a toothpick between his teeth. The unwelcome escorts huddled together at a nearby table. Veda and Natasha observed them closely. Both women wished they would just leave so they could eat in peace before going to the bus stop. Natasha handed Veda a bag and began eating fries from her own bag.

"We got enough money left for the Metro?" Veda asked Natasha between bites.

"Yeah. I wish these assholes would get lost," answered Natasha, loud enough for them to hear.

"Well hurry up then and let's get the hell outta here."

Veda turned to look over her shoulder to see if the three teenagers were leaving. That's when she saw them get up from the table and come towards them. The one who appeared to be the leader stood in front of Natasha, with his boys standing nearby and began yelling in Natasha's face.

"Who the hell you callin' an asshole? Don't nobody disrespect Little Bennie and get away with it."

Veda got up from the table. "Look kid, whatever your name is. We don't want no trouble. Let's go Natasha," she motioned with her hand for Natasha to follow, and they started up the street towards the bus stop.

Little Bennie wasn't buying it. He and his small band of followers, trailed behind Veda and Natasha. "Don't ya'll make me have to get ugly in front of my boys," yelled Little Bennie, "I demand ya'll apologize."

Little Bennie rushed forward and grabbed Natasha by the arm. She broke away from his grasp then elbowed him sharply in the chest. He took a few steps backward then came towards her again while his homeboys cheered him on.

"Think fast, asshole," said Veda suddenly.

She quickly retrieved the switchblade and pointed it at his throat. Little Bennie's crew stopped laughing. They stood perfectly still and speechless and waited for their leader to react.

"Okay, man. Just take it easy," said Little Bennie and backed away.

Veda did not take her eyes off him. Beads of sweat poured down his face. He dried the sweat with his hand then wiped his sweaty palm on his oversized T-shirt.

"Get the fuck outta here, you little bastards," yelled Veda, "or you'll have a short lifespan."

Little Bennie and his crew did not need to be told twice. He motioned to his entourage and they all left. As they walked away, Veda overheard one of the homeboys mumble something to Little Bennie about how familiar she looked.

"This is the second time this has come in handy," said Veda and tucked the knife back in its hiding place. Then she and Natasha continued towards the bus stop. Neither Veda nor Natasha saw the police car slowly pull up in front of curbside. When they did, it was too late. Veda tried to make a run for it, while Natasha stood motionless. Natasha realized she wouldn't get far in those platform heels. The cops jumped out of the car and ran after Veda.

"Stop. Police," shouted Sergeant Thaddeus Kane.

Veda kept running.

"Don't be stupid, Miss. Halt right now, I don't want to have to shoot you." Sergeant Kane had his gun drawn but he didn't shoot at her. Veda figured if she could just make it to the next block, she could catch the orange line at the Minnesota Avenue Metro Station. Then she'd be able to mingle in with the rest of the commuters and get away. She turned around for a quick glimpse and saw that Sergeant Kane was right on her heels. Veda was on the verge of collapse. The detective reached out and grabbed her collar. He held her arm, and twisted it behind her back. He slipped his gun in its holster and locked a pair of handcuffs on her.

They took her straight to the receiving area at D. C. Police headquarters. Once in the receiving area, Officer Kane handed Veda over to another officer who sat behind a metal divider like a bank teller separated from his customers. The receiving cop took Veda's purse and removed her handcuffs. He called for a female officer to conduct a search and a huge, battle-ax-looking woman appeared. The large-boned female officer searched her while another woman watched. The watcher had visible facial hair above her lip. While the big-boned officer conducted the search, the watcher stared at Veda with longing in her small, pig-like eyes. The searcher snatched the wig off of Veda's head and ordered Veda to remove her shoes and peered inside, then she patted her down.

After the search, Veda was escorted through a dark hallway that smelled like stale urine. The big-boned receiving officer who searched her informed Veda that she was being taken to a holding cell. She said Lieutenant Bradford would send down for her when he was ready to conduct his interrogation.

"Take me to a telephone," demanded Veda, "I know my rights."

"Shut the hell up," snapped the officer, "I know your rights too. You'll get your phone call when I say so." The receiving officer shoved her forward.

They passed a large open room that was separated down the middle by a concrete wall. On one side of the open room, four male prisoners wandered aimlessly about. The other half of the cell held a lone black female prisoner who looked so bad Veda couldn't even tell her age. She had a liverish skin tone and sunken in cheeks. She had fastened her coarse hair in a ponytail that stuck out at the nape of her neck. Fly-away frizz matted her roots and edges. The whole place smelled like urine and feces.

The officer took Veda to the section of the holding cell reserved for women. The woman who was to be her cellmate had on soiled, oversized clothing. Her hair stuck out in back and on the sides in uneven, broken off spikes and appeared matted with perspiration, hair grease, and dirt. She looked like a crack or heroin addict. The cell and the woman stank horribly. There was one steel toilette bowl without a lid. A metal slab stuck out of the wall that served as a cot. It had no pillow or mattress just the metal slab that was permanently bolted to the wall. Veda headed straight for the metal slab and buried her head in her hands. She felt an instant, throbbing headache emerge from the tension and anger at being thrown in this environment where she didn't belong. She held her breath for as long as she could to avoid the smell. Nothing but filth, stench, and cold metal surrounded her.

The men on the other side of the room kept yelling through the black metal bars at the guards.

"I wanna use the phone."

"I'm hungry."

"I need to go to the infirmary." The continuous echo of their voices made Veda's headache worse.

Veda felt the presence of her cellmate standing in front of her but she did not look up.

Finally, the woman spoke. "What you in here for?"

"I'm not in here to talk," said Veda.

"Oh, I get it, you ain't never been in jail before, huh?"

"No, I haven't."

"You look just like my eighth grade school teacher."

Veda did not respond. She wished the woman would go away and leave her alone. Apparently, the woman got the hint because she walked over to the bars and called out to one of the guards.

"Officer, Officer, you got any change so I can get somethin' out the vending machine?"

The woman yelled out to the guards repeatedly. No one came back to answer her. Other than periodically shouting to the prisoners to shut up, the guards completely ignored their calls.

It seemed like an eternity but finally the arresting officer, Sergeant Kane returned and called out her name. Veda stood up immediately and approached the bars.

"Alright, Lieutenant Bradford wants to see you now in the processing room, Miss Simms," he said. "I hope you're through playing games and ready to tell the truth."

Sgt. Kane unlocked the door to let Veda through. Veda looked up and followed the young detective's gaze back to the woman in the cell. She stood in front of him with a toothless grin on her face. With both hands, she held her dingy blouse wide open. Her large breasts jutted out in defiance. Sgt. Kane slammed the cell door shut and led Veda down the narrow hallway out of the holding area.

CHAPTER 33

▼

Renee placed a crusty bagel on the cutting board and sliced it open carefully. She couldn't afford to spend all day in the hospital emergency room because of a bagel-cutting injury. She was just about to carry her breakfast of coffee, bagel, and grapefruit juice down to her office when a news commentator interrupted the television program.

"Here is Susan Strattler who joins us with an exclusive report," said the morning show's anchor.

"Eyewitness News has just learned that Veda Simms, the prime suspect in last Saturday night's gruesome murder of a Washington attorney has been arrested at Minnesota Avenue and Benning Road, North East."

Renee clicked off the television set, grabbed her purse, and hurried out the door. She drove frantically, cursed at each red light, and weaved in and out of traffic until she reached Deek's house. She barely had time to knock when Deek's door flew open with him standing there.

"What took you so long?" he said, "Come on in. I guess you heard the news."

"Will I be able to see Veda Simms today?" asked Renee, worriedly, "She tried to get in touch with me yesterday, but I was with a patient when she called. I could tell she wanted to talk, but I had no way of contacting her."

"I should be able to arrange a visit," he said.

"Thank you. I suppose now that Veda's been arrested, you and Detective Bradford are ready to close the case."

"I haven't spoken to Mel, ... Lieutenant Bradford yet. Sergeant Kane called and told me they arrested our suspect."

"Deek, I don't want Veda to rot in that awful jail cell for something I know she didn't do."

"Follow me," he said, "I've found out some interesting things about LaMarr Coleman by tapping into his firm's e-mail system and downloading his messages."

"Did you identify anyone else with a motive to kill him?" asked Renee, hopefully, following him.

"Not exactly. Most of his messages are full of legalese and not relevant to our case. But from what I've read so far, this guy would have probably been up against sanctions from the Bar Counsel if he hadn't been murdered first."

Once in his office, Deek sat down at the computer and connected to the law firm of Davis & Bookerman. In minutes he was back into Coleman's e-mail.

"How were you able to break his code?" asked Renee.

"Simple," said Deek, "Just guessed LaMarr. Most people pick passwords that are easy for them to remember, like their own names or their birthday."

"And here I was just about to give you credit for being so clever," smiled Renee.

Deek pulled up an on-line file cabinet of stored e-mail messages that Coleman assumed had been permanently deleted and quickly scanned through the messages.

"I know I really shouldn't be showing you this, but what the hell," he shrugged. "Take a look at this one," he said and showed Renee a password protected document containing the names of confidential clients who Coleman apparently wanted to remain anonymous.

"Wonder why he wanted to keep these particular clients a secret."

At that moment the doorbell rang.

"It's probably Tyrone coming back from B-ball. He and his buddies went out to the basketball court earlier and I bet he forgot to take his keys again. Be right back," said Deek and dashed upstairs to get the door.

Renee glanced at Coleman's list of client names. She recognized one of them. He was the father of a former patient, Kenneth Blackwell. Renee had been very fond of Kenneth and regretted that his father removed him from therapy. Before she had time to consider why the name of Dr. Walter Blackwell at Georgetown Hospital was among Coleman's confidential clientele, she heard voices above. Next, came the sound of heavy footsteps galloping down the stairs. She expected to see Deek and Tyrone come through the door. Renee glanced up from Deek's laptop. It was Detective Melvin Bradford instead of Tyrone.

"I'm on my way to the station to finish interrogating the Simms woman and get a signed confession from her," said Bradford to Deek. "Just stopped by to tell you that me and Chief Riley went over the evidence again this morning. We agreed to seek an indictment just as soon as I get my signed confession." Bradford's specialty was extracting confessions. With all the evidence he had stacked up against the accused, he didn't anticipate any trouble getting one out of Veda Simms.

"Chief said to tell you that as of O-eight hundred this morning, you're back on the 'break-in murders' working with the FBI. Said he wants to show them 'good ole boys' our department's finest," smiled Bradford and patted Deek on the back, "Anyway, I'll have this Coleman thing wrapped by the end of the day."

"Hold up, Mel," said Deek, "I stumbled across some new information this morning that I think could have significant bearing on the Coleman Investigation."

Detective Bradford glanced at his watch, looked bored, but agreed to give Deek five minutes to hear what he had to say. Deek switched to a new screen and showed his partner an Internet web site created by Coleman eight months before his murder. Deek explained how Coleman was able to conduct illegal transactions across the network in order to receive blackmail payments without arousing suspicion.

"What the hell are you getting at Deek?" asked Bradford.

"Bottom line, Coleman set up a dummy corporation on the Internet," said Deek with excitement in his voice as he pointed to the screen. "I found copies of his incorporation documents in one of his protected work folders. It's just another one of these new millennium scams that's proliferating out there on the Web. And guess what? ... surprise, surprise, Coleman signed corporate by-laws and board resolutions naming himself as the president, vice-president, treasurer, secretary, and subscriber to the company's stock."

"So what if he was an entrepreneur on the side? Big deal," said Bradford and glanced briefly at his watch.

"Please Mel, just hear me out," begged Deek, "It's more to it than that. The records show that on January 5th of this year, Coleman opened a bank account for LDC Enterprises with his name on the signature card, allowing him to withdraw from the company funds. He also subscribed to a financial services company called NetCash. They specialize in linking customers and businesses with banks across the Internet. NetCash allowed electronic cash deposits to be made directly to LDC Enterprise's bank account. Get it now?"

"No Einstein, I don't get it. So what if this Coleman guy was into computers and put a store on the Internet? What the hell does that have to do with this homicide investigation?"

Deek urged Bradford to follow up with the people on Coleman's confidential client list and those who had been forced through blackmail to pay him regularly for fictitious products and services. Coleman was a clever attorney as well as a first class con artist. He knew how to structure the payments to avoid activating the banks reporting requirements on electronic cash transactions. Deek believed there could be other suspects besides Veda Simms who wanted Coleman dead, like any one of his Internet customers who were actually his blackmailed victims.

"Look, Young Blood, I already questioned everybody relevant to the case. And no one else had a better motive or opportunity than Veda Simms," said Bradford.

"But don't you see, Mel? This new information points to other mitigating circumstances."

Bradford did not look impressed.

"I agree with Deek," said Renee, "Any number of these other people could have wanted to kill LaMarr Coleman."

"Yeah, well wanting and doing is two different things," said Bradford as he got up and walked towards the stairs, "I don't have any number of other people fleeing the scene of the crime. Or having ample motive. Or having their fingerprints on a stolen weapon that just happens to be the gun that killed LaMarr Coleman."

Renee and Deek looked at each other in disbelief and then at Detective Bradford.

"You both heard me right. That gun we found hidden in the cereal box turned out to be reported stolen. The only set of fingerprints we could identify belonged to Veda Simms and the murder victim. Since we've clearly ruled out suicide, that leaves Miss Simms as my prime suspect."

"Detective Bradford, I've treated Veda and I know her well. I'm certain she's not the cold blooded killer you're after."

"Oh yeah, Doc? And what crystal ball are you looking at? Or is it your Psychic Friends network? 'Cause I'm just going on the evidence and it all points to her."

Bradford told Deek and Renee he expected to close the case as soon as he got that confession from Simms. He told them he planned to offer her a reduced charge of second degree murder if she pleaded guilty. He'd sweeten the pot by agreeing to inform the sentencing judge that she had cooperated with the government by pleading guilty. Thus, saving wear and tear on the overcrowded court system by confessing and avoiding a costly trial. Bradford knew he was a pro at this game. Especially when he had an open and shut case.

"Dr. Hayes asked me earlier if she could see her patient today," said Deek, "Is that possible?"

"No way. She'll be tied up with me in the interrogation room for most of the afternoon. Only her attorney or family members are allowed visitation. You might be able to see her tomorrow during visiting hours … if you arrange to get your name on the visitors list."

Bradford checked his watch before heading up the stairs to leave, "Looks like I've wasted enough time here. Gotta go greet my suspect."

Renee locked her fingers together and buried her forehead in clasped hands. The situation looked hopeless she thought. Deek didn't bother to see Bradford out the door, but instead took Renee by the arm and led her to the gray leather couch in his office. She felt the muscles of his strong arm as he guided her to the sofa where they both sat close together. Renee leaned back on the couch and closed her eyes. She felt the gentle force from his touch as he took one of her hands in his and massaged each finger, pulling and stroking the pressure points and rubbing inside the palm of her hand. Renee felt herself grow limp as the tension left her body. The only thing she could hear was the sound of his breathing. After he finished massaging both hands, he placed the open palm of one of her hands inside his loose cotton shirt and rested it against his chest. Renee felt the steady, rhythmic beat of his heart. She leaned her body into his chest and took in the spicy scent of his cologne. Renee knew that touching and inhaling his masculine fragrance was a guilty pleasure, but she could not resist being near him despite Veda's troubles with the law. Renee slowly opened her eyes and caught him staring at her with a look of concern. She outlined his trimmed mustache with her fingertips then traced the edges of his mouth. He pulled her into him and she felt his hardness against her body. She had sunk down on the couch almost to a full reclining position. Deek was now on top of her, but when he tried to kiss her, she turned her face away from him. "No Deek, we shouldn't. It's not right."

Deek stared down at her. "Why shouldn't we?" he asked. When his lips found hers again, she tasted its moist sweetness for too long before making him stop. If she didn't stop him now she knew they wouldn't be able to stop later. Bill knew about her affair with Deek and sleeping with him again could only make matters worse. When he saw that she still appeared conflicted, he rose and knelt down to a squatting position in front of her while clasping one of her hands. "What do you want me to say Renee?" he asked, staring into her eyes. She sat up and gently caressed his cheek with her other hand, but did not answer him. She still was not prepared to tell him about Bill's threats to find him and seriously hurt him.

Deek knew he might never get another opportunity to tell Renee how he felt about her. "Do you want me to make a complete fool of myself Renee and confess how I can't sleep at night anymore because all I do is lie there in bed and picture your eyes—how loving and caring they are when you look at me? How I pretend you're laying right next to me in bed and how much I wish I could just turn around and feel your body. And that's just at night."

Renee looked away, not trusting herself to gaze into his long-lashed dark eyes for too long. Then she spoke. "I'm glad you like me, Deek," is all she could manage to say.

"Like you?" he said, standing up before her. "I love you; that's the problem. I don't want to let you go. And I don't want to share you with Bill." He grabbed both her hands and pulled her from the couch to her feet, and slipped his arm around her waist to pull her close. Deek studied her face for a reaction to his declaration of love. "Why do you look so sad," he asked, "when I tell you I love you?"

"Why do you think?" she said, raising her chin to meet his gaze, "I'm in love with you too. And I'm afraid it's going to be my downfall."

CHAPTER 34

▼

Detective Bradford leaned back in the swivel chair in Interrogation Room One. He propped his feet on the table, and crossed his legs at the ankles. Sergeant Kane stood behind him. The suspect, Veda Simms, sat opposite Detective Bradford in a straight-back wooden chair.

Bradford turned on the tape recorder to identify the accused. He indicated on the recording that Veda Simms was being questioned in regards to the murder of LaMarr Coleman and appeared for questioning voluntarily without counsel. Detective Bradford folded his arms across his protruding belly.

"Did you kill LaMarr Desmond Coleman on the night of August 26?"

"I swear to God when I went back to LaMarr's to get something I left, he was already dead."

"What did you go back there to get?"

"My gun. Or the one I found in the streets a couple of nights ago."

"So you went to his apartment with a gun you found on the street and threatened him with it, right?"

"I suppose. But when I left that first time, LaMarr was alive. I didn't kill him."

"Earlier that week did you attempt to poison him with rat poison?"

"That was a mistake. I was just trying to scare him."

"Umhum. So, tell me. Why'd you leave when you discovered him dead?" asked Bradford, "Didn't it occur to you that fleeing the scene of a crime would incriminate you even more?"

"I didn't think about that, Detective. I'd had a few drinks before I got there, you know, so I could work up my nerve to say what I planned to say to him. I know I shouldn't have left without calling the cops. But when I saw him cut up like that, I just freaked out." Veda shook her head and covered her face with her hands.

"Wanna cigarette?" Bradford asked her. Veda lifted her head and eagerly nodded yes.

"Go get her a cigarette," he said to Kane who hurried out the door. Kane was back even before Bradford got around to the next question.

"Tell me, Simms ...," said Bradford after she had enjoyed a few puffs on her cigarette, "Why'd you go there in the first place?"

"Because he owed me some money ... a lot of money," Veda exhaled a cloud of smoke into Bradford's face, "I know it was stupid, but a few weeks ago, I borrowed $5,000 from my job's Petty Cash account and lent it to him."

Bradford removed his feet from the table and sat up. He rested his crossed arms on top of the table and stared at Veda as she continued.

"One of the senior partners was starting to get suspicious. He was having Price Waterhouse come and do an audit on our books."

"So you went to see LaMarr about paying back the money he owed the firm so you wouldn't get busted?"

"Exactly. I had to make it clear to LaMarr that I needed the money back by Monday or we'd both be in big trouble. Anyway, when I went to LaMarr's place I only meant to scare him with the gun. I could tell he was telling me the truth when he said he really didn't have the money, so I left. I was on my way to my aunt's in Luthersville, Virginia to see if I could borrow the money from her. Then I remembered I left my gun on his dresser and went back for it. But when I got there, he was dead. That's the God's honest truth, Detective."

"Well, Miss Simms," said Bradford, leaning back into his chair, "it seems mighty strange to me that you don't seem broken up about his death ... that is, for someone who claims to have been in love with the man for years."

"'Cause I finally realized LaMarr was only using me. I'm 38 years old, divorced, and I got a 15-year-old daughter who hates my guts because of LaMarr. But that's a long sad story and I'm not trying to get into all that."

"We've got time. So you also harbored some deep resentment against Mr. Coleman for totally screwing up your life, is that right Simms?"

"No, that's not right. You're turning everything I say around," she shouted, "LaMarr was a dog from day one. I just refused to see it. It was my choice to leave Louis and Sherrelle to be with LaMarr. It was my mistake and nobody else's." At that point, Veda broke down and the tears flowed. Saying it out loud was the first time she'd faced the reality of her choices. The hard shell that she revealed to others that had been concealing her inner pain for years, had finally cracked. Kane went out to get a box of tissues without having to be told. He came back and placed the tissues in front of her. After she had calmed down, Detective Bradford resumed his interrogation.

"It sounds to me like you're glad he's dead."

"I'm not happy to see anybody dead. That even applies to you, Detective Bradford."

"Hmm, I'm glad to hear that Simms. But your story sounds too convenient to me. You showing up at Coleman's place with a gun, leaving it behind. Then coming back later and finding him dead. It doesn't add up."

"Look here, Detective. I'm telling you straight up. I wasn't expecting to find what I did when I walked into that damn bedroom and saw what I saw. I guess you're just gonna believe whatever you wanna believe no matter what I say."

"You're right about that, Simms. And here's what I think happened, ... you committed this homicide. You had the motive and opportunity to do it. There's enough circumstantial evidence to charge you even without a witness," said Bradford, "Now, do you wanna cut a deal and confess or do you wanna continue to sit here and waste my goddamn time? Things could go a lot smoother for you, if you cooperate."

"But I didn't do it."

"That's what they all say. Right, Kane?"

After being returned to her cell, Veda collapsed in a heap on top of the thin mattress of her cot. The only thing she could be thankful for was that her cell mate wasn't there to bother her. She lay on her back and stared up at the cracked ceiling for what seemed like hours.

"Simms, phone call," said a burly female guard standing in the hallway. Keys jangled and the door screeched open. Stripped of her dignity, Veda looked downward as she shuffled her feet and followed along behind the guard that led her down the hallway to the telephone. "Five minutes," snapped the guard and cocked her head in the direction of the phone. Veda picked it up. "Hello," she whispered into the receiver.

"Mama, it's me," said the voice on the other end. It was her daughter, Sherrelle, speaking in a tone that was surprisingly without any malice. Veda's heart warmed. She wasn't able to speak for several seconds. She clasped her hand over her mouth and blinked rapidly through the tears that had begun to cloud her vision. Her voice cracked when she finally spoke. "How you doing, baby?" Veda wiped away the sniffles with the back of her hand.

"Mama, are you all right?" asked Sherrelle.

Veda took a deep breath before answering. "Sure baby, Mama's fine. How'd you know I was here?"

"Miss Natasha called Daddy last night."

"I'm sorry Sherrelle. For everything."

"I know Mama. Me and Daddy had a long talk. He said it's not about who's right, it's above forgiveness."

"Your father is a good man. I hope you know that."

"We wanna come see you tomorrow, Mama. When Daddy called to find out where to go, they said you had to put our names on the visitor's list. Can you do that for tomorrow?"

Just as Veda was about to answer, the sour-faced guard walked up and snatched the phone from her hand. "Time's up Simms," said the guard and hung up the phone. Veda wanted to slap the woman, but instead she clinched her fists at her sides and followed the guard back to her cell.

CHAPTER 35

▼

"Meet me at Oak Grove Marina. I'll be there in forty minutes. I have something important to tell you. And bring an overnight bag to spend the night on the boat."

Renee heard the urgency in Deek's voice. She looked at her watch. It was a little past eight o'clock. Bill hadn't arrived home from work yet so she wouldn't have to explain where she was going or why she was packing an overnight suitcase.

"Deek, are you crazy? I'm not driving all the way out to Edgewater tonight. Is it about the Coleman case?" she asked.

"I need to tell you in person. Can you throw a few things in a bag and meet me there in about hour? I'm ready to walk out the door now."

"Where's Tyrone?"

"He left this morning," said Deek, "He's spending the weekend with his family. But even if he hadn't gone home, Tyrone's a big boy and can take care of himself when I'm not here. So can you meet me? I really need to see you."

"I'm not sure that I remember how to get there, Deek."

Renee wrote down the directions that Deek gave her on a note pad that was next to the telephone. "Take New York Avenue NE and cross into Maryland. Then, take 665 Exit toward Riva Road," she repeated what he said as she hurriedly scribbled down the directions. "Then merge onto Solomons Island Road toward Edgewater. I know where to find the marina from there. Okay, I'll be there in less than an hour," said Renee.

"Thanks, honey. I'll be waiting for you," he said and hung up.

"This really is a beautiful still night. Just look at that sky," said Renee, gazing up at the stars and a crescent-shaped moon. They sat outside on a bench, facing the black night waters of the South River, illuminated only by a partial moonlight and the misty glare from a nearby lamppost. There was a slight chill in the night air. When he noticed her shivering, Deek rubbed her arms to warm them up. Then took off his jacket and draped it across her shoulders.

They stared at each other for only a few seconds, but it seemed like hours, each waiting for the other to speak first. Deek wanted to try to explain why he had not stopped his partner from interrogating her last week for LaMarr Coleman's murder. In the end, there was only one way he knew of to make it up to her. And that was to use his inside connections in law enforcement to locate her missing father. He knew how much she wanted to find her father even though she had stopped asking him how to track her father down. The information Deek found out would devastate her but he felt she had to know. This was the real reason for asking her to meet him there; that and his desire to be alone with her.

She leaned into him. He couldn't resist the soft lips that barely touched his. He grabbed her in his arms and kissed her passionately. Slowly, their lips parted but they remained close. He touched her face and she snuggled her cheek into the palm of his hand. Her body felt weak with pleasure from the scent of his cologne mingled with his perspiration brought on by the day's midday heat and a full day of active police work.

"Deek, I'm sorry but I'll have to go home soon. I know I said I would spend the night on the boat with you, but after giving it more thought while I was driving over here, I think that's a bad idea. Bill will be coming home soon and he'll wonder where I am. I don't want to risk antagonizing him further. What was it that you had to tell me?"

"You would have to break the spell with that bit of news flash, wouldn't you?" he said, still holding her tightly. Then, Deek agreed with her that it was probably time to go if she wasn't staying the night, but neither moved from the spot on the bench under the lamppost. She wrapped her arm around his waist while he stroked her back. He tried to think of a gentle way to break the news to her. Renee laid her cheek against his chest and felt his heart beat rapidly.

"Renee, there's something I have to tell you before we go. It's about your father, LeRoy Curtis."

"What?" Renee pulled back. She narrowed her eyes together and tried to interpret the look on Deek's face in order to prepare herself for what he had to say.

"I tracked him down using one of our latest on-line investigative International databases. He's been serving time in a prison in Paris for the last twelve months for manslaughter."

"No," cried Renee, "that can't be true."

"I'm so sorry Renee. I know how badly you wanted to find your father but not like this." He removed an envelope from his inside jacket pocket. "I received this document attachment in my email this afternoon from an Inspector in Paris familiar with your father's case. He's serving a three year sentence."

Renee buried her face in Deek's chest and cried, "I have to see him, Deek."

"I scanned in that picture of you I took by the lake and emailed it to the Inspector to give to your father," said Deek, "Renee, your father told the Inspector he doesn't want you to see him in prison."

"Is he well? I need to make arrangements to go there and find out for myself even if he doesn't know I'm there. Can you help me?"

"Of course. I'm already looking into it. For one thing, too many questionable circumstances surround his case. And two, he's a foreigner. But first I need to learn all the details about the city's case against him. I can't promise anything but with some intervention from our embassy we might be able to get him off with time served. I'll do everything I can."

"Thank you," she whispered and kissed his neck as he bent down to look at her, "Thank you so much for finding him. I lost my mother years ago when I was very young. He's all the family I have left."

When Deek said, "Tell me about your mother," Renee turned away from him. She stared out at the water. For nearly a full minute, she remained as still and lifeless as the South River. Slowly, Renee started to tell Deek what she remembered the last time she saw her mother.

"Her name was Bettina, but on stage she was known as Tina Joye," said Renee, "I was only 7 but I remember everything about her. She always gave me gifts just before going away on tour." Deek listened attentively without interrupting.

Renee explained that as she got older, she stopped looking forward to the presents because it meant her mother would be going away soon. On one particular cold March night in 1970, Bettina was about to leave again for New York City. Her chorus line's first stop on their eight-week tour was Broadway. The tour bus was departing at 5 o'clock the next morning. Renee knew it would be several weeks before she'd see her mother again. This time Bettina had bought something really special for her daughter.

At seven years old, Renee was too young to understand or care about her mother's career ambitions. Renee remembered how she had cried in her room almost all day. How she had pouted, sulked, and slammed doors. She was angry at her mother for choosing to go back on tour rather than stay home with her. Little Renee didn't understand why Bettina couldn't be a schoolteacher like her Aunt Clara. Then Bettina would be the one taking care of her instead of Aunt Clara.

Later that night before Bettina left for New York, she knelt down in front of her daughter and held out a box wrapped in pink foil and lace ribbons. Renee's face still looked puffy and sullen from crying. She refused to accept the gift. Bettina ripped open the package for her, and pulled out handfuls of pink tissue paper. She lifted up a porcelain doll dressed in red velvet and waited for her daughter's usual look of excitement. The doll's delicate features had been painted on with intricate detail. Bettina smiled and stroked the doll's face. "Isn't she lovely, Renee?" said Bettina, "Now, you be careful with her, you hear? She's a rare, collector's piece."

But Renee folded her arms across her chest and turned her head away. Renee felt the cool wetness of a single tear roll down her cheek, but stubbornly let it stay there. Bettina held the doll out to her daughter again. This time Renee snatched the doll from her mother's hand and hurled it to the hardwood floor, shattering the doll's face and breaking off one of her arms. Bettina stood up and gasped. Aunt Clara grabbed Renee by the arm and gave her a swift slap on her behind.

"Lord Jesus, child," said Aunt Clara sternly, "You march yourself straight on up those stairs to your room, young lady."

"I hate you," Renee screamed at her mother and Aunt Clara as she ran up the stairs.

Clara turned to face her younger sister and spoke with an 'I told you so' tone in her voice.

"You see there, Bettina. Just like I said. You've gone and spoiled that child rotten. As soon as you show up, all my good work goes straight to the devil."

Renee slammed the door shut and sat on the floor in front of her bed with her knees curled up to her chin and her face buried within folded arms. A few minutes later, she heard the door open slowly. Without looking up, she knew her mother had stepped inside because she smelled her rosewater fragrance.

Bettina slipped quietly into Renee's darkened bedroom and approached her daughter. Bettina bent down and gently touched Renee on the shoulder. The child glanced up at her mother and revealed red puffy eyes and plump cheeks lined with fresh tears. Renee wiped her face dry with the back of her hand. Bettina promised Renee that she'd return in eight weeks right after the tour was over. She said they would take a trip to Coney Island for a whole weekend just the two of them when she got back. Renee jumped up and clung to her mother's neck. Then she ran to her calendar and circled the date her mother told her in red crayon. Later that evening Renee drifted into a pleasant sleep.

Early the next morning just before it was time for Bettina to leave, her mother had tiptoed back into Renee's room while she slept. Renee heard the door creak as it opened and she sat straight up in bed. Her mother wore a black, fur-lined coat and a stylish, wide-brimmed hat. She tilted her head and bent down to give her daughter a hug and kiss good-bye. Her mother's neck was soft and smelled like rose water, sweet and light. Nothing like the awful, greasy night cream that Aunt Clara smeared on every night.

Renee puckered her lips to return her mother's good-bye kiss. The wide brim on Bettina's hat prevented their lips from actually touching. The hat started to slip off and Bettina arranged it neatly back in place. She turned once more and blew her daughter another kiss before closing the bedroom door. Renee jumped out of bed and ran to the window. She cried silently inside and watched her mother through the window until her shape disappeared. Renee relished the scent of her mother's sweet breath and her rosewater fragrance long after she was gone.

Renee vividly recalled this incident from her childhood thirty-seven years ago as if it had just happened yesterday. How could she forget the night her mother left on what turned out to be her last trip? A freak accident caused Bettina's tour bus to slide on a patch of ice early that morning and plunge over a guardrail, fifty feet down a steep embankment. There were no survivors. Renee missed her mother's lovely, smiling face and cursed the wide-brim hat that had kept their lips from touching one last time.

Renee sobbed gently into her open palms, still remembering that night. Deek rested his hand on her knee and didn't take his eyes off her.

"Are you all right, Renee?" he asked and gave her a handkerchief from his pocket.

She nodded and wiped her face. Suddenly thunder erupted from the sky and rain descended upon them. Deek covered Renee's head with his jacket and they ran towards their cars to escape the downpour.

When they reached their cars, Deek said, "Listen, Renee, I really want to be with you tonight. We're only a few minutes from where Phil keeps his yacht docked. I don't think you should drive home like this. Please spend the night with me on the yacht. What's the worse that can happen?"

Renee knew she'd only face the same loneliness she always felt at home tonight. Even when Bill lay right there next to her, she still felt alone, and she didn't want that. "The worse has already happened," she said, "All right, Deek. Let's go."

Deek retrieved his umbrella from the trunk of his car. They turned around and started to head back towards the marina where the Sarina's Joy was docked. Deek held the umbrella above their heads and wrapped his free arm around Renee's waist. They walked down the pier in the rain. No one else was in sight. The boats nestled side-by-side along each slip in the rain splattered waters.

CHAPTER 36

▼

The rainfall diminished to a drizzle. Renee felt a soft wind touch her neck. Gentle rain, a fresh breeze, and a full night of passion, she thought as she smiled to herself and defied a tinge of guilt that suddenly swept past her. Even the putrid smell of humidity and polluted water from dead fish, didn't mar her contentment. A few minutes later, Deek and Renee arrived at the marina's security guard's station. They went inside the building to see the security guard about getting the key to his friend Phil's yacht that he had left at the guard's station for him. Phil had apparently forgotten to leave instructions to give the key to Deek. The guard offered to try to get in touch with Phil and get his verbal permission. While he recognized Deek as an occasional visitor to the marina, he said he still had to follow proper procedures before granting access to the boat. Renee decided to go out and wait on the platform while Deek sorted everything out. She had been standing there less than a minute when someone who looked very familiar entered the marina. He checked his pass with the guard, and proceeded past her down the platform in the same direction as Phil's private slip on floating dock C. The young man looked just like Kenneth Blackwell.

Renee called out but Kenneth, walking at a brisk pace, apparently did not hear her. She followed him down the platform as fast as she could, being careful not to slip on the wet fiberglass dock. She wanted to catch up with him and find out how he had been doing. Seeing Kenneth reminded her about finding his father's name on LaMarr Coleman's confidential client file the day before. Perhaps Kenneth might know something about Dr. Blackwell's association with Coleman that would be worth Deek investigating.

From a short distance, Renee saw Kenneth board a cabin cruiser not far from the slip where the Sarina's Joy was docked. Her heart raced, but despite her fear, she stepped slowly across the wobbly gangplank and climbed aboard the cabin cruiser. Renee could see Kenneth through the window and was just about to knock when the shadow of a tall figure whisked by. She realized that Kenneth was not alone. Renee started to turn around and leave but then she heard Kenneth yell at the man, demanding to know if he had murdered LaMarr. Renee gasped in astonishment when she heard Kenneth ask the stranger that question. Every instinct told her to leave quietly and go find Deek, but instead Renee stood outside the door and listened. She stood there in a paralyzed state of fear, her feet cemented to the deck of the cruiser. As the man that Kenneth addressed spoke up, she recognized the other voice as that of Kenneth's father, Dr. Walter Blackwell. Renee took a few steps forward to get a better view.

Dr. Blackwell gave his son a crooked half-smile before answering. "What the hell do you expect me to say to a question like that?" He walked to the bar and poured himself a glass of bourbon on ice.

Kenneth stood trembling before his father, but would not back down. He took a step closer towards him. "Tell me the truth, Daddy. Did you kill LaMarr? He was the only friend I had and he really cared about me."

"LaMarr Coleman didn't care about anybody but himself. I had dealings with him in the past and I've always known him to be a greedy son-of-a-bitch, motivated purely by money. I didn't plan to kill Coleman when I went to his apartment that night. My intention was to try and buy him off. If I had known that my business association with him would lead to the two of you becoming lovers I would have never hired him to represent you. I thought if I could keep him away from you long enough for a competent psychiatrist to cure you, the problem would be resolved." He sat down on a cushioned loveseat, drink in hand. "So, now you know," he said matter-of-factly without remorse and took a gulp of his drink.

Kenneth bumped into an end table as he stumbled backwards and collapsed into a chair. Renee's heartbeat quickened and she felt a tightness pinch her stomach as she moved even closer to hear and see what was going on inside the cabin. Kenneth sat with his head bent low. She could hear him crying. Dr. Blackwell propped his feet up on the coffee table. He took out a pack of cigarettes from his pocket and lit one. He leaned back on the couch and blew out smoke, oblivious to the extent of his son's pain.

Kenneth spoke without looking at his father. "All you had to do was love me just as I am, Daddy—just as God made me. He made me this way and if I'm good enough for the Almighty I can't see why I'm not good enough for you."

Dr. Blackwell leaned forward and crushed out his cigarette in an ashtray on the end table. "Stop your blubbering. You sound like a little girl," he said in a biting tone that displayed disgust. "I only get one son and he turns out to be a blubbering sissy."

Without looking at his father, Kenneth spoke softly. "Real men cry, Daddy. It's not weak to show feelings, and it's not weak to need someone's love. That's all I ever wanted was your love and for you to make me feel safe growing up." Then Kenneth sat up in his chair and stared into his father's blank hazel eyes. "Do you remember that time you made me camp outside alone all night long in that tent when I was only 6 years old? You said it would toughen me up, you remember? It's taken me years of therapy and I still haven't gotten over that night. I was traumatized."

Dr. Blackwell shot up from the couch and gave his son a fierce look. "Traumatized hell! You were only in our backyard for christsakes, Kenneth. I had my eye on you the entire time. I was trying to help you get over that silly fear of the dark."

"I didn't know that, Daddy. I felt all alone out there." Kenneth rose and reached out his hands towards his father for emphasis and tried to explain how he felt. "I may as well have been alone in a jungle. Every dark shadow, every howl, and every rustling in the bushes terrified me. If you were really watching me then you knew I cried all night until I was so exhausted I couldn't help but fall asleep. I was always looking for love that I could never get from you, Dad. That could be the reason I've sought out male companionship as an adult."

Dr. Blackwell pointed a finger at Kenneth and shouted at him. "That's the most ridiculous bunch of horseshit I've ever heard. Don't try to blame your sick ways on me! I was always a good role model for you and a good father. It's your mother's fault. She treated you like a little baby. I blame her and I blame LaMarr Coleman for ruining your life. You damn straight I killed Coleman and I'm not sorry I did!"

Kenneth cried out that LaMarr didn't destroy him, his father did. He told Dr. Blackwell that growing up in emotional isolation, feeling rejected and constantly belittled made him feel invisible and worthless. He said there were many nights when he laid awake and thought about tying his sheet to the ceiling light fixture and hanging himself. The only thing that stopped him was thinking about how his mother would feel finding him there in the morning. Kenneth realized his father would never understand the depth of his suffering. He could never be what his father expected him to be.

Renee thought she felt something brush against her ankle. She jumped back and nearly slipped on the deck. Kenneth and Dr. Blackwell turned suddenly when they heard the noise outside. They both caught sight of her through the window. The cabin door swung open and the first thing Renee saw was the pistol in Dr. Blackwell's right hand.

"Come in, Dr. Hayes," he said softly and wore a brief, artificial smile.

The blood froze in her veins and her feet felt like lead bound to the floor. Renee couldn't move.

"I said come in," he repeated in a harsh tone.

Renee found herself inside the main salon and staring into the unflinching eyes of an unstable man. Her knees shook. "What the hell were you doing outside my door?" Blackwell demanded, pointing the gun at her, "Eavesdropping on a private conversation?" It was useless to explain what she was doing outside the door. The straight line of Blackwell's thin lips told her he knew she had heard every word of his disclosure to his son about killing LaMarr Coleman. She glanced at Kenneth who stood behind his father with a blank, catatonic stare on his face. His eyes were glazed and reddish. Dr. Blackwell stuck the gun sharply into Renee's ribs.

"Why did you kill LaMarr Coleman?" she asked. Renee tried to appear calm as her heart raced wildly.

"I told him I had ten thousand dollars in cash. All he had to do was agree to never see or contact my son again," said Dr. Blackwell, "He accepted the money but it was his smug attitude that set me off and I just snapped." Dr. Blackwell kept the gun thrust in her side as he spoke. He said LaMarr made fun of his beliefs and provided graphic details of what he and Kenneth had done in bed together as lovers. "When I called him a sick son-of-a-bitch and accused him of corrupting my son, he laughed at me. I'll never forget the sound of his laughter, so damn sure of himself. He was still walking around and bragging about some video tape he had made of Kenneth when I spotted the gun lying on his dresser," said Dr. Blackwell, "Coleman was too busy telling me about his video and how it would show who the real aggressor was. He didn't notice me picking up the gun. The creep was in mid-sentence when I shot him."

Renee felt the thumping of her heart quicken its pace. Her entire body trembled inside.

"I knew I had to make it look like one of his enraged girlfriends or boyfriends had murdered him out of jealousy. LaMarr was a hedonist. All he cared about was his own pleasure, and he didn't care who he slept around with. So I took out the instrument that I had hidden in my coat pocket and castrated the bastard with surgical precision. I brought the sharpest instrument I could find from the hospital that day," said Dr. Blackwell with a smirk. "I didn't know what frame of mind Coleman would be in when I saw him. But I had only intended to frighten him. It came in handy after all." He waved the gun around as he spoke. "Now, Dr. Hayes, I bet you wished you had decided to mind your own damn business."

Suddenly, the door burst open and Deek stood before them with his weapon drawn. "Police! Freeze! Drop your weapon," demanded Deek.

Blackwell slowly lowered his weapon. Kenneth pushed Renee out of the way, as Deek glanced in her direction, but in the span of those few seconds, Renee heard Dr. Blackwell's gun make a clicking noise as he pulled the slide back. Next, there was a loud blast like the pop of a firecracker explosion. Renee felt time cease. She couldn't tell if she had been shot. She didn't feel anything at that moment. She watched everything happen before her in slow motion although it took place in the flash of a few moments. Renee screamed when she saw Deek lying on the floor.

Kenneth suddenly sprang forward, covered his face with both hands, shouted the word No and ran past his father and Renee out the door. Dr. Blackwell called after him, but he didn't stop. Blackwell grabbed Renee and dragged her outside on the deck, shouting for Kenneth. She felt powerless and scared, while Deek lay bleeding on the cabin floor.

Dr. Blackwell held onto her with his one free hand while she screamed, kicked, and twisted fiercely. She no longer cared about her own safety. Renee struggled with Dr. Blackwell so she could get back to Deek. She knew he had to be growing weaker from loss of blood and would soon be unconscious. Renee jerked frantically until Dr. Blackwell lost his hold on her. She found herself free of her captor but the force of his release sent her tumbling over the railing and into the cold black water. The sudden immersion in water almost sent Renee into shock. Fear and helplessness took over as her body sank. She felt completely out of control. She reached around for something solid to grab onto but found herself engulfed in nothing but water. She panicked when she realized her body wasn't moving forward but instead, descended deeper into the water with as much buoyancy as a lead pipe. The water sifted through her nose and mouth. She couldn't breath. Seconds felt like hours and each second was pure hell. No one would be coming to rescue her. Deek lay dying on Dr. Blackwell's boat, and Blackwell certainly wouldn't jump in the water to save her. She didn't want to die. She hadn't taken time to simply appreciate life, not until that moment.

Renee prayed for Deek's life and for deliverance from her own impending death. She couldn't blame God for not listening. Until now she had been too absorbed in searching for her own way to happiness to consider seeking God's help. No, before this moment God was a convenient target to blame for all her pain and disappointments. Losing her mother at seven years old and for the most part losing her father as well, being prevented from conceiving her own child, and destined to an unfulfilling marriage without love. But now that there was no need to blame anyone, she prayed for the first time in a long while and begged God to save her.

For a brief second Renee thought she felt someone else's presence in the water but it was too dark to see anything. Then she felt it again. Someone was trying to grasp hold of her. But her rescuer's movements appeared to be in slow motion. Was it just her imagination? Renee believed that at any moment her lungs would swell up with water and she would die. She continued to try to push forward through the water. Suddenly she felt the firm grip of an arm around her waist. The mysterious grip felt like a lifeline that gave her a shred of hope. But the smell of fear was still pungent. The water continued to rush through her mouth and nose, preventing her from breathing. Finally, she was able to grab the edge of the dock. With the help of her rescuer, Renee propelled herself upward and landed on the platform. She silently thanked God for bringing someone to save her and getting her out of that terrible ordeal alive.

She spit out water and shook uncontrollably from relief and the aftershock of the frigid water. Her chest heaved painfully. But she was grateful to be alive. She struggled to get to her feet and was aided by her rescuer. Her wet body molded itself into his strong arms. After blinking a few times, her vision began to slowly focus more clearly. Renee looked up and saw that her rescuer was her husband, Bill.

"What ... What are you doing here?" is all she could think to say.

"I won't lie," answered Bill, "I followed you. When I got home you weren't there. After what you confessed to me a few days ago, I went out and bought a miniature-sized telephone recorder and installed it on our home phone. That's how I knew where to follow you. Are you okay?"

Her ears were clogged up from all the water. She heard herself talking but could not clearly hear what Bill said. His voice sounded muffled but she did detect some of his words.

"You followed me here?" she asked.

Bill nodded. "I was scared you'd stopped loving me. I needed to find out the truth for myself." At that moment, they heard footsteps running down the platform. It was Kenneth and the Security Guard.

"We'll have to talk later," said Renee to Bill, "Deek's been wounded. He saved my life. Dr. Blackwell shot him." She ran back to the boat. Bill was right behind her. Dr. Blackwell was no where in sight. When the security guard and Kenneth caught up to them, the guard said he had called for help. He gave the police Blackwell's tag number and description of his car. The ambulance was on its way for the wounded officer.

Renee felt like she was floating around them outside of her body in spirit form. As if she had actually drowned and was already on the other side. She knew she had to board the boat and check on Deek. Renee realized she couldn't perform the EMS procedures on Deek that she practiced as an emergency room nurse because she was wet and filthy from the water. She told Kenneth that he would have to do exactly as she directed to try to control Deek's bleeding before the ambulance arrived. The guard said he would return to the front gate so that he would be able to direct the police and paramedics to Dr. Blackwell's slip when they arrived.

Renee, Kenneth, and Bill climbed on board the cabin cruiser. Renee rushed to Deek's side and collapsed on the floor next to him. He was lying face down on the rug. With Kenneth and Bill's help, she gently turned him over, realizing that her first concern was to stop the bleeding. Blood poured profusely from an open wound in his abdomen. Renee asked Kenneth to look for clean towels and blankets. Bill disappeared into one of the cabin's compartments.

"Deek? … Deek can you hear me? It's Renee." Deek moaned and tried to open his eyes but his eyelids only fluttered.

Kenneth rushed back into the room, carrying an armful of clean towels and blankets, which he laid down on the floor next to Renee.

"We've got to do something now to control the bleeding," Renee said to Kenneth who was standing behind her. "We can't wait for the ambulance. I'm sure you have a first aid kit here. Get it. We need lots of bandages."

"You'll be okay, Deek. The ambulance is on the way," she said, afraid he was not going to live. Deek's eyelids stopped moving. Renee panicked. This was not a good sign. She yelled at Kenneth to hurry.

Kenneth returned shortly, carrying a small metal box and rolls of bandages. Bill reappeared and kneeled down behind Renee. He had cleaned himself up in the bathroom. He wrapped a large towel around Renee's shoulders and gently wiped her hair, face and arms with another towel as she remained focused on Deek, telling Kenneth what to do step by step.

Renee was back in head nurse mode, giving orders to Kenneth as if he were in training. "First, put on the gloves, ..." Kenneth slipped on a pair of gloves from the medical kit. When Bill had done what he could for Renee, he stood back but remained transfixed on them.

"I'm afraid he's going into shock," said Renee, "You'll have to work faster. Cut open his shirt and wrap those bandages around him," instructed Renee.

Kenneth took the scissors from the first aid kit and cut off Deek's pale blue shirt, now heavily stained with blood. He wrapped the bandages around him. The first dressing immediately soaked through. Kenneth continued to place fresh bandages on top of each blood soaked one and to apply pressure the way Renee described to him. Finally, after several dressings, Kenneth was able to control Deek's bleeding. Following her instructions, Kenneth leaned over Deek and checked his breathing. He checked his pulse and laid his ear to Deek's chest to listen to his heart. In response to Renee's explicit inquiries, Kenneth described exactly what he heard and felt during his examination.

"Is he dying, Dr. Renee?" asked Kenneth.

"He's still breathing, but his pulse is weak and his heart is beating rapidly," she answered.

"Kenneth, roll up one of those blankets and place it under his legs and feet."

Renee wrapped another blanket loosely around Deek's chilled body.

"I always wanted to be a nurse," said Kenneth nervously to fill in the quiet.

"So what's stopping you now?" she asked, looking directly into Kenneth's eyes.

"My father said no son of his was going to be nurse. If anything he'd be a doctor like him."

Renee touched Kenneth's shoulder and looked deeper into his eyes, "Kenneth, just be yourself and run your own life. Don't let other people run it for you." Renee stood up and asked Kenneth to stay with Deek to make sure he remained calm and still while she went into the bathroom to wash up. She had forgotten that Bill was still there until she looked up and caught him staring at her.

When she returned from the bathroom, Renee knelt down and moved close to Deek. He was just barely conscious. She listened to the faint sound of each rasping breath that he struggled to make. She leaned close to his ear and hoped he could hear her voice.

"Deek, don't worry. You're going to be okay. The ambulance is on its way." She knew that was their only hope of saving his life now. When she heard a commotion outside and the blaring sound of sirens, Renee got up and looked out the cabin window. She saw the security guard leading the police and the EMS team to the cabin. She felt dazed and relieved all at once. She was not aware of Bill's presence nearby.

Kenneth held the door open and the emergency team rushed in with their stretcher. Renee watched as the paramedics quickly donned latex gloves and checked Deek's vital signs. They placed an oxygen mask over his face and said there was no time to lose. Deek was now unconscious. They slid him onto the stretcher and carefully lifted it up and maneuvered it back onto the pier's platform. Renee, Bill, and Kenneth followed the EMS team off the boat. They told Renee that the patient was being taken by helicopter to the MedSTAR Trauma Unit at Washington Hospital Center. The ambulance waited by the gate and a helicopter hovered over the empty parking lot.

"Whoever stabilized the victim until we got here did an excellent job," said one of the paramedics on the EMS team. Renee pointed to Kenneth. "Well buddy, if he pulls through this, it'll be your assistance that made all the difference," said the paramedic to Kenneth as he and his partner rushed towards the front gate.

"I'll take you home now, Renee so you can get some rest," said Bill, grabbing her hand, "You've been through a lot this evening."

"No," said Renee in tears, "I can't go home with you now. He could still die. I'm going to follow the ambulance to the Trauma Center. I'll ask Kenneth to drive me. I'm too upset to drive myself."

"Who is that guy Renee and what does he mean to you?"

When Renee didn't answer, Bill saw from the look on her face that there was no use pursuing it.

"Guess I'll see you when you get home then," he said, "Looks like I found out what I wanted to know. This is as far as I go." A single tear seeped into his eye without warning. He quickly wiped his face.

"You're wrong, Bill," she whispered, "you haven't found out what you wanted to know because I still don't know. I don't know what I want in my life right now."

"What're you gonna do?" he asked, while turning his face away.

"I don't know. I'm beginning to see my life through new eyes," she said and grabbed his arm to get him to turn and look at her. "I can blink back the tears now and face whatever comes next. I'm tired of waiting and hoping for things to be different. I feel so grateful that God's given me another chance to live. Can you understand?" Bill gently removed her hand from his arm and walked away.

Watching him walk away, she remembered that she hadn't even thanked Bill for jumping in the river and saving her life. But the sound of the helicopter lifting off, brought her back to the reality that Deek could die. All she could think of was that she had lost them both because she hadn't been able to choose.

CHAPTER 37

▼

After the ambulance and helicopter left, Renee retrieved her black overnight bag from her car and got in the passenger's seat of Kenneth's automobile. She had packed a change of clothes, a makeup kit, toiletries, and a sexy nightgown, thinking she would be spending the night with Deek. Once Deek was out of danger Renee hoped she would be able to shower and change in the nurses' quarters. She did not intend to leave the hospital until he regained consciousness, no matter how bad she looked or felt.

Renee and Kenneth exited the gates of the marina. A dark blue Ford Crown Victoria sped up alongside them and came to an abrupt stop. The driver side window slid down and Detective Bradford leaned his head out.

"Need a lift to the hospital, Doc?" Bradford bellowed.

Renee realized she could get to the hospital faster riding with Lieutenant Bradford. She turned to thank Kenneth before getting out of his car. "You did great back there," she said to Kenneth. Once Renee got into Detective Bradford's car and fastened her seatbelt, he turned on the siren and sped off. On the way Bradford told her that he had contacted Tyrone at home and his mother was bringing him to the hospital. It was after midnight when they entered the emergency room waiting area. Renee jumped when she heard the public-address system announce a code yellow. Moments later, Renee and Detective Bradford saw the paramedics burst through the ambulance bay doors, pushing a stretcher carrying Deek's motionless body. The trauma team surrounded him and transferred his body from the stretcher onto a cot. Renee left Detective Bradford in the emergency waiting area while she raced through the hallway to keep up with the trauma team. They wheeled Deek's cot to the major trauma room. Renee stood by helpless.

"Can somebody get me a line?" asked the trauma surgeon.

One of the trauma technicians set up an IV to prevent Deek from dehydrating. Then she strapped a thin rubber tubing around his arm to draw blood. Another technician prepared to take X-rays. As this was going on, Renee watched an attendant wheel a stretcher past her, bearing a sheet-covered corpse and realized Deek was still not out of danger.

The surgeon snapped the X-ray up on the light board and immediately saw where the bullet was lodged in the abdomen. Once Deek was stabilized, they took him to the OR for surgery. A sheet covered him up to his chest. Various tubes and an IV were attached. The trauma team didn't notice Renee following them, but when she tried to follow them through a set of double doors where physicians and nurses scrubbed for surgery, she was stopped by one of the medical staff.

"There's an observation area to watch the procedure," said the nurse and pointed to a stairwell around the hall. Renee quickly went to the observation room. After several minutes, the surgical team appeared below Renee, garbed in faded green gowns and wearing latex gloves. She watched from the observation window above as the surgeon stuck a needle just outside the wound area. He bent over Deek and reached into the wound with a surgical instrument. The doctor raised up a bullet that he held within a clamped instrument. The surgical team made a gratifying sound of relief. They nodded their heads in approval and smiled under their masked faces. A nurse packed his wound with thin, sterile gauze then covered it with a sterile dressing. The surgeon scribbled something hurriedly on his chart. They cleaned up and left the operating room. Deek was being taken to the Intensive Care Unit to be closely monitored.

Renee ran down the stairs and grabbed the surgeon's arm just as he rushed by her. "Is he going to be all right, Doctor?"

"Looks like it. He'll be in ICU for the next few hours so we can monitor his vitals. I've prescribed an antibiotic to ward off infection or possible tetanus because of the missile-type injury he sustained," said the surgeon, "but I don't expect any complications. He's young and healthy. The bullet I took out was a low-velocity one so there wasn't as much damage. The pressure dressing that was done on him before he got here really helped curb blood loss and bought him some time. You can see him shortly in ICU. He should be coming out of the anesthesia soon."

A nurse approached the doctor and told him that a Detective Bradford was waiting in the emergency area. He needed the bullet they took out of his partner for evidence. The doctor nodded a brief farewell to Renee and rushed off. Renee went to ICU to wait for Deek to regain consciousness. Until he could recognize her, she planned to stay right there.

Renee stopped at the nurse's station and asked where she could clean up and change clothes. They were sympathetic when she explained to them what happened to her at the marina. One of the nurses escorted her to their private quarters. She felt much better after the quick shower, and once she changed out of her soiled clothing. Renee rubbed conditioning mouse into her freshly washed hair and brushed it back to air dry.

When Renee entered the ICU waiting area, she saw Tyrone's slender frame slumped over in a chair with his head down. He wiped his eyes with the end of his oversized T-shirt. He glanced up when Renee entered, but quickly turned away so she wouldn't see that he had been crying. He stared down at the speckled blue-gray carpet and punched a fist in the open palm of his hand. Renee sensed that he didn't want to talk. Tyrone's mother had just warned her in the hallway that Tyrone was confused and angry. She said she had to leave, but would return in about an hour to pick up her son. She told Renee that she would pray for Deek to recover. Tyrone had told his Mom he wasn't going anywhere until he saw Deek. While Renee wanted to try to comfort the boy, she thought better about approaching him at that moment. Detective Bradford stood gazing out the window in deep thought. He turned around when he heard Renee walk up behind him.

"You saved my partner's life, Dr. Hayes," said Bradford, "the trauma surgeon said the pressure dressing you instructed that kid on, is what gave them time to operate. Thanks, Doc."

"I was only able to be there by the grace of God, Detective. It's not me who should get the credit. By the way, is there any word on Dr. Blackwell's whereabouts?"

"Yeah. When the security guard called in his tag number and vehicle description, we had an APB put out. One of the units nearby arrested him about a mile from the marina last night.

"What's happened to Veda?" asked Renee.

"The paper work's being processed to have her released."

"Good. I'll go see her in a few days just to make sure she's all right."

Detective Bradford stuffed his hands in his pockets and paced the floor. "Wonder when they'll come tell us news about Hamilton."

"I stopped by the nurse's station and asked about him before I came in," said Renee. She noticed Tyrone perked up and listened intently while she gave news about Deek's condition. "They said he's still drowsy from the anesthesia, but at least he's out of danger now." She paused, then added, "But I'm not leaving until I can speak to him."

CHAPTER 38

▼

At the police station, a female officer handed Veda her belongings and told her she was free to go. When Veda stepped outside into the early morning light, the first thing she saw was a white van parked out front. A big man jumped out of the van when he spotted Veda on the steps and rushed towards her. Veda held her hand above her brow to shield the sunlight from her eyes. It was her ex-husband, Louis Simms. He had obviously been waiting for her to come out of the police station.

"Hey Veda, wanna ride home?" said Louis, smiling.

"You drove all the way from Baltimore just to give me a ride home, Louis?" she said, "We do have cabs runnin' in D.C., you know." Louis's smile faded. He looked hurt. Veda realized she had worn her tough veneer for too long. She touched his shoulder.

"Listen, Louis, I really appreciate this. Truth is, I don't have a penny to my name. And I sure ain't stoppin' no cabs on my good looks," she said smiling up at him, "Just look at this head. I look a mess."

Louis grinned back and pointed to his van parked on the street, "I'm right over there."

"Tell me something," she said, "How did you know I'd be released today? The cops just arrested the real killer late last night."

"Heard it on the news this mornin'. So I figure they bound to let you out sometime today."

They walked towards his van but before she could reach for the handle, the door on the rear passenger side opened and her daughter, Sherrelle stepped out. Veda looked cautiously at her, then at Louis.

"Was this your idea too?" she whispered to Louis.

"No, indeed. It was hers," answered Louis, "Sherrelle say she wanna come here wit me."

Veda noticed the small suitcase on the passenger seat.

"Daddy said I can stay with you for a few days, if it's okay with you, Mama," said Sherrelle, nervously, "I just thought you might need somebody to look after you for awhile."

Veda grabbed her daughter, hugged her fiercely around the neck, and rocked her back and forth. She was too emotional to speak and just nodded her head yes as the tears rolled down her cheeks. "You can stay with your mama as long as you want, baby," Veda finally managed to get out between sniffles.

Sherrelle grinned at her mother. Then Louis followed suit, showing all his pearly whites. Veda looked from her ex-husband back to her daughter.

"Umm, now I see where this child gets that big grin from." They all laughed. Louis told Veda he'd pick up Sherrelle on Saturday evening. Veda put her arm around her daughter one more time before hopping in the front seat. Sherrelle jumped in back and her father slid the door shut. When Louis climbed up in the driver's seat, Veda turned and whispered in his ear.

"Thank you, Louis. You always did know just what I needed."

CHAPTER 39

▼

Renee and Detective Bradford quietly stepped inside Deek's room. They would only allow two visitors at a time, so Tyrone waited in the visitor's area until it was his turn to see Deek. Deek appeared to still be asleep. A nurse held his hand and stared at her watch. She took the pressure belt and tightened it around his arm, pumped on the rubber ball, then let it drop. She watched the dial then jotted down the number on her chart. She stuck a thermometer in his mouth and waited for the electronic beep.

"Normal," she told Renee and Bradford, "Everything looks fine. No sign of infection. Let's see if he's ready to wake up."

The nurse held Deek's face in her hands, and shook lightly. "Mr. Hamilton? Time to wake up, hon."

Renee felt her checks getting hot. She wanted to be the first person Deek saw when he woke up. His eyes blinked several times as he tried to focus. Renee and Bradford stood up and approached the bed.

"How do you feel Mr. Hamilton?" asked the nurse.

"What?" He was still groggy and disoriented.

"Let me try," said Renee, gently shoving the nurse aside.

Renee sat on the bed next to Deek and bent over close to his ear.

"If you need me just press that buzzer," said the nurse and left the room.

"Deek? You're at Washington Hospital Center. Do you remember what happened last night at the marina?"

Suddenly, he grabbed hold of her with such strength, she almost fell on top of him.

"Renee are you ..."

"I'm fine," Renee said, regaining her balance. "You're going to be fine too. The police arrested Dr. Blackwell last night."

He still looked weak and tired but he turned his head to check his surroundings and saw his partner, Detective Bradford.

"Look here, Young Blood, don't make a vacation outta this place. We still got work to do." said Bradford.

"I don't plan on it," said Deek with a weak smile.

"Well, I better get the hell outta here. I got work to do. Hang tough, buddy," said Bradford and gave his partner the high-five. "Hey, want me to send the kid in now? He's been out there waiting to see you."

"Give us about five minutes before you send him in," said Renee, answering for Deek.

"Thanks for being here, Renee ... for caring about me," said Deek.

"It goes a little deeper than that," she said.

Deek smiled, showing both dimples.

Renee wanted to melt at his vulnerability. Even though she knew he would recover from his injuries, now was not the time to tell him what she had decided—that she needed time to figure out what was best for her.

Deek saw the worry in her troubled face. How could she explain that she needed time alone? She had become infatuated with him the moment she laid eyes on him. He made her crave passion again. But her attachment feelings to her husband were too deep to simply throw away her life with Bill. Things were moving too fast for her to figure out what she really wanted. But she didn't have to say anything. It was if he could read her mind.

"Take your time, Renee," he said, "I'm not going anywhere."

Renee hugged him so hard that he grimaced in pain. She kissed him briefly on the lips then looked into his eyes. They appeared so black they resembled the cobalt, blue-blackness of a starless, country night. She felt a tear began to settle in the corner of her eye. Then she left the room quickly to get Tyrone.

When Renee returned to the room with Tyrone, Deek's eyes lit up and he smiled broadly. It was obvious that seeing Tyrone lifted Deek's spirits. Tyrone cautiously walked up to the bed and gave the man who had been like a father to him a gentle hug. Renee adjusted the controls at the foot of the bed to raise Deek's head slightly and fluffed his pillows. Once he was comfortable she sat in a chair against the wall while Tyrone scooted his chair up close to the bed.

"You sure you gonna be okay Man?" said Tyrone, trying to sound brave.

"Sure, I'm gonna be okay. Don't worry about me. To prove it, why don't you bring our PSPs tomorrow so I can beat you in another game of Madden?" Deek gave a sly grin.

"For money?" Tyrone lifted his brows.

"You got money Tyrone?"

"I don't need none, after I beat you," said Tyrone with bravado. They both laughed. Renee noticed Deek's face contort in pain, though he tried to hide it from Tyrone.

"Are you forgetting the last time we played Madden 07 Football?" said Deek, wearing a confident smile, "the score was 27 to 6." At that reminder, Tyrone frowned. "That was just luck, Deek. Wait 'til I come back here tomorrow with the PSPs."

Renee looked puzzled. "What's a PSP?" she asked.

"a portable playstation," Tyrone answered.

Renee frowned, "Deek, don't you think you should wait until they discharge you from the hospital before you try to get back to your normal routine? Anyway, how're you going to hook up game equipment in your hospital room?"

"You don't need any cords. It's wireless," said Deek, giving Tyrone a playful punch in the arm, "Besides, I'm feeling fine. I'll be out of here in no time, right Big T?" he said, smiling at Tyrone. "Having you guys here has already made me feel much better." Deek paused, then looked at Tyrone, "Okay, buddy let's do this—if you win tomorrow I'll give you ten bucks and if I win you gotta wash my car. Deal?" Deek held out his hand for Tyrone to shake. Tyrone grinned, grabbing Deek's hand. "Deal!"

Tyrone and Deek joked around for another 15 minutes. Renee stayed out of their conversation, but kept a close watch on Deek. They talked about Tyrone's upcoming flying lesson and the book that Deek had loaned him to read over the summer, Makes Me Wanna Holler: A Young Black Man in America by Nathan McCall. The two of them were having a lively discussion about the book when Renee noticed signs of fatigue on Deek's face. She rose from the chair and went over to the bed. She kissed Deek softly and touched his cheek. Then she turned to Tyrone and said they should leave now so Deek could get his rest. Tyrone got up from the chair and gave Deek a parting hug while Renee stood by. Tyrone stopped at the door. "Get ready to get your feelings hurt. I'll be back tomorrow with the game," said Tyrone, grinning. Renee ushered him out the door and turned to take one last look at Deek before she left. His eyes followed her until she was out of view.

Tyrone's mother was waiting for him in the hallway to take him home. Renee took the opportunity to talk to her privately about Tyrone. She wanted to make her understand that Deek didn't want to worry Tyrone and was pushing himself to appear normal, but he was still in pain and had almost died. He needed to allow his body to heal. She asked Tyrone's mother to do her best to encourage her son to keep the video games at home for awhile and to keep his visits brief. Fortunately, the woman understood and agreed. She was very grateful for everything Deek had done for her son. She promised to talk to Tyrone when they got home.

As Renee headed for the exit, she noticed Bill coming out of the elevator and looking around the ICU area. She struggled to compose herself but it was too late. A teary red film had already clouded her eyes. When he saw her standing inside the waiting area, he walked up to her.

"How's your friend, ... the detective?"

"Fine. He'll be fine," answered Renee in a clipped voice.

"So, would you like me to take you home now?" he asked guardedly.

"No thanks, I'll catch one of those cabs parked out front of the hospital."

A full minute of silence followed until Bill spoke again.

"Where do we go from here Renee?"

Suddenly, Renee broke down crying. Hugging her, Bill led her to a nearby chair in the waiting room. She cried nonstop for about twenty minutes. She cried for her parents, for the hurt she had caused Bill, for Veda, for all the children like Susanna that she tried to save but couldn't. But most of all, she cried to release all the pent up emotions that had been locked away in order to maintain control of her passions. Bill gently rocked her in his arms and rubbed her hair and back.

Through her tears, more questions than answers floated inside her head. She couldn't wipe away the last three years of loneliness with Bill. Ever since he had lost that thirty thousand dollars on his failed business venture, he'd seemed to believe he had to compete with her success in order to earn her love and respect. Renee never cared about the money. All she ever wanted was his love but she had failed to get him to understand that. She thought of her feelings for Deek. Her desire for him still burned strong. But how long would that passion last? She was more than ten years older than he was. What happens when her looks begin to fade? Or if he should meet a woman his own age who could have his children? A future with him seemed elusive, just a beautiful fantasy that would one day slip through her fingers when she woke up.

Renee considered her desire to adopt a child and to help sick children who have no one else to turn to. Would either Bill or Deek be supportive of who she really was inside? She remembered the noted psychologist C. G. Jung once saying that, "Most people believe they are only what they know about themselves." Renee realized there was a great deal more to be discovered. She didn't want any relationship to hinder her self-discovery of the real Renee Janette Hayes.

She realized that her mother had chosen to live her life unstructured and spontaneous and didn't bother with other people's rules and expectations. Bettina 'Tina Joye' Johnson had been a free spirit and her aunt had resented it. Renee realized that she too was born a free spirit and could choose to be herself, not just what others expected. That was the advice she had given Kenneth Blackwell. Now she was ready to believe it for herself. Suddenly, everything made sense.

Bill went to the bathroom and brought back a wad of tissues. Renee wiped her face and took several deep breaths until she felt calm again. Only then did Bill speak.

"Listen Renee, I don't know what happened between you and Detective Hamilton and I don't want to know. All I know is that I love you and I want our marriage to work."

Renee stared at him, red-faced and puffy-eyed, without responding. He held her hand and continued.

"I want to take you to a romantic island to get away for awhile. Anywhere you like. I'll see a marriage counselor if you still think it'll help us. Give me another chance to try, Renee."

She knew this was difficult for Bill. She leaned into his body and they briefly caressed.

Then she pulled back. "Bill, if you had only said these things to me a month ago, it would have made all the difference in the world," explained Renee, "I hope you can understand. I do love you, but what I really need right now is time alone."

"What's going to happen to you and me?"

Renee shook her head. "I don't know. If I want a different life for myself—if I want happiness, it has to start with me. It's in my hands, nobody else's."

"Do you ... want me to move out?" he asked slowly.

Renee gently rubbed his cheek.

"No, that won't be necessary. My mentor, Helen Stone left for Senegal for a month. She gave me the key to her condo in Arlington and asked me to check on her plants periodically," explained Renee, "She invited me to stay anytime I needed some space to myself. I'll stop by tomorrow morning to get some of my things." She paused. "And in a few weeks, I'll be leaving for Paris. Deek ... Detective Hamilton found my father."

"I see." Bill sat back upright in the chair, the muscles in his face tightened, and he clinched the arms of the chair.

"Bill, please try to understand. This is important to me. It doesn't mean things are over between us." Renee placed her hand on top of his as she tried to explain. "When I was under that water, being pulled deeper and deeper, I prayed. I prayed for the first time in a long time because you see I had lost faith in a God that would let so many bad things happen to innocent people. I've been lost for a long time. Being under that water without any control was like a bad dream. I realized the only thing I had at that moment was God. I prayed, not knowing if he was even listening. Then out of nowhere I felt someone's strong arm around my waist, not knowing it was you. At that moment I let go of my fear and trusted God like I used to when I was a little girl before my mother died. When you were holding onto me, it felt just like my mother used to do at night when I'd wake up from a bad dream."

"Those were my arms you felt," said Bill, with a bitter tone in his voice.

"I know that now, and I'm forever grateful to you for saving my life. But I also believe it was God that led you there at the right time and place. Just seconds later and it would've been too late. It's time for me to start living my life on my own terms, the way I want to live it. Not the way I'm expected to live it." Renee got up slowly and walked towards the door. She stopped when she heard him call after her.

"You forgot this," he got up and retrieved her bag from the couch and handed it to her. They walked outside the hospital together in silence. The sign above the hospital entrance stated: Washington Hospital Center ... Where Miracles Happen Every Day.

Bill stared at the sign and smiled. Renee spotted an empty cab waiting for a passenger. She climbed into the back seat and gave the driver the address to the Concord House on Crystal Drive in Arlington, Virginia. Bill approached the open passenger side window in the back where Renee was seated and bent down until their eyes met.

"Will I be able to see you before you leave for Paris?" he asked, "Maybe come by Helen's condo and take you out someplace nice?"

"I don't see why not," she smiled.

"How about this Wednesday? Around seven?" He rested his folded arms on top the door ledge and leaned further inside the window, his face just inches away from hers.

"Until Wednesday then," said Renee. Their lips touched and lingered together for a moment. Bill stood up and moved away from the cab. She signaled the cabdriver to take off. The cabdriver adjusted his rearview mirror.

THE END

For Book Club DISCUSSION

1. How do you think Renee and Veda's childhood traumas shaped their destinies? What effect, if any, did their childhood experiences have on their self-esteem as women?

2. What do Veda and Renee think they want at the start of the novel? What do they really want?

3. Why does Renee stay with her husband, Bill Hayes? As a relationship therapist, why can't Renee communicate her needs to Bill?

4. What attracts Renee to Deek? What does Deek see in her?

5. What type of man is Deek? Why does Deek take on the responsibility for a troubled teenager like 16 year-old Tyrone Wallace who is not his biological son?

6. Explore Renee's relationship with her Aunt Clara growing up. Did Aunt Clara resent Renee or was her aunt's strictness a form of love? Did Aunt Clara resent Renee's mother, Tina Joye? If so, why?

7. Is Renee's restlessness actually genetic? Could she be more like her "free-spirited" mother than she thinks?

8. What do you think was the long term affect on Renee of having her father, LeRoy Curtis absent throughout most of her childhood?

9. Why does Veda fail to develop a maternal bond with her infant daughter, Sherrelle at birth and even into the child's pre-teen years? Would you consider Veda a "good" mother? Why or why not?

10. What prompts Sherrelle to forgive her mother by the end of the novel? Can you comment on a child's apparent need to connect to his or her biological parent despite that parent's shortcomings as a parent, nurturer, or role model? Think of other parent/child relationships illustrated in the book such as Kenneth with his Dad, Dr. Walter Blackwell.

11. Does Dr. Blackwell love his son, Kenneth? Backup your opinion with examples from the book and/or your own understanding of parent/child relationships.

12. How does Veda's childhood experiences (her relationship with her mother/ her exposure to the Pastor) affect her life choices and her psyche as a woman?

13. Comment on the depictions of the main characters' mother/daughter relationships, i.e. Veda/her mother and Renee/her mother.

14. How do you think Renee views the foster mother, Shirley Ann Turner?

15. What factors contributed to the collapse of Louis Simms and Veda's marriage? Could anything have saved that marriage?

16. Do you think Renee's marriage to Bill can be salvaged?

17. What is your opinion of Veda's boyfriend, LaMarr Coleman? Can you analyze what is driving him to behave as he does?

18. Renee's mentor and colleague, Dr. Helen Stone, acts as Renee's own therapist, not as a best friend. Why do you think it is easier for Veda to maintain a close girlfriend relationship with Natasha and have another female to share her problems with, whereas Renee does not appear to have any close girlfriends that she can confide in?

19. What is the significance of Renee's near death experience when she nearly drowns at the end of the book?

20. Reread the last few paragraphs of the novel, beginning with the text, "The sign above the hospital entrance stated: Washington Hospital Center … Where Miracles Happen Every Day." What do you see as the significance of this line and how the book ends?

21. What are some of the underlying themes revealed in this novel that you can identify as statements that the book makes?

DOROTHY PHAIRE ROMANTIC MYSTERY SERIES

The sequel to MURDER AND THE MASQUERADE coming Summer 2008

What happens to Renee and her husband Bill? Does she take a gamble on hand-some Deek Hamilton, her true soul mate—or does she stay in the familiar con-fines of her marriage? Will she adopt the baby she so desperately desires? Will Renee finally understand her own inner strength and capacity to love? What does Deek really want and will he ever attain it? Does Veda get in trouble with the law again? Is she able to become the type of loving and nurturing mother to her daughter that she herself never had growing up? What new characters and intrigues does the author have in store for the sequel?

Phaire promises that the luscious sequel will continue her pulsating and compel-ling storytelling genre in vivid details that takes the reader into the plot. Dr. Renee will not disappoint. She will encounter more challenges and complex choices both in her professional and personal life, as she struggles to find her inner strength and spirit. Most of the characters return in the sequel that is filled with more romance, deception and mystery, and still set in the Washington, D. C. area. The sequel will reveal deeply held dark explosive secrets and painful betrayals that shatter lives and are both transformative and life changing for its characters. Stay tuned.... Summer 2008!

About the Author

Dorothy Phaire is a novelist, playwright and educator. *Murder and the Masquerade* is her second novel. She currently teaches full-time in the English Department at the University of the District of Columbia in Washington, D. C. In addition to her romance/mystery series, she is working on a period fiction project, set during World War II. She has written, directed and produced two plays: *This Side of Jordan* (2004) and *Saving Us Saints* (2006, 2007) that were both staged at venues in Washington D. C. and Maryland. She is the president and founder of the Heralds of Hope Theater Company, Inc., a non-profit organization whose mission is to promote, mentor, and provide a platform of artistic expression for aspiring actors of all ages. Her poetry was published in *Beyond the Frontier: African-American Poetry for the 21st Century* (2002). For more information on the Heralds of Hope Theater Company as well as to find out more about Ms. Phaire's writing projects, visit www.dorothyphaire.com.